Praise for James Swain's Tony Valentine novels

"In this series about gambling, the main character is a big winner." —JANET MASLIN, *The New York Times*

"Swain's mysteries . . . are a sure bet." —*Chicago Tribune*

"James Swain is the real thing, a writer of pure, athletic prose, capable of bringing alive characters as original and three-dimensional as our best novelists." —JAMES W. HALL

"This smooth, funny series has got to be one of the finds of the decade." —*Kirkus*

"An expert on casino swindles, the author packs his books with mind-boggling cons and scams . . . along with entertaining dialogue and vivid characters." —*Publishers Weekly*

MR. LUCKY

"Bask in Swain's Las Vegas without having to set foot in the place and risk being skinned alive." —*Washington Post Book World*

"The momentum is great, the writing nimble, the action intricate. If you like Swain's formula, as I do, you'll get a lot of what you expect and love it." —*Los Angeles Times*

"Hits the jackpot. Impossible to put down." —MICHAEL CONNELLY

P9-ELS-685

FUNNY MONEY

GRIFT SENSE

Also by James Swain

GRIFT SENSE
FUNNY MONEY
SUCKER BET
LOADED DICE
MR. LUCKY

deadman's
POKER

A Novel

James Swain

BALLANTINE BOOKS · NEW YORK

A Ballantine Books Mass Market Original

Copyright © 2006 by James Swain
Excerpt from *Deadman's Bluff* by James Swain copyright © 2006 by James Swain

Published in the United States by Ballantine Books, an imprint of The Random House Publishing Group, a division of Random House, Inc.

BALLANTINE and colophon are registered trademarks of Random House, Inc.

This book contains an excerpt from the forthcoming paperback edition of *Deadman's Bluff* by James Swain. This excerpt has been set for this edition only and may not reflect the final content of the forthcoming edition.

ISBN 0-345-47549-6

Cover illustration: Don Sipley

Printed in the United States of America

www.ballantinebooks.com

OPM   9 8 7 6 5 4 3 2 1

For Margaret Swain

You're never so slick
that you can't stand another greasing.

—Old gambling expression

A Brief Glossary of Useful Cheating Terms

Action   Any gambling activity.

Beef   A complaint.

Bleed   To cheat a game slowly.

Bustout joint   A casino that cheats its customers.

Cheater   One who practices fraud or deception. Also known as an advantage player, grifter, hustler, mechanic, rounder, or scammer.

Classmates   Two people working in collusion in a card game.

Cooler   A prearranged deck that is secretly switched for a deck in play. Also known as iron man.

Cooler mob   A group of cheaters who switch decks of cards.

Crossroader   A cheater who specializes in ripping off casinos.

Doing business	Cheating.
Feel a breeze	When you feel something unnatural going on, but don't know what it is.
Gaff	A cheating device.
Gamer	Someone employed in the gambling industry.
Giving the office	Communicating through a secret code.
Greed factor	Winning too much, too often.
Grift sense	The ability to spot a scam or hustle. A compliment among hustlers.
Hairy leg	A moneyman who backs a game.
Half smart	Someone who thinks he's smart, but isn't.
Heat	Unwanted attention. Also called steam.
Hot seat	Where the sucker sits.
Joint	A casino.
Juice	Influence with the right people.
Muck	To switch cards.

Mucker — A cheater who specializes in switching cards.

On the square — A game that is played legitimately.

Peek joint — A setup allowing a hidden person to see someone's hand during a card game.

Paper — Marked cards. Also known as paint.

Proposition bet — A bet that you can't win, and won't win. Also known as a proposition.

Ring game — A side game in a poker tournament.

Shiner — A reflecting device used to spot cards as they are dealt.

Shoot the pickle — To make a huge bet. To go for it.

Suckers — 99 percent of the people who gamble. Also known as chumps, marks, pigeons, rubes, and vics (victims).

Tell — An unconscious signal that may be spotted by a knowledgeable player.

Texas Hold 'Em — A variation of poker invented by twelve ranch hands who had only a single deck of cards between them.

Tip your mitt — To inadvertently expose your hand or otherwise give away secret information.

Turn out   To teach somehow how to cheat.

Tush hog   A dangerous muscle man.

Whipsaw   Two partners in a poker game who try
             to force a third player out by raising
             and reraising each other.

Part I

Mr. Black and White

1

"I can beat any poker player in the world," Jack Donovan whispered.

Gerry Valentine leaned on the cold metal arm of the hospital bed while staring into the eyes of his dying friend. They'd gone to grade school together, gotten hauled into the principal's office a few dozen times, and when they'd gotten older, broken a bunch of laws together. They were as close as brothers, and to see lung cancer take Jack's life away had been one of the most painful things Gerry had ever experienced.

"Think we should go find a game?" Gerry asked.

A weak smile crossed Jack's lips. Gerry had flown into Atlantic City from Florida that morning and spent the afternoon at Jack's bedside, reminiscing with his friend. When nightfall had come, the nurse on duty had allowed Gerry to stay well past visiting hours.

"I'm serious," Jack whispered. "I can beat any player in any game."

"Is this a scam?"

Jack was on oxygen, his voice barely audible. "Yeah. Came to me when I was getting chemotherapy. The gaff is invisible, and there's no evidence left behind."

Jack had been a scammer since they were teenagers, and he knew all the angles. A scam that didn't leave evidence could make someone rich beyond their wildest dreams.

"And have you actually tried it out?" Gerry asked.

"What, you think I'm going to hustle the nurses?"

"So you don't really know if it works," Gerry said. "Stuff that looks good on paper doesn't always work in the real world. Remember that time you fell in the fountain outside Caesars, and nearly drowned?"

Jack rolled his eyes. "Did you have to bring that up?"

"Sorry."

"Look, Gerry, this is the crown jewels of poker cheating. I taught it to some guys who want to scam a poker tournament in Las Vegas. Only, now they're reneging on their end of the deal."

"How?"

"They won't pay me. They know I'm dying, so they think they can screw me."

Gerry didn't think there was anything lower than what Jack was describing. Whoever had said there was honor among thieves hadn't known many thieves.

"What do you want me to do?" Gerry asked.

"Remember Vinny Fountain?"

"Sure."

"Vinny wants to buy the scam for a hundred grand. I want you to sell it to him and give the money to my mom. She's living on federal assistance."

Jack's feet were sticking out at the end of the bed and Gerry pulled the blanket down to his toes. As a kid, Jack had been a runt, and everyone in the neighborhood had called him Little Jack. Then one summer he'd shot up like a beanpole, and lost the adjective.

"I need to stretch my legs," Gerry said. "Want me to get you something?"

"What's the matter?" his friend asked.

"I just need to think about this."

"You scared your father will find out?"

Jack knew him too well. Gerry had joined his father's casino consulting business a year ago. The casinos paid them to catch cheaters, and he didn't think his father would be too happy to find out his son was selling cheating secrets to scammers.

"I could get somebody else," Jack offered.

"No, I'll do it," Gerry said. "I just need to figure out how to keep my father in the dark. What's this scam, anyway?"

Jack lifted his head and looked straight down at the floor. Gerry looked as well, and spotted a canvas bag lying beneath the bed. He knelt down and parted the bag with his fingers. Inside were a dozen decks of cards, and a metal strongbox with the words DANGER, DO NOT OPEN! printed in white letters across the front. Jack had always liked practical jokes. Gerry closed the bag, stood, and went to the door.

"You want something?"

"Get me a Coca-Cola," Jack said.

The night Jack had fallen into the fountain outside Caesars Palace in Atlantic City and nearly drowned had been a classic example of a perfect scam gone wrong. Gerry knew this better than anyone else because he'd orchestrated it.

He walked through the hospital's cafeteria and found the bin with iced sodas. He pulled two out, then selected a couple of sandwiches from the pre-fixed food section. When he went to pay, he caught the cashier yawning.

The wall clock said eleven o'clock. That didn't seem real. He'd arrived at noon, and had been talking with Jack for most of the day. It was strange that the debacle

at Caesars hadn't come up before now; it had been the
first and last time they'd tried to scam a casino together.

Gerry had been eighteen at the time. His father was a
detective with the Atlantic City Police Department, and
had been assigned to protect the island's twelve casinos.
His father knew more scams and greasy hustles than
anyone around, and as a result, Gerry overheard a lot.
One night, while his parents were doing the dishes, his
father had told his mother that Caesars had seen a rash
of marked cards called luminous readers. These cards
could only be read by someone wearing glasses or contact lenses outfitted with special infrared material. Gerry,
who'd been in the next room watching TV, immediately
ran upstairs and called Jack on the phone.

"You're not going to believe this," Gerry told him.

Jack found an optometrist in town willing to fit him
with special contact lenses to read luminous paint. The
lenses were difficult to see through, and Jack spent several days walking around wearing them. When he stopped
bumping into things, he called Gerry on the phone and
told him he was ready to scam Caesars.

That night, Gerry drove Jack to Caesars in his father's
car. The casino was a replica of Caesars Palace in Las
Vegas, only smaller and not nearly as opulent. Nothing
in Atlantic City was as opulent as Las Vegas, yet it hadn't
stopped the place from making billions of dollars a year.

Caesars sat on Atlantic Avenue. Gerry pulled the car
in front, and watched Jack put drops into his eyes, then
pop the contact lenses in. Too many cops in Atlantic
City knew Gerry, and he couldn't walk into a casino
without someone recognizing him. So, it was up to Jack
to rip off the place.

"Good luck," Gerry said.

"This is going to be like stealing candy from a baby,"
Jack said.

Jack got out of the car, and walked across Caesars' promenade. The place was fancy, with lots of nude statues and gushing water fountains. Jack walked directly into the largest fountain, his body flipping over the metal railing and going headfirst into the water. He had not practiced with the lenses at night, and was almost blind.

Gerry jumped out of the car and saved his friend from drowning, but not without getting collared by casino security, and by a cop for leaving his car illegally parked. When neither authority liked the bullshit story Gerry concocted to explain what had happened, his father was summoned. It had been a long night.

That had been many years ago. Now it seemed funny as hell, but the truth was, they could have both ended up in jail. That was how Gerry saw his past now; there were consequences for breaking the law. Getting married and having a baby had changed his perspective.

Gerry pressed the elevator button while holding the sodas and sandwiches against his chest. The hospital was quiet, and he waited while humming a song he couldn't get out of his head. Finally he decided to take the stairs.

The stairwell had a dank smell. Halfway up, he heard footsteps, and looked up to see an Italian guy about his age coming down. The guy was dressed in black, had pocked skin and wore a scowl on his face. Normally, Italians were hospitable to other Italians. This guy wasn't, and grunted under his breath when Gerry said hello.

"Suit yourself," Gerry said when the guy was gone.

A minute later he walked into Jack's room. The monitor next to Jack's bed was beeping, and the oxygen tube that had been attached to his friend's nose had been ripped out, and lay on the floor. Jack lay with his arms by his side, his chest violently heaving.

"Jack!"

Gerry hit the red emergency button on the wall to summon the nurses. He stared at the monitor; Jack's oxygenation had fallen below 80 percent. He put his face a foot from his friend's.

"Who did this?"

Jack's eyes snapped open. *"Hitman . . ."*

"Hitman for who?"

"Guys I taught scam . . ."

"Why? You can't hurt them."

"Afraid I'd squeal . . ."

"Squeal about what?"

Jack's hand came out from beneath the sheet. Clutched between his trembling fingers was a playing card. Gerry took the card: It was an ace of spades from the Celebrity Casino in Las Vegas.

"Is this part of the poker scam?"

Right then two nurses ran into the room. They pushed Gerry away from the hospital bed as they worked to get Jack's oxygen intake back to normal. It was at that moment that Gerry noticed that the canvas bag underneath Jack's bed was gone. He shouldered his way between the nurses and lowered his face next to Jack's.

"What's the scam?" Gerry whispered.

Something resembling a smile crossed Jack Donovan's face, like he was happy to have pulled Gerry back into the fold. But then the look was replaced by one of pure fear.

"Tell me," Gerry said.

Jack's mouth moved up and down.

"I . . . so . . ."

"You so what?"

"I . . . so . . ."

"Come on."

"Bye . . . Gerry."

Jack's mouth stopped moving. And then he stopped breathing. Jack had accepted that he was dying, and he had asked his friends to accept it as well. Gerry had tried, yet it didn't make it any easier now that it had actually happened. He bowed his head and wept.

2

Tony Valentine could feel his son's eyes burning his face. *He knows the news isn't good,* Valentine thought. Still, it didn't make this any easier. Hanging up the phone, Tony sat down on the couch beside his son. He put his hand on Gerry's arm.

"The police are ruling it a suicide," he said.

"What? What are they smoking?"

"I'm sorry, Gerry, but all the evidence is pointing that way."

"For Christ's sake, Pop, don't take the company line on this." Gerry put his bottled water on the coffee table in his father's living room. "Jack was murdered. Take my word for it. I was there in the goddamn room."

Eight days had passed since Jack Donovan's death in the intensive care unit of the Atlantic City Medical Center. After Jack had been buried, Gerry had come home and asked his father to ride the coattails of the homicide detectives working the case. Still having juice with the Atlantic City Police Department, Valentine had obliged his son.

"Gerry, the only evidence you have is a suspicious-looking guy in the stairwell," Valentine said. "The nurses are saying that Jack talked about ending his life when things got bad. Maybe that's what he did."

Indignation rose in his son's face. "Jack was in the middle of telling me about this poker scam. Said it was the greatest thing since the baloney sandwich. I left, and that guy came into the room and pulled Jack's tubes and beat on Jack's chest. Jack said he was a hitman."

"The police checked Jack's room for fingerprints. The only prints besides Jack's and the nurses' were yours."

"The police also found a pair of rubber gloves in the garbage pail by the door," his son said. "The guy was a pro."

"There isn't any proof, Gerry."

"What about the playing card Jack gave me? Isn't that evidence?"

It was like déjà vu all over again. Valentine had examined Jack's playing card for hours, found nothing, then sent it to an FBI forensic lab in Langley, Virginia, where he had a friend. All the tests had come back negative.

"The FBI didn't find anything, Gerry. The card is normal."

"No, it's not," his son said. "Remember that scam you told me about at the Silver Slipper in Las Vegas? Major Riddle, the owner, lost his casino to a poker scam that one of his dealers pulled off. How long did the police examine those cards?"

"Two weeks," his father said.

"And the cards came up clean," Gerry said. "Then they sent them to you, and what did you find? The cheaters used an X-acto knife to draw tiny lines on the faces of all the high cards. The dealer felt when high cards were going to Major Riddle, and he signaled the other players."

"What does that have to do with this case, Gerry?"

"I'm saying that stuff gets missed. If Jack said that card was marked, then it was marked. You have to ask the Atlantic City police to start over."

Valentine blew out his cheeks. He'd already called in a bunch of favors with the police in his hometown; any more and he might start losing friends. It didn't help matters that Jack Donovan had been a scammer and had been run in many times.

"I'll see what I can do," Valentine said.

"What's that supposed to mean?"

"It means that I'm running out of options, Gerry."

"Come on, Pop. I'm begging you."

Valentine stared at the videotapes stacked next to his VCR/DVD player. He was on monthly retainer for dozens of casinos, and every day got a videotape from a client who thought his casino had been ripped off. He'd been neglecting his work to help Gerry, and couldn't continue to ignore his customers without it affecting his income.

"I'm trying, Gerry," he said.

His son pushed himself off the couch and walked out of the house.

Valentine believed that food was the antidote for most things that ailed you. Fixing two ham-and-Swiss-cheese sandwiches, he poured some potato chips onto the plates, stuck two cans of soda into his pockets, and went out the back door to where Gerry stood, smoking a cigarette in his postage-size backyard.

"You hungry?"

"No," his son said.

"I made you a sandwich."

"Pop, it's four o'clock in the afternoon."

"Eat something anyway. It will make you feel better."

Valentine put the food on the plastic table in his yard, and pulled up two plastic chairs. His son begrudgingly sat down and they began to eat. A few minutes later, Gerry pushed his empty plate to the center of the table, and stared at his father.

"Did I ever tell you that Jack came to Mom's funeral?"

Valentine was still eating his sandwich, and glanced at his son. His wife had died two weeks after they'd moved to Florida to retire. He'd taken her body back to Atlantic City, and buried her beside her parents. The ceremony was for friends and family, and Valentine was sure Jack Donovan had not been present.

"You could have fooled me."

"He was in a tree," Gerry said.

"Hanging out with his friends?"

"I'm being serious, Pop."

"Why was he doing that?"

"Because cops were there, and Jack was wanted at the time."

Valentine put his half-eaten sandwich onto his plate. "Why was he at your mother's funeral, is what I meant."

"Jack loved Mom, and he loved you."

Valentine put his elbows on the table, and gave his son a hard look. He'd always considered Jack something of a public menace as well as a bad influence on his son, and had never hidden those feelings. Now he waited for Gerry to explain himself.

"Remember when I was a kid, and the Donovans lived on our block?" his son asked.

"Sure," Valentine said.

"Mom used to ask Jack down on Christmas day to open presents, and have breakfast with us. Then, around noon, Jack would go back to his house, and open presents with his parents. We did that until the Donovans moved. Remember?"

Valentine nodded.

"When I got older, Jack explained to me that his parents were both drunks, and used to fight in the morning. Christmas day was always bad. He realized that you and

Mom invited him down so his Christmas wasn't spoiled by his parents' fighting. He loved you guys for that."

Valentine sipped his soda. His own father had been a drunk, and he'd always felt bad for kids whose parents abused the sauce. He picked up his sandwich, and noticed that an almost invisible line of ants had crawled onto the table, and they were attacking his food. He dropped his sandwich on his plate.

"You know that when Jack got older, he was involved in a lot of bad stuff," Gerry said. "But what you didn't know was that Jack protected you, Pop. None of the things he was involved with ever happened when you were on duty. And none of the gangs he ran with ever robbed anybody when you were on duty, either. That was the deal if someone worked with Jack, and he always stuck by it."

Valentine drummed the table. It would have been a Hallmark moment had Gerry told him that Jack had avoided a life of crime because of the Christmas mornings he'd spent at their house. This revelation was anything but.

"I'm touched," he said.

"Jack looked out for you, Pop. You should be grateful."

Valentine found himself wishing he'd arrested the kid and hauled him in front of a judge. That was the type of treatment that usually straightened out the Jack Donovan's of the world. He walked over to the garbage pails behind his house, and tossed the paper plate with his sandwich. Returning to the table, he said, "I'll continue to ride the Atlantic City detectives working the case and I'll continue to examine the evidence. But I can't promise you anything, Gerry."

Gerry rose from the table. From his pocket he removed a piece of paper and unfolded it. It was a composite that Gerry had paid a courthouse artist in Atlantic City to draw of the man he'd seen in the hospital stairwell. He handed the drawing to his father.

"Just look at the case some more, Pop, that's all I'm asking."

Valentine patted his son on the back. It was tough to lose a childhood friend, harder still when you thought the friend had been murdered.

"I'll do what I can," Valentine said.

3

Gerry left, and Valentine went inside and back to work. As he walked through the rooms to his office, he paused to dust off a stack of videotapes. Along with his collection of crooked gambling equipment and books, the house contained his massive library of casino surveillance tapes and DVDs. Twenty-five years of cases were shoved into the dwelling, and every inch of storage space was filled with boxes.

He hadn't intended for the house to be that way. When he'd retired from the Atlantic City Police Department and moved to Florida two years before, he'd been ready to turn his back on the gambling world. But then his wife had died, and his social life had vanished. His days had turned into treading water. Out of necessity he'd gone back to work and started his consulting business.

His office was in the rear of his house. Normally his office manager, Mabel Struck, was manning the phones, but she had taken a much-deserved vacation, and was cruising the Caribbean. The room felt lonely without her, and he sat at his desk and sorted through the mail.

Today's batch contained several letters from frantic casino bosses. Every day somewhere a casino got ripped off. Sometimes, an old-fashioned grifter was responsible. In other cases, high-tech whiz kids were using a new gadget to beat the house. In this game of cat-and-mouse, the mouse sometimes won.

As he tore open each envelope, he checked to see if the sender had enclosed a check. That meant they were serious, and not shopping for free advice. Today's mail had two checks. The first was from a French casino that was losing a few grand a night at baccarat. The second from a Houston oil man who believed he'd been ripped off in a private poker game. Each check was accompanied by a CD on which the sender had recorded the suspected cheater's play. As Valentine popped the oil man's CD into his computer, the office phone rang.

"Grift Sense," he answered.

"This is Mark Perrier, general manager at Celebrity Casino in Las Vegas," a man's voice said. "Is Tony Valentine available?"

Celebrity was one of the newer casino chains. Instead of hiring gamers to run their casinos, Celebrity employed stuffed suits from the corporate world.

"For a price," Valentine said.

"Excuse me?"

"He's available for a price," Valentine said, then added, "It's a joke."

There was a short silence on the line.

"I'd like to speak to him," Perrier said.

"He's busy right now, making a living. Can I tell him what this is about?"

"No, you cannot."

Valentine had never consulted for Celebrity's casinos, and didn't think this conversation would change that. He dropped the receiver loudly on the desk, then noisily ruffled some papers. After a few moments, he picked the phone back up.

"Valentine here."

"Wasn't I just speaking to you?" Perrier asked angrily.

"That was my associate, Mr. Lipschitz," Valentine said. "People tell us we sound a lot alike. What can I do for you?"

"Mr. Valentine, I'll get right to the point. My owner has asked me to contact you regarding a homicide investigation taking place in Atlantic City. It involves a known cheater named Jack Donovan."

Lying on Valentine's desk was the playing card that Jack Donovan had given Gerry. He picked the card up, and stared at the garish Celebrity logo on the back.

"What about it?" Valentine asked.

"Celebrity would like the case to go away."

"Is that so?"

"The Atlantic City police have informed us that you are the primary reason the case is still open. Celebrity is presently hosting the World Poker Showdown, the largest poker tournament in the world. Having our casino associated with a murder investigation of a known cheater could be a public relations nightmare. I don't want to threaten you, Mr. Valentine, but if this case were to hit the newspapers and damage our reputation, we would seek punitive damages against your company."

"That sounds like a threat to me," Valentine said.

"I hope you'll strongly consider what I've said."

"Jack Donovan had a Celebrity playing card in his possession when he died. Were you aware of that?"

There was another silence on the line, this one a little longer.

"Mr. Valentine, I don't like the course this conversation is taking," Perrier said. "I'd appreciate an answer to my question. Will you drop this case or won't you?"

"Get lost," Valentine said, and hung up the phone.

*   *   *

Valentine scratched his chin while staring at the Celebrity playing card lying on his blotter. Where there was smoke, there was usually fire. If Celebrity wanted the case to go away, it was not just because of the bad publicity. Casinos received bad publicity every day, and it didn't stop people from gambling in them.

He had an idea, and he went on his computer, opening the database of his friends who worked in the gaming industry. Information on close to a thousand people was kept on this database. He pulled up all the names of people he knew who'd gone to work for Celebrity. There were thirty files. Scanning through the names, one jumped out at him: Paul Cummins, an old crony from Atlantic City, and one of the top security men in the business. Paul had recently gone to work for Celebrity's casino in Detroit, and Valentine called him on his cell phone.

"Paul here," Cummins answered through a mouthful of food.

"Quit eating on the job."

"As I live and breathe, if it isn't Atlantic City's gift to the world."

"I miss you, too. Look, Paul, I need your help."

"Name it."

"A Celebrity playing card has turned up in a murder investigation," Valentine said. "The card is clean, but something tells me it's still a valuable clue, only I'm not seeing what it is."

"Well, for starters, our playing cards aren't in general circulation," Cummins said. "Whoever had our card shouldn't have, because they're not supposed to leave the casinos."

"They're not?"

"No, sir. Ever since we got scammed by our own

cards last year, we stopped selling them to the general public."

Valentine felt like a bucket of ice water had been poured down his back. Years ago, casinos had sold used playing cards in their gift shops. But then the used cards had started turning up on the tables, mucked in by skilled sleight-of-hand artists. Some casinos had started "canceling" the used cards before they sold them by punching a hole in them, while others had stopped the practice altogether.

"So how would someone get a card out of one of your casinos?" Valentine asked.

"They wouldn't," Cummins said. "Not legally, anyway. Our cards are printed by the U.S. Playing Card Company in Cincinnati, and shipped by armored truck to each casino. When the cards reach the casino, they're kept under lock and key until they're delivered to the tables. The cards are used for an eight-hour shift, then collected, inspected, and destroyed."

"How could someone get one of your cards?" Valentine asked.

"They'd have to bribe an employee. If that happened in Detroit, I'd find out about it, because every card is accounted for before it's destroyed."

Valentine picked up the card lying on his desk. "What would you do?"

"I'd have the employee arrested," Cummins said. "I'd also notify management, and we'd probably do something drastic, like have all our playing cards changed. Now, if you don't mind, I want to ask you a question. A Celebrity playing card has obviously been taken from one of our casinos. I'd like to know, which one?"

"Why?"

"Job security."

Valentine examined the card in his hand. Celebrity's

name was printed in bold colors on its back, but not the casino's location.

"I don't know," Valentine said.

"Just tell me the back color," Cummins said.

"Purple."

"Be still my beating heart."

"Not yours?"

"No," Cummins said. "Purple is from our new casino in Las Vegas that opened last week. They're hosting the World Poker Showdown."

"When last week?"

"The grand opening was Friday night. They didn't invite you?"

Valentine counted backward on his fingers. Last Friday was six days ago, and Jack Donovan had died eight days ago. Another bucket of water came splashing down his back, this one even colder than the first.

"Thanks, Paul," he said. "Thanks a lot."

4

Valentine said good-bye to Cummins and hung up, then weighed calling Gerry. He wanted to tell his son what he'd learned, and also to apologize. He hadn't believed that Jack Donovan was murdered. Now, he knew better.

He'd let it wait. Confirming what Gerry already knew wasn't going to make his son feel better. In fact, it would only get him more worked up. Better to let Gerry spend a peaceful night with his wife and baby, and tell him tomorrow.

His size twelves made the wooden floors creak as he padded through the house to his kitchen. He poured himself a glass of water from the tap, and had it halfway to his lips when he remembered how awful the water tasted in Florida. *Like a science experiment,* as Gerry was fond of saying. He took a long swallow anyway.

The kitchen window looked onto his backyard, and he watched a mother cardinal deliver an insect to a nest of babies. The babies' mouths were visible above the nest's branches, each screaming *Me!* The mother dropped the insect and flew away.

He poured the rest of the water down the drain. Jack Donovan had been in the hospital for several months. That meant the cards from Celebrity's Las Vegas casino had been delivered to him. Jack had doctore[...] some fashion, and given them back. Being [...] crook, he'd kept one for himself, just in case h[...] needed to blackmail his partners. That was the card ne'd given to Gerry. The blackmail card.

But why had his partners killed him? The poor guy didn't have much time left. His partners must have been afraid of something.

Valentine went outside and sat on the back stoop. The sun was setting, its dying rays turning the sky a burnt orange. Some nights, he crossed the bridge to Clearwater Beach, and watched the sun set over the Gulf of Mexico. It was painful without his wife, but he did it anyway, knowing that time was the only thing that could heal his wounds.

His stomach was making funny sounds, and he realized he didn't feel well. He went inside and opened the pantry in search of the Pepto. As he started to pour out a spoonful, he realized what was bothering him. Jack Donovan had been murdered while Gerry was visiting him. The murderer could have waited, but had obviously wanted to shut Jack up. Was the murderer afraid of Jack revealing the poker scam to Gerry?

He put the Pepto back on the shelf. It made all the sense in the world. No wonder Gerry was so upset. His visit to Atlantic City was why Jack Donovan had died.

Valentine took a turkey-and-cheese Subway sandwich out of the refrigerator, and ate half while standing at the kitchen sink. One of the great shortcomings of the male species was its unwillingness to cook food for one person, and Valentine had started buying sandwiches from Subway and storing them in the fridge. He ate an apple for dessert, then decided it was time to go across the street and have a talk with his son.

Gerry and his beautiful wife and baby lived on the same block, only across the street and at the other end. The distance kept things healthy, and he tossed the core of his apple into the bushes before crossing.

The burg they lived in was called Palm Harbor. It was sandwiched between several other burgs, and the residential streets saw little traffic. He and his late wife had bought their house right before real estate prices had gone through the stratosphere. These days, it seemed everyone wanted to live in a small town.

Parked in front of Gerry's house was a car with a Z license plate. A Z meant it was a rental. Exhaust was coming out of its tailpipe, music blaring out of its radio. As Valentine got closer, he glanced at the driver. An Italian guy around his son's age, with a drooping moustache and sunken eyes. Valentine slapped his hand on the sill of the open window.

"Good evening."

The driver stuck his head out and grunted like a caveman.

"Are you looking for someone?" Valentine inquired.

"Just enjoying the beautiful outdoors," the driver said.

Valentine walked to the end of the block, then turned around and walked back to the car. The driver was looking at him in a way meant to inspire fear. A famous criminologist had once claimed that career criminals could be typed by hostile attitudes. The guy parked in front of Gerry's house could have been the poster boy for that study. Valentine walked up to the driver's window.

"What's up?" the driver said.

"I lost my dog. You didn't happen to see him, did you?"

"What kinda dog?"

Valentine put his hands together. "He's about this big, black hair, a mutt."

"Can't say I've seen him." The driver lit the cigarette dangling from his lips and blew a cloud of smoke Valentine's way. "Sorry."

Valentine gave the guy a hard look. His gut told him the guy was up to no good. His gut also told him that the guy hadn't come here by himself, and that his friends were inside Gerry's house, and were also up to no good.

"Oh, look, for God's sake, he's under your car," Valentine said.

The driver sat up straight. "He is?"

"Yes. Come on, boy, come here."

Valentine knelt down, then grabbed his back in mock pain. "Oh, Christ, my sciatic nerve is acting up. Would you mind helping me?"

The driver snuffed his cigarette in the ashtray and opened his door. As he climbed out from behind the wheel, Valentine leaned his body against the door, and pinned him. The driver let out a yelp like he'd been kicked. Valentine continued to press the door.

"You carrying a gun, buddy?"

"No."

He didn't look like the trustworthy type. Valentine stuck his free hand through the open window, frisked him, then opened the door, and yanked the guy out. Holding the guy's arm, he gave it a twist, and the guy started to corkscrew into the ground.

"You claustrophobic?" Valentine asked.

"What's that?" he gasped.

"Didn't think so."

There were several buttons on the driver's open door. Valentine found one to open the trunk, and punched it. Then he led the driver around the vehicle, and made him climb in. To his credit, he didn't complain as Valentine slammed the trunk down.

Valentine climbed into the car. He liked to know who he was dealing with; he opened the glove compartment, and pulled out the rental agreement. The car had been rented that afternoon at Tampa International Airport to Vincent Fountain, whose driver's license was from Atlantic City, New Jersey.

Valentine ran home, got his loaded Sig Sauer from the hollowed out copy of *Crime and Punishment* on his desk, then ran back to Gerry's house. His heart was pounding as he opened Gerry's front door with a spare key, and slipped into the foyer.

The house was a New England–style clapboard with original wood floors, and it was hard to walk on them without making noise. He could hear talking from the kitchen and moved toward it, his feet telegraphing every step. He stopped at the swinging door, and tried to imagine the people he was dealing with.

He decided they weren't Mafia. He'd grown up around the mob, dealt with them plenty as a cop. The Mafia had a code of ethics, as hard as that was to imagine. One of those codes was never to mess with a guy's family. That told him that Vincent Fountain and company weren't connected.

He pushed the door gently and peeked inside the kitchen. Gerry and Yolanda sat at the kitchen table, his granddaughter asleep in Yolanda's lap. They looked remarkably calm. There was a mirror behind them, in its reflection two smarmy Italian guys. One was tall and thin and talked too much. The other was about six three and had the proud, damaged face of a boxer. The boxer stood behind the swinging door, his arms crossed in front of his chest.

Valentine put his foot to the door and gave it a healthy kick. He'd been the New Jersey state heavyweight judo champ five years running, and still took class three times a week. He wasn't the man he used to be, but could still deal with a couple of two-bit punks, and that was exactly what he had here.

Valentine entered the kitchen to find the boxer now lying on the tile floor with blood pooling around his mouth. The guy doing the talking stopped.

"You Vinny?" Valentine asked him.

"Yeah. Who the hell are you?"

The Sig Sauer was in Valentine's right hand. He tossed it into his left, then used his right to punch Vinny in the jaw. It was a move straight out of the Keystone Cops, and Vinny's head snapped. Then he fell backward and hit the floor. Valentine looked at his son.

"Get your wife and daughter out of here," he said. "Right now."

5

Gerry and Yolanda left the kitchen without saying a word. Valentine glanced into his granddaughter's face as her mother carried her out. Lois hadn't stirred throughout the whole commotion.

Hearing the front door close, Valentine frisked Vinny and the boxer while they lay on the floor. They were both clean, and he threw cold water on their faces and made them get up. With the Sig Sauer, he pointed at the sink.

"Get the blood off your face," he told the boxer.

The boxer splashed his face with cold water. When he was finished he pulled on his front teeth and seemed pleased that none were broken. Valentine picked up a dishrag and tossed it to him.

"Now clean up the floor."

The boxer got on his knees, and cleaned up the blood-stain. As a cop, Valentine had learned that there were two ways to deal with lowlifes. The first was through brute force, the second intimidation. He told Vinny and the boxer to take our their wallets and hand him their driver's licenses. The two men obeyed.

Valentine wrote their names, social security numbers, addresses, and driver ID numbers on a piece of paper. They were both residents of Atlantic City, and the boxer's name was Frank DeCesar. Valentine told him to pick up the digital camera on the windowsill above the sink.

"Toss it here."

Frank tossed him the camera, and Valentine pointed it at them.

"Say cheese," he said, and snapped a picture.

The picture came out just fine. Valentine placed the camera on the kitchen table, then pointed at the door with his Sig Sauer.

"Let's go."

"You're Gerry's father, aren't you?" Vinny said as they walked through the house.

"No, we just look alike," Valentine said.

"Look, Mr. Valentine, this isn't what you think. Frank and I came here to present Gerry with a business proposition, that's all."

"Let me guess. You want to open a pizza parlor together."

The two hoodlums stopped at the front door. Vinny was dumb enough to think he was being serious. "It's a little more involved than that, not that I want to bore you with the financial stuff. But our call is strictly business. We did not come here to harm your son or daughter-in-law, or granddaughter, who I must say is a beautiful little child."

Vinny had a face that only a mother could love—sallow eyes, crooked nose, and two rows of teeth that looked like a rotted picket fence. His strength seemed to be his ability to string words together. Valentine pointed the Sig Sauer at Vinny's chest.

"Don't ever mention her again."

"Her?"

"My granddaughter," Valentine said.

"No, sir, I won't."

They walked out the front door of Gerry's house. It had grown dark, and a lone streetlight illuminated the block that Valentine called home. He watched Vinny and the boxer get into the rental. Vinny looked around in a panic.

"Where's Nunzie?"

"Taking a siesta in the trunk," Valentine said.

The rear end of the car started to rock. Nunzie was banging around like a bear. Vinny turned and yelled at him to calm down.

"He your brother?" Valentine asked.

"Yeah, how did you know?"

"Inflection."

Valentine was standing by the driver's window, and he tucked his weapon behind his belt, then knelt down so he and Vinny were eyeball to eyeball.

"How much do you boys know about me?"

"You're an ex-cop from Atlantic City."

"Anything else?"

Vinny scratched the stubble on his chin. He knew he was getting off easy, yet seemed unwilling to acknowledge it. "You do work for the casinos, catch cheaters."

"That it?"

Frank leaned over, and whispered in his ear. Vinny's face turned dead serious.

"You whacked the Mollo brothers," Vinny said.

Valentine gave him his best, no-nonsense stare. The year before, some throwbacks in Atlantic City who'd been threatening Gerry had gotten blown up in a car. Even though Valentine had nothing to do with their murder, everyone on the island believed that he had. Sometimes, those things worked to your advantage, and he banged the rental loudly with his hand, then stood up.

"Don't ever come back here again," he said.

"Wouldn't dream of it," Vinny said.

*　　*　　*

Valentine watched the rental drive to the next block, then stop. Vinny hopped out, and let his brother out of the trunk. As Nunzie climbed into the backseat, they all started yelling at one another, and he found himself smiling. Three guys in their prime had gotten outfoxed by a retired sixty-three-year-old. It didn't get any better than that. He walked down the street to his house and was met by Gerry at the front door.

"What happened?"

"I let them go with a warning," Valentine said.

"You beat them up any more?"

"Just their egos."

Valentine went to his study and put the Sig Sauer back in the book, and then it hit him. While the suit from Celebrity had been threatening him, three punks had been threatening Gerry. Were the two events linked? He found Gerry waiting in the hall.

"Pop, I *know* those guys, for Christ's sake."

"Friends?"

"No, but I know them, from the old days."

"They have an invitation?"

"No, but—"

"No buts. They were up to no good. A man's house is off-limits, especially when his wife and daughter are there."

Gerry rolled his eyes and looked at the ceiling. Valentine went into the living room, and found his grand-daughter playing on the rug with Yolanda. His late wife had hooked the rug out of his old police uniforms and Yolanda was always trying to clean up the messes that the baby left on it. Valentine had told her not to worry about it. He'd been spit on, pissed on, and puked on plenty of times as a cop; what harm would a little more do? He sat on the couch, and the baby crawled toward him. She'd be walking soon, and he clapped his hands and saw her smile.

"What's the weather like in Puerto Rico this time of year?" he asked.

Yolanda lifted her head. Her parents lived in a bucolic town outside of San Juan, and she'd been talking about paying them a visit.

"It's beautiful," she said.

"I'd like the three of you to go down there. I'll spring for the airline tickets and rental car."

"Oh, Dad, that's awfully nice of you," Yolanda said. "I've got time off coming from the hospital, so it shouldn't be a problem."

Valentine picked up his squealing granddaughter while looking at his son. Gerry had a strange look on his face. He took his daughter from Valentine's arms and handed the child to her mother.

"I need to talk to my father," he said.

Yolanda started to speak, then thought better of it. She pushed herself off the floor and walked out of Valentine's house with the baby in her arms. The front door made a loud click as it shut behind her.

Gerry sat down across from his father on the couch. "Pop, Yolanda doesn't know I used to be a bookie."

"You ever going to tell her the truth?"

"Sure, someday I'll tell her."

"Who the hell is Vinny Fountain?"

"An old business acquaintance. He came here to tell me that a mobster out of Newark named George Scalzo was responsible for Jack Donovan's murder."

"George 'the Tuna' Scalzo?"

"That's right. The Tuna stole Jack's poker scam, and had Jack whacked. The Tuna is out in Las Vegas, backing a player named Skip DeMarco in the World Poker

Showdown. DeMarco is going to cheat the tournament using Jack's scam."

"What's Vinny's connection, besides his undying love for Jack?"

"Vinny agreed to buy the scam from Jack, with the money going to Jack's mother. She lives on federal assistance."

"And Vinny wants you to fly with him to Las Vegas, and get the scam back."

"That's right," his son said.

"I hope you weren't considering going."

"It crossed my mind."

"That's dumb, Gerry."

His son made a face like he wanted to argue, but knew it wouldn't get him anywhere. He said, "Jack was my buddy. I owe it to him."

Friendship had a way of making a person blind to certain realities. George Scalzo was a ruthless criminal who'd killed scores of men over the years. Vinny Fountain and his bumbling buddies were no match for someone like that.

"I've got a better idea," Valentine said.

"What?"

"Take your wife and daughter to Puerto Rico and lie low for a while."

A wall of resolution rose in his son's face. "You're saying I should put my tail between my legs, and run?" Gerry said.

"That's exactly what I'm saying. Whenever George Scalzo gets involved with something, dead bodies turn up. I don't want you to be one of them."

"I can take care of myself, Pop."

"What about your family?"

"I can take care of them, too."

Valentine stared long and hard into his son's handsome face. Gerry was thirty-six, and still young enough to think that nothing could harm him. Only age was going to teach him otherwise.

"Just do as I say, okay?"

"That doesn't sound like a partner talking to me," Gerry said.

Valentine took another deep breath. His son had joined his business with no money, and had been living off his father's largesse while he learned the ropes.

"No, it's your father talking," he said.

His son rose from the couch with a dark look on his face.

"Gee," he said, "and I thought we were in business together."

He walked out of the room before Valentine had a chance to reply.

6

Valentine went to his study and shut the door. Gerry had a way of getting under his skin that left him feeling battered, and he wished Mabel was there. His neighbor was good at refereeing when their arguments got heated.

He sat down at his desk. Sticking out of his computer's hard drive was the CD from the oil man that contained a clip of suspected poker cheating. Normally he didn't work late, but he felt out of sorts and decided to have a look.

His computer whirred as it accepted the disc. Within seconds he was studying a grainy film of a poker game in the back room of a neighborhood bar. Eight middle-aged guys smoking fat cigars sat around a table with a castle of colored chips in its center. It was not something Valentine normally dealt with, and he found the letter that had accompanied the CD.

A Houston oil man had been invited to join an on-going high-stakes game at a local watering hole. He had lost his shirt three weeks running. Suspecting foul play, on the fourth week the oil man secretly filmed the game with a video camera hidden in a briefcase.

Valentine put the letter down, and stared at the film playing on his computer. Cheating at private poker games was the largest unchecked crime in America. It cost unsuspecting players millions of dollars a year. He watched the game for a few minutes, then noticed a plastic Budweiser sign behind the table.

The oil man's cell phone number was given at the bottom of the letter. He punched the number into his phone, and moments later was talking to an older gentleman with a drawl so thick he could have cut it with a knife.

"You work fast, Mr. Valentine. You figure out what's going on?"

"Maybe," Valentine said. "Let me ask you a couple of questions first."

"Be my guest."

"I'm staring at the CD you sent me. There are eight players at the table. Are you the player wearing the string tie and twirling a toothpick in your mouth?"

"Well, I'll be darned. How did you know that?"

"It's because of where you're sitting at the table," Valentine said.

"It is?"

"Yes. You're in what gamblers call the hot seat. You sat in that chair every week, didn't you?"

"How the heck did you know that?"

"The guy who owns the bar is running a peek joint. The Budweiser sign behind the table is made of Plexiglas. It's tinted on the front, but not the back, and works like a two-way mirror. Someone standing behind the wall can see through the sign, and spot the cards you're holding. That information is transmitted to the guy who owns the bar either by radio or by a waitress who delivers it to him on a cocktail napkin."

"You're saying this whole thing was a setup designed to fleece me?"

"I'm afraid so. Did you lose much money?"

"Sixty grand, but that's not the point. The man who

owns that bar swore to me that he ran a clean game. He gave me his word."

"May I make a suggestion?" Valentine said.

"By all means."

"Show your local sheriff the film. Then have him call me. I'll explain what's going on, and he can file charges against the bar owner. If you'd like, I can fly to Texas, and act as an expert witness at a trial."

"That's awful generous of you, Mr. Valentine, but I have a better idea."

"What's that?"

"I'll just go and shoot the son-of-a-bitch."

Valentine hung up the phone, then picked up the oil man's check and endorsed it. He hadn't made much money as a cop, and felt a certain satisfaction each time he signed the back of a check that he'd received for solving a scam. His bank account was growing fatter by the week, and he supposed one day he'd go out and buy himself a new car, or some nice new clothes, or maybe even a boat. Someday, but not today.

As he started to shut down his computer, he remembered why he'd come back to his study in the first place. Digging into his pocket, he removed the sheet of paper on which he'd written down Vinny Fountain's and Frank DeCesar's social security numbers, driver ID numbers, and addresses. He canceled the shut down and went into his e-mail, hitting the button for NEW MESSAGE. Then he typed in the recipient's name: Eddie Davis.

Eddie was an undercover detective with the Atlantic City Police Department, a hip black guy whose resemblance to the actor Richard Roundtree from the first *Shaft* movie was uncanny. Eddie had joined the force after Valentine had retired. They'd never worked together, and had no mutual friends in the department.

But they did have a bond. Eddie had helped Valentine catch the people who'd murdered his partner, and they'd become good friends.

Valentine copied Vinny Fountain and Frank DeCesar's information into the body of the e-mail, and hit SEND. Picking up the phone, he called Eddie at home.

"Am I getting you at a bad time?" he asked when Eddie answered.

"Just entertaining a lady friend."

"I can call back."

"She was just leaving, weren't you, honey?"

Valentine heard a woman's angry voice, followed by an unpleasant exchange. The conversation ended with a door being slammed.

"I'm back," Eddie said.

"I hope I wasn't the cause of that," Valentine said.

"Not at all. She was starting to use offensive language, so I figured it was time to end things."

The mean streets of Atlantic City were as bad as any in the nation, and Valentine couldn't imagine any language that Eddie might find upsetting.

"What kind of offensive language?"

"You know, words like marriage and commitment. That sort of thing."

"You're never going to settle down, are you?"

"The fields are too green for a man to stop mowing."

"I guess that means no."

"I'll find the woman of my dreams someday," Eddie said.

Valentine's eyes found the framed photograph of his late wife that sat on his desk. She'd never stopped being the woman of his dreams, even after she'd died.

"So what's up?" Eddie asked.

"I just sent you an e-mail with the names of two punks in Atlantic City I'd like you to check out. I need everything you can tell me about these jokers. Criminal backgrounds, who they run with, crimes they've been accused of, the whole shooting match."

"Shouldn't be a problem. Anybody I know?"

"Vinny Fountain and Frank DeCesar. There's also a third one, Nunzie Fountain."

Eddie went silent, and Valentine said, "You know them?"

"Their names have come up."

"How so?"

"This is in strict confidence, okay?"

"Of course."

"Vinny and Frank are informants. There was a flood of bad heroin on the streets a year ago; lots of hookers were shooting up and dropping dead. Vinny and Frank came forward, gave us enough information to track the source, and shut the operation down. The department didn't pay them or anything."

"What are you saying, they're good Samaritans?"

"In a way, yeah," Eddie said. "Don't get me wrong. They're wise guys, but they're also locals. They didn't like what was happening, so they put a stop to it."

"Sounds like they want to go to heaven," Valentine said.

Eddie laughed. "I'll run a check on them first thing tomorrow."

7

At eight o'clock in the morning, Gerry drove his family across Highway 60 toward Tampa International Airport, the rush-hour traffic made bearable by the near-perfect spring weather. Warm temperatures, and not a cloud in the flawless blue sky. The baby was asleep in her car seat in the back, while his wife sat beside him reading the paper. He drove with his eyes glued to the road, even though traffic was hardly moving.

"What time did your father come over last night?" Yolanda asked.

"Late," Gerry replied.

"I'm surprised I didn't hear him."

"He tried to be quiet. He knows how lightly you sleep."

"What made him change his mind?" his wife asked.

Lying had never been Gerry's strong suit, and it was rare that he was able to pull the wool over his wife's eyes. Yolanda had a sixth sense when it came to knowing the truth, and he guessed it was why she hated it when he tried to break bad news to her over the phone.

"I don't know," he said.

"Come on. You must have some idea."

"I guess he realized I'm not a kid anymore," Gerry said.

"You're always going to be a kid in his eyes." His wife took out a sanitary wipe and cleaned off their daughter's chin. "You need to get used to it."

The traffic began to move and Gerry goosed the accelerator. Ahead was the Courtney Campbell Causeway, the four-lane highway bordered on both sides by the gently lapping sea. Yolanda had hit the nail on the head. His father was still treating him like a kid. Only he wasn't a kid anymore; he'd stopped being one the day he'd started taking bets from his classmates in high school. He'd done that for twenty years along with plenty of other illegal things, yet somehow his father had forgotten that.

"We're partners now," Gerry said. "My father can't be bossing me around if we're going to work in the same business together."

"Even if he knows it's for your own good?" his wife asked.

Gerry feigned a laugh. Yolanda was the best thing that had ever happened to him. She was beautiful and wickedly smart and loved him to a fault. But she didn't always back him up, especially when it came to disagreements with his old man.

"Even then," he said.

People who lived in Tampa liked to say that their airport was the best in the country. Gerry had used the airport a few times, and joined the chorus. The place worked like a fine Swiss watch. He parked in short term, and got his wife's suitcase out of the trunk along with his daughter's stroller. They took an elevator down to the second level, and headed for the American Airlines counter. Within ten minutes the suitcase had been vetted by two TSA agents, and Yolanda had the boarding passes to San Juan.

They strolled around the main concourse, looking inside the shop windows, then bought two coffees at the Starbucks stand and an oatmeal cookie for their daughter. Yolanda glanced at her watch and said, "Well, I guess we should be going."

The flight didn't leave for another hour, and Gerry knew that Yolanda would pre-board because of the baby. He asked, "Had enough of me, huh?"

Yolanda kissed him on the lips, then looked into her husband's eyes.

"What I mean is, it's time for you to go to work," she said.

"Think my old man will dock me if I show up late?"

"With that attitude, yes."

"Do I have a bad attitude?"

"You do with your father. He brought you into his business to help you, Gerry. That says a lot about what type of person he is. I know he can be a bear sometimes, but he has your best interests at heart and always will."

Gerry didn't doubt what Yolanda was saying for a minute. His old man had been there for him through thick and thin. But he also knew that if he didn't avenge Jack Donovan's murder, he wasn't going to be able to live with himself.

They walked over to the Concourse E shuttle and kissed again. Then he gave his daughter a kiss. His wife gave the security person her driver's license and the boarding passes, and a moment later was let through. Gerry waved good-bye, and watched Yolanda and his daughter board a tram that would take them to their airline gate.

Gerry drove his car out of short-term parking and handed the ticket attendant his stub. Moments later his charge was printed on a digital screen next to the attendant's booth. NO CHARGE.

"I get to park for free?" Gerry said.

"You just made it under the minimum amount of time," the attendant said.

"What a great place."

"Tell me about it. Have a nice day."

He followed the signs out of the airport until he saw one that said AIRPORT RETURN. He got in the left lane, and looped back the way he came. A minute later he reentered the parking area, and headed for long term. He spent several minutes finding a spot, parked, and sat behind the wheel watching a jet depart on a runway. He imagined Yolanda and his daughter on that jet, and how he would feel if something happened to them and he was not by their side. Pangs of guilt swept over him, and he supposed that was the penalty for being untruthful with his wife.

He got his suitcase from the trunk. He'd stowed it there the night before, when Yolanda was sleeping. His wife believed she was a light sleeper, but ever since she'd had the baby, she slept like a log.

He took a tram to the main concourse, then an elevator to the second level. As he exited the elevator, he stopped beneath a giant electronic board that showed the morning's arrivals and departures arranged alphabetically by city. There were three flights out that morning, and he didn't think he'd have trouble getting a seat. He went to the Delta counter and handed a reservation agent his driver's license and credit card.

"Where are we going today?" the agent asked.

"Las Vegas," Gerry said.

8

One of the curses of the retired was the excess of unstructured time. Though not yet retired, Valentine had read that in a magazine published by AARP and had taken it to heart. Every morning, he followed a strict routine—twenty minutes of exercise, followed by breakfast while reading the paper. By nine he was ready to start work, and would go to his study and check his e-mails. More often than not, a panicked casino boss in some part of the world had contacted him the night before, and his workday would officially begin.

But today felt a little strange. He had plenty to do—with six e-mails having come in since last night—but his enthusiasm was not there. Perhaps it had something to do with the cryptic note he'd found stuffed in his newspaper from Gerry. His son had taken his family to San Juan early that morning, and promised to call in a few days.

Valentine stared out the window onto his backyard, and tried to put his finger on why he felt out of sorts. It took only a moment for him to realize what was wrong.

He was alone.

He'd battled loneliness since his wife had died, and considered it his greatest nemesis. He needed to stay engaged, regardless of the task. He was still staring out the window when his office line rang. He answered the phone without enthusiasm.

"Tony, is that you?" It was the familiar voice of Bill Higgins. Director of the Nevada Gaming Control Board, Bill was responsible for policing Nevada's casinos. They had been close friends for over twenty-five years.

"Sure is. You're up early."

"Just doing the Lord's work," Bill said. "I've got a problem that I was hoping you could help me with."

"Help's my middle name," Valentine said.

"Good. Are you familiar with the World Poker Showdown?"

"Sure. Largest open poker tournament in the world, held in Las Vegas for eight days every year, over five thousand players competing for a ten-million-dollar grand prize. This year's event is being held at Celebrity's new casino."

"I didn't know you stayed up on the poker stuff," Bill said.

"Beats playing shuffleboard."

"There you go. There's an old-timer entered in the tournament named Rufus Steele. His nickname is the Thin Man. You know him?"

Valentine smiled into the receiver. Rufus was the last of the true Texas gamblers, and had never met a wager he didn't like. "I helped Rufus out of a jam in Atlantic City twenty years ago. You know what they used to say about Rufus? If he stood sideways and stuck his tongue out, he'd look like a zipper."

"Well, the zipper is kicking up a storm. He got knocked out of the tournament last night, and started yelling that he'd been cheated. The tournament is being televised this year by one of the sports channels, so of course they interviewed him. It's making all the casino owners in Las Vegas nervous."

"How so?"

"Poker has been Las Vegas's salvation since 9/11," Bill said. "It draws more players with money than any other game. It's keeping the casinos happy."

"And Rufus saying that he got cheated in the biggest game in town might kill the goose that laid the golden egg," Valentine said.

"Exactly."

"What do you want me to do?"

"Two things. The interview is going to be shown on television again. I'd like you to watch it, and see if you think Rufus has a legitimate beef. If he does, I'd like you to watch a surveillance tape of Rufus's table in an e-mail I'm about to send you."

Valentine stared at his computer screen. The six e-mails he'd received last night were from casinos that paid him monthly retainers. He needed to address them, but didn't want to leave Bill hanging. He didn't put money before friendship, and never would.

"When does the interview come on?"

"Ten minutes."

"I'll have a look, and let you know what I think."

The only new thing Valentine had purchased since moving to Florida was a giant-screen TV, and that was because his old TV had gotten blown out during a lightning storm. Sitting in his La-Z-Boy, he hit the power on the remote, then surfed through the hundreds of channels he paid for but never watched, until he hit upon the sports channel showing the World Poker Showdown.

To Valentine's way of thinking, poker tournaments were the only real competitive sport on TV. No one was getting paid except the blow-dried announcers, and every player paid an entry fee. He wondered how the prima donnas in baseball and football would feel if they had to pay to play their games in the hope of winning a prize.

An announcer named Gloria Curtis appeared on the screen. She'd been a big-time sports analyst for years, then gotten sent down to the minor leagues of cable. Valentine had always liked her and turned up the volume.

"This is Gloria Curtis, reporting from this year's World Poker Showdown in Las Vegas. I'm standing here with poker legend Rufus Steele, who was knocked out of the tournament last night and is crying foul over what happened at his table."

The camera pulled back, and Rufus Steele entered the picture. He still looked like an advance man for a famine. He wore his usual cowboy garb—boots, blue jeans, and a denim shirt buttoned to the neck—and could have stepped straight out of a rodeo. His Stetson was held politely in his hands.

"Rufus," Curtis said, "could you explain to our viewing audience what happened last night?"

"I was cheated," Rufus said, staring into the camera.

"Can you explain how you were cheated?"

"I'd be happy to. The tournament starts with everyone having two hundred dollars in chips. As a result, everyone plays tight. Now, the tournament directors also move players around every hour to keep things fair."

"I'm with you so far," Curtis said.

"Good. The second hour into the tournament, I was

up two hundred dollars, and doing the best at my table. Then the tournament director brought over a new player. This player had fourteen hundred dollars in chips, which put everyone at a disadvantage. Within an hour, this player knocked several players out, including myself."

"How is that cheating?" Curtis asked.

"The cheating occurred at that player's previous table," Rufus said. "It is statistically impossible for that player—who is an amateur—to have won that much money in such a short amount of time."

She looked flustered. "But Mr. Steele, you're playing cards. People get lucky."

Steele gave her an icy stare. "Ma'am, are you familiar with something called the Poisson distribution?"

Gloria Curtis shook her head no.

"The Poisson distribution is a mathematical method of analyzing rare events. One assumption of the Poisson distribution is that the chance of winning is equally distributed. Every individual should have an equal chance when it comes to a game of cards, or playing the lottery. Make sense?"

"Certainly," she said.

"Well, I went back to my room, and used the Poisson distribution to analyze the chance of that player being the *only* player in this tournament to have won that much money in such a short period of time. Would you care to know what the odds are?"

"Please."

"Six billion to one. Where I come from, that ain't called luck."

Valentine heard the phone ringing in his study. He killed the power, and walked to the back of the house while thinking about what Rufus had just said. Rufus looked like a bumpkin, but it was just an act. Otherwise, he wouldn't have lasted as long as he had.

He picked up the phone, and heard Bill say, "So, what do you think?"

"I'd say you've got a problem," Valentine told his friend.

9

"**Y**ou think Rufus was cheated?" Bill asked.

"It sure sounds that way."

"Come on, Tony, there's no smoking gun, just his word against the tournament director's. I thought Rufus might say during the interview that he saw this other player marking cards or stealing chips, but he didn't say anything like that. Quoting some obscure mathematical equation isn't grounds to say you were cheated."

"It is in poker," Valentine said.

There was a pause on the line. Valentine found a pad and pencil on his desk, and jotted down the number of players in the World Poker Showdown, then determined the likelihood of one player beating seven other players within an hour based upon the Poisson equation. Although his formal education had ended in high school, he'd become schooled in statistics and probability when he'd started policing Atlantic City's casinos, and as a result understood the math behind the games as well as anyone. Finished, he stared at the long number on the pad. Rufus had been dead on: six billion to one.

"Would you mind explaining?" Bill said.

Poker was not a big casino game, and not a lot of people in the gambling business understood it. He said, "Sure. Poker isn't like other casino games, where the players gamble against the house, and the house always has an edge. In those games, the house is expected to win."

"I'm with you so far."

"Good. In poker, every player has the same chance, *especially* at the beginning of a tournament, when players start with an equal number of chips. Now, the odds of an amateur beating seven other players out of all their chips within the first hour is off the chart."

"But it could happen," Bill said.

"Maybe, but not necessarily," Valentine said.

"What is that supposed to mean?"

"It means it could happen, but probably won't, especially in a tournament like the World Poker Showdown. There are a number of reasons. First, people always play tight on the first day, because they don't want to get bounced out. Second, amateurs tend to be picked on by pros or more experienced players, so the chance of an amateur knocking out seven other players is slim."

"Maybe the guy got lucky," Bill interrupted. "That's a big part of the game."

"I'll agree with you there."

"So, the amateur who beat Rufus Steele got lucky."

"That would be the natural assumption," Valentine said, "only the Poisson distribution rules that out in this situation."

"How?"

"When applied to gambling, the main assumption of the Poisson distribution is that the chance of winning is randomly distributed. Which means that every individual has an equal chance. For example, if someone won a million-dollar jackpot on a slot machine, that's luck. Right?"

"Of course."

"However, if someone won *two* million-dollar jackpots on the same machine within an hour, that's probably cheating. You agree?"

Bill let out an exasperated breath. "Yeah, probably."

"The same thing is true in poker. An amateur might beat a guy at his table out of all his chips in an hour. However, the chances of him beating *two* guys is unlikely, and the odds of him beating *everyone* is exactly what Rufus said during his interview."

"Six billion to one?"

"Yeah, give or take a few thousand."

"So the amateur was cheating."

"That would be my guess."

"You want the job?" Bill asked.

"What job?"

"I want to hire you to figure out how this amateur beat those seven players at his table. I'll send you the surveillance tapes, plus the footage Gloria Curtis's cameraman shot. Study them, and tell me what the guy's doing. Then we can bar him from the tournament, and everyone will be happy."

"Does Celebrity know you're hiring me?"

"No," Bill said. "They haven't been very cooperative. Between you and me, I think they'd just like this whole thing to go away."

Valentine thought back to the threatening phone call he'd received from the suit at Celebrity. Most casinos tried to expose cheating, and get the cheats barred or arrested. Celebrity was taking the opposite approach, and doing everything possible to pretend it didn't exist. It didn't smell right, and he stared at the Celebrity playing card on his desk.

"Who's the suspected cheat?" Valentine asked.

"An amateur named Skip DeMarco."

Skip DeMarco was the same player that Gerry had said was in Las Vegas using Jack Donovan's poker scam.

Maybe he could nail DeMarco, and give his son something to smile about.

"You want the job or not?" Bill asked.

"I want it," Valentine said.

A minute later, Bill's e-mail appeared on his computer screen with the surveillance tapes of Celebrity's poker room and the footage shot by Gloria Curtis's cameraman attached.

He watched the poker tape first. Celebrity's surveillance cameras were digital, and the tape's resolution was crystal clear. Eight men in their late twenties sat at a table along with a professional female dealer, who wore a red bow tie and starched white shirt.

Skip DeMarco sat in the center of the table. He wore purple shades and stared into space as he played. The game was Texas Hold 'Em, with each player dealt two cards to start. Instead of peeking at his cards like the other players, DeMarco brought his cards up to his nose, and stared at them. He enjoyed belittling his opponents and trumpeting his own wins. Had it been a private game, someone would have silenced him, either through words or a request to step outside. But this was a tournament, where anything was permissible. By the hour's end, he had everyone's chips.

Valentine paused the tape and got a diet soda from the rattling fridge in the kitchen. The fridge had come with the house, and he'd been meaning to buy a new one, only it still worked, and he'd never believed in getting rid of things simply because they were old. Back in his study, he resumed watching the tape.

Everything about the game looked on the square. DeMarco played smart, and got good cards when he needed them. Maybe the odds of him beating the other players were six billion to one, but sometimes those things happened. He decided to play Gloria Curtis's tape, and see if it revealed anything.

Curtis had interviewed DeMarco at the end of the first day of the tournament, right after DeMarco had beaten Rufus Steel. DeMarco was tall and good-looking, and she held the mike up to his face.

"I'm speaking with today's Cinderella story of the tournament, Skip 'Dead Money' DeMarco, an amateur player from New Jersey. Although this is your first tournament, I'm told you've played poker for many years."

"I got my chops in Atlantic City," he said, holding a beer to his chest.

"Can you tell us where the name Dead Money comes from?"

"It's what the old-timers call amateurs."

"Well, it looks like you knocked one of those old-timers out today," Curtis said. "Rufus 'the Thin Man' Steele wasn't very happy with how you beat him."

"Too bad," he said.

"Rufus claims you had an unfair advantage."

"Try disadvantage. I'm legally blind, and have been my whole life," he said. "Try playing poker and not being able to see your opponents' faces."

"What about Rufus's claim?"

"Rufus Steele is past his prime. I'm starting a petition to have his name changed."

"To what?"

"The Old Man."

"How far do you think you'll go in the tournament?"

"All the way," he said.

The camera switched to show DeMarco at the poker table, raking in the chips. Valentine froze the tape and stared at DeMarco's face. One thing that hadn't diminished as he'd gotten older was his memory; he'd never seen this guy play poker in Atlantic City.

So why had he lied? DeMarco could have said he'd learned to play on the Internet, just like millions of other people. Only he'd wanted to let Gloria Curtis know that he was experienced, and that his winning wasn't a fluke. Valentine picked up the phone, and punched in Bill Higgins's cell number.

"I want to see some more tapes," he said.

"You think he's cheating?" Bill asked.

"I sure do."

It took Bill several hours to get him the additional surveillance tapes from Celebrity. By law, Nevada's casinos were required to film any area of the casino where money changed hands. The buy-in for a poker tournament was no different, and at noon the tapes appeared on Valentine's computer.

The tapes were about as inspiring as watching paint dry. Endlessly long lines of men and women stood in front of dozens of tables, waiting to pay the ten thousand–dollar entry fee and get a table assignment.

It took an hour and a half of searching to find Skip DeMarco. He stood in a long line, drinking coffee and talking with several other players. He walked with a cane, his movements out of sync with everything around him.

Valentine scrutinized the players standing with DeMarco. It was the same seven guys who'd played with him the first day. People registering together in poker tournaments were never supposed to be placed at the same table. But the WPS had let DeMarco sit with his pals, and they'd folded to DeMarco, and let him amass a huge stack of chips that later let him beat Rufus Steele. It was cheating, pure and simple.

But what bothered Valentine most was the scope of it. DeMarco was involved, and so were seven of his friends. Someone in tournament registration was also involved. That made nine people. That was a lot of people to push one player into the next round.

"Sounds like a conspiracy," Bill said, after Valentine explained what he'd discovered.

"It does, except there's a flaw," Valentine said.

"What's that?"

"Eight members of the gang are now useless to DeMarco. His pals are out of the tournament, and whoever helped him in registration can't do him any good now. DeMarco is on his own, and there's another seven days to play."

"Then why did he do it?"

Valentine picked up the Celebrity playing card lying on his desk. He had a sneaking suspicion that there was something else going on, and he wasn't seeing it.

"I honestly don't know," he said.

"Have you ever heard of a blind person cheating at poker before? Or any game?"

"No."

"Neither have I. I think he's got something up his sleeve. Maybe he's doing a special for one of those reality-TV shows, and he's going to show how he swindled the world's biggest poker tournament. Stranger things have happened. In the meantime, he might end up ruining the tournament and hurting every casino in town."

"The guy is a world-class jerk," Valentine said.

"Meaning my scenario isn't so far-fetched."

"Not at all."

"So here's what I'd like to offer you," Bill said. "Come out here for a few days, and scrutinize DeMarco's play. If you catch him doing anything illegal—bending a card, peeking at another player's hand, copping a chip—we'll bust his ass and bar him for life. Say yes, and I'll fly you out first class, pay your daily fee, and put you up. On top of that, you'll earn my undying gratitude."

Valentine's gut had been telling him that something wasn't right at this tournament. Now he could find out what it was, and thumb his nose at the threatened lawsuit from Celebrity. It was a sweet deal if he'd ever heard one.

"For you, anything," Valentine said.

10

The day Gerry Valentine had become a partner in his father's business, he'd gotten a history lesson about Las Vegas. He hadn't wanted to get a history lesson, but his father had wagged a finger in his face, and made him listen.

"It's for your own good," his father said.

So Gerry pulled up a chair and let his father talk.

Back in the 1940s, Las Vegas had been a dumpy gambling destination that attracted illiterate cowboys and other rough trade. Then two men with long criminal backgrounds came to town and changed the place. The first was a New York mobster named Bugsy Siegel. Bugsy was famous for wearing tailored suits, murdering anyone who got in his way, and helping Meyer Lansky and Al Capone start organized crime in America. Bugsy believed Las Vegas could be turned into Monte Carlo, and had sunk millions of the mob's money into building the town's first mega-resort on Las Vegas Boulevard. It was called the Flamingo, and was the beginning of the fabled "Strip."

The second was a Texas gambler named Benny Binion. Benny had a police record a mile long, and liked to say, "I never killed a man that didn't deserve it." Benny left Texas after learning that the Rangers had orders to kill him on sight. Las Vegas welcomed him with open arms, and he bought the Horseshoe on Fremont Street in old downtown. His first day open, Benny hung out a sign that said WORLD'S HIGHEST LIMITS, and attracted every serious gambler around.

According to Gerry's father, these two men had created modern Las Vegas. It was the town's legacy, and no one was ashamed of it. But it did bother his father. His father believed that casinos, and the people who ran them, must have integrity. The majority of casino owners did not share this view, and had given his father a nickname. They called him Mr. Black and White.

This was on Gerry's mind as he stepped off the plane at McCarran International Airport. A lot of people in Las Vegas knew his father and didn't like him. And because Gerry was looking more like his father every day, people were going to recognize him. What were they going to call him? Mr. Black and White Jr.?

He ducked into a gift shop inside the terminal. Five minutes later he emerged wearing a Dodgers' baseball cap, cheap sunglasses, and his shirt pulled out of his pants. He glanced at himself in the reflection in the gift shop's window.

"Beautiful," he said.

He rented a car, and drove to a joint on Las Vegas Boulevard called the Laughing Jackalope. Las Vegas was always boasting about being the fastest-growing city in the country, and about all the great jobs the city offered, but only the casinos made serious money. Every other place struggled to make ends meet. The Jackalope was no exception.

He squeezed the rental between a maxed-out Harley and a mud-caked junker. The Jackalope's cross-eyed, albino bartender was considered a good source of information, and Gerry found him at the bar, standing like a statue beneath the TV. There was a hockey game on, a dozen guys slugging it out on the ice.

"A draft," Gerry said, taking a stool.

The albino filled a mug with beer. He put a giant head on it, and plunked it onto the water-stained bar; the beer rolled down the glass. Having once run a bar himself, Gerry realized he was being insulted.

"Two bucks fifty," the albino said.

"Can I get a scoop of ice cream with my drink?"

The albino didn't laugh, nor did the drunken prophets sitting at the bar.

"Two bucks fifty," the albino repeated.

"You always so hospitable?" Gerry asked as he paid up.

The albino eyed the C-note that Gerry had tugged out of his wallet. "I remember you," the albino said. "You're from New York."

"Was," Gerry said.

"Where you living now?"

"Sunny Florida."

"You like it down there?"

"Love it."

"I hear the summers are murder."

"They're not as bad as here."

"Here? Give me a break. You have the fucking humidity. We don't."

"No, you just step outside and burst into flames."

The albino's face cracked. Almost a smile, but not quite there.

"Drink your beer," he said.

The albino walked down the bar to take care of a female customer. The woman didn't have any money but wanted another drink. The albino showed her to the door, then returned.

"What do you want?" he asked.

"I'm looking for a couple of brothers who came into town yesterday," Gerry said, a frosty beer moustache painting his upper lip. "Their names are Nunzie and Vinny Fountain. There's a third guy with them, a gorilla named Frank."

"Tush hog?" the albino asked.

Gerry had never heard anyone use that expression except his father. A tush hog was a muscleman employed by mobsters who enjoyed putting the hurt on people. Usually, their presence was enough to settle things.

"Wouldn't know. I've never seen him fight," Gerry said.

"Let me make a phone call, see what I can find out," the albino said.

Gerry reached into his wallet and folded the C-note. He handed the money to the albino along with his empty mug. The albino walked down the bar, picked up the house phone, and made a call. Gerry lifted his gaze and stared at the TV. The hockey players were still fighting, their masks and gloves lying on the ice. He remembered going to a hockey game at Madison Square Garden with Jack Donovan, and Jack saying that hockey games *had* to have fights. Otherwise, they would last only about fifteen minutes.

The albino came back. "Your friends are staying at the Riviera."

"Thanks," Gerry said.

Going out, Gerry stopped to watch two guys at the pool table playing one-pocket. One-pocket was the favorite game among skilled players. Both players were too drunk to make any decent shots, and he left before the game ended.

He stepped outside into a blast of heat coming off the desert. The sunlight was fading, and the casinos' feverishly pulsing neon was beginning to define the skyline. Standing in the parking lot, he stared northward at the brilliant sphere of light coming out of the Luxor's towering green glass pyramid. The light had attracted thousands of moths, which in turn attracted hundreds of bats, and their wings beat furiously against the sky. He tried to remember the last time he'd seen a bat in the desert. Behind him, a car pulled into the lot, and two guys jumped out.

"Is that supposed to be a disguise?" one said sarcastically.

Gerry spun around. It was Vinny and the tush hog. He glanced into the idling car, and saw Nunzie behind the wheel.

"How did you find me?" Gerry asked.

"The albino called me," Vinny said. "We've got an arrangement."

"You sleeping with him?"

The tush hog laughed under his breath. Vinny threw an elbow into the bigger man's ribs. Then Vinny stared at Gerry for what seemed like an eternity.

"Is your father with you?" Vinny asked.

"No, I came alone," Gerry said.

Vinny rubbed his jaw. It was still swollen from where his father had popped him. Vinny's eyes were burning, the ignominy of the punch slow to fade.

"Let's go for a drive," Vinny said.

11

Valentine said good-bye to Bill and hung up the phone, then went to his bedroom and started packing for Las Vegas. Into his hanging bag went two pairs of black slacks, two white button-down cotton shirts, and two black sports jackets that dated back to his days policing Atlantic City's casinos. He threw in a gold necktie his wife had given him and zippered the bag closed. The clothes were the same ones he always wore when he was working—his uniform.

The phone rang while he was eating supper. He'd recently gotten Caller ID, and saw that it was Bill. He answered with a bite of sandwich still in his mouth.

"What would you say to appearing on TV when you come out here?" Bill asked.

He swallowed the food in his mouth and nearly choked.

"You're kidding, right?"

"Afraid not. Gloria Curtis won't let this story die, and neither will the network she works for. They're hounding me about Rufus Steele's allegations of being cheated. I told Gloria that I'd hired an outsider to investigate. Now she's wants an interview with you."

"You know how I feel about going on TV," Valentine said.

"Yes, that it's stupid and has ruined more investigations than it's helped," Bill said. "But here's my problem. Gloria broke this story. If you don't talk to her, she'll go on air, and start speculating about *why* the Nevada Gaming Control Board hired you. That would hurt your investigation and the tournament."

He put his dirty plate in the sink and ran warm water over it. He'd appeared on television a handful of times while working on cases, and always regretted it. His statements had been distorted, and he'd been challenged by nitwits who knew nothing about the gaming industry or cheating. Worse, his mug had gotten put out there for everyone to see, something that was unhealthy in his line of work.

"Sounds like you've gotten yourself painted into a corner," Valentine said. "How about we offer her a compromise?"

"Name it."

"I'll talk to Gloria, but not on the air, because showing my face would compromise the investigation. She can ask me questions, and I'll answer them to the best of my ability. Then she can tell her viewers what's going on."

"You'd be willing to do that?"

"Sure."

"Will you tell her anything?"

"Of course not," Valentine said. "It's none of her flipping business. Can I make another suggestion?"

"Of course."

"Get ahold of Rufus Steele, and tell him to keep his mouth shut until I get out there and get to the bottom of what's going on. If he gives you any lip, tell him I'll expose his sorry ass."

"Expose him how?"

"Rufus got arrested when he was a teenager. He rescued stray dogs from the pound, paid a groomer to make them look like an exotic breed, then went into wealthy neighborhoods, and sold them to widows with a sob story about needing money. At his trial, he told the judge he was doing the town a favor, because the women became attached to the dogs, and kept them after their coats grew out. The judge gave him ninety days."

He dried the plate with a towel and heard Bill laughing.

"That's wonderful," his friend said.

Valentine went into his study and printed his flight itinerary off the computer. His flight left Tampa at seven A.M., which meant he needed to get up by four thirty in order to drive to the airport and deal with security. It made him tired just thinking about it, and he folded the itinerary into a square and stuck it into his wallet.

He shuffled into his bedroom and set the alarm clock, then undressed and lay naked on his bed. Nighttime was the most difficult time, and sometimes he imagined that everything that had happened since Lois's death was a dream, and that she would walk into the room, and his life would return to normal. A stupid dream, but one he still held on to.

An hour later the phone rang. He answered it with a groggy "Hello."

"Hey, Tony, hope I didn't wake you," Eddie Davis's voice rang out.

"You did, but that's okay."

"I'm sorry it's taken me so long to get back to you," his friend from the Atlantic City Police Department said, "but it's been a long day. I did a background check on those three names you gave me. I also took it upon myself to ask my pal over at the New Jersey Gambling Commission if they had a file on those boys."

"Did they?"

"Yeah. Look, are you someplace where you can talk?"

Valentine's eyes opened wide. His bedroom was pitch dark, and except for the light creeping through the blinds from a streetlight, he couldn't see a blessed thing.

"I can talk. What did you find?"

"It isn't good, Tony."

He sat up straight and immediately felt light-headed. The phone had a short cord, and he heard it go crashing to the floor. He groped in the dark, found the phone, and clumsily replaced it on the night table.

"You still there, Eddie?"

"I sure am. Here's the down and dirty, Tony. According to police records, Vinny Fountain, Nunzie Fountain, and Frank DeCesar are small-time scammers who've had a hand in dozens of shady operations on the island in the past ten years. Mind you, they've never been arrested, but their names have come up during plenty of investigations."

"Wise guy wannabes," Valentine said.

"Exactly," Eddie said. "Now, here's what I got from the New Jersey Gambling Commission. The GC got a tip several years ago that the Fountains were conspiring to scam a casino in Atlantic City, and decided to conduct an investigation. The Fountains were followed and had their phones tapped."

Valentine threw his legs over the edge of the bed. What the hell was Eddie talking about? He'd never heard of the Fountains in conjunction with any scam, and there wasn't an Atlantic City scam that he hadn't known about when he was a cop.

"What year was this?" he asked.

"It was 1998."

That was three years before he'd retired.

"You're sure?" Valentine asked.

"Positive."

"But that's impossible. I would have known."

"Just listen," Eddie said. "The Fountains moved around a lot, and did most of their talking on pay phones. There was a bar in Brooklyn where they went a few times, and made some calls. Guess which one."

Valentine blinked in the dark. "My son's."

"There you go."

Which was why he'd never heard about the investigation. Someone over at the Gambling Commission had made the link, and decided to keep Valentine out of the loop. He thought back to the scene in Gerry's house the day before, and what Vinny Fountain had said to him. *We're just discussing a business proposition with your son.* He turned on the night table lamp, and flooded the bedroom with light.

"What happened to the investigation?" he asked.

"It fell apart," Eddie said. "The Fountains never went through with the scam for whatever reason. There wasn't enough evidence on the wiretaps to convict them of conspiracy, so the GC dropped it."

Valentine rubbed his face with his hand. It would have been nice to think that Gerry hadn't known what the Fountains were doing in his bar. After all, guys made phone calls in bars all the time. Only Gerry had run an illegal bookmaking operation and had known every scammer that had stepped into the joint. Gerry had been involved with these hoodlums, maybe even had a part in their scam. It was embarrassing as hell.

"Thanks, Eddie. I really appreciate you going to the trouble."

"Sorry to ruin your night," Eddie said.

12

"What the hell is a tush hog?" Frank asked.

They were in Vinny's rental, cruising the strip. Nunzie was driving, Frank riding shotgun, Vinny and Gerry in the backseat acting like sightseers. Nighttime in Vegas was a trip, the sky so brilliantly lit that it put the brain on overload. They'd been driving around for a while. Vinny had apologized to Gerry for coming to his house the day before without calling, and Gerry had apologized for his father roughing Vinny and Frank and Nunzie up. That had been the nature of their relationship for as long as Gerry could remember. He would do a deal with Vinny, they'd have a fight, then later end up apologizing.

"A tush hog is an old-timer's expression for an enforcer," Gerry said.

"Is that what I am, an enforcer?"

"You were a professional boxer once, weren't you?"

"Yeah, but all my fights were in Europe," Frank said. "So?"

"No one in the United States saw them. If my fights had been over here, people would be afraid of me, you know?"

"You're still a tush hog," Gerry said.

Frank shook his head, not liking it. "It makes it sound like I have a big ass."

"You do have a big ass," Nunzie said.

Everyone in the car laughed. Then Frank punched Nunzie in the arm, and the rental crossed the double line on the highway. Suddenly they were driving straight into oncoming traffic. Nunzie spun the wheel, and they recrossed the line to safety.

Gerry released his death grip on the door handle, took a few deep breaths, and felt his heartbeat slowly return to normal. That was the bad thing about working with the Fountain brothers. Everything would be going along just fine; then, without warning, your life was dangling in front of your face.

Vinny told Nunzie to drive to an area of town called Naked City. It was on the north end of Las Vegas, stuck between the strip and Fremont Street, and was filled with sleazy strip clubs, adult bookstores and fetish shops, and run-down massage parlors. Gerry had heard that every business in Naked City had ties to organized crime. The mob had once run the town's casinos; now they just ran the flesh trade.

Nunzie pulled up to the valet in front of a strip club called the Sugar Shack. The valets were all grown men and not moving terribly fast. Gerry had seen similar setups in strip joints up and down the East Coast. The mob ran the valet concession, and gave jobs to made guys just out of prison.

As they waited for a valet to take their car, Vinny said, "I set up a meeting with Jinky Harris. He owns this joint. He also runs the town's rackets. I wanted him to know what we were doing out here, make sure he was cool with it."

"I've got a question," Nunzie said.

"What?"

"If this guy's so important, how did he get a name like Jinky?"

Vinny reached around the headrest and grabbed Nunzie by the ear. No words were spoken, just a gentle twist of the lower lobe. Nunzie twisted painfully in his seat.

"All right, all right, it was a dumb question," Nunzie said.

The club's interior was upscale as far as strip clubs went. On three brightly lit stages, dozens of naked young women pranced and danced and gyrated on brass poles, their bodies showing more silicone than Palo Alto. It was a feast for the eyes, but what got Gerry's attention was the free buffet laid out on two long tables beside the main bar. He stared longingly at the steaming food while Vinny asked the bartender if the boss was in.

"Who wants to know?" the bartender replied.

"Vinny Fountain and associates," Vinny replied.

The bartender picked up the house phone and made a call. Gerry continued to stare at the food. He hadn't eaten since breakfast and was starving. He waited until the guy serving the food turned his head, and tried to pilfer an egg roll.

"The food's for customers," a booming voice said.

Gerry looked up into the face of a black guy easily seven feet tall. His head was shaved and the strobe lights in the club danced off his skull. Gerry removed his hand.

"Sorry."

"As well you should be," the giant said. "Which one of you is Vinny?"

"I am," Vinny said.

"Mr. Harris will see you now," the giant said.

They followed him through a red-beaded curtain,

then down a dimly lit hallway to a blue door. As the giant rapped on the door, Nunzie whispered to Frank, "Now, that's a tush hog."

Jinky's office was straight out of the movie *Scarface*, with thick white carpet, luxurious leather furniture, and ugly wall hangings. The boss sat in a motorized wheelchair behind a massive marble desk. In his fifties, he wore a purple velour tracksuit, had a full beard, and looked wider than he was tall. On the desk were four plates of food from the buffet, along with a tall glass of milk. The sizes of the portions were phenomenal. Jinky shook out a cloth napkin, and tucked it into his collar.

"You're from Atlantic City?" Jinky asked.

"That's right," Vinny said.

"I hate Atlantic City. What can I do for you?"

"We're in town to settle a score," Vinny said. "I didn't want to bother any of your operations."

Jinky plunged his fork into a steaming mound of chow mein. "A score with who?"

"George Scalzo. He's scamming World Poker Showdown," Vinny said.

"George 'the Tuna' Scalzo?"

"That's right."

"Another New Jersey scumbag. What did Scalzo do to you?"

"He stole something of mine, and killed our friend."

Jinky twirled the noodles on his fork, then stuck the fork into his mouth. He chewed and swallowed, then turned to glance at the giant, who stood behind him.

"We got any action at the WPS?" Jinky asked.

"Just the ring games," the giant replied.

"You rig them?"

"Yeah," the giant said.

Ring games were the side games at poker tournaments, and usually played for high stakes. By rigging these games, Jinky would make a killing without coming under the scrutiny of the tournament's rules and regulations.

"Stay away from the ring games," Jinky told them.

"Won't touch them," Vinny said.

Gerry's stomach emitted a growl. The smell of the food was too much for his digestive system to bear. Jinky dropped his fork onto his plate.

"What, your mother doesn't feed you?"

Gerry couldn't believe Jinky was treating them this way. Had Jinky walked into his bar in Brooklyn, he would have shown him a certain level of hospitality. Like a cup of coffee and a chair.

"I caught him stealing an egg roll," the giant said.

"Don't ever step into my club again," Jinky said.

Gerry nearly told him to shove it, but instead removed his baseball cap. "I haven't eaten all day, and my hunger got the best of me. I meant no disrespect."

Jinky leaned back in his wheelchair and scratched his beard. If he didn't accept the apology, he'd look like an ingrate. As the boss, he was supposed to be above that.

"Apology accepted," Jinky said.

Gerry put his baseball cap back on.

"Now get the hell out of my club, and don't ever come back."

Gerry felt like he'd been backhanded across the face. Had the giant not been standing there, he would have said something. He noticed a framed photo sitting on the desk. It showed Jinky holding a plaque outside the Acme Oyster House in New Orleans. Gerry had gone to New Orleans with Yolanda before the baby had been born, and had eaten at the Acme. He remembered seeing the plaque hanging above the main shucking area. He looked at his host.

"I can't believe it. You're the guy who ate forty-two

dozen oysters at the Acme Oyster House in New Orleans, aren't you?"

Jinky leaned forward. "Forty-two and a half. You been there?"

"Sure," Gerry said. "I could only eat two dozen."

"You like oysters?"

"Love 'em. I also love milk."

Jinky picked up the glass of milk on the desk. "Me too. Since I was a kid."

"How much do you drink a day?" Gerry asked.

Jinky counted on his fingers. "Ten glasses, at least."

"Over a gallon?"

"More than a gallon."

"Think you could drink a gallon of milk in an hour?"

"With my eyes closed," Jinky said.

Gerry took his wallet out and removed all his cash, which he tossed on the desk.

"Bet you can't," he said.

Hustlers have an expression: "Pigs get fed, hogs get slaughtered." Gerry had decided that it was time for Jinky to get slaughtered. He was going to pay this bastard back for not showing them any respect, and he was going to do it in a mean way.

The giant took Gerry's money and counted it on the desk. There was exactly four hundred dollars, which wasn't much by Vegas standards.

Jinky glanced up at Vinny. "You want some of this action?"

Vinny started to say no, but Gerry elbowed him in the ribs.

"Take the man's bet," Gerry said under his breath.

"What?"

"Just do as I say."

Vinny blew out his lungs and removed a wad of cash

from his pocket. He threw half of it onto the desk beside Gerry's money. The giant counted it as well. Twenty-six hundred bucks, all in C-notes.

"Three thousand bucks says I can't drink a gallon of milk in an hour?" Jinky said. "What if I drink it in half an hour?"

"We'll pay you double," Gerry said.

Vinny let out a gasp.

"You're on!" Jinky exclaimed.

The giant went down the hall to the kitchen. When he returned he was holding a fresh gallon of milk. He opened it, and poured a tall glass for his boss. Jinky raised it in a mock toast.

"Here's to the easiest six grand I've ever made. Thanks, boys."

Jinky drank the first four glasses of milk without a problem. But by the fifth glass, he began to slow down, the color of his face turning from deep red to a subdued pink. He was struggling to keep the liquid down, and placed the empty glass on his desk and filled his lungs with air. A little over half the gallon was gone.

"How much time have I used?" he asked.

"Fifteen minutes," the giant said. He sat on the edge of his boss's desk, guarding the money.

"Give me a minute to catch my breath."

"You've got another forty-five minutes, boss."

"Fifteen," Jinky said. "I'm going to drink the rest in fifteen."

"Don't hurt yourself, boss."

"Shut your mouth," Jinky said.

The sixth glass was a monumental achievement, and went down as slow as honey. By the time the seventh had been raised to Jinky's lips, five more minutes had passed, and Jinky's face had turned as white as the liquid in the glass. He was a goner, and Gerry tugged Vinny on the sleeve.

"Get out of his way," he said beneath his breath.

"He gonna blow?" Vinny whispered back.

"Any second."

"You slip something into his drink?"

"No. It's all the enzymes in the milk. The stomach can't tolerate them all at once. The king is about to be dethroned."

Vinny hid the smile on his lips. "Long live the king," he said.

13

Valentine landed at McCarran International Airport at nine thirty the next morning, and was greeted by Gloria Curtis as he stepped out of the jetway. She wore a striking blue suit and stood out among the poorly dressed tourists. He'd watched her announce sports for years, and always liked her direct, no-nonsense style. She looked younger than her age, which he guessed to be fifty. She was an attractive woman who'd opted for crow's feet instead of a face lift. He liked that, too.

"Mr. Valentine, I'm Gloria Curtis with WSPN Sports," she said.

He did not slow down, his clothing bag slung over his shoulder.

"How did you get out here without a ticket?" he asked.

It wasn't the best lead, and he saw a twinge of hurt on her face. "I was just wondering," he quickly added. "Being an ex-cop, my curiosity kind of runs away with my mouth sometimes."

"I was supposed to be leaving this afternoon," she said. "I used that ticket. Look, I'll get right to the point. I need to air my story in a few hours."

"Time's a-wasting, huh?"

"Yes. I have a deadline to meet, and I'm hoping you'll accommodate me."

"Off camera, as we agreed," he said.

"Yes. I rented one of the airport's conference rooms."

Valentine shook his head.

"Would you prefer one of the casinos, instead?" she asked.

He shook his head again. If there is anywhere in the world where the expression "The walls have ears" is true, it is in Las Vegas.

She made an annoyed face, and he said, "Don't worry. I know the perfect place we can talk."

There was something deliciously sweet about taking a woman that you'd always admired for a drive ten minutes after meeting her. But that was what Valentine was able to do, having rented a convertible at the Avis counter while convincing Gloria that a car would be the safest place to have their conversation about cheating at World Poker Showdown. As he opened the passenger door for her, she smiled.

"How nice. You're also a gentleman," she said.

Outside of the airport he got onto Tropicana Avenue and took it to Las Vegas Boulevard, then headed south, away from town. The pattern of two- and three-story condominiums broke after a few miles, the scenery changing to desert fields that lay in dusty rest. He glanced at his passenger and saw her eyeing the scenery.

"This feels like a date," she said with a laugh in her voice.

"Does that mean the interview's off?"

She turned in her seat, the shoulder harness pulling at her blouse.

"Don't try to wiggle out of this one."

He stared at the highway. "Fire away."

"First of all, I'm pretty sure that Skip DeMarco cheated during the first day of the tournament," she began.

"How did you do that?"

"I got my hands on the tournament registration log-book. DeMarco registered with the same seven guys he played with. I looked at the tapes from their table. They all folded to him, and gave him a huge advantage because he had so many chips. That let him beat Rufus Steele, plus a number of other top players. It was such an advantage that he's currently the chip leader in the tournament. I also ran a background check on him. His uncle is a gangster from Newark named George 'the Tuna' Scalzo. Scalzo is out here, backing him."

Gloria folded her hands in her lap, obviously pleased with herself.

"So what's the question?" Valentine asked.

She shot him a bite-your-head-off look. "Are you trying to be funny? I want you to confirm what I just said."

"Confirm what?"

"That DeMarco is a cheater."

"Can't."

"Why not?"

"Because you don't have any proof," Valentine said.

"But I just told you my proof."

"It won't hold up. Play devil's advocate with me for a minute. DeMarco registers with seven guys, and they end up at the same table. It looks suspicious, but maybe it's a coincidence. He is blind, so you can't blame him. Unless you can get one of those seven guys to admit it was done on purpose, you've got nothing."

He took his eyes off the road and glanced at her. "Agreed?"

Gloria bit her lower lip. "I guess."

"Now, those seven guys fold to DeMarco. Or did they

just lose to him? Unless one of them says they gave him their chips, you've got nothing. Agreed?"

"Come on. You and I both know that DeMarco cheated."

"That doesn't mean anything. There are plenty of cheaters playing in the World Poker Showdown, including your source, Rufus Steele."

"He is?"

"Yes. Rufus has been conning people for fifty years. Having one crook accuse another crook of cheating isn't credible."

"But Rufus has never been arrested," she said. "I checked him out."

"He's still a crook."

"But—"

"Trust me on this, okay?"

She acted wounded, and Valentine guessed she'd already written her story, and was just hoping he'd verify it so she could get in front of a camera and blow the lid off DeMarco's scam. That wasn't going to happen if he had a say in the matter, and he saw a gas station ahead and turned his indicator on.

"Look, Gloria," he said when they were sitting in the gas station's parking area. She had refused his offer of a hot drink, and stared coolly at him as he spoke. "A lot of gamblers are crooks. They try to get an edge whenever they can. Sometimes it means doing things that aren't kosher."

"And Rufus is one of these people."

"He sure is."

"Give me an example."

The gambling world was replete with stories of how Rufus Steele had conned suckers out of their hard-earned dough. He sensed that Gloria had taken a liking to Rufus, and he tried to pick a story that wouldn't offend her too badly.

"Rufus is the master of the proposition bet. Know what those are?"

She shook her head.

"A proposition bet is one that you can't win, even though it looks fair. Here's one of my favorites. Rufus showed up at a dog track in Miami one day. It was early in the morning, and the track wasn't officially open. With him is a greyhound with a big, lumpy belly. The dog looks like it's pregnant. Rufus starts chiding the trainers, and tells them that his dog is faster than theirs. Within five minutes, he's got everyone riled up, and a bunch of trainers willing to bet him otherwise. Needless to say, Rufus took them on."

"Did he win the bet?"

"Of course he won," Valentine said.

"But I thought you said the dog was pregnant."

"The dog *looked* pregnant. Rufus had fed her a bowl of hard-boiled eggs for breakfast. For some reason, they blow up a dog's stomach, but they don't affect their movement. The dog was also a world-class runner. It beat the field by two lengths."

"How clever."

"Clever like a fox. Rufus won thirty grand on that bet."

"Thirty grand? That's cheating."

"It sure is."

Gloria stared out the windshield at the convenience store. She looked defeated, and glanced at her watch, then across the seat at him.

"I think I'll take you up on that hot drink," she said.

Valentine bought two cups of coffee and shared a cinnamon doughnut with her. He felt he needed to impress her, yet at the same time, didn't want to get too close and blow his investigation. He pointed at the last piece of doughnut and said, "That's got your name on it."

She popped the piece into her mouth and smiled as she chewed.

"You sure know how to show a girl a good time," she said.

"I get the feeling that I've put you in a bad spot."

"Sort of."

"Tell me what the problem is. If I can help you, I will."

"Do you really mean that?"

"Of course I mean it."

She wiped her mouth with a paper napkin. "It's like this, Tony. Next year, I turn fifty. In the broadcast news business, that's a mature age for a man, ancient for a woman. I'm being put out to pasture. No more major league baseball games or NFL football analysis or any plum assignments. It's billiards tournaments and lumberjack competitions these days. Covering the World Poker Showdown was a favor by the head of the network. And I blew it."

"You mean by saying there was cheating."

"Yes. Based on what you just told me, I can't prove it. Mark Perrier, the guy who runs Celebrity, is threatening a lawsuit if I don't recant the story. If I *do* recant, I'll lose my job with the network. What's the expression? I'm stuck between a rock and a hard place, and I don't know what to do."

Perrier was the same guy who'd threatened him over the phone two nights ago. Valentine was seeing a pattern that he didn't like. Perrier should be trying to get to the bottom of these allegations instead of covering them up. He reached over and touched Gloria's sleeve. She looked into his face, her eyes hopeful.

"Do you know what the bad part about getting old is?" he asked.

"The wrinkles?"

"People don't think you count anymore."

"Oh," she said.

"As a result, you spend a lot of time showing people you *do* count. Sort of like when you were a kid, and no one took you seriously."

"You're saying growing old is like regressing."

"To other people it is. Now, I'm going to level with you, and I don't want it going any further than this car. Understood?"

"Certainly," Gloria said.

"I didn't travel three thousand miles to investigate some pissant scam. There's something seriously wrong with this tournament and I'm going to find out what it is. It might take me a few days, so here's what I suggest you do. Have your boss at the network call me. I'll tell him what I just told you. I'll also promise him that you'll get an exclusive once I'm done. That should get you off the hook."

"You mean that?"

"Of course I mean it."

The look on her face was something special. Surprise and happiness and something akin to admiration all rolled into one. She brought her body across the seat, placed her hand against his chin, and planted a kiss on his cheek. Her lips were soft, and brought back long-buried memories that made his heart stir.

"Thank you, Tony," she said.

14

Valentine took out his business card and wrote his cell number on the back. He'd only given his cell number to a handful of people over the years, yet handed it readily to Gloria Curtis. He started the car and pointed it toward Las Vegas.

"Tell your boss to call me anytime," he said.

"I will. His name is Ralph. He has a tough exterior, but deep down he's a real jerk."

Valentine laughed. "He ride you hard?"

"Like a mule." She pulled a pack of Kools from her purse and banged one out. "Mind if I smoke?"

"I might attack you."

"Trying to quit?"

"Yes. I kicked the habit when I was a cop, didn't smoke for twenty years. Two years ago I started again. Now, I'm not sure if I'll ever quit."

"Why did you start again?"

"My wife died."

"I'm terribly sorry."

"Then my son joined my business," he added, forcing a smile. "I think that was the clincher."

"May I ask you a question about your son?"

Valentine stiffened. Talking about Gerry with strangers

was never a favorite subject: too many surprises came up. He pointed out the window at the buff desert ringed with bluish mountains. "Sure is beautiful scenery," he said.

"Did you bring him to Las Vegas to help you with this case?"

The road back to town was as straight as an arrow. He stared at the double line in its center while playing her question back in his head. The first part was a statement of fact—Gerry was here, and somehow Gloria had found out—the second a question.

"How did you know my son was in Las Vegas?"

"Guess," she said. "I already gave you a clue."

"You did?"

"Yes. Remember how we met?"

Valentine continued to stare at the road. "You met me at my plane, meaning you have a contact with the airlines who told you what flight I was on."

"That's right," she said, lighting up.

"That's illegal, you know."

She choked on the cigarette's smoke. "You sound like a cop when you say that."

"Sorry."

"Do you want a cigarette or not?"

"Can I just have a puff of yours?"

She shook her head, and he took one and let her light it. He filled his lungs with the great-tasting smoke, and for about five seconds the world felt right again. It wasn't long, but sometimes that was all you needed.

"Your airport contact must have seen that Gerry flew here, and told you," he said.

"Your powers of deduction are amazing," Gloria replied, holding her cigarette like a movie starlet. "So, do you work cases often with your son?"

"Sometimes."

"Bringing a kid into a family business must be hard," she said.

The road had become super-sized, as had the cars passing by. Gerry was supposed to be in Puerto Rico, looking after his wife and baby, and not here in Sin City, doing whatever the hell he was doing. Valentine took several deep breaths and felt himself calm down.

"You have no idea," he said. "Where are you staying?"

"Celebrity," she said.

"Me too."

A mile before town he got onto Highway 105, and ten minutes later pulled into Celebrity's main entrance. Las Vegas casinos were designed like carnival attractions, the casino willing to say or do anything to get you inside its doors. Celebrity was no different. Its exterior looked like the entrance to Tarzan's lair, with elephants and giraffes and other jungle beasts roaming the grounds, the animals kept in check by natural deterrents. A valet dressed like Jungle Jim hustled over to take his car.

Gloria started to get out, then turned to face him. "I'm going to need filler to run while I'm waiting for your case to break. Any suggestions would be greatly appreciated."

"Filler?"

"Stories, human interest stuff."

"I can make some introductions. I know a lot of the famous players."

"Let's talk later about it, okay?"

The words were slow to sink in. He'd been wondering what kind of impression he'd made on her, and guessed it was several notches above what he'd thought. She scribbled her cell phone number on the back of her business card, then stuck the card between his fingers. "Call me when it's convenient," she said.

He watched Gloria walk away, then got out of his rental and pulled his garment bag from the trunk. Every dark cloud had a silver lining. Hearing that Gerry was in Las Vegas was bad news, yet meeting Gloria was not. There was a bounce in his step as he went inside.

Celebrity's lobby had an enormous atrium filled with screeching macaws and giant yellow-headed parrots. It was fun for about five minutes, which was how long he had to wait in line to get registered. After that, the panicked look on the birds' faces started to bother him, and he stopped looking at them.

His room wasn't clean, so he parked his garment bag with the concierge, and crossed the lobby to the casino. Like every joint in town, Celebrity's casino offered the same money-losing games, except for one difference. They had built a huge card room designed exclusively to hold the World Poker Showdown. It was as long as a football field, and had plush carpeting and real crystal chandeliers. Considering that most poker players would rather drink out of a toilet than tip a cocktail waitress, Celebrity's management had made a huge investment.

Two armed guards stood outside the card room. The WPS's main prize was ten million in cash, and it was on display inside in a Plexiglas box. Each night, the money was put into a vault. As publicity gimmicks went, there was nothing like it.

A giant-screen TV showed the action inside, with thousands of men and women sitting at green baize tables. The game was Texas Hold 'Em and each player was dealt two face-down cards to start. After a round of betting, three communal cards, called the flop, were dealt face up in the center of the table, followed by another round of betting. Then two more cards, known as Fourth Street, or the turn, and Fifth Street, called the river, were dealt face up, with a round of betting after each card. The five cards in the center were common to all players, who used them with their hole cards to make the best hand.

He went to the registration desk and asked for Bill Higgins. A man behind the desk picked up a walkie-talkie and called inside. Bill emerged through the doors thirty seconds later, all out of breath. Bill was Navajo by birth, and had the demeanor of a statue. Not only was he the most powerful law enforcement officer in Nevada, he was the best law enforcement person Valentine had ever known.

"One of the dealers is passed out cold," Bill said.

"Heart attack?"

"Could be. He keeled over during the middle of his deal." He turned to the guards. "An ambulance will be here soon. Be prepared to clear a path for them."

"Yes, sir," they both said.

Bill opened the doors, and Valentine followed him in. The unconscious dealer was in the room's center, being attended to by several other dealers. A crowd of gamblers stood off to one side, making wagers on whether or not the dealer was going to live. Valentine went over and told them to knock it off.

"You a cop?" a guy holding a fan of bills asked.

"How bad do you want to find out?" Valentine replied.

The parasites scattered. He joined Bill, and knelt down beside the dealer. One of the other dealers was shaking his head.

"He just had radiation treatment for cancer a few weeks ago," the dealer said. "I guess he wasn't as strong as he thought."

"What's his name?" Valentine asked.

"Ray Callahan."

The name was vaguely familiar. Valentine gently slapped Callahan on the cheek.

"Hey Ray, rise and shine. Breakfast is on, and everyone's waiting for you."

Callahan slowly came around. He blinked hard, and for a brief moment was wide awake. He stared at Valentine with a glint of recognition, then went back under. Three EMS guys pushing a gurney rushed into the room. They got Callahan on a stretcher, then rolled him out.

A gambler across the room called out, "Is he still alive?"

Valentine spotted the guy who asked this, and shook his fist at him.

"I met with Gloria Curtis earlier and got her under control," Valentine said when he and Bill were in the coffee shop. "She's willing to play ball."

"You going to give her an exclusive if you find anything?" Bill asked, blowing the steam off his drink.

"I didn't have a choice. Look, I need to level with you about something."

Valentine took out his wallet, and removed the playing card Jack Donovan had given Gerry. Bill stared at the card, then turned it over and stared at it some more.

"This is from this casino, isn't it?" Bill said.

"That's right. It turned up in a murder investigation in Atlantic City. The victim gave the card to my son before he died. He claimed he could beat any poker game in the world. Trouble is, we can't find anything wrong with the card."

Bill dropped the playing card on the table. "Was this person credible?"

"He was a scammer. He and my son were childhood friends."

"So the tournament is being cheated."

"Yes. The problem is, I have no idea how. I'd suggest you start checking every deck of cards before and after it's used. Especially those at Skip DeMarco's table."

Bill made a face. "So DeMarco *is* cheating."

"That's where the evidence is pointing."

"But he's legally blind. How could he be reading the cards?"

Valentine had thought about it during his flight out that morning, and had come to the conclusion that DeMarco, like many sight-impaired people, must have an elevated sense of hearing that compensated for his lack of sight. If someone at the table were reading the backs of the cards—such as the dealer—they could signal DeMarco by the way they breathed. Hustlers called this The Sniff and often used it to pass information.

"I think someone's reading them for him," Valentine said. "Start watching the dealers at DeMarco's table."

The waitress came and topped off their cups. As Valentine raised his to his lips, he stared at Bill. The look on his friend's face said he was frustrated as hell. Despite his obnoxious behavior, Skip DeMarco was the darling of the tournament. Busting him for cheating was the last thing Bill wanted to do.

"Rufus Steele called me earlier," Bill said. "He heard you were in town, and wants to talk to you. He's staying in the hotel."

Valentine put his cup down. Rufus's interview with

Gloria Curtis had bothered him. It was rare for a cheater to call another player a cheater. Rufus must have had good reason, and Valentine wanted to know what that reason was.

"Give me his room number," Valentine said.

15

"It's open, and I've got nothing worth stealing," Rufus Steele called out.

Valentine opened the door to Rufus's hotel room and poked his head in. Rufus was standing by the bed with the phone pressed to his chin, the look on his face pure agitation. Seeing Valentine in the doorway, he flashed a crooked grin, and motioned him inside.

"Hey, Tony, you're a sight for sore eyes. How you been?"

"Fine," Valentine said, shutting the door behind him.

Rufus hadn't changed that much since Valentine had last seen him. He was in his scruffy cowboy clothes and looked like he'd just stepped out of a spaghetti western. Back in his day, he'd been the greatest poker player in the world, but that had been a long time ago. Compared to the brash young kids who now ruled the poker world, Rufus looked sadly out of place.

"Hello," Rufus said into the phone. "Is this the hotel's general manager? Well, listen to what I'm about to say. You have as much chance of getting me to leave this room as you do getting French kissed by the Statue of Liberty. That's right, son. I know the law, and you can't throw me out. You think I'm mistaken? Well, here's an idea. Why don't you take this phone and shove it up your ass?"

Rufus dropped the receiver into its cradle. Then he grabbed two sodas from the minibar, and pointed at a pair of chairs by the room's window. They made themselves comfortable and clinked bottles.

"They trying to throw you out?" Valentine asked.

"They sure are. They're mad I blew the whistle on that smart-aleck DeMarco kid," Rufus said. He took a long swig of soda and let out a belch. "Besides, I can't leave the hotel even if I wanted to."

"Why not?"

"I can't pay the bill. I blew the last of my money on the entry fee."

"Times been hard?"

Rufus tilted back his cowboy hat. His forehead was covered with liver spots and his hair was a thin reminder of the mane he'd once sported. "Yeah, but I guess I should have expected it. They say a poker player spends the first twenty years of his life learning, the second twenty years earning, and the last twenty years yearning for what he once was. I believe I may have entered into that third stage."

"You can still beat ninety-nine percent of these kids," Valentine said.

"Thanks. I needed that."

"Bill Higgins said you had something to tell me."

Rufus raised the soda to his lips and all the liquid inside disappeared. "You need to grill the tournament director. He seated those boys together with DeMarco. It was fixed from the start."

"Can you prove that?"

Rufus frowned. "No, but it's obvious what happened."

Valentine leaned forward in his chair. He remembered

Rufus once telling him about poker games in Texas where they'd put guys with machine guns on the roof of the house to protect the players inside. Rufus had seen plenty of thieves in his day, and would undoubtedly run across plenty more. "Rufus, you're taking this personally. That's not like you. There will be other tournaments."

"This is different," Rufus said.

"How so?"

"That kid bad-mouthed me on national television. My ninety-eight-year-old momma called me from the Sunset Nursing Home. She said, 'You need to teach that loudmouth a lesson, Rufus.' "

Valentine put his soda on the windowsill. Then he pulled his chair a few inches closer to his host. "I want you to do me a favor."

"Name it."

"Stop calling DeMarco a cheater. That's my job."

"So what should I call him?"

"A worm, a toad, a snot-nosed schoolboy who doesn't know his ass from third base, a rank amateur, whatever you want."

Rufus grinned, getting his drift. "I'll do it, provided that you return the favor, and let me go about my business."

"Meaning what?"

"I made a bet with a guy in the tournament which I'm about to go downstairs and settle."

"A sucker?"

"I suppose you could call him that. He fancies himself a professional poker player."

"What's the bet?"

"I bet him ten thousand dollars that I could make a fly land on a sugar cube. The sucker thinks I'm off my rocker. I ask that you not tell him otherwise."

"I thought you said you were broke," Valentine said.

Rufus put down his drink, then pulled out both his pockets. There was nothing in either of them. "I am. That's what makes the bet so intriguing."

There was an impatient knock on the door. Rufus took his time getting to his feet, his old bones moaning and creaking. He'd been a cowboy all his life, had a wife and a bunch of screaming grandkids, and still called Texas home. He'd once told Valentine that he didn't permit gambling around the house, and Valentine had believed him.

Rufus opened the door and stuck his head into the hallway. A hotel maintenance man stood outside accompanied by a beefy security guard. The guard did the talking.

"Mr. Steele? I'm with hotel security. We'd like to come into your room."

"What for?" Rufus asked.

"The general manager informed me that you swore at him a few minutes ago," the guard said.

"All I did was ask him to shove the phone up his ass," Rufus said.

"He was deeply offended by the remark."

"Guess he doesn't spend much time inside his casino, huh?"

"The general manager has instructed our maintenance man to take your phone out of your room," the guard said.

"You're kidding me, aren't you?"

"Afraid not," the guard said. "Please step aside."

Rufus's shoulders sagged. He turned and looked back into the room at Valentine sitting by the window. "Can you talk to this guy, Tony?"

"I'm afraid it won't do any good," Valentine said.

"I thought you were here on behalf of the hotel."

"The Gaming Control Board hired me."

Rufus's shoulders sagged some more. He stepped away from the door, and gestured weakly with his arm. The two men entered the suite. The maintenance man took an electric screwdriver off his belt, and placed it on the bed. Then he dropped to his knees, and peered behind the bed, looking for the electrical outlet that the phone was plugged into. Valentine got out of his chair, and came over to where Rufus stood. He felt bad for Rufus, but didn't know how to express it without offending him any further. Take away a man's pride, and there wasn't much left.

Rufus turned to the guard. "Can I make one last call?"

The guard scratched his chin. "Is it local?"

"It's right here in the hotel," Rufus said.

"I don't see why not."

"I have your permission?"

"Sure," the guard said. "Go ahead."

The maintenance man got off the floor, and gave Rufus some room. Rufus picked up the phone's receiver, and punched in zero. An operator came on the line, and Rufus asked to speak to the hotel's general manager. A few moments later, he was put through.

"This is Rufus Steele," he said when the GM came on. "Remember that phone I suggested you shove up your ass? Well, hold on, son. They're about to deliver it to you."

16

The sucker was waiting for Rufus in one of the tournament side rooms. He was in his mid-twenties, wore his shirt out to hide his round stomach, and had yellow spiked hair. He was extremely loud, and jabbered away like he'd already won the bet. With him were a pair of tanned guys sporting expensive clothes and nice haircuts. Valentine guessed these were the hairy legs backing the sucker's play.

Hairy legs were a big part of gambling. They were the money men, and often had more capital than common sense. In Valentine's opinion, they were a major reason why high-stakes poker had exploded around the country. Most had gotten their wealth from the stock market or the high-tech boom, and frittered it away backing egotistical movie projects and professional poker players.

Introductions were made, with Rufus telling the sucker and his backers that Valentine was "an ex-police detective from the fair state of New Jersey who I asked to be here to keep things honest." The sucker eyed Valentine skeptically, as did the hairy legs.

Valentine nodded politely to them.

"I want to establish some rules before we start," the sucker said.

"By all means," Rufus replied.

"First of all, we get to provide the sugar cubes. We'll put them on the table, then you get to pick which cube you think the fly will land on."

"How many sugar cubes do you want to put on the table?" Rufus asked.

"Ten," the sucker said.

"That's a lot."

"Does it matter?"

"Yes, it makes it harder. Let's make the bet twenty thousand," Rufus said.

The sucker's mouth dropped down, as did his backers' mouths.

"You want to bet twenty thousand dollars instead of ten thousand?" the sucker said.

"That's right," Rufus replied. "If you put ten sugar cubes on the table, it will be harder for me to persuade the fly to land on a particular one. I'm willing to take the gamble, provided we bet twenty thousand dollars on the outcome. I think that's fair, don't you?"

One of the hairy legs let out a laugh. "Sure, why not?"

"There's one other stipulation," the sucker said. "We get to provide the fly."

Rufus tilted his Stetson back like he couldn't believe what he was hearing. "Excuse me, son, but I figured we'd use one of the flies that was buzzing around the place. It's never too hard to find a fly inside a casino, you know."

The sucker shook his head. It was obvious he'd thought this out, and decided that Rufus was somehow going to provide a trained fly to win the wager. They were standing beside a round table with a tablecloth draped over it, and the sucker reached beneath the table, and triumphantly came up with a glass mayonnaise jar.

The jar had the lid on, into which were poked several airholes. Buzzing around inside the jar was a large house fly.

"We'll use this one," the sucker said.

Rufus extended his hand, and the sucker handed him the jar. The old cowboy stared at the buzzing fly, then held the jar up to the light, and stared some more. After some thoughtful consideration, he handed the jar back to the sucker.

"You're on," Rufus said.

Rufus explained to the sucker that he was going to have to hypnotize the fly, and would need at least five minutes in order to do so. The sucker agreed, and placed the mayonnaise jar on the center of the table. Rufus sat down at the table, and stared into the jar while the fly flew around making an angry buzzing sound.

Valentine removed Gloria Curtis's business card from his wallet and retreated to the corner of the room. He flipped open his cell phone and punched in her number. She answered on the second ring, and sounded like she was in a restaurant.

"I've got a neat human interest story for you," he said.

"That was fast," she said.

"Come to the first side room next to where the tournament is being played. And bring a cameraman with you."

"I'm in the restaurant across the lobby, having lunch with my cameraman," she said. "We'll be right over."

Gloria and her cameraman appeared sixty seconds later. Valentine cornered them, and got them out of earshot of the sucker and his backers. Standing in the corner of the room, he explained Rufus's bet and the sucker's stipulations, then explained how Rufus was hypnotizing the fly to do his bidding. Gloria looked at him like he'd lost his mind.

"Excuse me, but you think this is suitable for TV?" she said, sounding more than a little put out. "For Christ's sake, Tony, we don't put crazy people on."

"He's crazy like a fox," Valentine said. "Rufus will win, trust me."

"But how?"

"I have no idea, but he will."

Gloria pointed at the sucker standing on the other side of the room. "That's Benjamin Gannon. He's a graduate of MIT, and a bona fide mathematical genius. I'm sure he's looked at every angle there is with this bet, and knows he can't lose. Rufus Steele is going to look like a fool. I'm not going to televise that."

She was really annoyed, and her cameraman seemed to mirror her feelings. He was a young guy, and wore a gold earring in each ear like a pirate. Valentine guessed they had never heard the Damon Runyon tale about the gambler betting the farmer that he had a deck of cards where the jack of spades would spit cider in your ear, and the farmer taking the bet, and proceeding to get an earful of cider. He made them both sit down, and explained what was going on.

"Rufus is pulling the hook, line, and sinker. Rufus met Gannon during the first day of the tournament. My guess is, there was a fly buzzing around, and Rufus made some offhand remark about flies being able to be trained. That's the hook. Then, Rufus wondered whether flies really could be trained. He tells Gannon he might have found a way. He knows Gannon is a genius, and will think he's crazy. That's the line, and Gannon bit on it. Now Rufus is performing the sinker. He's gotten Gannon's backers to double the bet, and if any more suckers come into the room, he'll get them to make wagers as well. That's how the game is played, and Rufus is a master at it."

"But you're leaving the most crucial part out," Gloria said. "How does Rufus make the fly land on the sugar cube?"

Rufus had risen from his chair, and was looking around the room for him. The fly was still buzzing around the mayo jar, looking no more hypnotized than when Rufus started staring at him. Valentine saw a smile crease the old cowboy's lips.

"I think we're about to find out," Valentine said.

"Okay cowboys and cowgirls, I'm ready," Rufus declared.

By now there were fifty-plus people in the room. Gloria got them to bunch up behind Rufus, which made the group look much bigger. She stuck her microphone into Rufus's face, and tried to get him to say a few words.

"Sorry, ma'am, but this takes a lot of concentration," he said.

The sucker tore open a box of sugar cubes. He removed ten, and laid them across the table in a line. Rufus took a plastic coffee stirrer from his shirt pocket. It had been resting there all along, and Valentine had not paid any attention to it. Rufus said, "Okay, now here's the deal. Everyone has to be clear on which sugar cube you want the fly to land on *before* the fly is released from the jar. Agreed?"

"Agreed," the sucker replied.

"Good. Now, which one do you want? And you can't change your mind, and confuse things. Whichever cube you pick, that's the one the fly lands on. Agreed?"

"Agreed."

"Then let's go. Which cube do you want, son?"

"Third from the left," the sucker said.

"Your left, or my left?"

"My left."

Rufus brought the tip of the coffee stirrer directly above the sugar cube that was third from the sucker's left. "You mean this one, son?"

"That one," the sucker said.

Gloria stood between them, moving her microphone back and forth as they spoke. She was cool under pressure, and reminded Valentine of a referee at a boxing match. You knew they were there, yet paid no attention to them. Rufus put the stirrer back into his shirt pocket. Then he picked up the mayo jar from the table. Staring into it, he said, "Third from *his* left, pardner."

He handed the mayo jar to the sucker.

"You open it, son. Good luck."

The sucker carefully unscrewed the jar, and allowed the inmate to escape. The fly flew around their heads like an angry kamikaze, causing several gamblers to duck. The fly flew straight up, and did several circles above their heads. Finally, its wings lost their steam, and it descended upon the table, where it landed upon the sugar cube third from the sucker's left. Gloria was filming the table when it happened, and got a shot for the ages. The sucker's mouth dropped open and his pink tongue fell out. One earful of cider, coming right up!

Valentine was watching Rufus, and saw the old cowboy wearily shake his head. All the talking had plumb worn him out, and he sat back down at the table, threw his cowboy boots onto a chair, and tilted back his Stetson.

"I win," he declared.

17

The fly remained on the sugar cube for half a minute, oblivious to the gamblers gawking at it, or the TV camera, or the pulsating sounds of the casino filtering in every time someone opened the door. It was just a fly, small and harmless, yet for those thirty seconds, it was the most important thing in the room. Finally it flew away, and Gannon's backers paid up and the gamblers drifted off and everything returned to normal.

"Rufus, would you mind doing a wrap-up interview?" Gloria asked.

"My pleasure," Rufus said, getting to his feet and straightening his string tie. Gloria stuck the microphone up to his face, and he flashed his best smile.

"This is Gloria Curtis, talking with world-famous poker player Rufus Steele, who just hypnotized a fly into landing on a sugar cube. Rufus, that was quite a performance. What are you going to do with the money you won?"

Rufus was a good foot taller than Gloria, and the microphone hung a few inches below his chin. He paused, then said, "Challenge that boy who beat me."

"Excuse me?" she said.

"I'm going to challenge that boy who beat me two days ago," Rufus declared.

"Skip DeMarco?"

"Yes. I'd like to play him again, heads-up, winner-take-all."

"This is the same man who you accused of cheating in the tournament," Gloria said. "Now, you're saying you'd like to play him again."

Rufus glanced briefly at Valentine, who was standing behind the cameraman, then back at Gloria. "I'll let the authorities decide whether anything inappropriate happened on Thursday. In the meantime, I'd like to play that boy again, see if he really knows anything about cards. My guess is, he doesn't."

"You do realize that DeMarco is currently the chip leader in the World Poker Showdown, and has won over a half-million dollars in just two days," Gloria said.

"Not to be impolite, but that doesn't mean much," Rufus said.

"Would you care to explain to our viewers?"

"This is a tournament, and you play for these little plastic coins called chips. I'm talking about playing for cold hard cash, the way we play down in Texas."

"Do you think that would give you an advantage?"

"Ma'am, that young man would be like a missionary with a bunch of hungry cannibals. I'd eat him alive."

Gloria knew an ending when she heard it, and faced the camera. "This is Gloria Curtis, reporting from the World Poker Showdown in Las Vegas. Back to you."

"I owe you a steak and an ice-cold beer," Gloria said a few minutes later. "That was really wonderful."

The room had emptied, leaving Gloria and Valentine and the empty mayonnaise jar. Gloria's cameraman stood off to the side, breaking down his equipment.

"I'll take you up on the steak," Valentine said.

"You don't drink?"

He shook his head. She looked surprised, like all cops were supposed to drink.

"My father was a drunk. I swore off the stuff before it ever touched my lips."

"Then I guess we'll just have to settle for a steak. Maybe over dinner I can bribe you into telling me how Rufus pulled that little stunt."

Valentine was not about to tell Gloria that he didn't have the slightest idea. She went to speak with her cameraman, giving him the opportunity to pick up the ten sugar cubes on the table. Most animals were attracted to sugar's sweet smell, and he wondered why the fly hadn't hopped around from cube to cube, instead of landing on the cube third from the left. He remembered his office manager once predicting where a fly would land on a table, and had the sneaking suspicion that the scam was older than he was. He went over to where Gloria stood with her cameraman.

"Would you do me a favor?" he asked.

"Name it," she said.

"Would you consider interviewing DeMarco, and informing him of Rufus's challenge? I'd like to see his expression when you break the news to him."

Her eyes sparked. "Think you'll see something in his face?"

"Yes, that's exactly what I'm thinking."

"What do gamblers call those?"

"Tells."

"Ooh," she said. "This is fun. If DeMarco really is a cheater, you think he'll cringe at the idea of playing Rufus again."

"I sure do."

"Will that help your investigation?"

"Let's just say it will put me one step closer to the truth."

"Ooh," she said. "I love it."

They went into the lobby, and found DeMarco standing outside the card room being interviewed by a Japanese TV crew. He was a shade under six feet, and looked like he worked out, his shoulders tapering down to a thin waist. He held a long metal cane in his hand, and was wearing thick dark glasses. Valentine had seen plenty of blind people in casinos—most liked to play the slot machines—and he'd seen people pretend to be blind as cover for a scam. DeMarco's body language said he was the real thing.

DeMarco's handlers stood behind him. One was big and looked like a bodyguard, the other an old man carrying a canvas bag. The old man was dressed in black, and had silver hair slicked back on both sides and lizard eyes. He was the epitome of an old-time gangster, and Valentine guessed this was George "the Tuna" Scalzo.

"Someone's done a marketing makeover on DeMarco," Gloria said under her breath. "New haircut, new wardrobe. Very smart."

"Think he's being groomed?"

"Sure looks that way." To her cameraman she said, "Zack, ready to rock?"

"Uh-huh," Zack said, hoisting the camera onto his shoulder.

DeMarco was wrapping up his interview as they approached him. Hearing them, he turned his head and offered the thinnest of smiles.

"Gloria Curtis, WSPN Sports Television," Gloria said, sticking the microphone in his face. "Congratulations on being the tournament money leader the second day in a row."

"Nice perfume," he said.

"Do you still feel confidant that you'll win the tournament?"

"Shouldn't I?"

"There are over two thousand players left in the field."

"And they're all chasing me," he said.

"Rufus Steele, an old-timer who accused you of cheating the other day, has issued a challenge. Are you aware of it?"

DeMarco froze, the bluster leaving his face. His Adam's apple bobbed, and then he squared his shoulders and shrugged it off. A nice recovery, Valentine thought.

"Rufus is challenging me?" he said.

"Yes," Gloria said. "He wants to play you heads up for cash."

"If I played every person I beat in this tournament, I'd never leave," he said. "No thanks. I've got more important things to do."

"Would you play him after the tournament was over?"

"You mean, after I win the tournament?" he said.

"Very well. After you win the tournament."

"Sure, I'd play him. A million bucks, heads up. Neither of us leaves the table until the other guy has all the money."

Gloria turned to the camera. "And there you have it. A pair of gamblers, one old, the other young, ready to lock horns and play poker for two million dollars, cash. It doesn't get any better than that. Back to you."

"That was great," Zack said, lowering his camera.

"We done?" DeMarco asked.

"Yes," Gloria said. "Thank you."

DeMarco lowered his cane and walked away. He was either blind as a bat, or up for serious Academy Award consideration for Best Actor. He entered one of the casino's noisy bars with his handlers behind him. Valentine felt a hand on his arm, and turned to find Gloria standing beside him.

"Did you ever think of being a producer?" she asked.

"No, should I?"

"Yes. You're filled with good ideas."

Gloria needed to review and edit the film before Zack sent it to the network. Still holding Valentine's sleeve, she said, "How about dinner tonight? The hotel has a steak house. I'll buy you a New York Strip, and you can explain how the sugar trick works."

"You've got a deal," he said.

"Eight o'clock at Bogart's," she said. "I'll make the reservations."

He watched her walk away. Then he crossed the casino, and found a bank of phone booths. He entered one, shut the door, and pulled out his cell. Mabel, his office manager, was coming home from her cruise today. He wanted to say hi, hear how it had gone, and find out how the damn sugar trick worked. He finished punching in her number when the white courtesy phone in the booth rang. Out of curiosity, he answered it.

"Tony, this is Bill Higgins," the caller said.

Valentine nearly dropped his cell phone on the floor. "How did you find me?"

"I'm in the Celebrity surveillance control room, watching the casino floor on the monitors," Bill said. "I saw you enter the phone booth, and called you."

Valentine stared at the domed ornamental light in the ceiling of the booth. If there was a hidden camera in the light, he couldn't see it.

"I know this is going to sound strange," Bill went on, "but I was just watching you in the bar."

"But I wasn't in the bar," Valentine said.

"Well, I saw you in the bar, drinking a beer. Then on another camera, I saw you duck into the phone booth. And I asked myself, how can he be in two places at once?"

It took a moment for what Bill was saying to register. *His son was in the bar.* Bill had never met Gerry, which explained the confusion. "This guy in the bar who looks like me," Valentine said. "Is he sitting with three Italian guys?"

"Yeah," Bill said. "They're at a table in the corner."

"Does one of them look like a boxer who went too many rounds?"

"Right again."

Valentine was still burned that Gerry had lied to him, and come to Las Vegas on the sly. A little payback was in order so he said, "I want you to backroom them."

"On what grounds?"

"The guy in the bar is my son. He needs to be humbled."

"Got it," Bill said.

Backrooming was a casino's way of dealing with undesirable people. The person or persons would be led by security to a windowless room, where they were read the riot act by someone who worked for the casino. It was about as much fun as getting arrested, and a perfect reality check for his son.

"You coming upstairs?" Bill asked.

"Of course I'm coming upstairs," Valentine said, opening his cell phone. "But first I'd like to make a phone call, if that's okay with you."

"Sorry," his friend said.

18

Mabel Struck had returned from her cruise ready to go back to work. It wasn't that cruising wasn't fun—seven days in the Caribbean was most people's idea of a dream vacation—and she'd enjoyed the food and nonstop activities. But after a couple of days it had become predictable, and by the week's end she'd been downright bored. Going away on vacation had convinced her that she had the best job in the world, and she'd come home eager to get back to it.

She unlocked the front door to Tony's house and punched the code into the security system, then took off her shoes and walked to Tony's office in the back. Tony had gotten her in the habit of taking her shoes off, and the house was usually so quiet she could hear a pin drop. Better to hear yourself think, her boss had explained.

She found a note from Tony Scotch-taped to the computer. Gerry and Yolanda were in San Juan, while Tony was in Las Vegas investigating a poker tournament. Her boss had left a stack of letters on the desk that needed to be addressed, plus a few dozen unopened e-mail messages. He ended by telling Mabel he hoped she'd had a good time, and hadn't gotten too sunburned.

Mabel found herself smiling. That was the thing she liked about Tony. He always cared about the personal things. As she started to go through the letters, she glanced at the clock in the shape of a roulette wheel on the desk. It was three P.M. Right about now, the square dancing lessons would be starting on the ship, and the midafternoon tea. It was fine if you liked prepackaged fun, only Mabel had decided that there was only so much of that kind of thing she could take. The nitty-gritty of the real world was more to her liking, and she was happy to be home.

The phone rang as she was scrolling through Tony's e-mails. Normally the afternoons were quiet around the office, no doubt because most casinos were quiet in the afternoon as well, and she answered the phone with a cheerful, "Grift Sense."

"Are you a shopping service for crooks?" a familiar voice said.

"Only if they have a sense of humor," she replied.

"Sign me up," Tony said. "It's nice to hear your voice."

The fun part about working for Tony was that he never took the job too seriously. As he was fond of saying, no one had ever cried when a casino lost money.

"Yours too. How is sunny Lost Wages?"

"Hasn't changed a bit. I read in the paper that they'd built a brand-new elementary school within five hundred feet of a brothel, so they're going to have to move it."

"The brothel?"

"No, the elementary school. Can't keep those girls out of work. So, how was your cruise? Did the unlimited buffet live up to your expectations?"

"The food was incredible," she said. "But there was one thing which happened on board that bothered me."

"Let me guess. You had to beat off all the eligible men who wanted to dance with you."

Mabel felt herself blush. Her late husband had been fond of calling her beautiful, but that was her husband. Hearing Tony say she was attractive made her wonder if there was something to it. "No, it was in the ship's casino. They shut it down one night, right when everyone was winning. When they reopened the next night, they'd lowered the limits on the table games to twenty-five dollars. Do you know why they did that?"

"I sure do," he said. "If I tell you, will you answer a question for me?"

"What is it?"

"How do you get a fly to land on a sugar cube?"

She burst out laughing. "Oh, Tony, my great-grandmother taught me that trick. Don't tell me someone pulled it on you?"

"Actually, he pulled it on a roomful of guys, and won twenty thousand bucks in the process. It kind of had me baffled."

"He's a fly whisperer."

"A what?"

"Just kidding," Mabel said. "You go first, then I'll explain."

"Here's the deal," Valentine said. "Cruise ship casinos have a problem. They're only open at night. As a result, they only have a limited amount of time to win money. Most casino games grind you down. A player's chances of winning are much greater in a casino the less amount of time they stay there."

"Really?" Mabel said.

"Yes. You lose in a casino, but only gradually. That's what keeps you playing. However, in the first few hours, you also have the best chance of winning some money, because you have your entire bankroll. Make sense?"

"Yes," Mabel said. "The cruise ship casinos are only open during the evening, and are susceptible to more losses than a casino that stays open longer."

"That's right. Because of this situation, some cruise ship casinos have been known to cheat their customers. They short the decks in blackjack and don't pay jackpots on slot machines. Since they operate in international waters, there isn't much the authorities can do about them."

"Is that why they call them 'cruises to nowhere'?"

"No, but it should be."

"Do you think the ship I was on was cheating?"

"No," Valentine said. "They closed down early because they were getting beaten. That's standard procedure. When the casino starts losing money, management stops the hemorrhaging."

"That hardly seems fair," Mabel said.

"Casinos don't gamble. Your turn."

Knowing a con or scam that Tony didn't know was rare, and Mabel could not help but savor the moment. Excusing herself, she went to the kitchen and poured herself an iced tea, then returned to the study and sat down in Tony's big comfortable chair. Only after she'd taken a gulp of her drink did she pick the phone back up.

"You're really enjoying this, aren't you?" he said.

"To the max. You're so hard to pull the wool over, I consider it a special occasion."

"It's really something stupid, isn't it?"

"Simple, but not stupid. Let's use your famous Logical Backward Progression, and analyze what happened," she said. "Explain to me what you saw."

"A sucker put ten sugar cubes on the table, and picked one. Rufus waved a coffee stirrer over it. A fly was let out of a mayonnaise jar, and it flew around, then landed on the sugar cube the sucker picked."

"What didn't the fly do?"

"You've lost me," he said.

"The fly didn't land on the other nine cubes," she said. "Why not?"

"I don't know."

"Because those cubes have no smell. Flies are attracted by smell. Sugar in its pure form doesn't have an odor. But, if you add moisture to sugar, it will release a powerful odor. That's what attracted the fly to the cube."

"So Rufus used the stirrer to drop moisture onto the cube."

"Yes," Mabel said. "It doesn't have to be very much for the fly to smell it."

"Well, I guess you learn something new every day," he said. " I've got to run. Gerry is being held in the back room of a casino, and I need to have a talk with him."

"I thought Gerry was in San Juan with Yolanda," Mabel said.

"He came out here on the sly. I'm about to go read the riot act to him."

"What should I tell Yolanda if she calls?" Mabel asked.

There was a long pause on the line.

"Tell her Gerry's doing a job with me," Valentine said.

Mabel smiled into the receiver. No matter what Gerry's

transgressions might be, Tony always stuck up for his son. It was Tony's biggest flaw, and a constant reminder to Mabel that no matter how much Tony fought with Gerry, he placed parenthood above all else.

"I will," she said.

19

Valentine killed the connection, thinking how impressed Gloria Curtis was going to be when he explained the sugar scam over dinner. It would make him seem more rounded, knowing that sugar didn't smell in its natural state. He hadn't had the urge to impress a woman in a long time, and liked the way it made him feel.

He took the stairs to the third floor of the casino and walked down a windowless hallway to a steel door marked PRIVATE. A surveillance camera was perched above the door, and he stared into its lenses. Moments later the door buzzed, and he entered Celebrity's surveillance control room.

The room's lighting was subdued, the air kept at a chilly sixty degrees so the electronic equipment would run properly. Valentine let his eyes adjust, then stared at the opposing wall of video monitors, the four-color digital pictures as clear as real life. Bill Higgins stood beside the monitors, talking on a cell phone. Bill shut his phone, and walked over with a grim look on his face.

"I don't know how to tell you this," his friend said, "but your son and his friends just robbed someone in the casino."

"What?"

"I was on the phone, telling hotel security to back-room your son when it happened," Bill said. "Your son and his three friends ran out to the parking lot, and got away. Your son's in serious trouble, Tony."

Trouble. It should have been Gerry's middle name. Bill spoke to a tech sitting at a desk. The tech typed on a keyboard, and a tape appeared on a monitor showing Skip DeMarco, his bodyguard, and the Tuna exiting the casino bar. The tape had a time and date code in the right-hand corner, and had been taken a short while ago.

"Watch," Bill said.

Gerry and his friends came out of the bar moments later. They were moving fast, and they threw themselves into the bodyguard and DeMarco, knocking them to the floor. Then Gerry grabbed the canvas bag from the Tuna, and with his friends ran out of the picture. The tech hit a button and froze the tape.

"Have you called the cops?" Valentine asked.

"No, I was waiting for you," Bill said.

Valentine tried to imagine his son in prison. Nevada's penal system was one of the harshest in the country, and Gerry would never be the same if he ended up doing time. If he hadn't asked Bill to backroom his son, Bill wouldn't have been watching Gerry on a surveillance camera. He felt responsible, even though it was Gerry who'd broken the law.

"Don't," Valentine said. "He's working with me."

Bill gave him a look of pure astonishment. "Tony, he just robbed a guy."

Valentine pointed at the frozen picture on the monitor. "See that old guy? That's George 'the Tuna' Scalzo, a mobster out of Newark. I'm convinced he's scamming the tournament. He's also backing DeMarco."

"You're saying your son robbed DeMarco with your permission?"

Valentine swallowed hard. "Yes."

"Do you have any proof against Scalzo?"

Valentine shook his head.

Bill crossed his arms in front of his chest and gave him a hard look. "Tony, listen to me. Scalzo is downstairs talking to hotel security. He's going to file charges. I have to show security the tape of your son, and identify him. It's the law."

Valentine glanced at the tech, then edged closer to Bill and dropped his voice. "The law? The Gaming Control Board routinely busts people you suspect of cheating without any proof. Correct?"

Bill slowly nodded.

"That means that you're the law, Bill. And since you hired me to investigate this tournament, you have to back me up. My son is helping me solve this case, and I don't want you to show security the tape. Okay?"

Bill thought it over. "What if Scalzo calls the police?"

"Let him."

"But the police will ask for the tape."

"Tell them the camera was taping something else."

One of the common fallacies of the casino business was that surveillance cameras taped everything on the casino floor. In reality, the cameras were constantly rotating, and missed a great deal of what was going on. Over 50 percent of the casino was not being watched most of the time. It was why casinos lost so much money to cheaters.

Bill went over to the tech and spoke to him. The tech stared up at Bill, his eyes wide. He slowly typed a command into his keyboard. Valentine stared at the frozen picture on the monitor. The picture went into reverse, and stopped just before Gerry and his friends exited the bar.

"You sure you want me to do this?" the tech asked.

"Yes," Bill said. "Erase the whole thing."

The screen went blank and stayed that way. Valentine felt the air trapped in his lungs escape, and he went over and slapped Bill on the back.

"I owe you," he said.

"I need to talk to you about the tournament," Bill said.

"I'm all ears."

Bill nodded at one of the offices. A casino's surveillance control room should have been the safest place in the world, but secrets often escaped from there as well. They went into the office and Bill shut the door. "I've been recording DeMarco's play, and having an old hustler watch the tapes to see if he can spot any hanky-panky," Bill said.

"Which old hustler?"

"Sammy Mann."

Sammy Mann was an old-time crossroader who'd given up his life of crime and gone to work helping casinos. He was a nice guy, as far as ex-crooks went.

"He find anything?" Valentine asked.

"Sammy says DeMarco is either incredibly good, or he's cheating."

"But not lucky."

"His luck stinks," Bill said. "He's gotten the worst draws of any player in the tournament. But, he's got this knack of knowing when to play his good cards."

Valentine considered what that meant. If DeMarco knew when to play his good cards, it also meant that he knew that his opponents were weak. Knowing those two things said that DeMarco knew every card on the table. Either the kid was psychic, or he was using marked cards, just like Gerry had been saying all along.

"Did you have today's cards examined?"

"Yes. We sent them over to the FBI's forensic lab after today's round was done. The FBI even gave the cards the burn test."

The burn test was a clever way to detect if a playing card was marked with a foreign substance. The suspected card was slowly burned while being examined under a microscope. If there was a foreign substance on the card, it would burn differently and reveal itself.

"What did they find?" Valentine asked.

"Absolutely nothing," Bill said.

There was nothing more frustrating than knowing a scam was taking place, but not having enough evidence to nail the cheaters and shut it down. They agreed to talk again later that night. Bill opened the office door, and they walked back into the surveillance control room.

As Valentine passed the wall of monitors, he saw a tape of the Tuna taken in the casino lobby right after he'd been robbed by Gerry and his friends. The Tuna was stomping his feet and cursing up a storm, and looked almost comical. Valentine walked over to the tech whom Bill had told to erase the tape. The tech was sucking a thick shake like it was the only food he'd had in days.

"Any particular reason you're watching this tape?" Valentine asked.

"Just covering my ass," the tech said.

"How so?"

"Mr. Higgins told me to erase the tape of that guy having his bag stolen. I figured I'd better erase the aftermath as well."

"I'd like to watch it before you erase it."

"Be my guest," the tech said.

Valentine went back to the monitor and watched the tape. The Tuna was poking DeMarco's bodyguard in the chest while yelling at him. The bodyguard whipped out a cell phone and made a call. Thirty seconds later a guy with pocked skin entered the picture. Valentine felt the icy chill of recognition and turned to the tech.

"Freeze this."

Instantly the image became frozen on the monitor.

"Now enlarge the guy's face."

"I can show you his pimples," the tech said.

"A head shot will do."

The face became enlarged, then appeared on every monitor on the wall. The tech was having fun, showing what his toys could do. It was enough of an overload to jolt Valentine's memory into remembering where he'd seen that face before. Taking out his wallet, he removed the composite that Gerry had paid a courthouse artist to draw of Jack Donovan's killer, and compared the composite to the face on the monitor. It was a match.

"Are your tapes digital?" Valentine asked.

"State of the art," the tech said. "We use Loronex."

Loronex was a digital surveillance system that could take a picture of a person, run it against ninety days of past tapes, and pull up any tapes the person appeared on.

"Find this guy in your digital database," Valentine said. "I want to see where he went after this tape was shot."

The tech's fingers were a blur on the keyboard. Moments later, the monitors came alive with a new tape. It showed the guy with the pocked skin walking through the front doors, and giving the valet a stub for his car. As he waited for his car, he removed a shiny business card from his pocket, and dialed his cell phone while staring at it.

"Can you enlarge that card?" Valentine asked.

The business card became enlarged on the monitor. It was for the Sugar Shack, and had a naked girl lying horizontally across it. Bill, who'd been talking to another tech, came over to where Valentine stood.

"That's Jinky Harris's club," Bill said. "He runs the local flesh market."

"Is he in the mob?"

"He sure is."

Valentine stared at the monitor while feeling his heart pound against his rib cage. Gerry and his friends were in real trouble, and not just because they'd stolen the Tuna's canvas bag. He took out his cell phone and called Gerry's cell. An automated voice answered, and told him to leave a voice or text message. His son was always picking up text messages from his wife, and Valentine typed a short message telling Gerry his life was in danger. He marked it urgent and hit send.

"Do you mind my asking you a question?" Bill asked.

Valentine snapped his cell phone shut. "What's that?"

"Is your son really working with you?"

A lie was only good if you kept it going.

"Yes," he said.

20

Las Vegas was like any other major city once you get away from the downtown, the roads and highways jammed with impossibly long lines of traffic. Highway 15, the main thoroughfare on the west side of town, was particularly bad, with lots of tire-burning stop-and-go. Gerry drove in the slow lane, searching for their exit.

"Boy, that was slick," Vinny said, the canvas bag Gerry had snatched from the Tuna sitting protectively in his lap. "Those assholes didn't know what hit them."

"You did a good job knocking down that bodyguard," Gerry said.

Vinny glanced into the backseat at Frank and Nunzie. "It was just like the good old days, wasn't it, guys?"

Frank and Nunzie both started laughing. They had spent their formative years doing hit-and-runs on drunks playing the slot machines in Atlantic City's casinos, knocking them off their stools and stealing their plastic buckets of coins. For a lot of bad kids, it had been the equivalent of having a summer job.

"So, when are we going to open the bag?" Nunzie wanted to know.

"Yeah," Frank said, leaning between the seat, "let's see what this secret is."

Gerry took his eyes off the highway and glanced at

Vinny. They'd talked about this earlier; Jack Donovan had lost his life because of this secret, and Gerry didn't think they should just open up the bag, and start playing with it like a toy.

"We're going to wait until we get back to the motel," Vinny said.

"Aw, come on," Frank said belligerently. "I want to know what it is."

"Me too," Nunzie said.

"Only when we're back at the motel," Vinny said.

Since Vinny was buying the secret, his word stood. Frank looked dejected, and popped an unlit cigarette into his mouth. It made him look like Marlon Brando from *On the Waterfront,* and he said, "I got a question. I know we were moving fast, but what if the cameras caught us? We could go to jail."

Gerry saw their exit and put his indicator on. "The cameras are always rotating. Which means we had a one-in-two shot of not being seen. Sort of like a coin toss."

Frank thought it over, then removed a quarter from his pocket, and tossed it into the air. Nunzie called heads, and Frank caught the coin, and slapped it on the back of his hand. He slowly pulled his hand away. Nunzie's face said it all. Tails.

"Gotcha," Frank said.

Gerry was in the motel parking lot when Vinny's cell phone rang. Vinny had downloaded Frank Sinatra singing "My Way" and used it as the chime for his cell phone. The novelty had already worn off, and Gerry felt like tossing it out the window. Vinny answered the call, then covered the phone's mouthpiece with his hand.

"It's Jinky Harris," he announced.

"Ask him if he's still cleaning up the milk," Gerry said.

"Shut up. That goes for everybody, okay?"

Everyone in the car quit talking, and Vinny took his hand away.

"I'm here, Jinky. What's shaking?"

Vinny's head bobbed up and down while he listened to Jinky talk. Vinny couldn't have a conversation without some part of his body acting like a metronome. If he was standing, it was his hands; sitting, his head or his foot.

"You got it," Vinny said. "We'll meet you at the Voodoo Lounge in twenty minutes. I know where it is. See you there."

Vinny killed the connection and gave Gerry instructions to the Voodoo Lounge. It was halfway between Las Vegas and the town of Henderson, and well off the beaten path. As Gerry headed back to Highway 15, Vinny explained that Jinky wasn't angry about the night before, and wanted to talk to them about a business proposition.

"Jinky says he's got a sweet deal for us," Vinny explained.

"What kind of deal?" Gerry asked.

"You think he was going to tell me over the phone?"

Gerry got back on the highway and followed the signs to Henderson. Jinky hadn't been willing to share his egg rolls, yet now was offering them some easy money. It didn't add up.

"We need to be careful," Gerry said.

"For Christ's sake, you think we're going to get gunned down, going into a bar in broad daylight?" Vinny asked.

Gerry stared at the curving highway. There was a break in the traffic, and he hit the gas, thinking that

Vinny didn't know Las Vegas the way he knew Las Vegas. He'd grown up hearing stories from his father. Las Vegas had more scumbags than any city in America. Anything could happen here, and often did.

"Yes," Gerry said.

The endless flow of money that was Las Vegas's life-blood did not stray far from the casinos, and the Voodoo Lounge looked like a desert outpost, the sand-blasted paint job suggesting a long-forgotten Mexican theme. They got out of the rental and went inside.

The lounge was a low-ceilinged fire trap, with posters of bikini-clad women supplied by beer companies covering the walls. There was a pool table with purple felt, some tables, and a silent jukebox. A barrel-chested bartender stood by the cash register, polishing a glass. His only customer, a construction worker at the far end of the bar, was drinking a beer while staring at the hypnotic curls of smoke coming off his cigarette.

Vinny, Frank, and Nunzie took seats at the bar. Gerry looked around before sitting.

"What's your pleasure?" the bartender asked.

"You have a happy hour?" Nunzie asked.

"We're always in a good mood," the bartender said.

"Any house drinks?" Frank asked.

"Ass juice."

"What's that?"

"Try one and find out," the bartender said.

Gerry turned in his seat, and stared at the front door. There was something not right about the place, only he couldn't put his finger on it. After a few moments of thinking, he realized what it was. No wheelchair access. He nudged Vinny with his elbow.

"This is a setup," Gerry said.

Vinny stiffened. "Why are you so paranoid?"

"Jinky isn't coming here."

"Why not?"

"He can't get his wheelchair through the fricking door."

Vinny looked over his shoulder at the front door. "You think it's an ambush?"

"I sure do," Gerry said.

Gerry felt the gentle pulsation of his cell phone against his leg. He pulled the phone from his pocket, and stared at the text message: SON. YOUR LIFE IS IN DANGER. BE CAREFUL! POP. He showed the message to Vinny.

"My father feels the same way," he said.

The most important aspect of a fight was the element of surprise. Whoever got the jump on his opponent usually won. Gerry ordered a draft, and as the bartender poured it, he jumped clean over the bar. At the same time, Vinny leaned over the bar, and grabbed the bartender by the wrists.

The bartender's .38 Magnum was in a leather holster wedged between two perspiring coolers. Gerry drew the gun, and alternated pointing it at the construction worker and the bartender. Both men stared at him without a trace of fear in their eyes.

"All my money's lying on the bar," the construction worker said.

"Mine's in the till," the bartender said.

"Lift up your shirts, and show me what you're carrying," Gerry said.

Both men complied. The construction worker's stomach was flat and white, the bartender's round and hairy. Neither man was carrying any heat. Gerry made them drop their shirts, and pointed at the front door with the Magnum.

"Any idea who's about to come through that door?"

The bartender had broken out in a wicked sweat. He shook his head.

"The mailman?" the construction worker asked.

Gerry looked at the bartender. "You know."

"No, I don't," the bartender said.

"You're lying."

"I swear to God, I'm not."

The bar's front door banged open. Sunlight flooded the room, and a hooded man wearing a bulletproof vest and carrying a shotgun came in. The hooded man hesitated, letting his eyes adjust. Although Gerry had been a bookie most of his life, he still went to church. He liked to think that God—in His infinite wisdom—watched over him. Like now, for instance. He was holding the most powerful handgun in the world, and had it pointed directly at the door. All he had to do was squeeze the trigger, and he wouldn't end up playing a harp.

He pumped two bullets into the hooded man's vest. The man flew backward like he had strings attached to him, the shotgun discharging into the ceiling and making the whole building shake. Gerry kept firing, and sent the man into the parking lot.

A getaway car was parked outside. The hooded man fell backward through the open passenger door, his face exposed to the sun. Gerry stared at his face, and realized it was the guy he'd seen in the hospital stairwell the night of Jack Donovan's murder. The getaway car sped away before he could squeeze off another round.

A stiff wind shut the front door, and the lounge fell quiet. Vinny, Nunzie, and Frank were frozen to their spots and looked like they'd seen a ghost. Gerry looked at the bartender, who appeared ready to cry.

"You were saying?" Gerry said.

*   *   *

The bartender fell to his knees, sobbing like he expected to die.

"Please don't kill me," he said.

"You work for Jinky Harris, don't you?" Gerry said.

"Never heard of him," the bartender said.

Gerry glanced down the bar at the construction worker, whose face still didn't show any emotion. Gerry wanted to believe the construction worker wasn't part of the plot to kill them, but his gut told him otherwise. The guy had a role. Maybe it was to drag their bodies away or bury them in the desert. Or something else.

Gerry led the construction worker and the bartender to the back room, and locked them in a broom closet. He told them to wait ten minutes before kicking the door down. Then he and Vinny searched the place, while Nunzie and Frank guarded the front door.

Beneath the bar Gerry found a stack of papers with World Poker Showdown printed across the top of each page. He leafed through them, and saw the names of every player in the tournament, along with their odds of winning. Skip DeMarco's odds were highlighted, and were 40 to 1. It was an angle Gerry hadn't considered. Anyone who bet on DeMarco to win would make a killing. He stuck the papers under his arm.

"Let's get out of this toilet," he said.

They went outside to the parking lot. The wind off the desert had picked up, and invisible particles of sand stung their faces. Vinny stuck his hand out, and asked Gerry for the keys to the rental.

"Let me drive," Vinny said.

Each time they'd worked together, Gerry had done the driving while Vinny rode in the passenger seat, and called the shots. Now Vinny was acknowledging that a shift had occurred. Gerry hadn't just saved their lives; he'd also taken charge.

"You sure?" Gerry asked him.

"Positive, man. Hand them over."

Gerry looked at Nunzie and Frank to make sure they were cool with what was happening. Both men dipped their chins, acknowledging they were okay with the change in leadership. Only then did Gerry take the car keys from his pocket, and drop them in Vinny's outstretched hand.

21

If there is any electronic device that casinos hate, it is the cell phone. Card counters, shuffle trackers, roulette cheaters, and other sophisticated scammers can use cell phones to transmit information and give themselves an unbeatable edge at different casino games. As a result, their use is banned from every casino in Las Vegas.

Valentine was crossing Celebrity's casino when his cell phone rang. Thirty minutes had passed since he'd contacted Gerry to tell him his life was in danger, and they'd been thirty of the longest minutes of his life. As he flipped the phone open, a hand came down squarely on his shoulder.

"Cell phones are not permitted inside the casino," a security guard said.

"It's an emergency."

"I'm sure it is. Please take the call over there."

He followed the direction of the guard's finger, and crossed the casino to the front lobby with its screeching exotic birds. By now his cell phone had gone quiet, and the message icon was flashing on its face. He retrieved the message, and heard his son's exuberant voice. The lobby noise was intense, and he pushed the volume control on high.

"Hey, Pop, it's me. I don't know how you knew my life was in danger, but your call saved my life."

Valentine felt the air trapped in his lungs escape. His son was okay.

"I'm sure you're pissed off that I didn't tell you I was coming to Las Vegas, but I decided I had to find Jack Donovan's killers," his son went on. *"You know what you're always telling me about following my heart? Well, my heart told me to do this, so here I am. I hope you can find it in you to forgive me for disobeying you.*

"I'll call you later tonight. Maybe we can hook up. I've got some dirt on cheating that's going on at ring games at the World Poker Showdown that I thought you'd like to hear. Oh, and Pop?—"

"What?" Valentine said without thinking.

"—Thanks for the save."

He erased the message. He and Gerry hadn't seen eye-to-eye since Gerry had been a teenager. After his wife had died, they'd tried to get back on neutral ground. Although the relationship wasn't perfect, Gerry was getting better at explaining himself, and he was getting better at listening. As he shut the cell phone, a yellow-headed parrot in a nearby cage began to flap its wings.

"Thanks for the save, thanks for the save," the bird screeched.

Taking the elevator upstairs, Valentine found himself thinking about his dinner with Gloria Curtis. He wanted to make a good impression, and wished Mabel were around to suggest what clothes he should wear. Not that he had much in the way of a wardrobe, but Mabel's help would quell the tiny butterflies dancing in his stomach. As he entered his room, he saw the red light on his phone flashing. He picked up the message.

"Hey, Tony," Rufus Steele's voice rang out. "I'm in a

jam and need your help. Would you mind coming down to my room? Thanks, pardner."

He glanced at his watch. He had a few hours to kill before dinner, and guessed he could get Rufus to help him pick out his clothes. It wasn't that Rufus was a great dresser either, but he needed another opinion to get his nerves calmed down. He took the elevator down to Rufus's floor. The old cowboy answered the door on the first knock.

"Hey, Tony. Sorry to bother you, but I've got a real problem here."

"What's wrong?"

"Come inside and see for yourself."

He entered the room expecting the worst, and was not disappointed. Everything was gone—the double bed, the night table, the couch, and the two chairs by the window they'd sat in earlier. Even the wall hangings and clock were gone. The place had been stripped clean, with Rufus's clothes left in a sloppy pile in the room's center.

"Who did this?" Valentine asked.

"The hotel," Rufus said. "They really want me out of here."

"Did they take any of your personal belongings?"

"No, they left those."

"What about the twenty grand you won?"

"That's in the vault behind the front desk," Rufus said.

"Did you go downstairs and lodge a complaint?" Valentine asked.

"Sure did. They acted real concerned. Guy at the front desk said someone would be sent up to 'look into things.' That was an hour ago. That's the thing I hate about this town. People will piss on your leg while swearing to you it's raining."

"How can I help?" Valentine asked.

The old cowboy removed his hat, and held it in front of his chest. "I hate to impose upon you, but I'm too old to be sleeping on the floor. I'd be forever grateful if you'd let me park these tired old bones on your couch."

Having a roommate during an investigation was never a good idea. But Rufus had his pluses. He'd been the first to nail DeMarco for a cheat, and knew as much about playing poker as anyone alive. Valentine pointed at the pile of clothes on the floor.

"Let me help you with those," he said.

They stowed Rufus's clothes in the closet of Valentine's room, his shaving kit beneath the sink. Rufus was testing the softness of the couch when Valentine approached him.

"I need a favor," Valentine said. "I'm having dinner with a woman tonight, and was going to buy a shirt down in the men's shop. I was thinking of blue."

Rufus threw his legs up onto the couch, and stretched out luxuriously. The couch was not long enough for him, and his cowboy boots dangled over the end.

"Light or navy?" he asked.

"Navy."

He decided the accommodations were to his liking, and brought his feet back to the floor. "Navy's strong. You seeing that newscaster woman?"

"Yeah, we're getting together later. Too strong?"

"No, navy's good, especially with your dark features. How long you known her?"

"We met this morning."

"Heck, I'm going to start calling you Sir Speedy."

Valentine laughed under his breath. "She likes hearing about scams."

Rufus patted the cushion beside him, indicating he

wanted Valentine to sit. Valentine accommodated him, and watched the old cowboy remove a pack of Lucky Strikes from his shirt pocket and bang out a smoke.

"Sounds like a match made in heaven. She's a smoker, isn't she?"

Valentine nodded. Rufus placed the cigarette between his lips and took out a book of matches. He hesitated before lighting up. "Do you think it's possible to light a cigarette, take four puffs, but not change the length of the cigarette?" he asked.

"No, I don't think it's possible," Valentine said.

Rufus lit the match, and placed the flame in the center of the cigarette. It quickly caught fire, and he took four puffs without the cigarette shrinking in length. Valentine saw himself having fun with that, showing Gloria over dessert.

"Know any other pearls?" he asked.

"I know hundreds of the damn things," Rufus said, exhaling two huge plumes of smoke. "Sometimes I think people take me up on them because they enjoy being hornswoggled. Say, do you mind if I help myself to something to drink?"

"Not at all," Valentine said. "The minibar's in the corner."

Rufus went to the minibar and Valentine saw him remove the last Diet Coke. He sat down on the couch and started to twist it open, then stopped.

"Heck, that's mighty rude of me. You want this?"

"Come to mention it, yes," Valentine said.

Rufus was still holding the matches, and he tore one from the pack, then handed it and the pack to Valentine. "Light the match, and hold the flame lower than your fingers."

Valentine lit the match and held the flame below his hand.

"How long do you think you can hold it that way?" Rufus asked.

The flame was racing up the paper match and starting to warm his fingers.

"I don't know—five seconds?"

"Betcha this soda pop I can hold it for a minute."

Valentine blew out the match that was starting to burn his fingers, and dropped it into an ashtray on the table. Then he tore a second match from the pack, and handed it and the pack to Rufus.

"You're on," he said.

Rufus put the soda down, then struck the match against the flint. It flamed, and he held it exactly as Valentine had, only moved his hand from side to side like a pendulum, effectively reducing the flame's head to the size of a pin. Valentine timed him with the minute hand of his watch. Sixty seconds later the match was still quietly burning.

"That's a keeper," Valentine said.

Rufus smiled his best aw-shucks smile, then got two glasses from the minibar, and split the soda between them. He was still smiling when they clinked glasses.

22

"How long have you been legally blind?" the newspaper reporter asked.

Skip DeMarco leaned back on the leather couch in his penthouse suite in Celebrity's hotel. He detected a faint Scottish brogue in the reporter's voice, and put his age at about thirty, with a college education in the states that had softened his vowels. DeMarco had been blind for as long as he could remember, his condition a hereditary one, not that he was going to tell this son-of-a-bitch that.

There was a glass coffee table with sharp edges in front of the couch, and he leaned forward and found the tall glass of ice water that had been placed there for him. He raised it to his lips and enjoyed its coldness against his dry throat. In the next room, he could faintly hear his uncle George, whom everyone called the Tuna, on the phone, cursing up a storm at hotel management. Back home, if someone had robbed his uncle in broad daylight, they'd end up dead in a garbage can by sundown. But Las Vegas wasn't home, and his uncle was having a hard time getting anyone to help him. He put his drink down, then raised his hands and held his hands approximately three feet apart.

"This long," he told the reporter. "Which paper did you say you were from?"

He heard the reporter's intake of breath. He had put him on the defensive. Good.

"I'm a stringer for the *International Herald Tribune*," the reporter said.

"I thought they went out of business."

He heard the reporter shift in his chair. It was made of wood, and it's feet moved slightly every time the reporter did.

"It's still published in Europe and the Far East," the reporter said.

DeMarco stared straight ahead. He knew where the reporter was sitting, but had decided not to gaze in his direction, further putting him on the defensive.

"Do you consider your blindness a handicap or an asset when you play poker?" the reporter asked him.

"An asset," DeMarco said.

"Do you feel your opponents play you differently, knowing you're blind?"

"Differently how?"

"Less competitively."

DeMarco felt himself stiffen. The reporter was treating him like a three-legged dog that had learned how to run, and he wanted to crack him in the head with something very hard. Only, he told himself not to. He'd already created enemies by calling Rufus Steele an old man, and ripping this asshole wouldn't win him any friends.

"No. When you sit down at a poker table, it's like a bunch of piranhas in a swimming pool. Everyone tries to eat everyone else."

He listened to the reporter scratch away on his notepad. The reporter had also brought a tape recorder, which sat on the coffee table in front of him.

"Can you tell me how your blindness is an asset?" the reporter asked.

"It helps me win," DeMarco said.

"Would you explain?"

"And give away my secrets?"

"Well . . . yes."

DeMarco sensed that the reporter was smiling, and he shifted his head so he was facing the reporter, and flashed a rare smile of his own. "It's like this. When I was a teenager, I couldn't play sports or do a lot of the things that my friends were doing. One day, my uncle George took me to Atlantic City and we went to a casino. There was a poker room, and my uncle sat me down, bought me some chips, and taught me how to play. He told me what the other players' cards were, and then how to play my hand. Even though I lost, I had a great time.

"When I got home, I went to the local bookstore, and bought every book on poker they had. Reading is difficult for me—I have to hold the book up to my nose—but where there's a will, there's a way, and I read all of them. One of the books mentioned a store in Las Vegas called the Gambler's Book Club, and I called there, and talked to the manager. He recommended a book that changed my life."

DeMarco could hear the reporter scribbling away, and picked up his drink of water and finished it. Then he resumed speaking. "It was called *Read the Dealer* and was written by a gambler named Steve Forte. The book explained how players could get an advantage against casinos at blackjack. The information was so powerful that the casinos had to completely revamp the way blackjack was played.

"The part of the book that fascinated me was about language. It showed how a player could elicit responses from dealers with simple questions, and how those responses told you if the dealer liked you, or didn't like you. The book also explained how language could be used to make dealers tip their hands.

"After I finished the book, I realized that the information could be used in poker. By listening to my opponents' voices when they bet or checked, I would know if their cards were weak or strong. And since I'm very good at listening, I knew that I could compete with anyone in the world."

"This must have been a wonderful revelation to you," the reporter said.

DeMarco nodded. He'd been interviewed several times in the past two days and hadn't enjoyed it, the reporters treating him either like a freak, or an object of sympathy. This was the first time a reporter had treated him seriously.

"It was like being handed the keys to the kingdom," he said.

The reporter finished scribbling and shut off his recorder. Not once during the interview had Rufus Steele's allegation of cheating come up, and DeMarco knew that he'd dodged a serious bullet. He heard the reporter rise from his chair.

"Thanks for the interview, and good luck," the reporter said.

The reporter left, and DeMarco rose from the couch and shuffled across the room to the big picture window that radiated heat late in the day. He placed his fingers against the glass, and imagined the snow-tipped mountains that rimmed the western desert of Nevada. When the tournament was over, he planned to get someone to drive him into those mountains, and let him walk around and smell the mountain air. He heard a door click, and his uncle's heavy footsteps as he crossed the suite and came up behind him.

"Hey, Skipper," his uncle said. "How was the interview? Another asshole?"

"This one was okay."

"You broke through to the guy?"

"Yeah, I broke through to him," DeMarco said.

"That's good. Really good."

For a while neither man said anything, which suited DeMarco just fine. Although he loved his uncle more than anyone in the world, he did not always enjoy their conversations. They were like conversations on TV cop shows, with the guy in charge asking a lot of pointed questions, and everyone else forced to give answers. Uncle George was like that: he was always the one asking questions, and never giving answers. It was a one-way street, and usually left his nephew feeling put out.

"Listen, about what happened in the lobby," his uncle said. "I'm sorry."

"There's no need to apologize, Uncle George."

"I called the local hospital. They're sending replacements. We're covered."

"Thanks, Uncle George."

His uncle snorted contemptuously under his breath. "Those motherfuckers are going to pay for stealing that bag, mark my words."

The bodyguard had told DeMarco how his uncle had been made to look like a fool, the bag being taken from his hands without his uncle putting up a fight, and that his uncle was going to have those responsible killed if it was the last thing he did.

"You know who did it?" DeMarco asked.

"Yeah," his uncle said. "I know."

"How did you find out?"

"A local mob guy fingered them for me."

"They from New Jersey?"

"Don't ask so many questions."

DeMarco turned from the window so he was facing his uncle. He hated it when his uncle addressed him like a child. "I have a right to know, Uncle George."

"According to who?"

"According to me. I want to know who's after me."

"Yeah, they're from Jersey."

"Atlantic City?"

There was a long pause.

"Yeah," his uncle finally said.

DeMarco felt himself shudder. There was only one good reason why four guys from Atlantic City would come to Las Vegas to rob them, and he found himself wishing he'd never allowed his uncle to talk him into playing in the World Poker Showdown. He felt his uncle put a reassuring hand on his shoulder, and leave it there.

"There ain't nothing to worry about, Skipper," his uncle said.

"You sure, Uncle George?"

"Yeah. Those guys will pay. Just leave everything to me."

23

While Vinny drove back to their motel, Gerry stared at the Tuna's canvas bag sitting on the floor between his feet. He'd come to Las Vegas for two reasons—to get Jack's poker secret, and to pay back Jack's killers—only now the payback scenario didn't seem like such a good idea. His father telling him that no job was worth getting killed over suddenly sounded real smart.

"What do you say we get this over with?" Gerry asked.

Vinny took his eyes off the highway and stared at him. "How so?"

"I'm ready to go home. Let's take a look at Jack's secret, then split up. I'll fly up to Atlantic City next week, collect the money you owe Jack, and give it to Jack's mom."

"You want to scram, huh?" Vinny asked.

"Let's just say I've had enough of this town. How about you?"

Vinny said yes, then looked in the mirror at Nunzie and Frank.

"What do you guys say?"

Nunzie and Frank nodded vigorously. The scene at the Voodoo Lounge had put the fear of God into them, and they'd hardly spoken a word since leaving.

"Then I guess it's unanimous," Vinny said.

They were on Tropicana Avenue heading into town, and Vinny aimed the car at an off-the-strip casino called Lucky Lou's. Lou's was a locals' hangout, and known for its homey atmosphere and endless buffet.

"Why are you going there?" Gerry asked.

"There's a blackjack dealer on the afternoon shift that flashes her hole card," Vinny said. "I figured we could see what Jack's secret is, and make a little pocket money."

"Who told you about the dealer?"

"The albino at the Laughing Jackalope," Vinny said. "He got the information from the newest edition of the notebook. He said this dealer was an easy target."

The notebook was the holy grail for Nevada hustlers, and contained the names of blackjack dealers who flashed their hole card during the deal. By knowing the dealer's hole card, the player had a 15 percent edge over the house. Gerry didn't like it, and shook his head. He wanted to get out of Vegas, not scam a BJ dealer.

"Come on, it's easy pickings," Vinny said.

"I'm out of the rackets, remember?"

"Then have a beer. Come on."

The car was drifting across the lanes, heading toward Lucky Lou's on its own. There was no stopping Vinny when there was easy money to be made, and Gerry picked up the canvas bag from the floor.

"All right," he said.

Like many off-the-strip casinos, Lucky Lou's gave gamblers good value, with slot machines that paid out more regularly, and table games that offered better rules. Gerry had always thought it wrong that Las Vegas casinos were allowed to control the odds they offered gamblers, but that was the way the town worked.

Lucky Lou's was busy, and they passed through a sea of denim and polyester to reach the bar. Gerry ordered draft beers all the way around, and when they were delivered, found a table in the corner of the room. When he was sure no one was watching, he put the canvas bag on the table, and opened it. Inside was a white plastic box wrapped in see-through plastic. Gerry undid the plastic, which was cold to the touch, and handed the box to Vinny.

"For me?" Vinny said, like it was a birthday gift.

"You paid for it," Gerry said.

Vinny shook the box, then looked at Nunzie and Frank.

"Maybe I should wait and open it later," he said teasingly.

"Come on, open the box," Frank said impatiently.

"Yeah, dickhead, open it," Nunzie chorused.

The box had a plastic clasp, which Vinny undid, then lifted the lid. The four men dropped their heads and stared. Inside were a dozen tiny bottles of yellow liquid, and a hypodermic with several spare needles. For a long moment, no one said anything. Vinny picked up one of the bottles, and held it up to the crummy bar light. He squinted to read the printing on the label, then cursed under his breath.

"We stole the guy's insulin," he said.

Gerry grabbed the bottle from Vinny. "Maybe this is the secret."

"Insulin?" Vinny asked.

"Jack said he came up with the scam while getting radiation treatment in the hospital," Gerry said. "Maybe he found a way to mark playing cards with insulin."

Gerry poured some insulin onto a white cocktail napkin. It had no color, and when he wiped it away a moment later, there was no stain. Substances used to mark playing cards were usually derived from ink, and almost always left marks on white surfaces.

"I don't think so," Vinny said in disgust.

A minute passed with no one saying anything. For Vinny, that was a rare event. Finally he blew out his lungs and looked at Frank and Nunzie.

"What do you say we go make some easy money?"

"Yeah," they both said.

The three men rose from the table. Without a word they left the bar and went into the casino. The bar's walls were made of tinted glass, and Gerry watched them roam the blackjack pit in search of their easy dealer. Then he stared at the box of insulin and felt his spirits drop. He felt like he'd dug himself a hole, and it was growing deeper by the minute. He needed to fix things, and then he needed to get the hell out of Las Vegas.

He spied a cute waitress circling the table. She wore a spandex outfit that was several sizes too small for her, and seemed embarrassed by all the skin she was showing. He motioned her over to the table.

"I need a bag of ice," he said.

She scurried away. From his pocket he removed the pages he'd lifted from the Voodoo Lounge showing the odds of each player winning the World Poker Showdown, and found the odds on Skip DeMarco. DeMarco was running at 40 to 1. Odds were only meaningful if there was real money being bet on the tournament. He knew plenty of bookies, and took his cell phone and called one in New York named Big Dave.

"As I live and breathe," Big Dave said. "I heard you'd gone legit."

"I have," Gerry said. "I need a favor."

"Fire away."

"How much action is on the World Poker Showdown?"

"The last I heard, over twelve million," the bookie said, a police siren wailing in the background. "And the tournament doesn't end until next week."

"Where do you think it will top out?"

"Twenty million, easy."

"Any idea where it's coming from?"

"Here, there, and everywhere," Big Dave said, the siren gradually fading. "There's a lot of money on that blind guy, DeMarco."

"How much is a lot?"

"A million, so far. Personally, I don't think he's got a snowball's chance in hell."

"Why not?"

"He bad-mouthed Rufus Steele. The other players will be gunning for him, mark my words."

Gerry thanked him and killed the connection. If the tournament ended up taking in twenty million in total wagers, it would be easy for DeMarco's backers to put a couple million on their boy without drawing suspicion. That would net them a cool eighty million bucks, along with the ten million first prize. It was a hell of a lot of money for a stinking poker tournament.

The waitress appeared with a large Ziplock filled with ice. He placed the ice in the canvas bag with the insulin, then fished out his wallet and tossed a twenty onto her tray. The help got paid dirt in Las Vegas, and she smiled appreciatively.

"Thanks a lot, mister."

Gerry walked into the blackjack pit, and found Vinny, Nunzie, and Frank sitting at a table with an older woman dealer. Each man had an imposing stack of chips, and was oblivious to the gray-haired pit boss standing nearby, watching them.

Gerry watched his friends read the dealer's hole card. Nunzie sat to the dealer's right, and stayed low in his chair. This allowed him to peek at the corner of the dealer's hole card as it was slipped under her face card. If he saw paint, indicating a king, jack, or queen, he puffed twice on his cigarette. If he saw white, indicating a number card, he puffed once. It was enough information to give everyone at the table an unbeatable edge.

Out of the corner of his eye, Gerry saw the pit boss lift a walkie-talkie to his face. He guessed the pit boss was talking to someone in the surveillance control room about what was happening at the table. It didn't matter if what was happening was legal, or illegal. The pit boss had a quota to meet for his shift, and if Nunzie, Frank, and Vinny prevented him from achieving that quota, he'd catch hell from his bosses.

Gerry felt the pit boss's eyes on him, and saw a look of recognition spread across the man's face. Gerry was sure he'd never laid eyes on the guy in his life. To his surprise, the man came out of the pit like he wanted to shake hands. Then it dawned on Gerry what was going on. The pit boss knew his father.

Gerry bumped Vinny's chair, and Vinny turned around to stare at him.

"Start losing," Gerry said under his breath.

"*What?*"

"Start losing. All of you."

"But—"

"*Do it.*"

The pit boss was a few feet away, and had stopped. Gerry turned around.

"I'm sorry," the pit boss said. "I thought you were someone else."

"I'm Gerry Valentine. My father's Tony Valentine." Gerry removed his business card from his wallet, and handed it to him. The pit boss's eyesight wasn't good, and he put his glasses on, read the card, then looked into Gerry's face.

"You're the spitting image of your father."

"I'll take that as a compliment."

"You here on a job?"

"Yes," Gerry said. "My associates and I are working with my father on a case."

The pit boss's expression changed. He looked at Vinny, Frank, and Nunzie, then back at Gerry. "These three guys are with you?" he asked.

Gerry could have cut the suspicion in the pit boss's voice with a chain saw, and he placed his hand firmly on the back of Vinny's chair. "Yes. We're all together."

"Your friends are taking us to the cleaners," the pit boss said.

The challenge in his voice was unmistakable. Gerry glanced at the table. Each man's stack of chips had dwindled to practically nothing. As Gerry watched, the three men drew cards on another hand, and all lost. Gerry looked innocently at the pit boss.

"You could have fooled me," he said.

"What the hell are you doing?" Vinny asked as they marched out the casino's front doors. "We were up three grand!"

"Yeah," Nunzie piped in. "That dealer was a piece of cake. I was thinking of asking her to marry me."

No one laughed. The late afternoon sun was blinding, and Gerry shielded his eyes and searched the endless rows of cars in the parking lot for their rental.

"The pit boss knows my father," Gerry said.

"And because of that, you told us to lose?"

"That's right."

"I don't get it," Vinny said. To Nunzie and Frank he asked, "Do you?"

"No," they both said.

Gerry could tell they wanted an explanation, only he didn't feel like giving it to them, and continued to look for their vehicle. He didn't like giving up a score any more than Vinny or Nunzie or Frank, but some things were more important than money, like his father's business.

It was strange how things worked out. Growing up, he'd hated that his father was a cop, and been glad when he retired. Then his mother had passed away, and his father had nearly died of a broken heart. One day, a casino in Atlantic City had asked his father to do some consulting work, and in no time his father was back on his feet, busting cheaters. The work had been his salvation, and Gerry wasn't going to screw that up.

He found the rental car sandwiched between two rusted old junkers that looked ready for the scrap heap. That was one of the bad things about casinos. They attracted people who'd run out of everything but dreams. The space between the cars was narrow, and Gerry was sliding between them to unlock the driver's door when he saw a long shadow on the asphalt. He turned around slowly, fearing the worst. Sensing his alarm, his friends also turned.

Standing twenty yards away was a man who looked familiar. Tall, lanky, wearing faded blue jeans and a dungaree shirt with a square bulge in the pocket, the man wore his hair straight back, and had a look on his face of pure menace. The handgun that dangled by his side rounded out the picture. Then Gerry recognized him. It was the construction worker from the Voodoo Lounge, the guy that Gerry knew was part of the scheme to kill them. Their eyes met, and the construction worker raised his gun.

24

"**G**reat shirt," Gloria Curtis said, spearing a shrimp in her shrimp cocktail.

"You like it?" Valentine asked.

"Yes. The color matches your eyes."

Valentine smiled as he buttered his roll. They were having dinner in Celebrity's revolving restaurant atop the hotel while watching the desert turn a burnt ochre color.

"I saw you buying it earlier," she added.

He looked into her face and saw her eyes twinkle. If he'd learned anything from the past two years of taking stabs at dating, it was that women appreciated when a man tried to look nice on their behalf. How this simple fact had escaped him during his forty years of marriage, he had no earthly idea.

"It's a new color for me," he said. "I'm glad you like it."

"New, as in you haven't worn it in a while?"

He shook his head. "I can't remember wearing blue as a kid. I wore it as a cop when I was in uniform and had a beat, then switched to jeans and sweatshirts when I went undercover. When I started policing casinos, I wore a black sports jacket and a white shirt."

"You always wore white shirts? No variations?"

He again shook his head. One year for Christmas, his wife had given him a pink button-down shirt, and he'd worn it to work. Everyone had made so much fun of him, he'd retired it to the closet and never worn it again.

"So why did you decide to wear blue today?" she asked.

The buttered roll still hadn't made it into his mouth. He hadn't wanted his shirt to become the main topic of their conversation, and said, "My closet is filled with white shirts. When I look at them, I see the past. I guess I felt it was time for a change."

Gloria stabbed another shrimp out of her cocktail. Las Vegas sold more shrimp than anywhere else in the world, and the ones swimming in cocktail sauce in Gloria's glass were of the monster variety. She chewed her food contemplatively.

"I have this bad habit of wondering about things until they start driving me crazy," she said. "I guess it's why I became a journalist. When I was talking to Rufus Steele the other day, I mentioned to him that the Nevada Gaming Control Board had hired you to investigate the tournament, and he made a comment that's been bothering me."

"What did he say?"

"Rufus said that the first time he played poker in Atlantic City, you saved his life, but also ruined his life. When I pressed him for an explanation, we got interrupted, and I never got my answer. Can you explain what he meant?"

A waiter appeared with their meals. He was a different guy from the one who'd taken their dinner order, who'd been a different guy from the one who'd taken their drink and appetizer order. The restaurant touted itself as the best in Las Vegas, only its service was nothing but asses and elbows. The waiter tried to take Gloria's shrimp cocktail away so he could set her plate down, and she grabbed it from his hand.

"I'm not finished with that," she said.

The waiter looked at her blankly. Normally Valentine would have given him a lesson in table etiquette, but instead told him to bring the plates back in five minutes.

"And make sure they're hot," he said as the waiter walked away.

"So, where were we?" Gloria said.

"Rufus's comment about my saving and ruining his life."

"Right. What did he mean?"

He decided his roll was not meant to be eaten, and put it down on his bread plate. He spent a few moments dredging his memory. He'd dealt with many situations during his years in Atlantic City, and Rufus Steele was buried deep in the past.

"If I remember correctly, this was in early 1980," he said. "Atlantic City had opened it's first casino a year and a half before, and we were attracting gamblers from all over the country, including a lot of poker players. Now, we didn't have any legal poker rooms in our casinos, so these guys were playing in private homes on the island, or in rooms in the casino."

"Was that legal?"

"No, but that never stopped a poker player from playing in a game. Especially Rufus. It's a risky proposition, too, when you consider how often these games get hijacked."

"Hijacked?"

"It's what poker players say when a game gets robbed. Did you happen to notice the thick rubber band Rufus wears around his wrist? A lot of the old-time poker players wear them."

Gloria thought about it while devouring another

shrimp. "Come to mention it, I did see a rubber band around his wrist. I assumed it had some meaning."

"It does. A poker player's best friend is a rubber band. If a guy comes out of a game, and thinks he's about to get hijacked, he'll pull his bankroll out of his pocket, and encircle it with a rubber band. Then he'll toss the bankroll under a car, or over a wall, and recover it later."

"That sounds awfully dangerous."

"They say playing poker is the most dangerous way to make an easy living."

"Okay, back to your story," Gloria said.

"Right. Rufus comes to Atlantic City to play poker in a private game in a casino hotel. Rufus looks me up, knowing I'm the head law enforcement officer, and introduces himself. He doesn't come out and say he's there to play poker, but I figured it out. He was famous even back then, and I realized he was asking me to look out for him. You know, make sure he doesn't get hijacked."

"Why would you do that? You knew the game was illegal."

"A lot of reasons. For one thing, if the game got hijacked, it would bring bad publicity to the casino. Another is that if people gamble inside a casino, it's hard to stop them from going up to their rooms, and playing cards. The third is, I liked the guy."

"The third reason is the best," she said.

"The next morning, I get to work, and call Rufus's hotel room, just to see how he's doing. The phone rings and rings, but he doesn't answer. I call the hotel's housekeeping, and ask them to send a maid up, and have her knock on the door. I get a call back, saying there's no answer. Now, either Rufus is a heavy sleeper or he's in trouble, so I called hotel security and alerted them. Then I ran over there."

"Ran?"

"Yes. My office was in one of the casinos. At the time, there were three casinos in Atlantic City, and they were all connected by the Boardwalk, so it was easier to run between them than taking my car. It was also a good way to stay in shape."

Gloria broke into a big smile. "That's a wonderful image."

He felt himself blush, not entirely sure what she meant. She reached across the table and placed her hand on his wrist.

"Please tell me the rest."

"Right. I reach the hotel, and go up to Rufus's room. Hotel security is standing outside, not knowing what to do. I kicked down the door, and ran in. Rufus was lying in the bathtub with a gag in his mouth. His wrists were tied behind his back with piano wire, and his ankles were tied as well. The piano wire had cut through the skin, and he was slowly bleeding to death."

"How horrible."

"I untied him, and he told me that he'd won fifty thousand bucks playing poker the night before, then come back to the room. Two guys had lock-picked the door, and jumped him at three o'clock in the morning. They had stockings over their faces, only one of the guys started coughing, and had to pull the stocking off. Rufus saw his face, so the guys decided to give him the piano wire treatment, and leave him."

"You mean they meant to kill him?"

"They sure did."

"Did Rufus know the man?"

"No, but he saw his face, and the guy was scared of Rufus fingering him. I rushed Rufus to the hospital, then tracked down the guys who'd robbed him, and hauled them in."

"But how did you do that, if Rufus didn't know them?"

"Piano wire isn't something most crooks carry around with them. Atlantic City is a small island, and there's only one piano store. I called it, and asked them if two guys had been in the day before, and purchased any wire. Turns out, they had. They'd paid for the wire with a credit card, so it was easy to track them down."

"Did you retrieve all of Rufus's money?"

"Every last cent. That was how I ruined him, so to speak."

"What do you mean?"

"The law required that I inform the Internal Revenue Service about the money Rufus had won, since it was income. I ran into Rufus about ten years later, and he told me that the IRS had been auditing him every year since."

"Couldn't you have prevented that?"

"You mean not tell the IRS?"

"Yes."

Valentine shook his head. "It would have meant breaking the law."

A look crept across Gloria's face that was neither a smile nor a frown. The shrimp had vanished from her shrimp cocktail, and the sun had dropped low enough in the horizon for dusk to have settled in. The real day for Las Vegas was about to start.

"Now I know why you always wore black and white," she said.

It took Valentine five minutes to flag down their waiter, and convince him to bring their food. He touched their plates as they were served, and was pleased they were hot. He and Gloria had both ordered plank-grilled salmon with garlic mashed potatoes. They seemed to have a lot in common, and dug into their meals.

"My producer loved the piece with Rufus and the fly," Gloria said. "He's going to run it tonight after they show the highlights from the tournament. You saved me with that call."

"Saved you how?" Valentine asked.

"I found out a few hours ago that my producer was going to call me home. It's the worst thing that can happen to a reporter when they're out on assignment. After he saw the segment, he told me to stay a few more days, and see what I could dig up."

"So you still have your job."

"It sure looks that way."

"Glad I could help."

"My producer thinks Rufus's stunt was a trick, and that he really didn't hypnotize the fly. I told him if anyone would know the secret, it was you."

Valentine put a piece of salmon into his mouth and chewed. He'd come to dinner prepared to explain the sugar cube trick to Gloria, but now found himself having second thoughts. He guessed it had something to do with seeing Rufus so down on his luck earlier, and all his clothes piled unceremoniously in the middle of his room. Rufus was slowing down, which was death for any gambler, and the vultures were starting to pick him apart. He had no desire to join the carnage.

"I don't have a clue," Valentine said.

25

Gerry watched the construction worker walk toward them, aiming his gun. It was a simple .22, a gun that was relatively quiet compared to most handguns. Gerry had heard that mob guys and hitmen liked .22s because once the bullet entered the body, it tended to ricochet and cause a lot of damage. Vinny and Nunzie dove between a pair of parked cars, and a bullet whistled over their heads.

The construction worker kept coming forward, his weapon now aimed at Gerry. Gerry followed the Fountain brothers' lead, and ducked behind a car.

"Gimme the keys," Frank said, standing beside the trunk of the rental.

Crouching, Vinny dug the rental keys from his pocket. "Here," he said, throwing them in Frank's direction.

Frank plucked the keys out of the air and unlocked the rental's trunk. He was amazingly calm, and it reminded Gerry of his mother's favorite expression: "Everyone is good for something." As a boxer, Frank had faced guys who were bigger than he was, and who punched harder than he did, but Frank had beaten them all. He was afraid of nothing. The other thing Frank was good at was seeing into the future. Before they'd left the

Voodoo Lounge, he'd gone back inside the bar, and returned carrying the bartender's .38 Magnum, which he'd placed in the rental's trunk.

"Never know when you'll need a gun," he'd remarked.

Frank now removed the .38 from the trunk as the construction worker took a shot at him. The bullet hit an SUV parked behind Frank, winging it and causing the car's alarm to go off. Gerry heard the construction worker curse, and knew the guy was making a classic mistake. It was hard enough to shoot someone while standing still, but moving forward made it doubly hard.

Grasping the .38 with both hands, Frank leveled its barrel at the construction worker, causing him to freeze in his tracks. Frank squeezed the trigger and nothing happened. He squeezed again, and heard another click.

"I need backup," Frank yelled.

Vinny, who was hiding across the aisle, pulled off one of his loafers, and threw it at the construction worker. The man ducked, not knowing what was being thrown at him. Then Nunzie threw one of his shoes, hitting the construction worker in the side. Gerry stared at Frank, who'd opened up the .38's chamber, and was inspecting the weapon. Satisfied, he snapped the chamber shut, aimed, and fired.

The bullet hit the construction worker in the chest, and he lurched violently to one side, his arms going straight into the air. The .38's bullet was a different animal than a .22's. It was meant to penetrate, and left a larger exit hole than most handguns. The construction worker's legs moved backward, like they'd taken on a life of their own, his fingers still clutching the .22.

Frank shot him again in the chest. The construction worker was dead, but didn't know it. Frank shot him a third time, and the .22 flew out of the construction worker's hand and disappeared beneath a parked car. The man continued going backward, only now his feet had stopped working. He hit the pavement and lay motionless on the ground.

Vinny and Nunzie ran out from their hiding places, and retrieved their shoes. They fitted them on while hopping on one leg. The construction worker stared up at the cloudless sky, the look on his face pure disbelief.

Gerry went over to Frank, and put his hand on the bigger man's shoulder.

"Jesus, Frank, you okay?"

Frank stared at the dead man and shook his head.

"I got lucky," Frank said.

Most hitmen worked in pairs, with one man doing the shooting, the other doing the driving. Gerry guessed the construction worker's driver was sitting in a car in the parking lot, waiting for his partner to run over and jump in.

"Time to get out of Dodge," Gerry said.

The four men climbed into the rental. Vinny made the tires squeal as he drove out Lucky Lou's back entrance, and onto a side street with little traffic.

"We need to get lost," Gerry said.

Vinny drove east and got onto the strip. It was dusk, and the city was starting to come alive, the streets and sidewalks teeming with tourists. It was comforting to be around so many people, and Vinny drove for several minutes without anyone in the car saying a word.

"How the hell did that guy find us?" Gerry suddenly asked. "We left the Voodoo Lounge and drove around.

Then we went to Lucky Lou's. How did that guy know where we were?"

Gerry turned around in his seat. Nunzie and Frank gave him blank looks. Neither man was big in the thinking department. He turned back around and looked at Vinny.

"Any ideas?"

Vinny gripped the wheel and stared at the road. Like Gerry, he'd gone to college for a few years, and had also worked in his father's business. He knew how to connect the dots, and scrunched his face in concentration.

"He didn't find us," Vinny finally said. "He was there in the parking lot, waiting for us. He found the car."

"So what you're saying is, this car is being traced."

"Must be," Vinny said.

Gerry stared straight ahead. A pack of young women were jaywalking in front of the car. One stopped to wink at him. When Gerry ignored her, she stuck her tongue out, then moved on, her friends laughing hysterically.

"Get off at the next intersection and find a gas station," Gerry said. "We need to fly speck this car."

Vinny hung a left on Sahara, and drove until he found a gas station. He pulled into the lot and parked beside the station's convenience store. The four men hopped out, and Frank grabbed a newspaper out of the trash and laid it on the ground, then slid beneath the car, while Vinny popped the hood and examined the engine with Nunzie. Gerry leaned against the car and watched the street, wary of someone pulling into the gas station and blindsiding them. After a minute he heard Frank speak up.

"Underbody's clean," Frank said.

"So's the engine," Vinny said, slamming the hood.

Frank slid out from beneath the car. Gerry offered his hand, and helped pull Frank to his feet. The four men huddled beside the building.

"What do we do now?" Vinny asked.

Gerry felt his friends staring at him, and tried to think what his father would do in a situation like this. Whenever his father had a pressing problem, he usually ate something and drank a cup of coffee. Gerry had always thought it was something that cops did, but now saw the value in it. A little break in the action was needed, and he went inside the convenience store.

He emerged a few minutes later with a cardboard tray containing four cups of coffee and a bag of doughnuts. The sun was setting, and the fractured light lit up the sky. He offered the food to his partners. As he did, a tiny sparkle of light on the roof of their rental caught his eye. It was there for an instant, then disappeared.

Nunzie grabbed the bag out of Gerry's hand, and peeked inside.

"Jelly doughnuts. These all for me?"

"Share them," Gerry said. He handed Vinny the tray of drinks, then started to take off his shoes and socks. The three men stared at him.

"What are you doing?" Vinny asked.

"What does it look like I'm doing?"

"It looks like you're taking off your shoes and socks. You going to walk around barefoot?"

"That's right."

Gerry climbed onto the hood of their rental, then slid his body onto the roof. In its center he found a small, circular reflector similar to the kind used on bicycles. He peeled it off the roof, then climbed down.

"Look what I found," he said.

The three men stared at the reflector while eating the doughnuts.

"The reflector can be seen from up in the sky," Gerry explained. "We were being followed by helicopter. That's how the construction worker from Voodoo Lounge traced our car."

Vinny took the reflector from Gerry's hand, and stared at it.

"Jinky was using a helicopter?"

"Not Jinky," Gerry said. "The cops. This is how the cops follow people."

Vinny stopped eating his doughnut, and his face turned pale. Gerry knew exactly what Vinny was thinking, because it was the same thing he was thinking. Jinky Harris had a cop with the Metro Las Vegas Police on his payroll, and was using that person to track their whereabouts with a helicopter, then send hitmen to whack them. They didn't stand a chance against someone with those kinds of resources.

"So, what do we do?" Vinny asked.

Gerry took the last doughnut from the bag and bit into it. There was only one thing to do, and that was find his father, and ask for his help. He'd been doing that most of his life, and his old man had never let him down.

"Call my father," Gerry said.

"So, call him."

A white Impala pulled into the gas station and parked in front of the convenience store. It was an unmarked police car, and a uniformed sheriff got out. He touched the brim of his hat as he passed them, and entered the store.

Gerry took the reflector out of Vinny's fingers, and walked over to the Impala. He glanced inside the store, and saw that the sheriff was at the counter with his back to him. Gerry placed the reflector onto the Impala's roof, and pressed down firmly. Then he walked over to his friends.

"That should keep them off our trail for a while," he said.

Part II

Juice

26

"I think I'm being watched," Gloria Curtis said.

Valentine had insisted on paying their dinner bill, and was struggling to figure the tip. The service had bordered on comical, with none of their courses coming out when they were supposed to. But the waiter still had to pay his rent and put food on the table, and Valentine didn't see any point in penalizing him just because the guy hadn't been properly trained. He calculated 20 percent before tax, and added it to the bill.

Then he looked into Gloria's eyes. They were a hazel green, and very soft. She had a face that got prettier every time he looked at her. They'd been eating dinner for an hour, and not once had the conversation lagged.

"By who?" he asked.

She'd lit up a cigarette after they'd finished their desserts, and it had taken all his resolve not to bum one off her. She drew back in her chair, and took a deep drag.

"Someone inside the hotel."

"Any idea who it might be?"

She shrugged, and seemed to be wrestling with how to proceed.

"I don't know if I should be telling you this," she said.

He studied her face. He'd learned a long time ago that

a woman wouldn't confide in a man until she trusted him. It didn't matter who that man was—a cop, a lawyer, or even a judge. If she didn't think he was trustworthy, she wouldn't talk. He sensed the same thing was taking place with Gloria. She'd spent dinner getting to know him, but still had reservations. He decided to take a stab in the dark.

"I was hired by the Nevada Gaming Control Board to investigate the tournament," he said quietly. "I don't work for the hotel, or the tournament, or the casino. I've also never been employed by any of them before."

"No ties, huh?"

"None whatsoever."

She crushed her cigarette in the ashtray. "So what you're saying is, if I can't trust you, there probably isn't anyone in the hotel I can trust."

"That would be a fair assumption," he said. Then he added, "If there's someone spying on you, I'd be happy to help you get to the bottom of it."

"You can do that?"

He glanced at his cell phone lying on the table. As a rule, he kept his cell turned off, and in his pocket. But being that his son was in Las Vegas and had hitmen trailing him, he'd decided to make an exception and keep his phone within reach.

"With a single phone call," he said.

Her face took on a new look. "Really? You have that kind of juice?"

"Yes," he said.

The waiter came and took the bill. He thanked Valentine, and as he was walking away, opened up the bill holder and stared at the tip. Satisfied, he began to whistle.

"Looks like you made his day," Gloria said.

*   *   *

No sooner was the waiter gone than a Hispanic bus boy appeared. He cleared off the table, oblivious to the fact that they were still sitting there. Valentine decided it was time to give the maitre d' a piece of his mind when Gloria stopped him. She wanted to talk, and suggested the bar next door.

A hostess dressed in black greeted them at the bar's entrance. She explained that the bar was full, and she couldn't let them in without reservations. Valentine slipped a twenty into her hand, and she led them inside and seated them at an empty table.

The bar was typical of Las Vegas drinking holes, and filled with loud, obnoxious men. A bottle blonde with gravity-defying breasts was behind the bar, simultaneously mixing martinis, Manhattans, and Latin-style drinks as the men cheered her on.

"Scotch and soda," Gloria told the waitress.

"I'll have a water," Valentine said.

"Perrier or sparkling?" the waitress asked. She was also in black, from her nail polish to her nose ring.

"Tap, if you have it," he said.

The waitress frowned, then picked up the drinks menu from the table, studying it to see if his request was printed with the other outrageously expensive drinks.

"I'll have to ask the bartender," she said.

"Please," he said.

Gloria waited until the waitress was out of earshot before slapping the table and breaking out in uncontrollable giggles. Valentine was glad one of them found the situation funny. It made it almost tolerable.

"Who do you think is watching you?" he asked.

Gloria lit another cigarette. "Let me tell you what happened, and then maybe you can tell me. I got a call from Zack in my room this afternoon. He said another dealer in the tournament had passed out, and been sent to the hospital. We decided to go downstairs, and check it out. When I was in the elevator, I realized I'd left my wallet on the bedside table. I went back to my room, and found two hotel employees inside. They were standing by the closet, and jumped when I came in. They claimed they were restocking the minibar, but that was bogus."

"How can you be sure?"

"They'd closed the door to my room. They're not supposed to do that when they're servicing a room. One of them was wearing a tool belt. He was going to open my room safe." She glanced at the bar, then looked at him. "I had my notes and copies of my interviews locked in the safe."

"Did you take them out?"

"Yes. They're hidden now."

What Gloria was describing was a serious crime. Hotel employees could not open room safes unless the person occupying the room requested it. Employees who got caught breaking this rule not only got fired, but often went to jail. The waitress appeared with their drinks balanced on a tray.

"Tap water is on the house," she said.

The waitress left, and they clinked glasses with smiles on their faces.

"Based upon what you just told me, I'd say someone from the hotel is keeping tabs on you," Valentine said. "They legally can do that a number of ways. They can listen to your voice messages, and they can monitor your room through the door lock. Each time the door is opened, it's seen. There are also surveillance cameras in the hallways which can follow you around."

"This is all legal?"

"It is in Las Vegas."

"You don't approve of that, do you?"

"Not in the least. But I don't make the rules."

Gloria held her drink in one hand, her burning cigarette in the other. It was a pose straight out of a Humphrey
Bogart movie, and he didn't think she was doing it on
purpose.

"Who's behind it? The tournament?"

"That would be my guess," he said. "You aired the
piece with Rufus, and all hell broke loose. Someone at
the tournament pressured the hotel to start following
you, and maybe break into your room safe. It's not a
pretty picture."

"You mean for me?"

He nodded. He didn't want to tell Gloria that Las
Vegas was notorious for keeping scandals out of the
news. The city spent a hundred million dollars a year
marketing itself, and the money bought a lot of favors
with the press. Gloria glanced at his cell phone, which
he'd placed on the table when they'd sat down.

"Can you really call someone, and make this stop?"

Valentine nodded again. He would call Bill Higgins
later, and tell him Gloria was being electronically tailed
by the hotel for no good reason. Bill would send his
agents to Celebrity's surveillance control room, and have
them read the riot act to Celebrity's technicians. Hope-
fully, that would stop the problem.

Gloria smiled at him with her eyes. Her face had become enveloped in a curl of cigarette smoke, and it gave
her features a dreamy quality.

Valentine's cell phone began to move across the table,
and they both stared at it. He remembered that he'd put
it on vibrate, and he picked it up and stared at its face.
It was Gerry, the prodigal son. He answered it.

"What's up?" Valentine said.

"Frank just shot a guy to death," his son said.

Valentine brought his hand up to his eyes. Just when

everything was moving along in brilliant fashion, his son spoiled the party. Sensing his distress, Gloria shot him a concerned look.

"Where are you?" Valentine asked.

"At a gas station on Sahara, just off the strip," his son said.

"I'll be right over."

"Thanks, Pop. Thanks a lot."

Valentine killed the connection while shaking his head.

"Is something wrong?" Gloria asked.

"It's my son."

"Problem?"

"Yes. A big problem."

"Well, he certainly called the right person," she said.

27

Mark Perrier, Celebrity's forty-two-year-old general manager, sat in his office on the top floor of the casino, staring at the burnt orange desert that was his property's backyard. The desert stretched as far as his eyes could see, and he often imagined himself taking a long walk across it. *Maybe someday,* he thought.

His eyes fell on the spreadsheet lying on his desk. It contained yesterday's take from the casino, and showed the money they'd made for slots, video poker, keno, the Asian games, Caribbean stud poker, blackjack, craps, and roulette. The total was one million, one hundred thousand dollars, or fifty thousand dollars over their nut. The casino had made money yesterday, but just barely.

He pulled off his necktie, then took a bottle of Scotch out of his desk and poured a finger into a glass on his desk, then gulped it down. The Scotch made his throat burn; he shut his eyes, and felt himself relax. He didn't think anyone in his life understood the pressure he was under.

His wife, Tori, was a perfect example. She looked at the opening of Celebrity's Las Vegas hotel like the opening of any other hotel that her husband had been involved with. Mark had opened five-star hotels from Perth to Paris, and all of them had been wildly successful. Why should this be any different?

His bosses at corporate headquarters in Chicago also didn't understand. To them, Celebrity's Las Vegas hotel was one more casino in the chain. They didn't want to discuss the fact that Celebrity had never run a property in Las Vegas, the company content to stay in smaller, less competitive markets. They had never swum with sharks this large.

Celebrity's stockholders didn't understand, either. When construction of Celebrity's Las Vegas hotel had been announced two years ago, the company's stock had shot up 20 percent and become the darling of Wall Street. The stockholders were banking on the property to pay huge dividends, and had no idea how tough the market really was.

But Perrier knew better. He'd been a hotel guy his whole life, and had cut his teeth running resorts all over the world. He could spot a good property in a minute. It was all about location, location, location. Everything else was camouflage.

Celebrity's Las Vegas hotel was a dog. The property was four miles from the strip, which was too damn far. His bosses had tried to buy property on the strip, but had been turned off by the high prices. Instead, they'd bought a hundred-acre tract out in the desert, and called it paradise.

The other problem was the staff. Corporate had promised to transfer the best people from their other casinos to run the Las Vegas hotel. Only no one had wanted to come, forcing Perrier to fill hundreds of positions with retreads and high school dropouts.

Which left Perrier sitting on a nine hundred million dollar white elephant. Long term, the hotel wouldn't survive. But short term was a different story. The World

Poker Showdown was being shown live on national television. It was the best advertising going, and would keep the place filled long enough for him to find another hotel to run.

The phone on his desk rang. His private line.

"Perrier here."

"Are you watching Valentine?" his caller asked.

"That you, Jasper?"

Karl Jasper growled at him. He was the founder and president of the WPS, and as trustworthy as a snake oil salesman. On television, Jasper projected the image of a devoted family man and all-around good guy. In person, he was a foul-mouthed thug, and would go to any extreme to get what he wanted.

"Are you watching him or not?" Jasper asked.

Perrier played with the keyboard on his desk. A picture appeared on his computer screen, showing Valentine in the rooftop bar with Gloria Curtis.

"Yes. He's with the newswoman, Gloria Curtis."

"Are you taping their conversation? I want to know what they talking about. That woman is poison, and so is he."

Perrier shut his eyes. Jasper had a pattern. He would ask you to break the law, then explain why it had to be done. The reasons were always logical.

"Wiretapping is illegal in Nevada," Perrier said.

"I thought that was just for telephones," Jasper said.

"All private conversations."

"What's he doing now?"

Perrier opened his eyes. Valentine was talking to the waitress. The resolution of the picture was so clear, Perrier could see a tiny stain on his blue shirt.

"Nothing much," he said.

"I want you to keep watching him," Jasper said. "This goddamn situation has to go away. Rufus Steele is stirring the pot, and Valentine is sniffing around the bushes like a bloodhound. That son-of-a-bitch could spoil a picnic if you gave him the chance. He's cost more casinos money than any cheater he's ever busted."

"Cost them how?" Perrier asked.

"By making them play by the rules," Jasper said. "What's he doing now?"

Perrier stared at the screen. The waitress had brought the check, and Valentine and Gloria were fighting over it, only they were doing it in a way that was making them both laugh. They liked each other. He groaned.

"What's the matter?" Jasper asked.

"You really want to know?" Perrier asked.

"Yes."

"This tournament is what's the matter," Perrier said.

"What the hell is that supposed to mean?"

"I'll tell you. First, your tournament director screws up, and lets DeMarco play with his friends. Now everyone thinks he's a cheater. Then, your dealers forget to get Sheriff's Cards from the Metro Las Vegas Police Department, and the chief of police is calling me every hour. Oh yeah, and your dealers keep dropping like flies. I feel like I'm sitting on a nuclear bomb, Jasper."

"Last night's ratings were through the roof," Jasper said.

Perrier didn't think Jasper had heard a word of what he'd just said. Television ratings were all Jasper talked about, and cared about.

"So I heard," Perrier said.

"Where is Valentine now?"

Perrier stared at the screen. Valentine and Gloria Curtis had settled the bill and were getting up from their table, sharing meaningful looks.

"He's leaving the bar," he said.

"I need to get him out of Las Vegas," Jasper said. "And that goes for Rufus Steele, and that newscaster woman. My ass is on the line, and so is yours, my friend."

Perrier shook his head. One of his great assets was his ability to watch his mouth. Then he'd had drinks with Jasper, and let it slip that he thought the hotel was a dog. He'd regretted it ever since.

"What do you want me to do?" Perrier asked.

"Keeps tabs on Valentine and the newscaster," Jasper said.

"We're already watching them."

"Beef it up," Jasper said. "Record everything they do, who they talk to, the works."

"What about Rufus? Isn't he the one causing all the trouble?"

"I've got Rufus taken care of," Jasper said.

Perrier didn't like the sound of that. He played with his keyboard, and checked the hotel's res system. Rufus Steele had left his room a few hours ago, and was now sharing a room with Valentine. The information had been filed by a maid.

He typed a command into his keyboard, and found the hallway outside Valentine's room. As luck would have it, Rufus was coming out of the room. Perrier followed him down a hallway to an elevator. He switched cameras, and watched Rufus get into the elevator, and push the button for the sixth floor.

"You going to beat him up?" Perrier asked.

"No, no," Jasper said. "No rough stuff."

"Then what?"

"Trust me. He won't give us any more trouble."

Perrier watched Rufus depart the elevator, and walk to a room on the sixth floor. The door opened, and a guy with a grin on his face greeted him. Perrier saw a card table inside the room. Then the door closed. They were going to fleece him, Perrier thought. He could live with that.

"Will you do it?" Jasper asked.

"Do what?" Perrier asked.

"Keep tabs on Valentine and Gloria Curtis. Come on, Mark. Help me out here."

Perrier hesitated. He could get in a ton of trouble for spying on people. But if he didn't do it, Valentine and Gloria Curtis might bring the tournament down in flames, and he'd be out on the street looking for work.

"All right," he heard himself say.

Jasper exhaled deeply on the line.

"I knew I could count on you," the president of the WPS said.

28

"**Y**our father is crazy," Vinny said after Gerry explained his father's solution.

"No, he's not," Gerry replied. "This is the best way to handle what's happened."

Vinny shook his head in exasperation. "Go back to the scene of the crime? Call the cops and tell them what happened? Those are suicide tactics."

Vinny, Gerry, Nunzie, and Frank were sitting in the rental in the convenience store parking lot. Vinny was sweating like he was going to the electric chair, and dabbed his forehead with a napkin stained with jelly doughnut. The jelly was cherry, and made Vinny look like he'd been stabbed in the face. Gerry tilted the mirror so Vinny could see what he'd done to himself.

"For the love of Christ," Vinny said, and went inside to clean himself off.

Gerry turned so he was facing Nunzie and Frank in the backseat. They didn't looked too thrilled with the idea of going back to Lucky Lou's, either. They'd been running away from the law since they were teenagers. A minute later, Vinny returned to the car. "Explain it to me again, will you?" Vinny asked.

"It's like this," Gerry said. "My father has already

told Bill Higgins, the director of the Nevada Gaming Control Board, that we're in Las Vegas helping him with a job. My old man fronted for us, okay?"

"I thought your old man hated us," Nunzie said.

"That's beside the point," Gerry said. "He did it, which means when we talk to the police, Bill Higgins will back our story. My father just gave us a Get-Out-of-Jail-Free card."

"But why go back to Lucky Lou's?" Vinny asked. "We didn't see a single camera in that section of the parking lot. There wasn't one at the exit, either. We got away without being photographed."

Vinny didn't know it, but he was dead wrong. Gerry's father had explained it to him. Every major intersection in Las Vegas had a surveillance camera hidden in its traffic light. It was part of a massive surveillance campaign that had begun right after 9/11. The police would review the tapes of the intersections around Lucky Lou's, and match their departure time with the approximate time of the shooting. They'd also get the license of the rental they were driving, and eventually track them down.

"Because it's the smart thing to do," Gerry said. "My father has established an alibi for us. We're law-abiding citizens, working for my father's company. That's our story, and I'm sticking to it. Now, are you in, or are you out?"

Fifteen minutes later, Gerry's father pulled into the lot and parked by the front door to the convenience store. The look on his father's face was one Gerry had seen countless times before. Frustration mixed with anger mixed with resignation. Gerry walked over to his father's car, and knelt down by the open driver's window.

"Hey, Pop, thanks for coming so fast."

"You okay?" his father asked.

"Yeah, I'm okay. Are you sure going to the police is a such good idea?"

His father glared at him. "Sure, I'm sure. Why, you getting cold feet?"

"My friends think Jinky Harris has the police department in his back pocket," Gerry said. "They don't think turning ourselves in is such a smart idea."

His father frowned. It was a look that made Gerry feel ten years old.

"Hoods don't have police departments in their back pockets," his father said. "At best, they have a cop they pay off to do them favors. This is the best way to go, trust me."

"I still think they're apprehensive," Gerry said. "These are street guys, Pop."

"Want me to talk to them?" his father asked.

"Sure. But don't yell, okay?"

His father got out of the car and gave him a look. Gerry stared at the ground.

"Sorry," he said.

Cops were pricks, especially the good ones. It wasn't just what they said, but how they came on to you, rough and hard and full of piss and vinegar. It was the only advantage they had when dealing with lowlifes and scumbags. That veneer didn't wear off when a cop got older. It sure hadn't with his old man.

His father slid into the passenger seat of the rental, and faced the Fountain brothers and Frank. For a long moment, his father did nothing but stare at the three men. Gerry stayed outside, listening through the open window.

"Which one of you did the shooting?" his father asked.

Frank raised his hand like a kid in sixth grade. "I did."

"You ever kill anyone before?"

"In the ring," Frank said.

"How did it make you feel?"

"Shitty."

"How about this time?"

" 'Bout the same," Frank said.

"Where's the gun you used?"

Frank took a paper bag off the floor of the backseat and carefully handed it to Valentine. He looked inside the bag, then placed it on the seat. "Here's the deal," Valentine said. "We're going back to Lucky Lou's, and you're going to tell the police what happened. I want the cops to know you're out here, doing a job for me. I know you don't have police records, but if the Metro Las Vegas sheriff starts digging, he might discover there's a file on you with the Atlantic City Casino Commission, and that file has you tied to a scam several years ago." Valentine turned, and glanced out the window at his son. "*All* of you. So, let's go back there, and get this settled while we still can. Okay?"

Gerry swallowed the lump rising in his throat. His old man had a sixth sense when it came to knowing all the dumb things he'd done in his life, yet he still stuck with him. He was going to have to remember that when his daughter grew up.

"You're going to vouch for us, Mr. Valentine?" Vinny asked.

"Isn't that what I just said?" Valentine snapped.

"I just wanted to be sure."

Valentine growled at Vinny. Then he took the paper bag off the seat and climbed out of the rental. Valentine crossed the lot and got into his own car without a word. Gerry slid into the rental and looked at his friends.

"Let's go," Gerry said.

Expectations and reality were never the same. Expectations took place inside your head, reality on the street. Gerry had expected Lucky Lou's parking lot to be packed with police cars and an ambulance, but when Vinny pulled into the lot a few minutes later, the place was no different from when they'd left it.

As Vinny drove the rental down the aisle, Gerry saw why. The construction worker's body was gone. Gerry jumped out, and went to where the construction worker had gone down. There was a pancake-size bloodstain that was slowly blending into the jet black macadam, but otherwise no evidence of what had happened.

Gerry glanced over his shoulder. His father was sitting in his car behind Vinny, his face demanding an explanation. Gerry raised his palms to the sky, then saw a silver-haired security guard speeding toward him in a golf cart. Gerry waved the guard down.

"What's up?" the guard said, braking the cart.

"Sorry to bother you," Gerry said, "but we heard some gunshots, and ran over to see what was going on."

"Gunshots?" The guard tapped the hearing aid in his ear to make sure the battery was working. "There weren't no gunshots here."

"You sure about that?"

"Positive. How many did you hear?"

"Five or six," Gerry said.

"Five or six? You're making it sound like this here's the OK Corral," the guard said, now sounding annoyed.

"I'm just telling you what we heard."

"You all heard it?"

"Yeah, didn't you?"

The guard didn't like being challenged and picked up the walkie-talkie lying on the dashboard of his cart. "No, I didn't. Unless you've got some business here, I'd suggest you boys get off the premises immediately. Understand?"

Gerry didn't need another invitation to leave. He walked over to his father's car and knelt down to his open window. "The body's gone, and the security guard swears there wasn't any shoot-out. I honestly don't know what's going on, Pop."

His father tapped the steering wheel with his fingers. The look on his face said he was thinking hard. It was a look that Gerry always identified with hope. Like the time his father had bought him a ten-speed bicycle that had come in pieces through the mail, and needed to be assembled from scratch. His father had read the instructions aloud several times with that same look on his face. The thinking look.

"Get in the car," his father said.

29

Raising a kid was the hardest thing Valentine had ever done. It wasn't the discipline of teaching his son right from wrong that he'd found so challenging, or the sense of futility that had come from not succeeding. What had made it hard was the realization that his son was his own person, and could not be molded into the person Valentine wanted him to be.

Because the body of the construction worker was gone from the parking lot, Gerry assumed that the shooting was no longer a problem. He was ready to walk away, and get back to whatever he'd been doing. Valentine knew better. A dead man was always a problem, even if you couldn't find the body.

"Pop, you can't be serious," his son said.

"I'm dead serious," Valentine said.

"You want us to confess to the police?"

"Yes. That guy's body is going to turn up."

"How can you be so sure?"

Valentine blew out his cheeks in exasperation. Sometimes, reasoning with his son was like talking to an atheist about religion. "Think about it, Gerry. Twice today you had guys try to whack you. You kill one of them, and the body disappears. It's going to turn up, and when it does, it's going to be tied to you. If you don't talk to the police before that happens, you and your friends are screwed."

"We're screwed if we *do* talk to the police," Gerry said. "Frank and Nunzie didn't graduate high school. Do you honestly think either one of them can keep his story straight? A smart detective will trip them up in five minutes. Then we'll all be in real hot water."

Valentine realized that his son had a point. If the Las Vegas police thought Frank or Nunzie were lying, they'd arrest them, and individually interrogate each man until they got a straight story.

"There's our motel," Gerry said, pointing up the block. "Why don't we dump the bag I stole, and talk about this some more?"

Valentine tapped his fingers on the wheel. He hadn't told his son that he'd seen him rob the Tuna earlier, and now he decided to see how truthful Gerry was being with him.

"You stole something?"

Gerry nodded. "I stole a bag from George Scalzo in the lobby of Celebrity's hotel this afternoon. I thought it was Jack Donovan's secret. Turns out it was a bag of insulin."

"What are you going to do with it?"

"Give it back to him, I guess."

It was the smartest thing his son had said so far.

"Okay," Valentine said.

His son's motel was a two-story run-down stucco building that looked like a hooker's hangout. As Valentine pulled into the parking lot, he spotted three Metro Las Vegas Police Department cruisers and an ambulance in the lot, then a pair of medics wheeling a gurney out of a ground-floor room. Lying on the gurney was a black body bag. His son jumped in his seat like he'd been jolted with a cattle prod.

"Holy shit," Gerry said.

"Let me guess," Valentine said. "That's your room."

His son nodded vigorously. Instead of pulling in, Valentine spun the wheel, and drove past the motel. At the next intersection was a traffic light, and he hit his brakes while glancing in his mirror. Vinny had pulled up behind him, and was trying to calm Nunzie and Frank down, both of whom looked petrified.

"Nunzie and Frank didn't graduate high school, huh?" Valentine said.

"No," Gerry said.

Valentine stared at the road in front of him. His son was right: Nunzie and Frank would crack once a smart detective started to press them. The light changed and he pumped the accelerator. "Time to regroup," he said.

Once you got away from the glitz and glitter of the strip, Las Vegas was a wasteland. Two blocks later, Valentine pulled into a graffiti-covered grocery with metal bars covering its windows, and parked behind the building. Moments later, Vinny pulled in behind and parked next to him.

Valentine got out, walked around the car to his son's side, and had Gerry hand him the paper bag with the .38. There was an overflowing Dumpster behind the building, and he opened the lid, untied the drawstring to a bag of rotting food, and tossed the weapon in. When he turned around, Gerry, Vinny, Nunzie, and Frank were standing behind him. They had expectant looks on their faces, and looked ready to play ball.

"Do any of you know what K-I-S-S means?" Valentine said.

The four men shook their heads.

"It means Keep It Simple Stupid," Valentine said. "You need to remember that when you talk to the police. Keep your story simple, and you shouldn't have any problems. With me so far?"

They all nodded. The Dumpster was a magnet for flies, and they were starting to buzz around their heads. Valentine kept talking.

"Now, when was the last time you were in your motel room?"

"Late this morning," Vinny said.

"Good. An autopsy will show that the guy you shot in the parking lot of Lucky Lou's was killed after that. So, here's the story I want you to tell the police. Ready?"

The four men moved a little closer. They were more than ready.

"You came to Las Vegas to help me investigate allegations of cheating at the World Poker Showdown," Valentine said. "You left your motel this morning, and went to Celebrity's casino to do some scouting around. I saw you there, and so did Bill Higgins, who believes you're working for me. That establishes your first alibi. With me so far?"

Their heads went up and down.

"Good," Valentine said. "You left Celebrity in the early afternoon, and decided you needed a break. You drove to Lucky Lou's casino, and hung around for a while."

"I talked to a cocktail waitress and a pit boss there," Gerry said.

"Think either of them will remember you?"

"I gave the waitress a twenty-dollar tip for a bag of ice to keep the insulin cold," his son said. "I also had a conversation with a pit boss. The guy knew you, and I gave him my business card."

Valentine saw a funny look cross Vinny, Frank, and Nunzie's faces, and sensed that something had happened inside Lucky Lou's casino that wasn't kosher. He said, "You weren't scamming Lucky Lou's, were you?"

The three men all stared at the ground.

"Gerry talked us out of it," Vinny said quietly.

Valentine looked at his son. "That true?"

"Yeah, Pop."

"Mind my asking why?"

"I thought it could end up hurting our business."

It was the second smart thing his son had said.

"Okay," Valentine said. "That's your second alibi. After leaving Lucky Lou's, you drove to a convenience store and got coffee and doughnuts. Did you get a receipt?"

Gerry dug into his pocket and triumphantly pulled out a crumpled receipt.

"Alibi number three," Valentine said. "After you finished your coffee, you called me. We met up, came back here, and discovered the police at the motel. You don't know who the dead guy is, or how he got in your room. This all make sense?"

"Yeah, Pop," his son said.

Valentine looked at the other three. The flies were swarming around them like roadkill. He had always marveled at how guys this dumb could survive in such a hostile world, and had come to the conclusion that God even looked out for scumbags some of the time. The three men slowly lifted their gazes. They had lost their deer-in-the-headlights expressions, and looked relieved. They nodded as well.

"That's beautiful, Mr. Valentine," Vinny said quietly.

"Glad you think so," Valentine told him.

*   *   *

Valentine drove back to the motel with Gerry sitting beside him. The motel was called the Casablanca, although he didn't think he'd find a guy wearing a white dinner jacket running the place. As he parked, he spotted a guy in a baggy suit standing outside the door to his son's room. It looked like a thinned-down Pete Longo, chief detective of the Metro Las Vegas Police Department's Homicide Division, and he muttered under his breath.

"Something wrong?" his son asked.

Valentine did not respond. The last time he'd seen Longo, the detective had been having an affair with a stripper that nearly cost him his career and his marriage. Longo had been out of his mind, and had picked a fight with Valentine. It had been ugly, and Valentine had ended up breaking Longo's nose.

Valentine had kept tabs on Longo since then. He'd heard that Pete had publicly apologized to his colleagues for what he'd done. He'd also patched up things with his wife and two teenage daughters. He was attempting to redeem himself, and Valentine gave him a lot of credit. Falling on your sword and starting over was never easy.

As Valentine got out of his car, Longo spotted him, and a jolt of recognition spread across the detective's face. He said something to one of the cops, then hustled over. He'd lost a lot of weight, and his suit swayed from side to side as he walked.

"Tony Valentine, what the hell are you doing here?"

Valentine spread his palms to the sky. "I love the outdoors. How about you?"

"I'm investigating a murder. You here on a job?"

"Bill Higgins hired me to look into some cheating at the World Poker Showdown. My son and his colleagues are helping me."

Longo glanced at Gerry sitting in the car, then into the second car at Vinny, Frank, and Nunzie. Cops were good at picking out lowlifes, and Longo's brain was telling him that these boys hadn't been to choir practice in a long time.

Valentine decided to take the bull by the horns, and pointed at the door to his son's room. "That's my son's room. What's going on?"

"The hotel manager found a dead body in it," Longo said. "Your son been with you today?"

"Part of it."

"What was he doing the rest of the time?"

"A job for me. Who's the stiff?"

"A local dirtbag named Russell John Watson," Longo said. "His death is no great loss to the world. Watson was put in your son's room, then shot again in the head."

Longo's admission was surprising. The detective was saying more than he was supposed to, considering it was Gerry's room the stiff had ended up in.

"How can you tell that?" Valentine asked.

"Lack of blood," Longo said. "Whoever brought Watson here propped him up in a chair, stuck a gun in his mouth, and pulled the trigger. His head had already drained, so there wasn't much blood on the wall when the bullet came out, just bone and brain tissue. Believe it or not, I've seen this before."

"Sorry."

Longo smiled thinly. He looked different from the last time Valentine had seen him, and it wasn't just the loss of weight. His face had taken on a gravity, like he knew how lucky he was to be getting a second chance at life.

"I need to talk to your son and his friends," the detective said.

"Of course."

"Any idea why someone might be trying to set up your son?"

"It's a bad world, Pete. I have no idea."

A uniformed cop standing in the doorway to Gerry's room called to Longo, and the detective turned and hurried across the lot to where the cop was standing. Valentine went back to his car, and saw Gerry roll down his window.

"You fix it, Pop?"

"Yeah, I fixed it. You're going to need to talk to the cops. Stick to your story, and you're home free."

"Oh man, Pop, that's great."

Gerry was smiling like he'd won the lottery. It was a look that Valentine had seen on Gerry's face many times before, and had always reminded him of a pardoned man on death row. He knelt down so he was eyeball-to-eyeball with his son.

"Where's the bag of insulin you stole?"

Gerry produced the bag and passed it through the window. Valentine peered into it, and saw a white plastic box and a baggie of melting ice. Gerry had been telling him the truth, and planned to give the insulin back. His son was learning, even if he was doing it the hard way, and Valentine guessed that was all he could ask for.

"Call me when you're finished with the police," Valentine said.

30

Las Vegas sat in a desert basin surrounded by mountains, and nighttime seemed to settle over the town more slowly than anyplace else Valentine had ever been. It was like a big party was about to begin, the house lights slowly being dimmed.

By the time he pulled into Celebrity's valet stand, the casino's blazing neon was the only thing visible across the vast desert. He grabbed the bag of insulin off the front seat and got out. Tossing his keys to the valet, he glanced at the tiny TV sitting in the valet's alcove. It was tuned to the World Poker Showdown, and showed Skip DeMarco playing earlier that day. The kid looked good on TV, and the camera was showing him to the exclusion of the other players at the table. As Valentine went into the hotel, a concierge appeared before him.

"Mr. Valentine?"

"That's me."

"There's a call for you on the house phone."

He followed the concierge to his desk, and was handed a white house phone. He guessed it was Bill Higgins, spying on him from the surveillance control room.

"Valentine, here."

"Sammy Mann, at your service," a man's voice said.

"Not *the* Sammy Mann, king of the cooler mobs?"

"In the flesh," Sammy said. "I'm upstairs in surveillance, doing a job for Bill Higgins."

"So I heard. Want to get together?"

"Yeah, but don't bother coming up here," the retired hustler said. "I'll meet you in the lobby bar, if that's okay with you."

Valentine was tired, and felt like going to his room and taking a nap. Only he'd learned a long time ago that when crooks wanted to talk, he needed to listen.

"Sure. I'll grab us a table inside."

"See you in ten minutes," Sammy said.

Hanging up, Valentine turned to the concierge, and handed him the canvas bag with the insulin. "I need you to put this someplace cold for a little while."

"Certainly, Mr. Valentine," the concierge said.

"I took your advice, and started hiring myself out to the casinos," Sammy said ten minutes later, nursing a ginger ale while untying his necktie. In his day, Sammy had been the epitome of a classy cheat, and had gone back to wearing his trademark clothes—a navy sports jacket with mother-of-pearl buttons, silk tie, and white shirt with French cuffs. He'd once run with a cooler mob, and could take eight decks of prearranged playing cards out of an arm sling he was wearing, and exchange it with eight decks being held by a crooked blackjack dealer, all in three seconds flat.

"They paying you good?" Valentine asked, sipping a decaf.

"Like a king. I went through chemotherapy two years ago, and came out a new man. I decided the best way to stay alive was by working."

"What did you think of DeMarco?" Valentine asked.

"What do *you* think of him?"

"I never played poker, so I don't know," Valentine said.

Sammy's coal dark eyes scanned the crowded casino bar. He was Arab, and had the dark good looks of an aging movie star. Valentine was glad to see that he was doing well, but still wouldn't confide in him. Sammy had been a thief for too long to be fully trusted.

"He's cheating," Sammy said quietly.

There were plenty of people inside the bar, many of them associated with the WPS. Valentine raised his glass to his lips. "How?"

Sammy smiled. "My guess is, he's being fed information."

"By who?"

"The dealer. The cards are marked. The dealer reads the marks during the deal, and signals DeMarco what his opponents are holding."

"But the kid is blind."

Sammy leaned back in his chair. The bar had a plasma-screen TV, and was broadcasting the same rerun of the tournament Valentine had seen at the valet stand. DeMarco was on, and had just knocked another world-class player out of the tournament.

"Doesn't mean a thing," Sammy said. "Maybe the signal is verbal—you know, by breathing loudly. Or maybe it's the way the dealer pitches the cards to DeMarco during the deal. DeMarco has some vision."

Valentine had already considered those methods, and ruled them out. Breathing loudly—called The Sniff— was too noticeable, and so was The Pitch. He sensed that Sammy was taking stabs in the dark.

"Any other ideas?" Valentine asked.

Sammy stared at him coolly. "You think I'm wrong?"

"Yes."

Sammy grabbed a passing waitress and bummed a cigarette off her. He could have been the greatest salesman who'd ever lived, so natural were his charms of persuasion. He lit up, and blew a perfect smoke ring into the air. "Tony, that's the only explanation for what's going on. The kid is getting outside help. Period."

There was real resentment in Sammy's voice, and Valentine guessed he'd heard DeMarco call Rufus Steele an old man on TV, and taken exception to it.

"Maybe he's lucky," Valentine said.

"Poker isn't about luck, and it isn't about the cards you get dealt," Sammy said. "It's about playing your opponent, and knowing when he's strong or weak. That's the entire formula in a nutshell. This kid is being fed information."

The smell of Sammy's cigarette reminded Valentine of every cigarette he'd ever smoked. He tagged the waitress and talked her into giving him a cigarette as well.

"The cards aren't marked," he said after he'd lit up.

Sammy turned and gave him a long stare. "Who checked them?"

"The Gaming Control Board and the FBI. Every single card in the tournament has been checked."

"Like I told you before, that doesn't mean anything," Sammy said.

Valentine choked on his cigarette smoke. When he finally got his breath, he saw the old hustler smiling at him. Sammy had gotten his choppers whitened, and they looked like a million bucks.

"Why not?"

"Because there are ways to mark cards that you don't see," Sammy said.

"That's a new one," Valentine said.

"New to you," Sammy replied.

Valentine shifted uncomfortably in his chair. He'd recognized long ago that no matter how much he knew about cheating, there would still be things he didn't know.

"If I admitted I was a sucker, would you smarten me up?"

"Sure," Sammy said.

"I'm a sucker," Valentine said.

"It's like this," Sammy said, an impossibly long ash dangling from his cigarette. "Twenty years ago, you arrested me for ringing in a cooler in Atlantic City, and assumed that was my speciality. Well, it wasn't."

"Switching decks wasn't your speciality?"

"No," Sammy said.

"But at the sentencing you told the judge you'd switched decks in casinos over a hundred times," Valentine said.

"That's right," Sammy said. "And remember my sob story? I said I was turned out by my uncle, who was a cheater, and that he started training me when I was six years old."

"Let me guess, you didn't have an uncle."

"No, but I had eight aunts."

Valentine laughed through a cloud of smoke. The judge at Sammy's sentencing had been a woman, and she'd gone soft on Sammy, and put him in a work-release program.

"All right, I'm stumped," Valentine said. "If you weren't a specialist at switching cards, then what were you a specialist at?"

Sammy gave him a sly look. He was holding back, as if this piece of information would somehow change things. Cheaters wore many layers, and it was rare that they ever pulled them all back at the same time. Only after a long moment had passed did he speak.

"My speciality was marked cards."

It took a long moment for the words to sink in, and then Valentine felt like someone had hit him in the head with a lead pipe. Marked cards. Sammy was telling him that the decks of cards he'd switched in casinos were stacked *and* marked, which let the cards be used more than once to rip off the house.

"That's brilliant," Valentine said. "You must have made a fortune."

Sammy gave him the best smile of the night. "We ate steak and lobster a lot."

"Who marked the cards?"

"I did. I also trained the other members in how to use the information. One player would read the dealer's hole card in blackjack, and signal its value to the other players at the table. The other players all were small betters, so their wins didn't look too horrifying to the house. They would leave, and another team would sit down, and do the same thing. It was like taking candy from a baby."

"The marks must have been spotted later on," Valentine said. "Every casino checks for them when the cards are taken out of play."

"They were never spotted," Sammy said.

"What about by a forensic lab?"

"I imagine it would fool them as well."

"You've lost me," Valentine said. "If the mark can't be seen, and can't be tested for, it doesn't exist."

Sammy shot him the You're-So-Stupid look, and Valentine swallowed hard. There was a paddle for everyone's ass in this town, and his was getting royally spanked.

"Or does it?" he said.

*   *   *

"I came up with this marking system by accident," Sammy said. "My crew used it for over twenty years. When we retired, so did the system."

There was a glass of water sitting on the table in front of them. Sammy stuck his fingertips into it, then sprinkled several drops on the tabletop. After several moments he brushed the drops away with his napkin, and pointed at the tabletop. Valentine stared at the tiny marks left on the table's finish.

"Water stains," he said.

"Exactly. They reduce the shine on the back of the card. It's not uncommon for water to get sprayed on cards in casinos. The casino people who were looking for marks were used to seeing water stains, so they didn't pay any attention to ours. We used a lot of clever patterns to mark the cards. I used to be able to read them from across the room."

"That's brilliant," Valentine said.

"Thank you. Over time, we also made the marks fainter. We would record each casino's lighting with a light sensitivity machine, then learn to read the marks under those conditions. I used to practice for an hour a day reading those marks, and so did the members of my crew."

Sammy had finished his ginger ale and was looking at his watch. Valentine took out his wallet and settled the bill. It was rare for a hustler to reveal his secrets, especially one that had worked so well, and Valentine guessed there was a motive behind Sammy's generosity. Leaning forward, he said, "Do you think this is what DeMarco is doing?"

Sammy coughed into his hand. "Or something like it."

It slowly dawned on him what Sammy was saying.

DeMarco had a marking system that wasn't immediately obvious, just like Sammy's.

"So what do I do?"

"Keep examining the cards," the retired hustler said. "You'll find the marks eventually."

Sammy's eyes drifted to the plasma-screen TV showing DeMarco playing poker. DeMarco's image was larger-than-life, and dwarfed everything else in the bar. Sammy gritted his teeth in displeasure, then took out his business card and handed it to Valentine. They shook hands, and Valentine watched him walk away, then stared at the card.

SAMMY MANN

Casino Cheating Consultant

"It takes one to know one."

702-616-0279

31

Valentine left the bar shaking his head. Everyone seemed to know that DeMarco was cheating, yet no one could do anything about it. There was an old baseball expression—"It ain't cheating if you don't get caught"—and it applied perfectly to this situation. Until they found evidence that proved DeMarco was rigging the game, the tournament had to let him play.

At the concierge's desk he got the bag of insulin and asked to use the house phone. The concierge obliged him, and after a moment the house operator came on. Valentine asked to be put through to Skip DeMarco's room.

"I'm sorry, sir, but we've been instructed not to put any calls through to Mr. DeMarco," the operator informed him.

"Tell him I've got his bag of insulin, then call me back," Valentine said.

He hung up, and waited for the callback while tapping his foot to the live music coming from the casino. If Las Vegas had anything in abundance, it was good live music, and he kept time to an old Count Basie tune until the phone rang.

"You found my bag?" a gravelly voice said.

The voice had a lot of years behind it, and Valentine

guessed it was the Tuna. He said, "A bag of insulin was found in the parking lot which I believe belongs to you."

"How much you want?"

"Excuse me?"

"How much money you want for it? That's what this is about, isn't it?"

"I don't want your money," Valentine said. "I just wanted to return the bag to its rightful owner."

"Who *is* this?"

"My name's Tony Valentine."

A short silence, then, "There was a cop in Atlantic City named Tony Valentine. A real prick, if I remember."

"That's me," Valentine said.

The hallways in casino hotels were the longest hallways in the world, and Valentine beat a path to DeMarco's room while smothering a yawn. He'd been going non-stop all day, and the three-hour jet lag was starting to wear on him. That was one of the tough things about getting old. You no longer told your body what to do. Your body told you.

DeMarco was staying at the hallway's end. Valentine rapped on the door, and stepped back so the person on the other side could see him through the peephole. He heard the door being unlatched, then saw a bodyguard dressed in black standing before him.

"You Valentine?" the bodyguard asked.

Hoods had a tendency to ask ridiculously stupid questions, and Valentine had discovered that he couldn't answer them without insulting someone. He handed the guy his business card. The bodyguard stared at it in a way that suggested his inability to read had driven him from seeking a higher education, and motioned him inside.

DeMarco was staying in a high-roller suite, and Valentine entered a large living area with ornate furniture that looked straight out of Buckingham Palace and with a view of the city that matched anything he'd ever seen. He wondered how DeMarco rated such digs, as he knew that hotels did not normally rent their high-roller pads, preferring to offer them as freebies to their best customers, called whales. In all his years in the business, he'd never heard of a single poker player getting this kind of treatment.

"You must be Valentine," a voice said.

An older Italian guy with slicked back hair stood by the window, gazing at him through the reflection. Stocky, about five ten, wearing black slacks and a flowing black shirt that hid his paunch, hands festooned with gold jewelry, mouth retracted in permanent distaste. Valentine assumed this was the Tuna and nodded, then placed the bag of insulin on a chair.

"It probably went bad, you know," the Tuna said.

He still hadn't turned around, preferring to let Valentine see the back of his head.

"What went bad?" Valentine asked.

"My nephew's insulin."

"I kept it cold for you," Valentine said.

Valentine could see the Tuna's face in the reflection. He look surprised.

"I appreciate that," the Tuna said. "You like something to drink?"

"A glass of water would be fine."

"You on duty?"

Valentine realized the Tuna thought he was still a cop.

"I'm retired. I don't drink the hard stuff."

The Tuna nodded that this was acceptable, then snapped his fingers. The bodyguard went to the bar, which was filled with bottles of top shelf brands. He poured a

Scotch for his boss and a glass of tap water for his guest, then delivered them to the two men. The Tuna turned around but remained by the window, as if getting too close to a cop, even a retired one, was not anything he planned on doing in this lifetime.

"*Salute,*" he said, raising his glass.

Valentine raised his glass and took a sip. He could hear someone in the next room, and glanced over his shoulder through an open door. Skip DeMarco was standing in the next room with his shirt off. He was built like a martial artist, his body lean and sinewy, and he practiced his exercises in slow motion, his movements quick and fluid. Valentine stared at the ugly red scars that marred his arms and chest and spoiled his otherwise perfect physique. He'd seen scars like that before, when he'd been an undercover cop assigned to narcotics in Atlantic City. He'd seen them on little kids whose parents were crackheads. They were cigarette burns. He shifted his gaze to the Tuna, and lowered his glass.

"You once threw me out of a casino in Atlantic City," the Tuna said.

"When was this?"

"June 7, 1987."

Valentine tried to remember the incident, but came up blank. The Tuna was good at reading faces, and said, "You said I was an undesirable. You let the niggers and Spics into the casinos, but not me. I always resented that."

Valentine had heard a lot of hoods use this argument, as if blacks and Hispanics were some social yardstick by which acceptance should be measured, instead of who you were, and what you'd done.

"Just doing my job," Valentine said.

The Tuna twirled the ice cubes in his drink. "I had

you checked out after that. You know, we're alike in a lot of ways."

Valentine didn't think the Tuna could have insulted him any worse than he just had. Nothing about them was alike; not one damn thing.

"How so?"

"We're Sicilian. Both our fathers were immigrants; both came through Ellis Island. You had a tough upbringing, so did I. You know anything about Sicily's history?"

Valentine decided to indulge him and nodded.

"For hundreds of years, the Italians treated us like dogs. The island was lawless, people were poor, there was no electricity, no running water, and no one in Rome gave a rat's ass. Only one thing kept Sicily from falling apart. The dons. They were the law, and everyone respected them."

"Do you see yourself like a don?" Valentine asked.

The Tuna downed his drink. "Yeah, I do."

As a child, Valentine's father had told him about the Sicilian dons who'd traveled to Rome during the early 1900s, and convinced Italy's leaders to give Sicily food and money to keep its people alive. For the Tuna to liken himself to those men was like comparing the Sistine Chapel to an outhouse.

"Afraid I don't see it that way," Valentine said.

"You don't?"

"No. Those dons saved lives. You destroyed them."

An ice cube spilled out of his host's drink. He came forward very quickly, halving the distance between them. But that was as far as he came. Valentine held his ground.

"This isn't Atlantic City," the Tuna said. "You watch yourself, Valentine, you hear me?"

Valentine realized he was being threatened, and again found himself looking at the ornate furnishings. DeMarco was getting the royal treatment, which meant that either he, or his uncle, had juice with someone.

"Thanks for the drink and the fun conversation," Valentine said.

The Tuna turned to the bodyguard. "Guido."

The bodyguard was standing behind the bar with a bored look on his face.

"Yes, Mr. Scalzo," he said.

"Throw this asshole out of here."

"My pleasure, Mr. Scalzo."

Guido came around from behind the minibar and dropped a massive paw on Valentine's shoulder. Valentine guessed it was his gray hair, or maybe that he'd said he was retired, that had gotten Guido to drop his guard. He kicked Guido in the instep, a spot that people who practiced judo called a vital point. Guido grunted and began to hop around on one leg. Valentine kicked him again, this time in the ass. He put a lot behind the kick, and Guido hurtled across the room, his arms flapping like he was trying to fly.

"What's going on?" a voice said.

DeMarco appeared in the open doorway separating the rooms, a towel draped across his glistening torso, his walking cane clutched in his right hand. The two men collided with a bang of heads, and DeMarco hit the floor hard.

"Skipper!"

The Tuna ran across the room to his nephew's aid. Kneeling, he cradled DeMarco's head in his arms. When he looked up at Valentine, there were tears in his eyes.

"You'll pay for this," he said.

32

It was late, and Mabel was still in the office when Tony's phone rang. One week of mindless inactivity aboard the Love Boat had turned her brain to mush, and when Tony's computer had frozen right before quitting time, she'd found herself on the phone with a polite but utterly worthless support technician in New Delhi trying to fix it. She'd wanted Tony to get rid of his desktop in favor of a notebook computer, but was now grateful for the bulkier model. It was less tempting to throw out the window.

"Grift Sense," she answered.

"Is this a rare coin shop?" her boss's voice rang out.

"Sometimes I wish it was," she said, staring at the blank screen.

"What are you doing there so late? It's eleven thirty."

"I froze your computer, and have been talking on the telephone with a young man named Vijay trying to get it straightened out."

"Any luck?"

"None whatsoever."

"Try whacking it. That always works for me."

Whacking things was Tony's answer to a number of problems that demanded more concrete solutions. Still, it was the one thing Mabel hadn't tried, and in frustration she whacked the PC with the palm of her hand, and saw a lightning bolt flash across the screen. Moments later, Tony's screen saver appeared She let out a heavy sigh.

"Oh my," she said.

"Let me guess," he said. "It worked."

"Yes, it did. How's Las Vegas?"

"Still the fun capital of the United States. I have a job for you. I was going to leave a message. If you want to go home, I can call back, and leave it on voice mail."

Mabel picked up a pen and notepad lying on the desk. She'd downed several cups of coffee while talking with Vijay, and felt like she had toothpicks holding her eyelids apart. "Fire away."

"I want you to do a background check on two individuals. One is a mobster out of Newark named George Scalzo, aka the Tuna. The second is Scalzo's blind nephew named Chris 'Skip' DeMarco. I'm interested in finding out what Scalzo's relationship is with DeMarco. Scalzo might have adopted him, or is the kid's legal guardian. See what you can find. I'd suggest you start with the FBI first."

"But they're always such brats," Mabel said.

"They are. But the FBI has extensive files on every Mafia boss in the country. The files include a lot of personal information. Some of these guys are followed twenty-four hours a day, seven days a week. If Scalzo did adopt DeMarco, the bureau would know about it."

"Not to be a pill, but just exactly how do I convince the FBI to give me this information?" she said, having scribbled down the names. "The last time I checked, the FBI didn't have a help line you could call."

"Easy," Tony said. "On my desk is an overnight envelope from Special Agent Romero of the FBI. He wants my opinion on a cheating case he's handling. Tell Romero I won't charge him, provided he lets us see Scalzo's file."

"A horse trade?"

"Exactly. If Romero agrees, you'll need to look at his cheating case, and see what you think. If you can't figure out what's going on, send me an e-mail, and I'll have a crack at it."

Mabel felt the color in her face change. A few weeks ago, she'd spotted a woman using her coffee cup to filch chips inside a casino. There was a piece of adhesive on the bottom of her cup, allowing her to steal chips from other players while casually chatting with them. Ever since the bust, Tony had been letting her look at cases.

"Do you have any idea what Special Agent Romero's case is about?" she asked.

"Craps cheating in the basement of a guy's house. The guy's attorney claims he had the table there for fun. Romero believes the guy is cheating people, only the victims are too embarrassed to testify, and Romero doesn't have any solid evidence. He said the craps table's position in the basement bothered him, and asked me to study some pictures."

"And by looking at some pictures, you'll know how this guy was cheating at dice?"

Her boss laughed. "I already think I do."

Mabel felt the tingle of excitement that came whenever Tony challenged her. Her boss was saying the mystery could be solved by looking at how the craps table was positioned in the basement. Those were all the clues she needed.

"Talk to you later," she said.

If there was anything about police work that Mabel enjoyed, it was the sense of immediacy the work demanded. It wasn't like the real world, where people promised to get back to you, and never did. Law enforcement people understood the importance of time when solving a case. Like grains of sand slipping through an hourglass, every minute meant something.

She found Special Agent Romero's overnight envelope within a stack of mail on Tony's desk. The envelope contained a typed letter, and a manila file folder stuffed with crime scene photographs. She read the letter first, and learned the suspect had also been transporting illegal gambling equipment across state lines, which was against federal law and probably why the FBI had gotten involved. Romero also mentioned finding a great deal of money in the house, several hundred thousand dollars.

Finishing the letter, she opened the file folder, and stared at the eight-by-ten glossy on top. The suspect's basement was decorated like a nightclub, and she immediately found herself disliking the suspect's defense attorney. Any dimwit could see that his client had pumped a small fortune into turning his basement into a gambling den.

She focused her attention on the craps table in the photograph. It was shaped like a tub, and positioned in the rear of the room, backed up to the wall. The basement was good-sized, and there was no reason the craps table should be in such tight quarters. She flipped through several other photographs. The table was definitely in a strange spot.

Tony had taught her a thing or two about craps cheating. When the house cheated, it was with crooked dice, called bust outs. Bust outs were either shaved dice, which rolled more unfavorable combinations than normal, or loaded dice, which had mercury loads hidden in the numbers, and were controlled by electromagnets in the table. Shaved dice beat the unsuspecting players gradually; loaded dice took their money right away.

She closed the folder and leaned back in her chair. The last time she'd spoken to Tony, he'd explained why casinos on cruise ships were more susceptible to losses because their hours were limited. She guessed the same time restraints applied to casinos that cheated. The fewer hours you were open, the more blatant the cheating had to be. If the cheating wasn't blatant, you still might lose money. Which led to her next conclusion. The casino in his basement was using loaded dice.

She found herself smiling. Tony was fond of saying that the toughest scams often had the simplest solutions. She picked up the photograph, and instantly understood why the craps table had been positioned near the wall. It was the only way the loaded dice would work.

She picked up Romero's letter, and looked to see if it had an e-mail address. It didn't, but Romero had included his phone number. Mabel decided to call it, and leave a message. She punched the number in, and was surprised when a person answered her call.

"Hello," a man said.

"I'm sorry," Mabel said. "I was calling to leave a message."

"Who is this?"

"My name is Mabel Struck and I'm with Grift Sense. Are you the cleaning man?"

"This is Special Agent Romero of the FBI," the voice said curtly.

Mabel brought her hand up to her face. "I'm sorry. I didn't realize the FBI worked so late."

"We do when it's an emergency," Romero said. "I hope you're calling about the case I wrote to your boss about."

"Why yes, I am."

"Good, because a judge is going to let our suspect walk if we can't come up with any evidence, and six months of work will go down the drain."

"The FBI spent six months investigating a man running a casino in his basement?"

"He runs two dozen of these operations around the country," Romero said. "His net worth is in the neighborhood of twenty million dollars a year."

"You're saying this man's a public menace."

"That's a polite term for him."

"I think I can help you," Mabel said. "Do you have any agents near the suspect's house?"

"There are a team of agents there right now," Romero said. "They're combing the basement for clues we may have missed. We had the craps table taken out, and examined by our forensics lab. The table was absolutely clean."

"That doesn't mean a magnet wasn't in play," Mabel said.

"It doesn't?"

"No. Would your agents by chance have a mallet handy?"

"You mean to break down a door?"

"A wall, actually. They'll need something with a little heft."

"They have a battering ram in the trunk of their car," Romero said. "It's standard equipment. I'd like to put you on speakerphone with Special Agent Darling who's in charge at the house. I want him to hear this directly from you."

"Certainly."

Romero put her on hold. Mabel took the top glossy off the stack, and stared at it once again. The electromagnet used to control the loaded dice was hidden behind the wall the craps table had been so auspiciously shoved up against. Somewhere in the room was a switch that activated the magnet. With a simple flip, the dice could be made to roll losers. That was how the suspect was making twenty million dollars a year.

Romero came back on the line, and introduced Special Agent Darling. Holding the glossy up to her face, Mabel told Darling which wall in the basement needed to be knocked down.

33

Valentine lay in his hotel bed staring at the ceiling. The drapes in his room wouldn't properly close and tiny neon angels danced above his head. One of the great injustices of old age was the mind's unwillingness to do what the body told it to. In this case, it was not falling asleep, even though he was exhausted. Something was bothering him, and no amount of counting sheep was going to let him rest until he figured out what it was.

He climbed out of bed and heard his joints creak. He still took judo classes three days a week, and did exercises every day at home, but some days he felt like he was fooling himself, and that his body kept going on memory.

He slipped into a bathrobe supplied by the hotel. It was a size too small, and felt like a straitjacket. He went into the living room, and not seeing Rufus, parked his tired bones on the living room couch. The casino's giant neon sign was directly below the room's window, and bathed him in a rainbow of garish colors. He stared into space, trying to put his finger on what was wrong.

He'd always been adept at finding incongruities. It was what made him good as a cop, and especially good as a casino cop. Sometimes, those incongruities were obvious, like the night he'd spotted a wedding party in Atlantic City walking across a casino carrying balloons and table decorations from the nuptials they'd just attended. He'd called down to security, and told a guard to follow them. Going into the slot machine area, the party had released their balloons and let them float to the ceiling, hiding the view of a surveillance camera as they opened a machine with a skeleton key, and set the reel for a million dollar jackpot. Later, after everyone was arrested, Valentine had told the guard why he'd acted so quickly.

"I've never seen balloons at a wedding before," he'd said.

Other times, those incongruities weren't so obvious. Like tonight. He'd been in Skip DeMarco's suite an hour ago, and seen DeMarco practicing his martial arts exercises in the next room. There was nothing unusual about that—he'd met plenty of impaired people who practiced karate and judo—only DeMarco doing it just didn't feel right. The problem was, he couldn't put his finger on why.

He got up from the couch and went to the minibar. It had been restocked, and he weighed drinking a diet soda. Caffeine usually put his brain into another gear, but with it came the penalty of not being able to sleep. Of course, if he didn't figure out what was bothering him, he wouldn't sleep anyway. He said to hell with it, and drank the soda.

Returning to the couch, he noticed a deck of playing cards scattered across the coffee table. He guessed they belonged to Rufus, and he gathered them up, and began to shuffle them. The cards were old and dog-eared, but had a nice feel to them, and he imagined Rufus's bony fingers playing with them. Most poker players kept a deck in their pockets at all times. Poker was easy to learn but difficult to master, and even the best players spent hours analyzing a bad hand or strategy.

As he shuffled the cards, he realized what was bothering him. People who played poker for a living lived the game every waking minute. When they weren't playing in tournaments, they were playing in private games, and when they weren't doing that, they were fiddling with cards and working out strategies in their heads. That was true for every single player in the tournament, except one. Skip DeMarco.

He hadn't seen any playing cards in DeMarco's suite, nor any evidence that DeMarco was a player. Guys who played in tournaments always went back to their rooms, and examined what they'd done wrong during the day. There had been no evidence of that in DeMarco's suite. That was why DeMarco doing exercises seemed so out of place. It wasn't what tournament chip leaders did.

He heard a knock on the door, and went to the peephole and peered into the hallway. Rufus Steele stood outside looking drunker than a sailor on a Saturday night. Valentine let him in.

"Having a bad night?"

Rufus belched whiskey in his face.

"I just lost all my money," he said, falling forward in Valentine's arms.

Rufus was as light as a feather. He didn't look that light, and Valentine guessed it was because he stood about six one. But it was all bone and a little sinew. As he shut the door, Rufus straightened up. It was a startling transformation, the old cowboy snapping to attention. With his eyes downcast, he walked into the suite.

"Sorry, pardner, but I'm pretending to be drunk."

"Pretending for who?"

"Whoever in this stinking hotel is watching me. Too many coincidences in the past couple of hours for someone not to be."

Gloria had said the same thing. Someone in the hotel was playing Big Brother. He followed Rufus into the living room, and pulled up a chair as Rufus sank into the couch.

"Ever hear the expression, 'Seldom do the sheep slaughter the butcher'?" the old cowboy asked.

"A couple of times, sure."

"Well, this butcher just got slaughtered."

Rufus doffed his Stetson and examined the crease in it. His eyes had yet to reach Valentine's face, and he spoke in a monotone. "Got fleeced in a ring game. Lost my twenty thousand bucks, and then some. They were all in on it."

"How many players?"

"Six guys and a professional dealer."

"What were they doing?"

Rufus picked up the dog-eared deck from the coffee table, then placed one of the couch's pillows onto his lap. He put the cards on the pillow and riffle-shuffled them. It was the same shuffle used by every professional dealer in the world, and he did it slowly and efficiently.

"You familiar with riffle-stacking?" Rufus asked.

"I saw a demonstration a few years ago by Darwin Ortiz. It was pretty amazing."

"Amazing is right. Not many mechanics can riffle-stack. It's too damn hard. I'm told there are five guys who are any good. Well, I met one of them tonight."

Rufus stopped the shuffle on his left side while holding back a small number of cards. He dropped the remaining cards on his right, then dropped all of those on his left. The tiny seesaw motion was the move's only tell.

"I caught the dealer doing that tonight and knew I was screwed," Rufus said.

"What did you do?"

"Nothing. There were six of them, and little ole me. I figured out that I'd been set up, and the dealer hired to wipe me out. My guess is, the World Poker Showdown is behind this."

Valentine didn't see the jump. People got fleeced in poker games every day. "How can you know for certain? Tournaments always attract cheats."

"Easy," Rufus said. "The cost."

"The cost of what?"

"Do you have any idea how much a skilled mechanic—especially one who can riffle-stack—gets paid to fleece a poker game in this town?"

"I have no idea."

"Try fifty grand, plus a cut of the take," Rufus said. "They won't get out of bed for less. I lost twenty grand, which didn't cover the cost of the mechanic. Somebody *paid* that guy to fleece me. And since I am one of the most beloved figures in the world of gambling, my assumption is that the WPS is behind it. They want me gone."

"Anyone in particular?"

"Yeah. Karl Jasper, the president of that crummy organization."

"Jasper's no good?"

"He's a rattlesnake," Rufus said.

Rufus squared the weathered cards, then placed them back in his pocket and stuck his Stetson on his head. He looked ready to jump on his horse and fade into the sunset, and Valentine found himself feeling sorry for him.

"What are you going to do?"

"Pay them back," Rufus said.

There was a twinkle in his eye, and Valentine sensed he was up to no good.

"How you going to do that? You're broke."

"That's where you come in, pardner," Rufus said.

"You did *what*?" Valentine said in astonishment thirty seconds later.

"You heard me," Rufus said, lying on the couch with his legs spread out, his cowboy boots kicked across the floor. "Since those sons-of-bitches fleeced me at poker, I decided to pay them back, and fleece them at a proposition bet. I pretended to get drunk, and told them I had X-ray vision. Before you could say Jack Daniels, those boys had bet me a sizable sum I didn't. Since I'm broke, I told them you would back me."

It sounded like something Gerry would do. Valentine took that back; even his son wasn't this dumb.

"When is this bet going to take place?"

"Tomorrow morning at nine, before the tournament starts."

"Don't you think you should have asked me?"

"Don't go getting hinky on me," Rufus said, smothering a yawn. "I'm flat broke right now, and can't pull this off without your help. I need a hairy leg."

"But what if you lose?"

"I'm not going to lose," Rufus said. "It's a scam."

Valentine shifted uncomfortably in his chair. He'd never gambled a single day in his life, and had no intention of starting now. "I really don't like the sound of this," he told his guest.

Rufus showed him his best smile. He could be as charming as a senator when he wanted to, and Valentine felt his resolve give way, and threw up his arms.

"At least tell me what you've got me involved with."

Rufus continued to smile, clearly pleased with himself. "I told these boys I could see through things. I told them I developed my X-ray vision after I got in a car wreck, and had a concussion."

"And they bought that?"

"We were playing Seven-Card Stud. I pointed to a card in my opponent's hand, and asked him to pick it up, and hold it with its back toward me. Then I named it."

"Did you mark it?"

"Of course I marked it. I used the ash from my cigarette. The mark was huge."

"And they bought it?"

"Of course not! That's the hook. It's a dumb trick, and they all knew it. Hell, I think one of them even spotted the cigarette ash on my finger. When they started to challenge me, I insisted I had X-ray vision, and offered to bet them a hundred thousand bucks that I could prove it. Needless to say, the suckers bit on the line."

"You bet them a hundred thousand bucks of my money?"

"In a manner of speaking, yes."

Valentine slowly got to his feet. There was no way he was participating in this scam, no matter how sorry he felt for Rufus's situation. The phone rang, and he crossed the suite and answered it. It was Gloria Curtis.

"I hope I'm not calling too late," she said. "I just wanted to thank you for dinner tonight."

"My pleasure," he said.

"Rufus Steele called a little while ago, and told me you were helping him with another proposition bet," she said. "I was hoping you and I could get together before. How's eight o'clock in the lobby restaurant?"

"You're going to film it?"

"Of course I'm going to film it," Gloria said. "Rufus's last bet was a huge hit with my boss. I already called him, and told him another segment was on its way."

Valentine knew when he was beaten and glanced at Rufus. The old cowboy had lowered his Stetson over his eyes, and was feigning sleep. If nothing else, the guy was a fighter, and Valentine had always liked fighters.

"Eight o'clock it is," he said.

34

"**D**o you believe in second chances?" a voice asked.
Gerry was standing in the hallway of Metro Las Vegas Police Department headquarters trying to call his father on his cell phone. Glancing over his shoulder, he saw Detective Longo standing behind him with two cups of steaming coffee in his hands. Gerry flipped his cell phone shut.

"Sure," he said. "My wife gives me one every week."

The detective offered something resembling a smile and handed him a cup. Being a cop's son had given Gerry good police etiquette, and he followed the detective down the hallway to a conference room with a long wooden desk and a couple of metal chairs. The room had a single window, which was wide open, the evening air twenty degrees cooler than what had been blowing earlier that afternoon. The open window was not lost on Gerry. This was not a normal interrogation room. If it was, the window would have been shut and barred. Longo took a chair, and Gerry sat across from him.

"I believe in second chances, too," Longo said. "And I'm about to give you and your friends one."

"Really?"

"Yes, really."

Gerry blew on his drink, waiting to hear what was coming.

"Your story has more holes in it than the *Titanic*," Longo said. "Never mind the fact that the Fountain brothers and Frank DeCesar have never worked for your father until this afternoon, when your old man decided to vouch for them."

Gerry sipped his drink. "This sure is good coffee."

"Glad you like it. Now, I could be a prick and a half, and sweat your friends until I get something resembling the truth out of them. My guess is, it would take me a day or two, and Nunzie would be the one to crack. He's the weakest."

"Did you brew it yourself?"

"Got it from a machine, believe it or not. But I really don't want to go there. You boys obviously pissed someone in this town off, and Russell John Watson was sent to kill you. The fact that he ended up getting killed is a blessing in disguise.

"The other thing in your favor is that Bill Higgins personally vouched for you, even though I have the sneaking suspicion he's never met you. How your old man pulled that off, I have no idea, but that's just my opinion."

"Can I get another cup when I'm done with this one?"

"Sure. Have as many as you like. So here's what I'm proposing we do. I let you and your pals skate, in return for you answering a couple of questions for me. I just want to know a couple of things to put my mind at rest. Sound fair?"

Gerry leaned back in his chair and looked around the room. No two-way mirrors, no tape recorder on the table, just him and Longo talking man to man. Longo had a right to know what was going on, and Gerry saw no reason to trample on that right.

"Sounds fair."

"Who sent Russell John Watson to kill you?"

"I honestly don't know."

"You must have a suspicion."

"Jinky Harris."

A knowing expression spread across Longo's face, and he put his elbows on the table and gave Gerry a long look. His father once said that in every town, there were a handful of creeps that were responsible for the majority of serious crimes, and that every cop's dream was to rid the streets of one or more of those individuals during a career. Longo's dream, Gerry guessed, was to put an eraser to Jinky Harris.

"How did you get mixed up with Jinky?"

"We didn't," Gerry said. "Vinny suggested we pay a visit to Jinky, and tell him we were in town investigating a scam at the WPS. Vinny's feeling was that he didn't want to cross paths with Jinky, or anything he might be doing."

Longo scratched the stubble on his chin. "Your friend Vinny is a crook, isn't he?"

"You want some more coffee?" Gerry asked, rising from his chair.

"Sit down. I'll rephrase the question. Vinny's relationship with the law could best be described as tenuous."

"Vinny knows how the game is played," Gerry said, returning to his seat. "We went to see Jinky out of respect."

"And Jinky turned on you."

"That would be my guess."

"Think it has something to do with the case you're investigating?"

Gerry considered the detective's question. He hadn't told Longo that Jinky had rigged the ring games at the WPS because he had yet to tell his father, and it would be his father's call if he chose to pass the information on to the Metro LVPD. But telling Longo that Jinky was up to something had its merits. For one thing, it might lead to getting Jinky thrown in jail, which would suit Gerry just fine.

"Yes," he said.

Longo raised his coffee cup to his lips, took a sip, and grimaced. "This has to be the worst coffee I've ever tasted. You're some actor."

"My mother taught me never to be disrespectful to my hosts," Gerry said.

The detective grinned and put his cup down. "I've gone through my life believing that if we all listened to our mothers, the world would be free of problems. I have a proposition for you, which I'd like you to share with your friends."

"Shoot."

"I'm going to let you walk. Furthermore, I'm going to write up this case so it will never come back to haunt you, or your friends. Sound good so far?"

"Like a dream," Gerry said.

Longo nodded. He had put all his cards on the table, something law enforcement people seldom did. Leaning forward, he dropped his voice to a conspiratorial whisper. "Good. Here's what I want in return. Jinky Harris has slipped through my fingers more times than I can count. If I didn't know better, I'd swear he was tapping my phone.

"I need to put this piece of garbage away, and not just

because he's a pimp. We have thousands of whores in this town, and always will. Furthermore, a lot of people make money from pimping these girls—cabbies, bartenders, bellhops, concierges, motel managers, even valets get in the act. Where there's easy money, there are whores, and people making money off them.

"If Jinky was just a pimp, I wouldn't be asking for your help. But he's more than that. He caters to teenage runaways and underage girls. He gives them jobs in his club, then gets them freebasing on cocaine until they owe him money. Then he starts pimping them to his clients. The girls can't escape because there's nowhere to go, Las Vegas being the kind of hospitable town that it is. When the girls are used up, he gives them a bus ticket, and kicks them out."

"You're saying Jinky is in the slave trade," Gerry said.

"Yes," Longo said. He took out his wallet and unfolded it, letting Gerry see the snapshot of two beaming high school beauties that he kept next to his heart. "I've been a cop in this town for twenty-plus years. I didn't pay attention to this kind of stuff until my babies hit puberty. Then one day it hit me what a hypocrite I was. I don't want that happening to my girls, or for that matter, anyone else's. Jinky Harris needs to be put away for the rest of his life. If you can help me do that, I'll be eternally grateful."

A cool breeze blew through the open window, and invisible particles of sand grated against Gerry's face. Over the years, he'd heard stories from his father about strange alliances that police formed with crooks, and the uneasy trust that these alliances produced. But he sensed that this was something different. By talking about his girls, Longo had confided in him. Gerry hadn't done anything to deserve that, and he assumed it was because of the respect Longo had for his father. Longo wasn't treating him like a crook at all. He was treating him like a good cop's son.

"I'll do whatever I can to help you," Gerry said. Then he added, "And so will my friends."

35

"**I** want to go home," Skip DeMarco said.

DeMarco sat on the couch with an ice pack pressed to his head, his uncle sitting beside him. It was midnight, and his head had finally cleared from the fall he'd taken. He still wasn't sure what had happened. One minute he was standing in the doorway, listening to his uncle have a conversation with a visitor, the next he was being given smelling salts. His uncle said he'd been out cold for fifteen minutes.

"Once the tournament is over, we'll go right home," his uncle said.

"I want to go home right now," DeMarco said.

"We can't do that, Skipper."

DeMarco snapped his head in his uncle's direction. "We?"

"You can't do that, Skipper."

"Why not, Uncle George? Why not?"

"Because we're committed, that's why."

DeMarco could hear his heart banging in his ears, drowning out the rest of the world. Being the nephew of a Mafia kingpin, he understood exactly what that meant. A lot of people were involved in this. His uncle had struck deals, paid people off, made promises that he was bound to keep. His cojones were on the chopping block.

"I don't give a rat's ass," DeMarco said.

"You sound like you're twelve when you say that," his uncle scolded him. "Talk like a man, for Christ's sake."

"I want to go home. I don't feel safe here."

His uncle didn't have an answer for that. DeMarco lowered the ice pack and took several deep breaths. The fifteen minutes he'd been unconscious had done a number on his head, and he'd woken up knowing something that had been lurking in his subconscious for a long time. He was in over his head. Way over.

"Skipper, I'm sorry for what happened. It won't happen again."

"Twice today I've been knocked flat on my ass," DeMarco said, seeing his opening. "Twice. Once in the lobby by a gang; then tonight, right here in my own suite. How can you make a promise like that, considering what's happened? I don't feel safe here. Is this deal more important than my safety?"

His uncle's breathing grew labored. When DeMarco was younger and his vision better, he'd memorized everything about anybody that mattered to him, his uncle George especially. At this very moment, his uncle was staring at the floor, at a loss for words.

"Nothing means more to me than your safety," his uncle said.

"Even being committed?"

"I cannot back out of my commitments, Skipper, and neither can you. I'm deeply sorry about what happened. And it won't happen again. I've made sure of that."

DeMarco didn't doubt that. He'd heard his uncle on the phone, telling someone named Jinky Harris how he wanted Tony Valentine taken out of the picture. Over a dozen times his uncle had called Jinky either a fat fuck, or a worthless piece of shit, obscenities that his uncle used when he wanted to make a point. But that still didn't change things. His uncle had decided to stay in Las Vegas without consulting him. He pushed himself off the couch in anger.

"Skipper, sit down."

"No thanks, Uncle George. You could have asked me, you know?"

"I gave these men my word. You wouldn't ask me to go back on my word?"

It was his uncle's argument for everything. That a man's word was more important than his relationships. It said everything you needed to know about the Mafia.

"Would you put my *life* above your word?" DeMarco asked, bumping into the coffee table because he'd risen too fast, the sudden pain making him wince. He heard his uncle's body leave the couch. "Don't. I'm okay."

"You sure?"

"Yes."

"Skipper, I would not put your life above *anything*. But these men are not trying to kill you. They want to discredit you, so you'll be thrown out of the tournament. You don't want that, do you?"

DeMarco's leg was singing the blues where he'd banged it. He hated pain; it ignited too many memories buried deep in his soul. His uncle came over, and offered his arm. DeMarco pushed it away.

"Put yourself in my shoes for once," he said.

"What's that supposed to mean?" his uncle said.

"I'm blind. I don't see this shit coming. It's like running into a tree. I did that when I was little, hit the tree as fast as I could. I was on the ground for ten minutes."

"I'm sorry, Skipper."

"You're always sorry, Uncle George, but you never do anything different."

"I don't like the way this conversation is going," his uncle said.

"You don't? You know what I think, Uncle George?"

"I never know what you're thinking, Skipper."

"I think this is another of your deals."

"What did you say?"

"You heard me. This is just another deal. You figured out a way to make a killing on this tournament, and sweet-talked me into being your shill. Only you didn't bother to tell me that I was going to get the shit kicked out of me in the process. Thanks, Uncle George, thanks—"

There was only so much lip that his uncle George would take and he slapped his nephew's face. DeMarco grabbed his uncle's wrist, and twisted it. His uncle tried to resist. DeMarco twisted harder.

"How does it feel, Uncle George? How does being helpless feel?"

"Skipper!"

"These are my shoes, Uncle George. Try them on."

"Let me go!"

"It really stinks, doesn't it, Uncle George?"

"Guido! Help me!"

DeMarco heard a door bang open and Guido's patent leather shoes come plodding across the suite's inch-thick carpet. As Guido's hands came down on his arms, DeMarco shoved his uncle aside, and found Guido with his hands. He had enrolled in self-defense classes when he was a teenager and been a disciple of the martial arts ever since. If he managed to get his hands on someone, he could beat anyone.

Guido had hands shaped like cow udders. DeMarco got one of his thumbs and bent it back, paralyzing him.

Guido groaned, and DeMarco pulled him close. "You know something, Guido? You were the first person to cheat me in cards. We were playing for nickels at the kitchen table and I felt the bends you were putting in them. Can you believe that, Uncle George? Guido picked the one way to cheat me that I'd catch on to. He bent the cards."

"Let him go," his uncle declared.

"Took a couple of steps back, didn't you, Uncle George?" DeMarco said. "Not used to this dynamic, are you?"

"Please, Skipper."

His uncle was using his nice voice. He didn't do that very often. Like maybe five times since the turn of the century. DeMarco obliged him, and released the bodyguard. Guido stalked away, muttering under his breath.

"I did this for you, Skipper," his uncle said. "This isn't just another deal. I did it for you."

"For me? That's a new one."

His uncle stepped very close. He was shaking his head emphatically, and wanted DeMarco so see it. He did this sometimes when he was desperate to make a point.

"For you, Skipper. As payback. How many times did you get cheated in those poker tournaments you entered in Atlantic City? Every time! You said the other players saw the injured animal, and took you out. You said they whipsawed you, by raising the bets so early that you couldn't afford to stay in. Am I right?"

DeMarco nodded reluctantly. Whipsawing was a form of collusion between two players. The pair would raise and reraise early in the hand, convincing the other players to fold. Usually, the players had nothing, and would later split the pot between them.

"You also told me that your opponents played cousins,

and signaled their hands when they thought you were weak. They used hand signals that you couldn't see."

DeMarco nodded again. It was becoming a night of painful memories.

"So this is payback, Skipper. You're the best poker player in the world; you told me so yourself."

DeMarco found himself nodding. He *was* the best poker player in the world, at least on the Internet. He'd won over twenty online tournaments and nearly a half a million dollars in prize money. Several poker Web sites had banned him, forcing DeMarco to play under pseudonyms. He was a blind guy playing under a fake name and he was beating everyone out there. Sure, it wasn't the same as playing in live events, but in time, he was certain he would win all of those as well.

His uncle pinched DeMarco's arm. He'd been doing that since DeMarco had gone to live with him. It was his way of being affectionate.

"Yes, Uncle George."

"I'm sorry," his uncle said. "You'll be included in all decisions from now on."

"No more keeping me in the dark?"

His uncle laughed under his breath. "That's a good one."

His uncle led him across the room, and parted a curtain. The suite looked down upon the casino, the neon lighting the glass so brilliantly that DeMarco could see it a foot from his face. It made him feel normal, even if just for a little while, and he continued to stand there long after his uncle had said good night.

36

Nothing worked quickly in law enforcement, and it was nearly three A.M. before Gerry was given a sworn statement by Detective Longo regarding the discovery of Russell John Watson's body in Gerry's motel room. The statement was three pages long, and typed on legal paper. Gerry read it twice, just to make sure the details were right, then scribbled his signature across the bottom and slid the statement across the desk to the detective. Longo stood up, and the two men shook hands.

"How long you planning to stay in Las Vegas?"

"A couple more days," Gerry said.

"Try to stay out of trouble, okay?"

Longo led him to the reception area in the front of the station house, which was filled with angry-looking people and several mothers with screaming babies. The area had plastic benches molded to the walls and steel chairs hex-bolted to the floor, and Gerry felt like he'd been dropped into an asylum. The detective shook his hand again.

"Your friends should be out in another ten minutes or so," Longo said.

Gerry thanked him again, then found an empty seat on a bench, and watched Longo be buzzed back into the station house. Then he spent a few minutes unwinding.

He'd been in plenty of tight spots in his life, but today took the cake. He needed to call his father and tell him he was okay, and also to thank him. Mr. Black and White had pulled through again.

He took out his cell phone and powered it up. Several bars of music came out of the phone, indicating it was ready to be used. The large African American sitting beside him emitted a menacing growl. Gerry glanced at him.

"What's up?"

"Make a cell call in here, and I'll make you eat that thing," the man said loudly.

The reception area got still, with even the babies quieting down. Gerry looked around the room, and noticed that he was the only person with a cell phone. Leave it to him to find the one place in the country where people were gathered, and weren't talking on cell phones. He snapped his phone shut, then rose and went to the front doors. Pushing them open, he glanced back at the man who'd threatened him.

"Save my seat?"

No one in the reception area laughed. *Tough crowd,* Gerry thought.

He stood on the edge of the parking lot and made the call. His father's cell phone was turned off, and he left a rambling message on voice mail, thanking his father more times than was necessary, which he guessed was his way of compensating for not thanking him enough for saving his neck when he'd been a kid. Someday it would all balance out, although Gerry knew that day was a long ways off.

He heard the front doors open and someone come out. There was a breeze in the air, and he smelled perfume, then felt a hand touch his sleeve.

"Excuse me, are you a cop?"

He turned to find a woman who resembled Heather Locklear standing beside him. She wore jeans that fit like baloney skins and a sweater molded to her ample bosom.

"No, are you?"

She let out a little-girl giggle. "I was just wondering if you'd walk me to my car."

Gerry obliged her, and they walked across the visitor parking lot. He was able to pick out her car before they reached it, a bloodred Mustang convertible. She opened it by pressing a button on her key chain, then thanked him with a smile.

He walked back to find Vinny, Nunzie, and Frank waiting by the front doors.

"Where you been?" Nunzie wanted to know.

"Being a good Boy Scout. Ready to go?"

The three men nodded. The apprehension of being inside a police station was slow to leave their faces, and Vinny took out a pack of cigarettes and offered it around. They all accepted, and shared a silence while allowing themselves to relax.

"How we ever going to pay your father back for this?" Vinny asked.

Gerry stared at the cigarette he'd just lit up. Yolanda was bugging him to quit, and he guessed now was as good a time as any. He dropped the cigarette and ground it out with his shoe, then said, "You're not."

"Your father isn't going to demand something in return?"

Gerry shook his head. He took a deep breath, sucking in the secondhand smoke all around him. Vinny had survived as a hoodlum because he'd learned that favors must always be paid back. Except it was different with his old man. You couldn't pay him back because there wasn't anything his old man wanted.

"I'd still like to do something for him," Vinny said. "You know, show my respect."

"Maybe you could send him a turkey at Thanksgiving," Nunzie suggested.

"Or a ham," Frank said, speaking for the first time. "They've got these places that precook them, and deliver."

"You think he'd like a ham?" Vinny asked.

Gerry realized they were being serious, and tried to imagine what his father would do with a baked ham sent to him by a bunch of hoodlums. He'd either take it to a local homeless shelter, or to the neighbors, but he wouldn't eat it himself.

"Sure," Gerry said.

"*Bah-zoom,*" Nunzie said under his breath. "What do we have here?"

The four men's attention shifted to the attractive member of the opposite sex coming across the visitor parking lot toward them. It was the young woman Gerry had escorted to her car, only now she had a pissed-off look on her face, and her car keys dangling from her fingertips.

"I'm sorry to bother you again, but my car's engine is as dead as a doornail," she said. "Is there any way you could give me a ride home? I don't live that far."

Gerry looked at his friends, and not seeing any objections, said, "Sure, but I've got to warn you, it's not that big a car."

"I'll squeeze in," she said.

Her name was Cindy Dupree, and she sat sandwiched between Vinny and Gerry in the front seat, and told them how she'd come to Las Vegas expecting to get a job as a blackjack dealer in a casino—"I heard you could live pretty decently on tips"—but had ended up working the graveyard shift as a bartender—"The tips suck"—and was hoping to scrounge up enough money to move to Los Angeles and enroll in a beautician's school. She called Las Vegas a whorehouse sitting on a hot plate, and hoped never to return for as long as she lived.

While she talked, Cindy directed Vinny to a nameless subdivision on the northern outskirts of town. There were no streetlights, and Gerry squinted to see the street names, trying to remember them so they could get back to town. They passed a billboard for a smiling attorney named Ed Bernstein, then turned down a dead-end street named Cortez, and Cindy said, "This is it," and pointed at a single-story ranch house in the middle of the block. Vinny pulled up to the curb, and threw the rental in park.

"Well, I guess this is where we part ways, gents," Cindy said. "Thanks for helping a girl out of a tight spot. I really appreciate it."

Gerry slid out of the car and offered his hand to her. She took it, gave him a friendly kiss on the cheek when she was out of the car, then brushed past him on her way up the front path. She had her key ring out, and he saw her press a button that made her garage door automatically open. His father was always telling him that where there was smoke, there was usually fire, and he found himself questioning why she'd come to the police station by herself. She hadn't felt safe walking across the parking lot, yet had been willing to let four strange guys give her a ride home. It didn't make sense, and he jumped into the car while looking back at Cindy's garage. The door had come up, and as she went inside, two men hiding in the garage swept out past her.

"Cute broad," Vinny said.

"Get out of here!"

"What's wrong—"

"I said go!"

A Pontiac Firebird was parked in front of them, twenty yards down the street. Its headlights came on, bathing their rental in light. The car's engine roared, and it came forward as if to hit them, then suddenly stopped. Two men wearing jeans and sweatshirts jumped out. Together with the two men from Cindy's garage, they surrounded the rental. In their hands were automatic pistols with silencers, and Gerry heard the quiet *pop, pop, pop* as they shot out their tires, the rental slowly sinking several inches. He glanced at the house, and saw Cindy standing in the garage. She'd turned the light on, and was watching the action. Their eyes briefly met, and she shrugged and killed the light.

One of the armed men tapped Vinny's window with the tip of his silencer. Vinny rolled down his window while keeping his other hand visible on the wheel.

"Which one of you is Gerry Valentine?" the man asked.

Gerry said that he was. He'd put his hands on the dashboard and was trying to stop his bowels from exploding. The only thing worse than getting whacked was soiling yourself before it happened, and he struggled to retain his dignity.

"You and the driver get out of the car," the man said.

Gerry got out of the rental and faced the man doing the talking. He'd inherited a lot of things from his father, one of which was his phenomenal memory. He'd seen this guy before, then it clicked where: the guy was a valet at the Sugar Shack. The fact that he wasn't wearing a mask did not bode well for what was about to happen to them.

The valet made them empty their pockets, frisked them, led them to the back of the Firebird, and made Gerry and Vinny climb into the open trunk. He slammed the trunk down hard, and they were instantly enveloped in suffocating darkness.

They listened to Nunzie and Frank being put through the same drill; and put in the trunk of another vehicle. This was how hoodlums executed people, and they both knew it.

"It's been nice knowing you," Vinny said.

37

Valentine had never used an alarm clock in his entire life. When the sun rose, so did he.

His hotel bedroom wasn't big enough for him to get on the floor and do his exercises, so he went into the living room, and did his push-ups and sit-ups to the accompaniment of Rufus Steele's apocalyptic snoring. He'd told Rufus off before going to bed, and sensed the old cowboy was faking sleep, his Stetson conveniently hiding his face. Valentine stole glances at him while he worked up a sweat.

He'd always thought of Rufus as a man born a hundred years too late. He had uncanny street smarts, and a century ago might have become a prominent businessman or politician. But those days were long past, and his lot in life was playing cards.

Finishing his exercises, he sat on his haunches in front of the window, watching the sun rise. Dawn was the best part of the day, the first rays of sun filled with promise and hope. His mother had taught him that, and he had never forgotten it.

He shaved, then took a hot shower. His exercises consumed twenty minutes of every day. That, his walking, and his judo classes kept him sharp. He wasn't the man he used to be, but he was a hell of a lot closer than most guys his age.

He took his time dressing, and was ready to go downstairs to have breakfast with Gloria Curtis at eight. His cell phone was on his night table, and he powered it up and found a message from Gerry. He listened to it, his son's overapologizing making him smile. If only his wife were alive to hear this. He walked out of his bedroom with the cell phone in his hand. As he passed the couch, Rufus spoke up.

"You ain't running out on me, are you?"

Valentine reached over and removed the Stetson from Rufus's face. The old cowboy was wide awake and twirling a wooden toothpick between his gums.

"Wouldn't dream of it," Valentine said, tossing the hat into Rufus's lap. "I'm meeting Gloria Curtis for breakfast, and then we'll both come over to the poker room to film you and your X-ray eyes. I sure hope you know what you're doing."

"Well, there is one thing I failed to mention, come to think of it."

The words had a serious tone to them, and Valentine stared at him. "What's that?"

"The boys who fleeced me last night—the ones I'm about to fleece back?"

"What about them?"

"I told them they could invite their friends to the demonstration this morning, and that if their friends wanted in on the action, they could have some."

Valentine felt something drop in his stomach. He'd reluctantly agreed to front Rufus the hundred grand he was going to need to fleece the boys who'd cheated him at poker. Now, Rufus was telling him that there was going to be more action, and that he was going to have to cover it, since Rufus was flat broke. He pulled up a chair and sat in it so he was facing his guest.

"Their friends?"

"You know, some of the boys."

"In other words, more suckers."

"Now, I didn't say that, but I wouldn't call these boys the most knowledgeable gamblers who've ever lived, just some of the greediest."

"How much additional action will I have to cover?"

Rufus scratched the steel-gray stubble on his chin. His posture on the couch reminded Valentine of the uneasy sleepers he used to have to run off from the public places in Atlantic City when he was a street cop. "That's hard to say," Rufus said.

"Take a wild guess."

"Okay. Another hundred and fifty grand. Maybe two hundred, if we're lucky."

Valentine blew out his cheeks and stared at the carpet. He'd retired on his pension and social security and a little money squirreled away in the bank. Opening Grift Sense had been a windfall, and the last time he'd checked his bank statement, the account was hovering at three hundred thousand dollars. The notion that he might lose all of it covering Rufus Steele's bet did not seem real, and he forced himself to his feet.

"You look slightly perturbed," Rufus said.

"I am," Valentine said. "This is my life savings we're talking about."

"Stop worrying, pardner. This is a sure thing."

If there was any lesson Valentine had learned from the gambling business, it was that you didn't mail in the results, and there was no such thing as a sure thing. People who believed otherwise ended up in the poorhouse, and he left the suite without saying another word to his guest.

*   *   *

Talking to Rufus had made him late for his breakfast with Gloria Curtis, and he found her sitting at a secluded table in the hotel restaurant, the simmering look in her eyes suggesting she was ready to walk out. He slid into the seat across from her.

"Oversleep?" she asked.

Her question had a bite to it, like a guy as old as him might need to get his rest.

"Actually, I was up with the sunrise," he said. "My roommate dropped a bombshell on me, and I needed to have a chat with him. I'm sorry I'm late."

"Care to share?"

A waitress filled their cups with coffee, then glanced into their faces, and said she'd come back. She was the first competent person Valentine had encountered in the hotel.

"Rufus has bet some guys that he has X-ray vision," he said.

"So I've heard."

"Well, it appears I'll be fading the action on his wager. Since we're talking about several hundred thousand dollars, I wanted to talk it over with him."

"Fading the action?"

Valentine sipped his coffee and nodded. "It's one of gambling's little secrets. A gambler will use another gambler's money to play with, only he doesn't tell anyone. The problem with this wager is that Rufus didn't bother to tell me."

His words slowly registered across Gloria's face, and her anger was replaced by a look of concern. Her hand came across the table and encircled his wrist.

"How much money are we talking about?"

"Three hundred thousand dollars."

"Are you serious?"

"I'm always serious."

"Can you cover it?"

He was tempted to say just barely, but nodded instead. Her fingers felt comforting against his skin, and he suddenly knew exactly what she was thinking. Before the words could come out of her mouth, he said, "I know, he's wrong, and I shouldn't be backing him, but these guys cheated him in a poker game, so Rufus is going to cheat them right back."

"What if he loses the bet?" Gloria said. "Then what?"

Her hand was still on top of his wrist. She'd done that the night before at dinner to gain his confidence, and Valentine decided he liked it. The world of gambling was new to her, and she wanted to learn, so long as the person teaching her was someone she could trust. He decided he liked that, too.

"Then I pay up," Valentine said.

"You would?"

"Every last cent."

"But these men that Rufus is gambling with, they don't know he's using your money," she said, lowering her voice. "What if you told Rufus to forget it, that he'd have to find the money someplace else. What then?"

"Then Rufus would have to tell them he didn't have the money, and give the men IOUs. The gamblers would be angry, and they'd sell the IOUs to wise guys, who'd show up on Rufus's doorstep in a few days, looking for payment."

"What if Rufus refused, or was flat broke? What then?"

Valentine looked into Gloria's eyes while considering the best way to answer her. He'd lived in a violent world for the better part of his life, and had done a good job of shielding the people he cared about from that world. His role was that of a filter, and it was not a responsibility he took lightly. He said, "There used to be this famous gambler in New York City named Arnold Rothstein. Supposedly, Rothstein was responsible for fixing the 1919 baseball World Series."

"The infamous Black Sox scandal," Gloria said.

"That's right. One night in New York, Rothstein got in a poker game with a gambler named Titanic Thompson, and ended up losing half a million bucks. Rothstein gave Thompson an IOU, and Thompson sold the IOU to some hoodlums. They tried to collect, and Rothstein welshed. Guess what happened."

"That was the end of Arnold Rothstein."

"Exactly."

"Would you do that to Rufus?"

Valentine's coffee cup had mysteriously emptied itself, and he stared at the grounds in its bottom. He was angry with Rufus for putting him in such a bad spot, and also afraid of losing his life savings. But deep down, he wanted to believe that Rufus had one last trick up his sleeve, and was still capable of pulling the wool over the eyes of any gambler in the world. Belief was the only thing a person had in this world, and he realized he was willing to put every cent he had behind Rufus pulling this off.

"Never," he said.

38

At ten minutes of nine, Valentine and Gloria left the restaurant, and met up with Zack in front of the poker room. Over breakfast, Gloria had explained how she and Zack had worked together for fifteen years, and developed a level of communication that bordered on telepathic.

"We've already got a good crowd in there, so we won't have to make people bunch up like yesterday," Zack said. "I talked a maintenance man into dimming the lights, so there won't be a glare problem. And I convinced two security guards to keep the crowd noise down, so we won't have to redub the sound before we send it to the network."

"You're a genius," Gloria said.

"In my own mind," Zack replied. His camera was lying on the floor, and he picked it up and hoisted it onto his shoulder. Pointing the lens at Valentine, he said, "So Tony, you have a reputation for being able to see through any con or swindle. How is Rufus Steele going to pull this X-ray vision stunt off, anyway?"

There was no one standing within earshot, and Valentine stared into the lens and said, "I honestly don't know."

"I'm not filming," Zack said. "You can be honest."

"I am being honest. I don't know."

Zack lowered his camera, and a disbelieving look spread across his face.

"Do you think he's off his rocker?" the cameraman asked.

Gloria edged up beside Valentine, and locked her arm into his.

"Tony's backing him, so he'd better not be," she said.

The elevator doors on the other side of the lobby parted, and Rufus Steele emerged, wearing black pants, a gleaming white shirt, and a black bow tie with two long tails, western style. Seeing them, he hustled over, and Valentine read the words inscribed on each tail of his tie: *Thin Man*.

Rufus doffed his Stetson and bowed to Gloria Curtis, then gave Valentine a friendly whack on the arm. "Hey pardner, you ready to win some money?"

His eyes were twinkling, and Valentine sensed Rufus was prepared to dig down deep into his bag of tricks, and do something really wonderful. He'd never helped anyone win a bet before, and supposed there was a first time for everything.

"Ready when you are," Valentine said.

Over two hundred men were gathered inside the poker room. They were the gray-faced, unshaven variety of male who populated casinos during the early morning hours; their hotel rooms used for shaving, showering, fornicating, and little else. They applauded politely as Rufus crossed the room with his entourage.

Taking off his Stetson, Rufus gave the crowd a big Roy Rogers wave, then approached the round table in the center of the room where the six players who'd cheated him the night before were assembled. Valentine edged up beside Zack.

"Do me a favor while you're filming, and get a clear shot of those six guys, okay?"

"Sure," Zack said.

"I'm also going to need to get a copy of the tape."

"No problem. You saving their pictures for something?"

Valentine nodded. Back home on his computer was the largest database of cheaters in the world, and he planned to add these six jokers' pictures to the mix.

"Before we start, I want to establish some rules," Rufus began. "You gentlemen obviously will take great pains to make sure that I don't swindle or cheat you, and I understand why you feel the need to take such precautions. I, too, feel the need to take precautions. Since I'm going to be blindfolded, I have asked the house physician, Dr. Robinson, to act as a neutral third party."

A red-haired, red-bearded man wearing a tailored suit stepped out of the crowd. He wore an annoyed look on his face, and Valentine wondered if Rufus had conned Dr. Robinson into helping as well.

"Here's the deal," Rufus went on. "I don't want someone holding something up to my blindfolded face, and asking me what it is—such as a coin—and then switching it. So, whatever object you'd like me to read with my X-ray vision, you will have to hand to Dr. Robinson to hold. Fair enough?"

The six cheaters went into a huddle and conferred among themselves. After a few moments, one stepped forward. He was a brutish-looking guy with swirls of dark hair sprouting from both ears. Above the pocket of his bowling shirt was his name: *The Greek.*

"Okay," the Greek said. "You can use Dr. Robinson, provided you let our doctor—Dr. Carlson—examine you for any hidden transmitters or receiving devices."

"Sure," Rufus said obligingly. "Should I strip?"

Dr. Carlson stepped out of the huddle. He was one of the six cheaters, and had the superior air of a man who made too much money. "That won't be necessary."

"Shucks," Rufus said.

Dr. Carlson went over Rufus with a fine-tooth comb, and ended the examination looking down Rufus's ears with a pen light. Intercanal earpieces were commonly used by cheaters wanting to transmit information inside a casino, and Carlson did everything but stick an ice pick down Rufus's ears to make sure he wasn't wearing one. Satisfied, the doctor stepped back.

"He's clean as a whistle," Carlson said.

"Okay," the Greek said, "now, examine Dr. Robinson."

A hush fell over the crowd. There were common courtesies among gamblers. The Greek had just broken one, but didn't seem to care. He took Carlson by the arm.

"Do it."

Carlson looked at Dr. Robinson. "Do you mind?"

Dr. Robinson looked at the ceiling, as if asking God what the hell he was doing there, then nodded his compliance. Dr. Carlson went over him with the same painstaking precision he'd used on Rufus. Again he stepped back.

"He's clean," Carlson said.

"Good," the Greek said.

Taking a paper bag off a chair, the Greek removed a pair of wraparound glasses made of stainless steel. The glasses were the same design worn by Arnold Schwarzenneger in the Terminator movies, and completely covered the wearer's eyes. As the Greek showed them to the crowd, Valentine got closer, and had a look. The glasses were half-inch thick, and the idea that someone might be able to see through them seemed impossible.

When the Greek was finished showing the glasses around, Gloria Curtis stepped forward and stuck her mike in Rufus's face.

"This is Gloria Curtis reporting from the poker room at the World Poker Showdown. Standing beside me is Rufus Steele, who has bet a number of gamblers that he has X-ray vision. Rufus, when did you discover you had X-ray vision?"

"About two years ago," Rufus replied.

"Do you know what brought this on?"

"Happened after I wrecked my car. I'd been drinking."

Gloria tried not to laugh, although several gamblers in the crowd did.

"How much money have you wagered?" Gloria asked.

"A hundred thousand dollars," Rufus said. His eyes swept the sea of faces. "If there's anyone else who'd like a piece of action, please step right up, and talk to this handsome fellow standing to my right. He'll take care of you."

Two dozen gamblers formed a line in front of Valentine. He had come prepared, and wrote down each man's name on a pad of paper he'd gotten in the restaurant, and the amount of his wager. He kept a running tally in his head, not wanting to go over the three hundred thousand bucks he was responsible for, and when the last man was done, did another re-adding. One hundred and ninety-seven thousand dollars in additional bets had been placed. Rufus had called it perfectly.

He went over to Rufus, and showed him the amount.

"That's a nice number," Rufus said. "Let's get this show on the road."

*　　　*　　　*

A folding chair was placed in the center of the room. Rufus sat down with a smile on his face, and was quickly surrounded by the crowd. Stepping forward, the Greek fitted the steel glasses onto Rufus's face, then produced a piece of twine, and tied the glasses behind Rufus's head.

"That's a little snug," Rufus complained.

"Does it hurt?" the Greek asked.

"Come to mention it, yes."

The Greek added another knot, then another. He wore the twisted look of someone who enjoyed inflicting pain. Finished, he stepped back with a triumphant look on his face.

"You done?" Rufus asked.

"Sure am," the Greek said.

Rufus stuck his hand into his pants pocket, and produced a leather bag with a drawstring. He tossed the bag in the Greek's direction, and the Greek plucked it out of the air. "Put that over my head, will you?"

The Greek looked at the other gamblers, a suspicious look on his face. Then he tried the bag on over his own head, then tugged it off, his hair standing on end like he'd been shocked.

"I can't see through it," he announced.

"That's the whole idea," Rufus said.

Several gamblers who'd made bets with Rufus wanted to examine the bag, and it was passed around the room. Valentine caught Gloria flashing him a nervous smile. When the gamblers were finished examining the bag, it was handed to the Greek. He stepped forward, and began to fit it over Rufus's head, when the old cowboy stopped him. "One last thing. We need to agree on how many items I have to identify."

The Greek hesitated, and glanced at his partners.

"Three," one of the men called out.

"Three?" Rufus asked. "I was thinking more like one."

"You could guess with one," the man shot back. "Three is fair."

"I'll do three," Rufus said, "if you'll make it double or nothing."

The Greek looked at his partners, then at the other men who'd made wagers with Rufus. Gamblers were good at communicating with their eyes, and without a word being spoken, everyone who'd made a wager with Rufus agreed to double it.

Valentine felt his knees buckle. The only way he could cover the bet now would be to sell his house and his car and probably his giant-screen TV. If there hadn't been so many witnesses and a camera rolling, he would have dragged Rufus across the room and beaten the living crap out of him.

"Double or nothing it is," the Greek said.

With a smile on his face, the Greek placed the leather bag over Rufus's head, and tied the drawstring as tightly as he could.

Dr. Robinson stepped forward with the annoyed look still on his face. He didn't look like a gambler, or the kind of person who enjoyed gamblers' company, and Valentine imagined him going straight home after this, and taking a long shower. The doctor looked at the Greek and said, "Ready when you are."

The Greek fished a worn deck of playing cards from his pocket. Removing one, he held it up to the crowd. It was the four of clubs. He handed the card to Robinson. Without a word, the doctor held the card a few feet from Rufus's bagged head.

"It's a playing card," Rufus's muffled voice said.

Another hush fell over the group. The Greek acted like he'd been kicked in the groin with a steel boot.

"Which one?" the Greek asked.

"Four of clubs," the muffled voice said.

Valentine could not believe what he was seeing. There was only one way to pull this stunt off—by having Robinson "cue" Rufus through a verbal code. These codes, called second sight, were the staple of mind-reading acts, and known by cheaters. Only Robinson hadn't said a word, the annoyed look still painted across his face.

The Greek took a stack of chips from his pocket. They were a rainbow of colors, indicating several different denominations. He plucked out a purple chip, and gave it to Robinson. The doctor held the chip in his outstretched hand.

"It's a chip," Rufus's muffled voice said.

"What denomination?" the Greek asked.

"Ten grand," the voice said.

The Greek angrily threw the chip to the ground. "You're cheating!"

Valentine stepped forward to defend his man. "How can he be cheating?"

"He's somehow seeing through the glasses and the bag," the Greek said. "He has to be. There's no such thing as X-ray vision."

Valentine got in the Greek's breathing space. "Then why did you bet with him?"

The Greek started to reply, then thought better of it, and shut his mouth.

"Cover my eyes with your hands," Rufus's muffled voice said.

Valentine's head snapped.

"You heard me," the voice said.

The Greek took the bait, and scurried around to the back of Rufus's folding chair. Leaning forward, he placed his enormous palms directly over Rufus's eyes. One of the Greek's partners stepped forward, and removed a handful of change from his pocket. The man selected a coin—an old-looking silver quarter—and bypassing Dr. Robinson, held the coin up to Rufus's face.

"What's this?"

"A dirty fingernail," Rufus's muffled voice said.

Everyone in the room who wasn't part of the wager started laughing. Those who *were* part of the wager looked like candidates for Siberia. After a few moments, the room quieted down.

"You're holding a quarter," the muffled voice said.

The man holding the quarter started to shake. "What's the date?"

"It's 1947."

Dr. Robinson took the quarter out of the man's hand and, in a loud voice, verified the date. It was indeed 1947. The doctor handed the quarter back to the man, who passed it to his partners. The other men examined the coin while shaking their heads in disbelief.

No one was more despondent than the Greek, who hurriedly came around Rufus's chair, and examined the coin. The Greek began to dab at his eyes, and Valentine realized he was crying, never a pretty sight inside a casino.

"Hey, Tony, help me out, will you?" Rufus asked.

Valentine went to where Rufus sat, and untied the drawstring of the leather bag around the old cowboy's head. He pulled the bag off, then untied the twine holding the steel glasses to Rufus's face. To his surprise, the glasses hadn't moved, and he wondered how Rufus had managed to see through them.

Rufus rubbed at his eyes, and then patted down his hair. Standing, he faced Gloria Curtis's microphone and the camera, and raised his arms triumphantly into the air.

"I win," he declared.

39

"We're not going to kill you," Jinky Harris said.

Gerry Valentine stared at his captor, the rhythmic pounding of flesh reverberating across the dusty warehouse. He was sitting bound to a chair and sweat was pouring off his body. Jinky's men hadn't driven very far after abducting them, and Gerry had seen the casinos' blazing neon in the distance as he'd been pulled from the trunk.

"You could have fooled me," Gerry said.

The warehouse was shaped like a small airplane hangar. On the other end, Vinny and Nunzie and Frank also sat bound in chairs. Jinky's henchmen had been slapping them around for a while, then decided to gang up on Frank, their punches sounding like sledgehammers hitting a side of beef.

"You want me to stop it?" Jinky asked.

"Of course I want you to stop it," Gerry replied.

Jinky played with the automatic controls on the arm of his wheelchair, and pulled around so he was facing Gerry. He'd been eating nonstop since their arrival, and crumbs of food peppered his beard. He pointed across the warehouse.

"Which one of them shot Russ Watson in the parking lot yesterday?" Jinky asked. "That's all I want to know."

"Who's Russ Watson?"

Jinky pulled a candy bar from the pocket of his purple velour tracksuit and tore off the wrapper. "You're making this hard on your friends."

Gerry stared across the warehouse at the guy punching Frank in the face. The guy was a gorilla, yet Frank kept smiling at him in between getting hit. Frank had boxed as a pro for six years, and won all his fights except a couple of hometown decisions. His fight philosophy had been simple: he'd been willing to take punishment in order to deliver punishment. They'd picked the wrong guy to beat up.

Gerry's eyes returned to Jinky. "Let me guess. Russ Watson is the dead guy that turned up in my motel room yesterday."

"That's right," Jinky said. "I want to know who shot him."

On the other side of the warehouse, Frank let out a sickening grunt. It echoed across the room, and made Gerry's stomach do a flip-flop.

"Will you tell me something if I tell you?" Gerry asked.

Jinky bit into the candy bar like he had a grudge with it. "Depends."

"We came to you in good faith, and told you what we were doing in Las Vegas," Gerry said. "You got in touch with the Tuna, and ratted us out. The Tuna sent a hitman, who killed my best friend, to kill us. When that went south, *you* tried to have us killed. Why did you do that?"

The candy bar was a memory. Jinky fingered the control on the armrest of his chair, like he was considering taking off. The question obviously made him uncomfortable. Gerry, tied to a chair, had just called him a piece of shit.

"You don't know how things work in Las Vegas," Jinky said.

"I don't?"

"Nope."

"Then why don't you educate me?"

Jinky snorted under his breath. "This town is run on juice."

"It is?"

"Absolutely. The Tuna has juice with people in town, so it was in my best interest to strike a deal with him. Your father has juice with people in town, so it's in my best interest not to kill you. Get it?"

Gerry gazed across the warehouse. "What about my friends?"

"Your friends are fucked," Jinky said. "Nobody knows them from Adam. They could die and it would be like they never existed. That's what happens when you don't have any juice in Las Vegas."

"Can I ask you something else?"

"What's that?"

"Who does the Tuna have juice with?"

Jinky's laughter filled the warehouse. "You don't know anything, do you?"

"I guess not," Gerry said.

"Now, it's your turn to answer a question. Who shot Russ Watson yesterday?"

"Why do you care?"

"What the hell is that supposed to mean?" Jinky said angrily.

"He was a hitman," Gerry said.

Jinky's face went blank. "So?"

"One of the job dangers of being a hitman is that sometimes people fight back."

"You think Russ got what was coming to him?"

"You sent Russ into battle and he lost."

A look of rage flashed over Jinky's face, and it occurred to Gerry that he wasn't used to back talk. The big man touched the arm control on his wheelchair and crashed into him, sending Gerry's chair scraping several feet across the concrete floor.

"Don't give me any of that philosophy shit," Jinky roared. "Which one of you shot Russ Watson?"

Gerry studied Jinky's face. Every time Jinky mentioned Russ Watson, his eyes went soft, and Gerry guessed they'd had a relationship like the one he'd had with Jack Donovan. Telling Jinky the truth would only lead to Frank getting killed.

"It was the security guard," Gerry said.

"Which one?"

"The guard in the parking lot."

Jinky had to think. "The old geezer with the hearing aids?"

"Yeah. Your friend got fresh, and the guard shot him. It wasn't pretty."

Jinky crashed into him again. Seeing it coming lessened the impact, and Gerry felt his chair tip dangerously to one side, then right itself like a tightrope walker.

"If your father wasn't tight with Bill Higgins, I'd put a bullet in your head," Jinky said.

A harsh cry went up across the warehouse. Jinky stared, and Gerry followed his gaze. The man who'd been punishing Frank was clutching his hand while cursing up a storm.

"What happened?" Jinky yelled to him.

"I broke my hand against his face," the man called back.

"I told you to wrap a towel around your hand, didn't I?"

"I did wrap a towel around it," the man said.

"So, walk it off."

Easy for you to say, Gerry nearly said. He watched the man walk a serpentine pattern across the warehouse. If the look on his face was any indication, he was going to need a doctor. Frank had beaten the guy without ever laying a finger on him. Gerry caught Frank's eye, and Frank winked. His friend's face looked like a pepperoni pizza that had been left out for too long in the sun. Gerry winked back.

"Who's got the digital camera?" Jinky called out.

"I do," the man with the broken hand said.

"Bring it over here."

The man came over and handed Jinky a digital camera. Jinky monkeyed with it for a little bit, then aimed at Gerry and snapped a picture. Jinky held the camera away from his face and stared at the picture, then showed it to the man with the broken hand.

"What do you think?"

"He looks too pretty," the man said.

"Then make him look unpretty."

The man came over and popped Gerry in the face with his good hand. Gerry felt something run out of his left nostril and knew it wasn't snot. He stared down at the blood sheeting his neck and the front of his shirt, then saw another flash from Jinky's camera.

"Take a look," Jinky said.

The man came around Jinky's wheelchair and appraised his handiwork.

"Much better," the man said.

40

Valentine hung around the poker room for a few minutes and helped Rufus Steele collect his money. Poker players were a lot of things, but it was rare that one welshed on a bet. By Valentine's calculations, Rufus was owed five hundred and ninety-four thousand dollars, and that was exactly the amount collected. When Rufus tried to hand him some, Valentine balked.

"Come on, it's your cut," Rufus protested.

"I did it as a favor," Valentine said, refusing to touch the packets of money being shoved his way. It was at least fifty grand, maybe more.

"I'm well aware of that," Rufus said, "but I'm not a charity case. Take it."

The tone of his voice hadn't changed, but there was a bite to his words nonetheless. Gloria was standing nearby with Zack, and they both turned their backs, and pretended to be watching the segment they'd just shot. Valentine didn't want to make an enemy of Rufus, and stared long and hard at the money.

"I'm here on someone else's nickel," he said quietly. "If word got around that I'd gone into business with you, my real business would suffer. So let's just say you owe me one, okay?"

"No one ever worked with Rufus Steele and didn't get

paid," the old cowboy said, waving the stacks in Valentine's face. "This is your money. I'm going to hold it for you until your job is over. Then it's yours. Understand?"

Rufus wasn't going to back down, and Valentine guessed there was a worthwhile charity he could donate the money to before he left town.

"I'll do it, provided one thing."

Rufus had eyebrows that looked like fluffy sandpaper. They both went up.

"What's that, pardner?"

"Explain how you pulled that stunt."

The old cowboy laughed like someone was tickling both his feet.

"Never in a thousand years," he said.

"What kind of man puts up nearly six hundred thousand dollars to back a crazy bet?" Gloria Curtis asked when Rufus was gone. There was a bemused look in her eyes, and Valentine didn't know if she thought he was a fool or an idiot or both.

"I think it has something to do with Rufus's unique powers of persuasion," he said. "I'd normally never do anything like that."

"I sensed that," she said. "You old guys really stick together."

"Is that what I am? An old guy?"

She put her hand on his wrist and gave it a squeeze. "A good old guy."

Gloria had innocently touched him several times in the past two days, and he found himself liking it. Each time they had a conversation, he felt the need to continue it, and he said, "Would you like to have lunch with me?"

She smiled at him with her eyes. "Sure. I have to cover the tournament this morning. Is twelve thirty all right?"

"That's my nap time."

"Stop that."

He felt a smile coming on. "Twelve thirty it is. I'll meet you in the lobby restaurant."

"See you then."

She gave his wrist another squeeze and left with her cameraman. When they were gone, Valentine asked himself where this was going. She was part of the case. Even if this relationship went no further than the platonic stages, it was the wrong thing to be doing. Business was business, pleasure was pleasure, and they weren't supposed to mix.

He felt his cell phone vibrate, and pulled it from his pocket. The Caller ID said BILL HIGGINS. As he flipped the phone open, he realized he didn't care. Gloria was smart and pretty and he liked talking to her. His partner in Atlantic City had liked to say that it was easy to find a woman to have sex with, but finding one whom you wanted to talk to, that was tough.

"Hey, Bill, what's up?" he said into his phone.

"I need to talk to you," his friend said. "It's urgent."

"Just say where."

"Meet me at Gardunos in twenty minutes."

Gardunos was a local Mexican restaurant they sometimes frequented. It was away from the casinos, and the food was homemade and exceptionally good.

"I'll see you in twenty," Valentine said.

Going outside, he handed the valet his stub, then went to the curb and waited for his rental to come up. Celebrity's valet stand was decorated with African flora and fauna, and had Congo music playing over a loudspeaker. It was like walking onto a movie set, and at any moment he expected to see Tarzan come swinging through the trees.

While he waited, Valentine found himself staring at a man standing at the end of the curb. The man wore tailored slacks and a white dress shirt that clashed with a floppy tennis hat and Ray-Bans. He sensed the guy was trying to keep a low profile, and guessed he was a celebrity visiting the hotel incognito. The man looked impatiently at his watch, and Valentine got a good look at his face. It was Dr. Robinson, the house physician.

A decrepit Toyota Corolla pulled up to the curb. Robinson picked up a gym bag lying at his feet, and went to the car. He gave the valet his stub and climbed in behind the wheel.

Valentine felt his radar go up. Robinson was driving a junker and hadn't tipped the valet. Valentine had known plenty of house physicians at hotels, and they all made a decent buck. Something wasn't adding up here. He walked down the curb, and glanced into the Toyota just as Robinson pulled away. A tattered black suitcase occupied one of the backseats. Stenciled across its front were the words RENFO & COMPANY in bold white letters. It looked like something an entertainer might use, and he went to the valet stand, and found the kid who'd brought up the car.

"Let me see that guy's stub," Valentine said.

The kid wore his hair in his face and shot him a defiant sneer. "No way. It's against hotel rules."

"I'm a dick doing a job for the hotel."

"You're a dick?" the kid said, hiding a laugh.

"It's short for detective. Let me see it."

The kid stared at his clothes. Sometimes, looking like a cop had its advantages. The kid produced the stub from his pocket, and Valentine read the name printed across the top: *Renfo*. He stuck ten bucks in the kid's hand, then returned to the curb and waited for his rental to come up.

* * *

He waited until he was on the highway driving toward Garduno's before pulling out his cell phone and dialing Las Vegas information. A chatty female operator came on, and he asked for any listings in Clark County for Renfo. Within seconds she had found four. Two were businesses, the other two residential.

"The residential, please," he said.

She gave him the numbers and he memorized them, then called them while driving one-handed. Both were disconnected. He called information again, and this time got the two business listings. The first number led him to a long-haul trucking company and a friendly guy named Jack. The second number was answered by a middle-aged woman with a smoker's raspy voice. She was not nearly as friendly.

"Good morning, Renfo and Company," she said. "What can I do for you?"

"Hi," Valentine said. "I met Mr. Renfo this morning, and he gave me his business card. I'd like to talk to him about some work."

"You'd like to hire Renfo?" the women asked, sounding skeptical.

"That's right."

"What kind of engagement do you have in mind?"

The woman had a cutting edge to her voice, and Valentine felt himself feeling sorry for Renfo. Whatever he did for a living, she sure wasn't helping.

"Engagement?"

"Yeah, as in work. Are you hiring Renfo for a birthday party, a corporate event, a bar mitzvah, or what? How big is the group? How long do you want him to work? The standard questions, you know?"

She sounded ready to slam down the phone, and Valentine quickly improvised.

"It's my son's birthday party next Saturday. There will be about thirty children and ten adults. I'd like Renfo to work for half an hour."

"How old are the kids?" the woman asked.

"Ten- to twelve-year-olds."

"That's good to know. I'll tell Renfo to leave out the blue stuff."

"Blue stuff?"

"Yeah, the dirty jokes."

Renfo was a comedian? That didn't make sense, and he started wondering if this was another dead end.

"Some of them are actually pretty funny," the woman added.

"You don't say."

"Really, they are," the woman said. "Renfo's got one where he says, 'What's your favorite bird?' And Freddy, his dummy, says, 'A wood*pecker*.' And Renfo says, 'I bet you've always wanted one of those.' Ha, you get it?"

Valentine stared at the bluish bank of mountains rimming the horizon, thinking back to everything that had happened in the poker room that morning. Now he understood why Rufus had wanted a leather bag put over his head. It had muffled his voice, and made it impossible to tell if he was actually doing the talking. Dr. Robinson, aka Renfo, wasn't a doctor at all. He was a professional ventriloquist.

"Got it," he said.

Part III

Shoot the Pickle

41

Mabel Struck was about to leave for a late lunch when the phone rang. She'd spent the morning soothing the nerves of several panicked casino bosses, and had worked up an appetite. She looked at the phone, and saw that it was Tony's private line. Only a few people had the number, and she stared at the Caller ID. It was the boss himself.

"Grift Sense," she answered cheerfully.

"Is this a money-laundering operation?"

"There you are. How's sunny Las Vegas?"

"Fine. I saw something this morning that you would have really enjoyed."

"What was that?"

"I saw a ventriloquist turn a crowd of smart people into a bunch of dummies."

"A ventriloquist? I thought you were out there working."

"I am out here working," he said. "I'm on my way to a meeting with Bill Higgins. I called to see if Romero had sent the FBI's file on George Scalzo."

Mabel spun in her chair so she faced Tony's computer, and opened his e-mail account. Six new messages had arrived in the last twenty minutes, and she quickly

scrolled through them. The last was from Special Agent
Romero.

"Got it. Would you like me to read it while you
drive?"

"You're psychic," he said.

Mabel stuck the phone into the crook of her neck and
opened Romero's e-mail. The special agent had sent a
thank-you note, and she read the note first.

"Dear Ms. Struck: Thanks for your help last night.
When our agents knocked down the wall in the basement, they discovered the hidden electromagnets, plus a
large bag of cash. Our suspect has decided to change his
plea, and is cooperating with the prosecutor.

"Unfortunately, I cannot fulfill your request and provide you with the FBI's current case file on George
Scalzo, since the law does not allow me to share information regarding ongoing investigations. However, I did
remove from the file information regarding Scalzo's relationship with Chris DeMarco, and have pasted it into
the body of this e-mail. Feel free to contact me if I
can be of further assistance. Yours truly, Special Agent
Romero."

"You helped the FBI crack a case?" Valentine asked.

"Why, yes, I did," Mabel said.

"That's great. Now I can retire, and get out of this
racket."

"Listen to you! Are you ready to hear what Romero
sent?"

"Fire away."

Mabel scrolled down the e-mail. "Let's see. Special
Agent Romero included some background information
about George Scalzo. Would you like to hear that?"

"Why not? Mobsters are always good for a few
laughs."

"Okay. Scalzo was initiated into the New Jersey mob

at eighteen. By twenty-two, he had been involved in over a dozen crimes, including kidnapping, murder, loan-sharking, bookmaking, racketeering, fire-bombing, extortion, and aggravated assault with a deadly weapon. He'd been to state prison three times, and it didn't do him any good."

"What a charmer," Valentine said.

"Okay, here's the case file. It's broken down by date. On September 19, 1981, a prostitute named Danielle DeMarco and her blind four-year-old son, Chris, rented a house two blocks south of Washington Street in Newark, New Jersey, where George Scalzo lived. Living with Danielle was a black pimp named Jester (real name unknown)."

"Chris DeMarco's mother was a hooker?"

"That's what it says here. Two weeks later, Danielle DeMarco was arrested for rolling a john in a motel. Jester posted her bail, but left Chris alone at home. The boy left the house somehow, and made his way over to Washington Street. He ended up walking into a restaurant called Carmine's where a birthday party was taking place. Scalzo was there playing the piano, and talked Chris into sitting on the piano stool with him."

"Scalzo plays the piano? I sure hope he doesn't sing."

"You're hysterical. The next day, Scalzo turns Chris over to the police, and the boy is reunited with his mother. That night, while Danielle is working the streets, Jester decides to punish Chris for leaving the house. According to neighbors who listened through an open window, Jester beat him with a coat hanger, then burned his arms and chest with a cigarette."

The connection had gone quiet. Then she heard Tony cough, and continued.

"Word of the boy's abuse spread through the neighborhood, and the police were summoned the next morning. Danielle refused to open the front door, and said nothing was wrong. The police left to get a warrant. Not long after their departure, a town car containing four men pulled up in front of the house. The four men got out, and forced their way inside. They pulled Jester from bed and started to beat him up. When Danielle came to her pimp's aid, the men threw her down a flight of stairs."

"Nice guys."

"At twelve fifty-five that afternoon, Jester and Danielle were admitted to the emergency room of a local hospital. Every major bone in Jester's body was broken, and Danielle was suffering from a broken leg and a broken back. Two hours later, they were both pronounced dead."

"Jesus."

"The police went to Danielle's house but could not find Chris. Although scores of neighbors saw the men break in, none of the neighbors were willing to identify the four men for police."

"Sounds familiar."

"The next day, Scalzo contacts the police, and tells them that Chris had come to his house. When the boy is turned over to the police, he is wearing new clothes, and his cigarette burns have been treated by a doctor. The police turn him over to Health and Human Resources, who put him in a foster home. Four weeks later, George Scalzo's sister, Lydia, files papers to become Chris's legal guardian. Lydia tells friends in the neighborhood she is doing this for her brother, who never had children.

"Three months later, a judge in Newark bestows legal guardianship of Chris DeMarco to Lydia Scalzo, and the boy is transferred from his foster home to Lydia's house. Within a few days, he is living with his 'Uncle

George' next door. And . . . that's where the e-mail ends."

"Well, that explains a lot," he said.

Mabel saved the e-mail message, then turned away from the computer. "You need to be careful with this one, Tony."

"I'm always careful," he replied.

"I know that. But this isn't your ordinary hoodlum."

"It isn't?"

"No, it's a psychotic who had a woman killed, and stole her child."

"That's one way to look at it. I'll be doubly careful."

"Thank you."

"You're welcome. Here's my exit. Oh, by the way, lunch is on me today."

"Why, that's awfully nice of you," she said.

"You broke a case, you deserve it. Talk to you soon."

Mabel said good-bye and hung up the phone. Reading about George Scalzo getting custody of Chris DeMarco had an unsettling effect on her, and she realized she wasn't hungry anymore. Men could be such monsters when they wanted things. She decided to take a walk instead, and slipped on her shoes. It was a beautiful day, and she felt certain that a leisurely stroll around the neighborhood was just the thing to lift her spirits.

42

Gardunos served the best Mexican food in Las Vegas, with a terrific waitstaff and homemade dishes you couldn't find anywhere else. It was ten o'clock when Valentine slid into the booth across from Bill Higgins. The restaurant had just opened it doors, and they were its only customers. The look on Bill's face said he did not feel well.

"What's wrong?" Valentine asked.

"I've got some bad news this morning," his friend said.

"Concerning me?"

"Yes, concerning you."

Since getting into the consulting racket, Valentine had discovered that he wasn't doing his job if he wasn't regularly pissing someone off.

"I'm a big boy, I can take it," he replied.

Bill removed an envelope from his pocket, and handed it to him.

"It isn't pretty," Bill said.

A waiter delivered bowls of homemade chips and salsa, and Valentine stuffed a chip into his mouth. He'd tried to call Gerry several times during the ride over, and now nearly choked as he pulled a photograph of his son bound to a chair from the envelope. The lower half of Gerry's face was sheeted in blood, and there was a cornered look in his eyes, like he knew he'd reached the end of his rope. Paper-clipped to the photograph was a note that had been banged out on an old-fashioned typewriter.

Bill Higgins: There is a nonstop Delta flight to Tampa this afternoon at 5:25. Tell Tony Valentine to be on it, or he'll never see his son alive again.

He put the note down, and looked across the table at Bill.

"They delivered this to you?"

"A kid on a bike brought it to my office an hour ago," Bill said.

"It was nice of them to check out flight arrangements for me."

Bill drummed the table with his fingertips. Their waitress took that as a cue, and scurried over. Bill tried to wave her away, and a hurt look crossed her face. Valentine intervened and ordered the homemade guacamole, a house specialty. She smiled and disappeared through swinging doors into the kitchen.

Valentine stared at his friend's face. Bill was in a tough spot. The kidnappers had put Gerry's fate in Bill's hands. Bill continued to drum the table and the waitress reappeared. Valentine ordered two iced teas.

"You're going to have to order the whole menu if you keep that up," he said when she was gone.

"You're not making this any easier," Bill said.

"I'm not leaving town, if that's what you want to know," Valentine said.

"You're not?"

"No. I step on that plane, and they'll put a bullet in Gerry's head."

"How can you be sure?"

Valentine picked up the photograph and pointed at his son's face. "He's not wearing a mask. My guess is, neither are the guys who abducted him. Gerry saw their faces, which is as good as a death sentence."

"Who do you think is behind this?"

It was Valentine's turn to drum the table. Skip DeMarco's cheating, Jinky Harris's wanting to kill Gerry and his friends, and the strange things taking place at the World Poker Showdown were all connected, even if he didn't know exactly how. Their iced teas came, and he took a long swallow of his unsweetened drink.

"I have a good idea," he said.

"Then let's go to the police," Bill said.

Their booth looked onto the parking lot, and Valentine paused to stare at the dusty bumper of his own rental. "My son said he thought a cop was tailing them yesterday. If that's true, then the police are the last people we should contact."

Bill poured enough artificial sweetener into his tea to kill a horse. "Dirty cops or not, the police need to be involved. If they find out Gerry's been abducted and we didn't tell them, they'll haul us in. We need to do this by the book, Tony."

Valentine felt himself slowly exhale. The memory of Gerry's first car had popped into his head, and how Gerry had wrapped the vehicle around a telephone pole within forty-eight hours of owning it. It was always something, and he looked at Bill.

"Let's call Pete Longo," he said.

Twenty-five minutes later, Longo slipped into their booth at Gardunos. He wore old jeans and a polo shirt and hadn't shaved, and Valentine guessed it was his day off.

"How's your son doing?" Longo asked.

Valentine slipped the photograph of Gerry across the table. The detective's eyes grew wide, and he put down the chip dripping with salsa he was about to stuff into his mouth. He read the note accompanying the photo.

"When did you get this?" he asked Bill.

"Nine o'clock this morning."

Longo shifted his gaze to Valentine. "I walked your son out of the station house this morning at three A.M."

"I know," Valentine said. "He called and left me a voice mail."

Longo turned the photograph face down on the glistening table. The loss of weight had given his face gravity beyond his years, and he shook his head sadly. "I was talking to your son about Jinky Harris, and the problems I've been having nailing him. I told your son it's like my phones are being tapped."

"Maybe they are," Valentine said.

Longo picked up the chip he'd been meaning to eat. "That's why you asked me to come here, isn't it? You think I have a dirty cop in my department, and he'd find out we were meeting."

"That's right."

The salsa had made the chip soggy, and it split in half before it reached Longo's mouth, and landed with a plop on his place setting. He stared at it, then at them.

"Shit," the detective said.

Cops held grudges. It came with the job. You worked the streets long enough, and you ended up hating people. Longo had a grudge with Jinky Harris, and he made it clear he would break as many rules as necessary to help them find Gerry. It was a good start, and Valentine leaned across the table and dropped his voice.

"I once nabbed a gang of dice cheaters in Atlantic City. They took the casino's dice, and switched them in plain view for shaved dice. There was no subtlety. These guys had been around for a while, and I finally got one of them to open up. He told me it was all about distraction. Right before they did the switch, a drunk started arguing at a blackjack table, while a pretty girl started peeling off her clothes at the roulette table, while a couple staged a fight in the aisle. They were all part of the gang."

"Like a giant smoke screen," Longo said.

"Exactly," Valentine said. "This afternoon, I'm going to create a smoke screen, and distract everyone who I think had something to do with my son and his friends being abducted. Once that happens, I want to have a chat with Jinky Harris."

"By yourself?" Longo said skeptically.

"Yes."

"The guy has twenty guys on his staff, and a seven-foot-tall bodyguard."

Valentine glanced at Bill. "Think your agents can handle twenty guys?"

"Not a problem," Bill said.

Valentine looked back at Longo. "Anything else about Jinky we should know?"

"Yeah," the detective said. "The bodyguard fancies himself a karate expert. He fights in those tough-man competitions."

"What's his name?"

"He calls himself Finesse."

Valentine had never cared for fighters who gave themselves comic book names, and decided he could deal with Finesse. "There are two things I'm going to need from you, Pete."

"Name them," Longo said.

"First, I want you to pull any cops from the vicinity of Jinky's club when Bill's agents raid the place."

Longo looked at Bill. "I'll need you to coordinate the time of the raid with me."

"Done," Bill said.

Longo looked at Valentine. "No problem."

"Second, I'm going to need a SWAT team at my disposal," Valentine said. "Once I get Jinky to tell me where Gerry is being held, I want that team to rescue him."

"Consider it done," Longo said.

The three men shook hands, and the deal was struck.

Longo picked up the tab, then leaned forward on his elbows. His eyes swept the room the way only a cop's can before he spoke. "Since we're putting our cards on the table, I guess it's time for me to show mine. Tony, does the name Ray Callahan ring any bells?"

Valentine gave it some thought. "Not particularly."

"You busted him in Atlantic City fifteen years ago."

Valentine hated hearing that his mind was going, and struggled with the name some more. "I arrested a Raymond Callahan at Resorts International in 1991 for cold-decking a poker game where he was the dealer. The prosecutor let him cop a lesser charge, and he did probation. Same guy?"

"Same guy," Longo said. "Callahan's a dealer in the World Poker Showdown. He collapsed yesterday and was rushed to the hospital. The hospital ran a background check and his rap sheet popped up. How do you cold-deck a poker game?"

There were many ways to switch a deck of cards during a game of poker. Some involved wastepaper baskets, others, umbrellas and sports jackets with large pockets. But in the end, what made any deck switch fly was a pair of steady hands and nerves of steel. Raymond Callahan, as Valentine recalled, had an abundance of nerve.

"Practice," he said. "How can Callahan be a dealer at the World Poker Showdown when he has a criminal record?"

"I asked myself the same question, and decided to talk to my boss about it," Longo said. "Karl Jasper, the president of the WPS, didn't submit a list of names of their poker dealers to us. Those dealers are working without Sheriff's Cards."

By state law, employees of Las Vegas casinos could not work without Sheriff's Cards. Possessing one meant you'd been vetted, and had a clean record.

"How can that be possible?" Bill asked.

Longo's eyes again swept the room. His voice dropped an octave lower. "Jasper is claiming that this is a private event, and that his organization did the vetting."

"Your boss isn't buying that, is he?" Bill asked.

"My boss says he's going to put the screws to Jasper, but we're now into day four of the tournament, and so far, nothing has happened," Longo said. "I've seen him act this way before. He talks a big game, but doesn't do anything."

"Why?" Bill said.

"High jingo."

High jingo meant the sheriff was getting pressure from above not to interfere with the tournament, and Valentine wondered if it was coming from the mayor or even the governor. To them, the World Poker Showdown was a good thing, since it brought money and exposure to Las Vegas. They didn't see the harm a crooked tournament could cause, simply because it was easier to look the other way. He tossed his napkin onto the table and slipped out of the booth.

"I need to talk to Callahan," Valentine said. "Where is he?"

43

Valentine drove to the University Medical Center of Southern Nevada where Ray Callahan was a patient, and parked in the visitor parking lot. Bill had let him keep the photograph of Gerry, and he placed it on the steering wheel. For a long while he stared at his son's bloody face and the cornered look in his eyes. Saving his son's ass had become something of a specialty over the years, but each time he'd done it, it had been with the knowledge that one day he'd run out of luck and his son would take a hard fall. Closing his eyes, he prayed that this was not that day.

Inside the hospital he found a friendly receptionist who directed him to Callahan's room on the fourth floor. Callahan was in the intensive care wing, the cancer he'd been battling having come back with a vengeance. Valentine explained that he was doing an investigation for the Gaming Control Board, and asked if Callahan had had any recent visitors. The receptionist opened up the visitor logbook, and thumbed through its pages.

"Just his lawyer," she said.

Valentine wrote down the lawyer's name and put it into his wallet. He thanked the receptionist, and took the elevator to the fourth floor.

Of all the employees who worked in a casino, the

dealers were a casino's biggest concern. There were a lot of reasons for this. Dealers handled large sums of money at the tables, but rarely got to keep any of it. They tended to make scale, and relied on tips to pay their bills. And they usually gambled on the side.

Some dealers ended up resenting the casinos, and decided to pay them back. There were dozens of ways a dealer could do this, from using sleight-of-hand to rig a game, to collusion with outside agents, and sometimes even forming a conspiracy with other dealers. Whatever the method, the end result was almost always the same. The casinos lost their shirts.

The elevator parked on the fourth floor and he got out. A sign pointed the way toward ICU and he started walking. During the drive, his memory of Callahan had come back. Callahan had used a cold-deck machine to switch during a game in the casino's card room. A cold-deck machine was a black bag concealed behind the waist of the dealer's pants. Inside the bag was a metal clip that held a stacked deck. At the appropriate time, the deck in use would be dropped in the bag, and the stacked deck grabbed. The term *cold-deck* came from the fact that the switched deck was colder to the touch. As he recalled, Callahan had made the bag disappear during the bust, which had helped reduce his sentence.

Callahan's room was at the hallway's end. Valentine stuck his head in, and saw that Callahan was propped up in bed on oxygen, taking a nap. He walked into the room and stood by the bed. After a moment, Callahan's eyelids flickered open. A look of fear spread across the dealer's face.

"Did I die and go to hell?"

Valentine grinned. "You remember me, huh?"

"Of course I remember you. You nailed me in Atlantic City. That crummy partner of yours isn't with you, is he?"

Doyle Flanagan, Valentine's partner, had been the bad cop of the team, and liked to kick the chairs out from underneath any cheater they hauled in. Landing on your ass had a way of staying with you, and most cheaters never forgot the experience.

"He's downstairs in the lobby," Valentine said.

"Very funny. What do you want?"

"Can I sit down?"

"No."

Valentine got a chair anyway, and sat down beside Callahan's bed. There was a faraway look in Callahan's eyes, and he shifted his gaze to the view of distant mountains circling the pinkish horizon.

"Nice view," Valentine said.

"It's pollution."

"I busted you how many years ago?"

"Fifteen," Callahan said.

"And you've been doing business ever since."

The muscles in Callahan's neck tightened, and he continued to look away. "I haven't been cheating, if that's what you mean. What happened in Atlantic City was a one-time thing. I was down on my luck, and made a mistake. I paid my debt to society."

It sounded like a speech a lawyer had written for him. Valentine found himself staring at Callahan's hands, which rested above the sheets. The nails were manicured by decades spent riffle-shuffling cards and were polished by smooth felt tables. They were a card mechanic's hands, and Callahan guiltily pulled them beneath the covers.

"I want you to leave," Callahan said.

"Just answer one question for me."

"No."

"Why did you do it?"

"Cold-deck the game in Atlantic City? I needed the money."

"No, why did you cheat the World Poker Showdown, and signal the cards you were dealing to Skip DeMarco?"

Callahan's face clouded with anger. "I don't know what you're talking about."

"I think you do."

Callahan pulled himself up in his bed, and looked around for the call button, which was attached to a string and hung from the wall. The string was hanging behind the bed, out of Callahan's reach, and Valentine made no attempt to retrieve it for him. "Get out of here, or I'll start yelling my head off, and have you thrown out."

Valentine rose from his chair. He'd forgotten how much he enjoyed making creeps uncomfortable; it was one of the great perks that came with being a cop.

"I want you to think about something. You've beaten your cancer before, and you just might beat it again. If you do walk out of here, you'll be facing a murder rap. Is that how you want to spend the rest of your life, in jail?"

"A murder rap?"

"That's right."

"What the hell are you talking about?"

Valentine put the chair back against the wall, and went to the door. "It's been nice catching up with you. I'll tell my partner you said hello."

"Come back here," Callahan said angrily.

"You're not going to have me thrown out?"

"No, I want to hear about this."

Valentine got the chair back, and returned to Callahan's bedside. This time when he rested his elbows on the metal arm, Callahan did not look away.

"It's like this," Valentine said. "George Scalzo stole a poker scam from a guy named Jack Donovan. Jack was dying at the time, and Scalzo had Jack murdered so he wouldn't squeal. Only, Jack did squeal."

Taking out his wallet, Valentine removed the playing card that Jack had given Gerry, and showed it to Callahan. "This is our evidence. George Scalzo is going down, and so is his nephew. The question is, do you want to go down with them?"

"Can I see it?"

He let Callahan hold the playing card. Callahan stared at the card for a few moments, then handed it back.

"Is that your evidence?" he asked.

"That's part of it," Valentine said. "Do you want to go down the river with them or not?"

"Tell me something first," Callahan said.

"What's that?"

"This guy Donovan, what was he dying of?"

The hairs on the back of Valentine's neck went straight up. He wanted to ask Callahan what that had to do with anything, but sensed that he'd blow whatever rapport he'd established.

"Cancer."   •

"You said he was terminal."

"Yes," Valentine said.

Valentine saw Callahan's eyes shift, and stare at the playing card that Valentine held in his hand. There was a connection here that he wasn't getting, and he didn't know how to press Callahan without revealing that he didn't know how the scam worked. That was the problem when working with too little information. Sometimes, you got yourself painted in a corner and couldn't get out.

"Afraid I can't help you," Callahan said.

Valentine stood up. "We're talking about life in prison, Ray."

Callahan's face was vacant. He'd seen through the ruse, and wasn't buying it.

"Don't let the door bang you in the ass on the way out," he said.

44

If there was a dead time on the congested highways of Las Vegas, it was midday, when everyone was at work. Valentine made it back to Celebrity in fifteen minutes, and walked through the hotel's front doors with the picture of Gerry clutched in his hand. His son was being held somewhere in Las Vegas, and he wasn't going to leave until he rescued him. Upstairs in his suite he found Rufus Steele sitting on the couch, counting the money he'd won that morning.

"Hey pardner, long time no see."

The money was stacked in piles on the floor. Real gamblers did not use checks, and nearly all of Rufus's winnings were in hundred dollar bills, most of them brand-new. Over the years he'd heard gamblers call money "units," and learned that it wasn't the value that was important, just the level of the action that the units allowed the gambler to play.

"I need your help," Valentine said.

Rufus was wrapping the stacks with rubber bands, and looked up. "Well, it's about time I returned you a favor. Name it."

"I need for you to stage one of your scams later today, and get as many gamblers as you can involved. I'll make sure Gloria Curtis is there. I'm going to alert the World

Poker Showdown people to be there, and I want you to say some things about the tournament which aren't particularly flattering."

"Sounds right up my alley," Rufus said. "What exactly am I going to say?"

"You're going to announce that you've learned that the dealers in the WPS haven't been cleared by the Metro Las Vegas Police Department, which makes them the only dealers in the state of Las Vegas who haven't. You're also going to say that you're aware that one of these dealers has a criminal record for cheating."

The fun drained from Rufus's face and he gazed at Valentine with renewed respect. "Sounds like your investigation is moving right along."

"It sure is."

"The World Poker Showdown is behind this whole thing, aren't they?"

"Let's just say there's a link which I need to get to the bottom of."

"Just so I don't get sued for slander, who's this dirty dealer?"

"His name is Ray Callahan," Valentine said, "and I busted him in Atlantic City for cold-decking a game fifteen years ago. He's got a record."

Rufus glanced at the piles of money at his feet. Just a few short hours ago, he'd been poorer than a church mouse, but that, as gamblers liked to say, was ancient history. Still looking at the money, he said, "Tony, your timing is impeccable. Right after you left, I got into a verbal altercation with the Greek and his friends. Seems they thought about my X-ray vision stunt, and didn't like the fact I had a bag over my head."

"You think they knew you were using a ventriloquist?" Valentine asked.

Rufus did a double take. The look on his face was

priceless, and Valentine wished he had a camera with some film in it. The old cowboy coughed into his hand.

"Who the hell told you that?"

"Nobody. I figured it out myself."

"You're pretty damn smart for a cop."

Valentine had heard that for most of his adult life. Cops were supposed to be dumb. When people ran into a smart one, it tended to surprise them.

"Thanks a lot."

"You're welcome," Rufus said. "Like I was saying, I decided to give the Greek and his cronies a chance to win their money back, and bet them I could beat a race-horse in the hundred-yard dash. They were skeptical at first, but when I told them that they could pick the horse *and* the jockey *and* the field to run on, they took me up on the wager."

"You're going to do what?"

"You heard me. I was the state champion runner in high school, and still can burn rubber when I have to."

Rufus was seventy years old if he was a day, and he still chain-smoked cigarettes, drank whiskey, and played cards all night long. He did all the things you weren't supposed to do when you got old, and Valentine couldn't envision him beating a ten-year-old kid in a footrace, much less a racehorse.

"You're serious about this?"

Rufus took out a pack of smokes and banged one out. "Dead serious."

"When's this going to happen?"

"Around nine o'clock tonight. The Greek is keeping the field location a secret. He'll call me right before, and we'll meet there and run the race."

"Where's he getting the horse from?"

"Wayne Newton has a bunch of horses out at his place. I hear he's going to pull the fastest one."

"How much are you betting?"

The old cowboy indicated the stacks of money lying on the floor, then spread his arms as wide as possible.

"You're betting *all* of it?"

"Yes, sir. That DeMarco kid says he'll play me for a cool million bucks. Well, right now I've got about half that much. It's time to shoot the pickle."

"Shoot the what?"

"The pickle. It means to go for it."

Had the situation been different—and Gerry's life hadn't been hanging in the balance—Valentine would have tried to talk some sense into Rufus. The Greek and his cronies weren't going to let the same dog bite them twice, and would make sure that the racehorse Rufus ran against was lightning fast. But every man had his poison, and he guessed Rufus's was making outlandish wagers.

"What time do you want me downstairs, stirring up the pot?" Rufus asked.

Valentine checked the time. It was twelve forty. Something had been nagging at him, and he realized what it was. His lunch date with Gloria Curtis had been for twelve thirty, and he said, "I'll call you once I've got everything in place."

Rufus picked up a stack of hundreds lying at his feet. He licked his thumb, and began counting them. "I'll be waiting," he said.

Valentine found Gloria sitting by herself at a corner table in the lobby restaurant, and she shot him a dagger as he pulled up a chair. Relationships between men and women were defined by how they fought, and he guessed theirs was about to be tested.

"I'm sorry I'm so late," he said. "Something came up, and I had to deal with it."

Gloria's cell phone was sitting on the table beside her plate. She fixed him reproachfully with her green eyes. "Did you forget how to dial a phone?"

He swallowed hard. The polite thing would have been to call, and tell her he was running late and not to wait for him. But he hadn't done that. He considered taking out the photograph of his bloodied son and showing it to her, only that was what a kid in the sixth grade would do, beg forgiveness and ask for sympathy at the same time. He needed to take his medicine like a man, and said, "No, I just forgot about our lunch date. It was wrong of me, and it won't happen again. Scout's honor."

The look on her face said she wasn't buying it. She looked incredibly sexy when she was angry, and he guessed if he told her so, she'd slap him right across the face.

"Look, Tony," she said, "you're my life support system right now. Every story I've gotten in the past two days has come from you. Understand?"

He wasn't sure that he did, but nodded anyway.

"My job and my career are on the line," she went on. "I'm depending upon you to come through. On top of that, I've decided that I really like you."

"I like you, too," he said.

"I don't think that's such a good idea. I can't turn into your shadow, or be a puppy dog that waits for its master to come along and toss it a bone when he feels like it. I've got too much pride for that."

He stared down at the white tablecloth. If anything good had come out of this job, it was meeting her, and now that was going up in flames. He looked up into her eyes.

"Let me make it up to you."

"I don't think that's possible."

"Let me try, anyway," he said. "I feel very bad about

this. I don't mean to lead you and Zack around. I'm not that kind of guy."

"You're not?"

"No. I just . . ."

"Suffer from short-term memory loss?"

No matter how old he got, Valentine was never going to use his age as an excuse for bad behavior.

"I get preoccupied sometimes," he explained. "It drove my late wife crazy. She used to make me write appointments on my hand so I wouldn't forget them."

"On your hand? I used to do that as a little kid."

"Hey," he said, "it works."

Gloria leaned forward, and gave him another hard look. Her own look was neither friendly nor unfriendly, and he sensed that she wanted to believe him, and get things back on track, only she wasn't going to let him wound her a second time.

"All right," she said, "I'll give you another chance."

Valentine took his hand, and placed it upon her hand resting on the table.

"I won't let you down," he said.

45

Gerry Valentine had decided that people who couldn't fit in anywhere else, fit in just fine in Las Vegas.

Take the four goons working for Jinky who'd been beating the daylights out of Frank, Vinny, and Nunzie for the past two hours. As enforcers went they were laughable, and did not know the first thing about getting someone to talk. Rule number one was that you never used your bare fists to hit someone, because knuckles usually broke before jaws did. Rule number two was that if you started out by hitting someone hard, they'd never cooperate with you. But these guys had never been to that school, and after two hours of abuse, two of them had broken hands, and no one had spoken a word.

"How's your face feel?" Gerry asked Vinny, who'd been dragged in his chair to where Gerry was sitting, his face a bloody pulp.

"My nose is broken, my teeth are broken, and I can't see out of my left eye," Vinny said through horribly swollen lips. "But you know me, I can't complain."

Gerry forced himself to smile. Even in the worst of times, you had to find reasons to smile. He looked across the warehouse at Nunzie and Frank. The goons were beating up Nunzie, and making Frank watch. They still were asking the same question—"Which one of you shot Russ Watson in the parking lot?"—and neither Nunzie nor Frank had uttered a peep in response.

"You think Nunzie will crack?" Gerry whispered.

Vinny shook his head. "Not the Nunz. He's solid as a rock."

"Glad to hear it."

"So, what's the plan?" Vinny asked.

Gerry stared at the steel door across from where they sat. Sunlight seeped through the bottom and had formed a small puddle of light. Twenty minutes ago, Jinky Harris had driven his wheelchair through that door, and moments later they'd heard a car drive away. Not having Jinky around had bothered Gerry. He could talk with Jinky, maybe strike some kind of bargain. He couldn't do that with the guys he'd left behind.

"What plan?" he asked Vinny.

"The plan to get us out of this rat hole," Vinny said.

"I don't have a plan."

"So, come up with one. You were always the man with the plan when it came to disaster relief."

"I was?"

"Yeah. Remember the time I owed that money to those gangsters in Atlantic City? You came up with the best plan."

"I did?"

Vinny spit something onto the floor, and Gerry watched it roll past his feet and stop. It was small and white. A tooth.

"Yeah," Vinny said, making himself talk so he wouldn't be scared. "I borrowed five grand from two gumbas who ran the Italian Men's Social Club on Fairmont Avenue. I was supposed to pay them back on Wednesday at noon, only I wasn't going to have the money to pay them back until Saturday. You remembering this?"

Gerry was watching two of the goons take turns whacking Nunzie in the kisser. Nunzie had a neck like a weight lifter and his head hardly moved from the blows.

"A little," he said.

"So, I called you up, and you came up with the best plan."

"Refresh my memory."

"You knew two squares who worked at a bank," Vinny said. "They had short hair and wore blue suits and neckties. You called them, and talked them into helping me out. They agreed to meet me on Wednesday at a few minutes before noon in the parking lot of Harold's House of Pancakes where I was supposed to be paying off the gumbas."

One of the goons connected with a solid right cross. Nunzie let out a soft grunt, the sound being amplified in the warehouse's high ceiling.

"You left a part out," Gerry said.

"I did?"

"Yeah. I also told you to buy the bank guys attaché cases and dark sunglasses to wear so they'd look like FBI agents."

"Oh yeah, that's right," Vinny said. "It was a nice touch."

"Thanks."

"So, I pull into Harold's at a minute before noon on Wednesday, and the gumbas are sitting there in their Caddy, waiting for me. I hop out of my car holding a brown paper bag stuffed with crumpled newspaper—"

"I think that was my idea, too."

"It was, and as I'm crossing the parking lot, the two bank guys jump out of their car holding their attaché cases. They stopped me, pulled out their wallets, and shoved them in my face. I never understood that part."

"They were supposed to be showing you their badges," Gerry explained. "You know, like they were FBI agents."

Vinny looked stunned. "So that was what it was about. Well, they hustled me across the parking lot, shoved me into their car, and we drove away. I was in the backseat with the paper bag in my lap, and saw the gumbas standing in the parking lot by their Caddy with these looks on their face. It was fucking priceless."

"Did you give them their money?"

"Oh yeah," Vinny said. "On Saturday I went to the club and paid them off. They took me aside and said, 'We saw what happened. You took it like a man.'"

"You made two new friends."

"That's right. So, come up with a plan like that."

Gerry stared at the ceiling. Bound to a chair in a warehouse in the middle of the desert and Vinny was telling him to come up with a plan to let them escape. If he had that kind of power, he wouldn't have gotten himself in this situation to begin with.

"Let me think about it."

"Hey," Vinny said, "we've got all day."

The sound of a man screaming snapped their heads. Gerry stared across the warehouse at one of the goons who'd been punishing Nunzie. He was clutching his hand and dancing around in agony. Nunzie, his face swollen and distorted, was laughing at him. Frank was laughing as well. Three down, one to go, Gerry thought.

"We need to keep stalling these guys," Gerry said.

"That's your plan?" Vinny asked.

"Yeah. My guess is, my old man has the cavalry looking for us. If we keep stalling and don't tell them what they want to know, they won't kill us right away."

Vinny spit some bloody mucus on the floor. His eyes had been bulging out of his head, his heart racing out of control, and now, finally, he was beginning to look normal.

"If we get out of this alive, you've got to explain how it works between you and your old man."

"How what works?"

"How you manage to get along, but not always like each other."

That was a good question, and one that Gerry wasn't sure he knew the answer to. He and his old man had always been civil to each other. Over the years, that civility had turned into tolerance, and now it was bordering on something that felt like what a father and son were supposed to feel toward each other. But it sure hadn't started out that way.

The guy who'd broken his hand came over to where Gerry and Vinny were sitting. The look on his face said he'd had enough screwing around, and wanted a straight answer out of one of them.

"You assholes going to tell us which one of you killed Russ?" he asked.

"You want to know who killed Russ?" Vinny replied.

"Yeah," he said.

"Russ died of a broken heart," Vinny said. "He couldn't stand being in love with Jinky, and not having his love returned. So Russ shot himself."

There was only so much nonsense a person could take, and Gerry thought the mutt was going to shoot Vinny right there. Instead, he walked to the center of the warehouse, and took out a cell phone. He made a call, and spoke to someone in a hushed voice while glaring at them. Hanging up, he turned to his partners and called out in a loud voice.

"They're bringing over the flamethrower," he said.

46

At exactly two o'clock in the afternoon, Gloria Curtis appeared in the lobby of Celebrity's hotel with her cameraman. She wore a white blouse and a black suit with a diamond broach on the lapel that made her look like a million bucks. Valentine stood near the lobby phone booth, watching. She saw him as she passed, and winked.

Gloria walked over to the doors leading to the World Poker Showdown, and stood a few yards away from the pair of stern-faced security guards blocking the entrance. Zack's camera had a light, and it basked Gloria in its artificial glow. Her presence immediately drew a crowd of curious passersby coming out of the casino.

"Good afternoon. This is Gloria Curtis reporting from the World Poker Showdown in Las Vegas. Today is day four of the tournament, and folks, if you don't mind my saying so, we've got a couple of bombshells for you."

Valentine saw three men in tailored suits standing on the far side of the lobby. The man in the middle appeared to be in charge, and had dyed black hair, padded shoulders, and teeth so artificially white they appeared to glow. Valentine guessed this was Karl Jasper, president of the WPS. He had called Jasper's room ten minutes ago, and left an anonymous message to be in the lobby at two if Jasper knew what was good for him.

"But first, a rundown on today's tournament," Gloria said, her eyes focused on the camera. "Skip DeMarco, the blind poker phenom from New Jersey, is still in first place, and has accumulated four million dollars in chips. In second place with two million dollars is last year's winner, Gene Mydlowski. The rest of the pack is far, far behind.

"But the real story is not the action taking place behind these doors. The *real* story comes from Rufus Steele, the legendary poker player who lost in the first round, and claims he was cheated. Rufus has told me that he's learned from the Metro Las Vegas Police Department that a dealer who was working the tournament is a known cheater, and was prosecuted in New Jersey for cold-decking a poker game. For those of our viewers who don't know what cold-decking a poker game means, we're going to show you a clip of this cheating move in action."

Gloria went silent and lowered her mike. Mabel had e-mailed Gloria a surveillance tape of a poker dealer cold-decking a game, which Zack would later edit into the segment. After ten seconds had passed, Gloria brought the mike up to her face.

"Rufus Steele has also told me that the dealers being used in this tournament are not from this casino, and in fact have not been cleared by the Las Vegas sheriff's department to deal these games. That's the law here in Las Vegas, and the folks running the World Poker Showdown are breaking it."

Valentine was watching Jasper, and saw the president of the WPS ball his hands into fists while his face turned the color of a fire truck. Jasper was standing next to a large bird cage, and seemed oblivious to the yellow-headed parrot flapping its wings and screeching at him.

"Now, let's talk to Rufus Steele, the man who broke this story," Gloria said. "Here he comes right now."

Zack turned and pointed his camera at the elevator banks. Rufus had stepped out of a car a few moments before, and was waiting to make his entrance. He wore a fluffy white hotel bathrobe, white socks and sneakers, and his Stetson. As he crossed the lobby, he began punching the air like a prizefighter. Many in the crowd applauded, and Rufus waved to them good-naturedly, then sidled up beside Gloria.

"Rufus, it's good to see you again," Gloria said.

"The pleasure's mine, Miss Curtis," he said.

"During the first day of the tournament, you claimed you'd been cheated by a player. Now, you're claiming the whole tournament is cheating."

"That's right."

"Would you please explain for the folks at home."

"This tournament stinks like a three-day-old fish left out in the sun," Rufus said, a smile plastered across his leathery face. "The dealers haven't been checked out. One dealer actually got arrested for switching decks in Atlantic City a few years ago. That's like having a bank robber working as a teller. The people running the World Poker Showdown have some explaining to do."

Valentine continued to stare at Karl Jasper. If there was ever a good time for Jasper to step forward and defend his tournament, this was it. Only Jasper wasn't having any part of the discussion and looked genuinely scared.

"Well, Rufus, I suppose our viewers would like you to explain the unique getup you have on," Gloria said. "Are you becoming a boxer?"

"Just getting ready for my race tonight," Rufus said.

"Your race?"

"Yes. As you know, I'm going to play Skip DeMarco in a heads-up poker game for one million dollars. In order to raise the cash, I've agreed to run a footrace against a racehorse, winner-take-all."

"A real racehorse?" Gloria said, her eyes widening.

Rufus put on his serious face, and nodded. "Yes, ma'am. My sources have told me that I'll be up against a champion, no less. The horse I'll be running against is being loaned out from Wayne Newton, who has a number of prize horses on his farm. This one's a thoroughbred, and is being used for stud."

"And the horse is a champion?"

"I believe it ran in the Kentucky Derby a few years ago, and is still competitive."

"How much are you betting on yourself to win?"

"Five hundred thousand dollars," Rufus said with a toothy smile.

"How long will the race be?"

"We'll be competing in the one-hundred-yard dash."

"Rufus, I don't mean to be disrespectful, but don't you think you've bitten off more than you can chew?" Gloria asked, her tone one of genuine concern. "There isn't an athlete in the world who can outrun a racehorse."

"I can," he said with a positive air, "and I *will*."

Before Gloria could pose another question, Rufus undid the knot in his bathrobe, then pulled off the garment and let it drop to the floor. He was wearing a white T-shirt and a pair of black boxing trunks and had the physique of a telephone pole. He began to do jumping jacks for the camera, and the crowd, which had swelled to over a hundred people, cheered him on. If people in Las Vegas loved anything, it was an underdog, and a chant quickly went up.

"Rufus! Rufus! Rufus!"

"I want you folks to all come out and see me tonight," Rufus said, his face red from exertion. "You too, Miss Curtis."

Gloria was holding the mike by her side, and doing all she could not to burst into laughter. "Trust me, I'll be there," she said.

"Rufus! Rufus! Rufus!"

"Remember, folks," Rufus said, still doing his jumping jacks. "Roses are red, violets are blue. Horses that lose to cowboys are turned into glue."

"Rufus! Rufus! Rufus!"

Valentine stared across the lobby at Jasper by the birdcage. The president of the WPS had company. George Scalzo was standing beside him, and looked ready to kill Rufus with his bare hands. Valentine wondered how it felt to rig a poker tournament so his nephew could win, only to have all the glory stolen by a sly old fox.

Valentine suddenly had an idea, and elbowed his way through the crowd. It was illegal for anyone who worked in a casino to be in the company of gangsters, and he assumed the same was true for presidents of poker tournaments. He got up behind Zack, and whispered in the cameraman's ear. Zack nodded, and pointed his camera at Jasper and Scalzo on the other side of the lobby.

"Got them," Zack said.

47

At two thirty Valentine was on the road and driving to his rendezvous with Bill Higgins. He'd called Bill before leaving Celebrity, and told him how he'd caught Jasper and Scalzo together on tape.

"That's a home run," Bill said.

Valentine certainly thought so. He had everything he needed to put the screws to Jasper. Las Vegas did not let casino people fraternize with mob guys, and Jasper would be run out of town on a rail, and the tournament shut down. The World Poker Showdown was as crooked as a carnival, and needed to be exposed.

Fifteen minutes later, he pulled into the parking lot of a McDonald's on the north side of town and found Bill parked beside the kid's play area. He got out of his rental, and hopped into Bill's unmarked car.

"I hear you really shook them up at the WPS," Bill said.

Valentine fastened his seat belt. "Good news travels fast, huh?"

"Jasper is screaming his head off, calling everyone under the sun."

"Let him scream all he wants," Valentine said. "He broke the law."

Bill flipped open his cell phone, and called one of his

agents. While Valentine had been setting the WPS's house on fire, Bill had marshaled three dozen of his best field agents and put them inside Jinky Harris's strip joint. When Bill gave them the word, the agents would raid the club under the pretense of looking for gambling activity. That would give Valentine time to find Jinky, and persuade him to reveal where Gerry and his friends were being held hostage.

"I need a gun," Valentine said.

Bill pointed at the glove compartment. Valentine popped it open, and took out a Sig Sauer. "You remembered," he said, slipping it into his jacket pocket.

"It's the gun of choice of old farts," Bill said.

"Speaking of old farts, I need to find a walking cane."

"What for?"

"It goes good with my gray hair," Valentine said.

Bill drove to Naked City. Naked City sold sex in the private VIP rooms of strip clubs, in massage parlors, and behind closed doors of dirty bookstores. The only place you couldn't find sex in Naked City was on the streets. Bill pulled up in front of a medical supply store called ABC Medical and Valentine hopped out.

Five minutes later, Valentine emerged from the store walking with a burnished wood walking stick. He'd also purchased a pair of dark sunglasses, and a white captain's fishing hat. As he slid into the passenger seat, Bill stared at him.

"You bought the hat and glasses in there?"

"I bought them from the guy behind the counter," Valentine said.

"How much?"

"Thirty bucks."

"You got hosed."

As Bill pulled out of the lot, Valentine adjusted his hat and glasses. The guy behind the counter had worn the hat with the sides pulled down, like Gilligan on the old TV show. It had a comical effect, and he tried it, then appraised himself in the reflection of his window. He looked like the captain of a shuffleboard team. Perfect.

Bill drove several blocks, then turned down the street to Jinky's club. The Sugar Shack was at the very end of the street. The club was doing brisk business, with several black stretch limousines parked by the curb.

"You sure you're up for this?" Bill asked.

"Sure, I'm sure," Valentine said.

Bill looked at his watch. "The raid will take place in exactly five minutes."

Valentine didn't need to look at his watch. He knew how long five minutes was, and whacked the burnished walking stick against the palm of his hand.

The Sugar Shack's admission fee was fifteen bucks. Valentine asked for a senior discount and thought the cashier was going to physically throw him out the door. He paid up, got his hand stamped, and ventured inside.

The club was a sprawling, multilevel room filled with pulsating strobe lights, blaring disco music, and exposed female flesh. There were three stages, just like at Barnum & Bailey's circus, and they were filled with naked women doing exotic dances and swinging on brass poles. He guessed the crowd of guys watching them to number eighty, which meant almost half of them were Bill's agents. He found an empty spot at the bar and ordered a club soda.

"Seven bucks," the bartender said, serving him the drink.

Valentine slid a twenty his way. "Tell Jinky his appointment is here."

The bartender gave him the hairy eyeball. "Who are you?"

"George Scalzo's brother, Louie."

The bartender walked down to the end of the bar and disappeared through a beaded curtain. Valentine followed him, practicing his limp. The short time he'd been living in Florida had convinced him that older people were invisible, and were therefore entitled to go wherever they pleased. He passed through the beaded curtain without anyone saying anything, and entered a narrow hallway illuminated by a red bulb hanging from the ceiling. He spied the bartender at the hallway's end. The bartender rapped three times on a blue door, then spotted Valentine.

"Hey mister, you're not supposed to be back here."

"I thought you told me to follow you," Valentine said, shuffling toward him.

"I didn't say no such thing."

"You sure?"

"Positive. You need to go back inside."

Valentine caught up to him, and pretended to be breathing heavily. He put his free hand on the bartender's shoulder and took several deep breaths.

"Sorry, son. My hearing's going. Old age ain't for sissies."

The blue door opened, and a seven-foot-tall black guy emerged. Valentine guessed this was Finesse, the guy with designs on being a professional fighter. Finesse looked like he'd been lifting weights, his pectoral muscles bulging through his turtleneck sweater. He glared down at the tops of their heads.

"Who's this guy?" Finesse asked the bartender.

"Permit me to introduce myself," Valentine said, touching the brim of his hat. "Louis Scalzo, also known as Louie the Lip. I believe you're expecting me."

"He's George Scalzo's brother," the bartender explained.

Finesse scratched his chin like a great thinker. "George Scalzo's brother? How come I never heard of you?"

Valentine leaned on his cane with both hands and looked up into the giant's face.

"Your boss has," he said.

Finesse motioned him inside and shut the door. Jinky's office had a large desk, several plush leather chairs, and several ugly paintings hanging on the walls. Next to the desk was a trestle tray loaded with food, and Valentine eyed the chicken chow mein and barbecue spare ribs.

"You guys throwing a party?" Valentine asked.

Finesse put his finger to his lips and shushed him. Jinky was at his desk, talking on the phone while gnawing on a spare rib. He had a napkin tucked into his collar, yet had managed to smear sauce all over his face. Hanging up, he stared at his bodyguard.

"Who's this clown?" Jinky asked.

"Your appointment," Finesse said.

"I don't have an appointment," Jinky said.

"You don't?"

"No. Get rid of him."

Valentine had edged up beside Finesse. Holding his walking stick by its center, he whacked Finesse in the kneecap with the round handle. It made a clean sound against the bone, and Finesse's mouth opened in a perfect O. Valentine brought the stick straight up, and caught him on the tip of the nose. A torrent of blood spurted across the desk, and Finesse went down clutching his face with both hands.

There was only so much threat in a walking stick, and Valentine dropped it on the floor, then drew the Sig Sauer from behind his belt, and aimed it a few feet above

Jinky's head. Jinky did not seem terribly concerned, and continued eating.

"You shouldn't have done that," Jinky said.

Valentine squeezed the trigger. The bullet hit the frame of the painting hanging behind Jinky, ruining it. Jinky's napkin slowly fell from his collar.

"You're crazy, mister."

Taking the snapshot of his bloodied son from his pocket, Valentine dropped it on Jinky's desk, then aimed the gun at an imaginary bull's eye on Jinky's forehead.

"You have something of mine," Valentine said, "and I want it back."

"I don't know what you're talking about," Jinky said.

Valentine picked up the walking stick from the floor. He was prepared to beat the information out of Jinky if he had to. Jinky looked at him defiantly.

"Hit me all you want," Jinky said. "It won't get you anywhere."

Valentine sensed Jinky wasn't the type to squeal. He patted Jinky down, then made him go down the hallway in his electric wheelchair and through the beaded curtain into the club. The raid was in progress, with club employees and strippers lined up against one wall, the scared-out-of-their-wits patrons on the other. Valentine pulled a Gaming Control Board agent aside, and asked him where Bill Higgins was.

"By the VIP rooms," the agent replied. "I think he found the mother lode."

"What do you mean?"

"They're running a gambling den," the agent said.

Next to murder, there was no worse crime in Las Vegas than running an illegal casino, and Valentine tapped Jinky's chair with his walking stick.

"You're going down," Valentine told him.

Valentine made Jinky lead him to the VIP rooms. A swarm of agents was standing by a door marked PRIVATE and parted as the two men entered. The room had plush carpeting and subdued lighting, with a bar covering one wall, and four blackjack tables, a roulette table, and a craps table in the room's center. Bill was standing by one of the blackjack tables and had pulled several decks of playing cards out of the shoe. He looked up as they entered.

"You crummy piece of shit," Bill said to Jinky. "You're running a bust-out joint!"

Jinky sunk low in his chair. "I don't know what you're talking about,"

"This shoe is short twenty high-valued cards," Bill said, throwing down a handful of cards in disgust. "You were cheating the players."

"I swear to God, it must have been one of the dealers," Jinky said.

Bill approached Jinky with a look of rage distorting his face. It was bad enough that Jinky had been running an illegal casino in his own club, but it was worse that he'd been running a casino that cheated. Las Vegas had spent twenty-five years trying to convince people it was a safe place to gamble, and the stain from this would hurt every casino in town, and make Bill Higgins look bad. Bill put his hands on Jinky's shoulders and shook him.

"You're lying," Bill said.

"I swear on my mother's grave, I'm not," Jinky said. "We just ran the casino to keep the patrons happy. I didn't know there was cheating going on."

Valentine found himself staring at the craps table. It was shaped like a tub, and reminded him of a table he'd seen during a raid of an illegal casino in Atlantic City years ago. That table had been manufactured by a crooked gambling supply house out of Miami. Crossing the room, he went to where the stickman stood at the table, and felt around the polished wood. His fingers found an indentation and he tapped it, and heard a hollow sound.

"Hey, Bill," he called across the room.

Bill turned his head. "What?"

"Look at this."

Valentine pressed the indentation and a hidden compartment in the table popped open, revealing a small shelf containing six pairs of dice. He removed a pair and threw them on the table. They came up a two, or snake eyes. A loser.

"They're loaded," Valentine called out.

Bill turned, and smacked Jinky in the face with the palm of his hand.

"That was for your mother," Bill said.

48

Jinky Harris wouldn't talk.

Bill had hauled Jinky into one of the VIP rooms, and was giving him the third degree. There were only so many things Bill Higgins could do to make Jinky talk, and none of them were working. Being a law enforcement officer, Bill had to follow the rules, even when someone's life was at stake. It was one of the job's great drawbacks.

Being retired, Valentine didn't have to follow the rules, and he went back to Jinky's office and retrieved his walking stick from the floor. Finesse was sitting on the couch and nursing a large purple welt on the bridge of his nose. Valentine removed the photograph of Gerry from his pocket, and tossed it on the coffee table. Then he pointed at it.

"That's my son. Know where he is?"

Finesse looked at him blankly. Valentine was sure he knew something, and raised the stick like he was going to take his head off. The giant cowered in fear.

"I don't know anything!"

"You're a sorry excuse for a bodyguard, you know that?"

Finesse didn't take the bait.

"I just do as I'm told."

Valentine got behind Jinky's desk and started looking for a scrap of paper with an address or some other clue that would lead him to Gerry. The blotter was splattered with drops of blood, as was the phone receiver. He stared at the giant.

"You made a phone call, didn't you?"

Finesse did not reply. Valentine whacked the cane against his palm.

"I'm prepared to beat it out of you, buddy."

Finesse jumped off the couch and bolted out the door. He was dragging his bad knee but still moved pretty fast. Valentine followed him down the hall, and saw Finesse raise his arms over his head as he entered the strip club. He was going to let himself be arrested, rather than let Valentine work him over.

Valentine returned to Jinky's office and slammed the door behind him. In anger he raised the cane and smashed a framed photograph of Jinky with a naked stripper hanging on the wall. He had blown it. If he'd handled Finesse right, he could have made him talk, instead of letting his temper take over.

He checked Jinky's desk a second time, just to be sure he hadn't missed anything. He picked up the phone, and hit the redial button. He got a frantic busy signal and let out a curse. He decided to go back to the club, and see if Bill had gotten Jinky to open up. Gerry's photograph was lying on the coffee table. As he picked it up, he noticed something he hadn't seen before. A red smudge on Gerry's right cheek.

It was too bright to be blood. On Jinky's desk was a magnifying glass used for reading. Valentine picked up the magnifying glass, and examined the smudge.

It was a woman's lipstick. A kiss.

*   *   *

Now he had a clue, only he didn't know what it
meant. He went to the minibar behind Jinky's desk and
stole a Diet Coke. He always thought better with caffeine rushing through his bloodstream, and he sucked it
down while staring at the photograph. Gerry had called
him right after he'd been released from the police station, and said he was going straight to the motel. If
Valentine remembered correctly, the motel's name was
the Casablanca. On a hunch he got the motel's phone
number from information, and called it.

"Haven't seen your son since yesterday," the manager
said after Valentine identified himself.

"He didn't come around early this morning with his
friends?"

"Nope."

"Mind answering a question for me?"

"Go ahead," the manager said.

"How far are you from the Metro Las Vegas police
station?"

"Two point three miles."

"Thanks. I really appreciate it."

Valentine hung up. Gerry and his friends had never
reached their motel. Chances were, they'd been nabbed
right as they'd left the police station. A pretty girl had
talked them into driving her someplace, and given Gerry
a kiss for his trouble. His son had always been a sucker
for a pretty face.

He finished his soda still looking at his son's face. Pete
Longo had practically admitted that he had a dirty cop
in his department. That cop must have orchestrated this.
There was no other way it could have worked so well.
He tossed his empty bottle into the trash, then picked up
the phone, and dialed the Las Vegas Metro Police De-

partment's phone number from memory. An operator answered on the fifth ring.

"Let me speak to Detective Longo," he said.

Pete Longo was having the day from hell. Besides being asked by Bill Higgins to stay out of a major bust, he'd just learned that Jinky Harris had been operating a bust-out joint right under their noses. It was a big black eye for the city, and no one was going to get more heat over it than the police department. His secretary stuck her head into his office.

"Some guy named Tony Valentine is holding on line two," she said. "Want me to get rid of him?"

"No, I'll take it."

The door closed and Longo picked up the mug of coffee that had been sitting on his desk since early that morning and slurped it down. Then he picked up his phone and punched in line two. "This is Detective Longo. Can I help you?"

"This is Tony Valentine," the caller said. "How would you like to do a horse trade?"

Longo pulled himself closer to his desk. "What are you offering?"

"I think I've nailed your dirty cop."

The words were slow to register. Maybe the day from hell was about to show its silver lining. Longo removed a fresh legal pad from his drawer along with a pen.

"What do you want in return?"

"Jinky Harris won't tell us where my son and his friends are," Valentine said. "I want you to promise me that you'll make this cop talk, no matter what."

"You want me to hurt him?"

"Just do whatever you have to do. You don't have to tell me how."

Longo realized his hand was shaking. He had suspected there was a dirty cop in the department for over a year, and had lost many nights' sleep over it.

"Give it to me from the top," Longo said.

"Is that a promise?"

"You have my word," the detective said.

Longo meticulously wrote down Valentine's theory of how his son and friends had been abducted outside the station house. When Valentine was finished, Longo read it back to him, making sure the times corresponded to the correct events.

"That's it," Valentine said. "A pretty girl was waiting for my son at the station house. She was bait. She convinced him and his friends to drive her someplace, where Jinky's boys were waiting. That's my theory."

Longo thought back to early that morning when he'd released Gerry and walked him to the reception area. He'd done a quick scan of the visitors, like he always did. There hadn't been any pretty girls sitting on the plastic chairs bolted to the floor. Had she come from somewhere inside the station house? He put his pen down.

"Let me look into this," Longo said. "Give me a number where I can get back to you."

Longo wrote Valentine's cell number on his blotter and hung up. Then he sat at his desk, deep in thought. He had to handle this right, and not make any accusations until he was certain he had the right cop. He pushed himself out of his chair, and walked to the front of the station house with the legal pad pressed to his chest.

The receptionist on duty was a no-nonsense female sergeant named Cobb. Cobb sat behind a three-inch piece of bulletproof Plexiglas, her eyes riveted to the reception area. No matter what time of day it was, the reception area was always filled with angry and sometimes desperate people. Longo came up behind her, and asked to see the logbook. Cobb pulled it off the desk.

"Don't go too far with that," she snapped.

Longo pointed at the chair behind her own. "Here okay?"

"Perfect," she said.

He sat down, opened the logbook on his lap, and found the entries from early that morning. The station house had several hundred visitors a day, and it took him over a minute to find Gerry Valentine's entry. Gerry had signed out at 3:04 A.M. According to Tony Valentine's theory, the girl who'd baited Gerry had done so right after he'd been released, which meant she'd probably signed out around the same time. Longo checked the names of the visitors who'd signed out around the same time as Gerry, and found only one. A woman named Bonnie Vitucci.

Longo stared at the *Person Here to See* box next to Vitucci's name. It was blank. Rising from his chair, he tapped Cobb on the arm.

"Who was working the graveyard shift last night?"

"Boy, your memory's going," the sergeant said.

"Why do you say that?"

"I was working the graveyard shift. Fannie got sick, so I took her shift."

Longo pointed at Bonnie Vitucci's name in the logbook. "Does this woman's name ring any bells?"

Cobb had eyes like a lizard, and looked at the name in the log without shifting her head. She cracked her bubble gum and nodded at the same time.

"Who is she?"

"A stripper who also does tricks on the side," Cobb said. "She got arrested for offering an undercover detective a BJ."

"When was this?"

"About a year ago."

"How can you remember that clearly?"

"It was her walk," Cobb said.

"Her walk?"

"Yeah. The way she sashayed through here when she got arrested, you'd swear she was sleeping with somebody in the department. That's what we thought."

"We?"

"The other ladies on the staff. *We.*"

Longo realized he was nodding his head. Everything Cobb had said made perfect sense. Jinky Harris had gotten one of his strippers to start sleeping with a detective, and the stripper had pulled the detective over to the dark side. That was how those kinds of things worked. He knew that for a fact, because he'd fallen for a stripper himself once. Sex made you blind and it made you stupid. He put the log back in its place and thanked Cobb for her help.

Longo returned to his office and shut the door. He sat down in front of his ancient PC and pulled up Bonnie Vitucci's rap sheet. The mug shot showed a pretty blonde in her late twenties with a faraway look in her eyes. He read the rap sheet, and saw that the charge had been reduced to a misdemeanor when the arresting officer had not shown up in court for her trial. Longo guessed that this was when the affair had started.

The arresting officer's signature was at the bottom of the sheet, and he hesitated before scrolling down. He knew every detective on the force, and considered nearly all of them his friends. He found himself almost not wanting to know who it was.

Longo took a deep breath. His own affair had nearly cost him his career, and his marriage. But his buddies on the force had closed ranks, and so had his wife and two daughters. They had given him a second chance, and he'd sworn to them that he'd never screw up again.

But this situation was different. This dirty cop had fed information to Jinky Harris, who'd ruined the lives of more young girls than anyone in Las Vegas. Longo took out his wallet, and stared at the plastic-enclosed snapshot of his two teenage daughters. The girls Jinky had ruined were just like them, he reminded himself.

Longo put his finger on the mouse and scrolled down to the name of the arresting officer on the rap sheet. Detective Hector Frangos. He'd known Hector since they were both rookie cops, and had been to his house in Henderson a couple of times for backyard barbecues. Hector had a wife and three small children, and if he remembered correctly, the youngest was autistic. He'd considered him a friend, up until now.

He picked up his phone and started to dial Hector's three-digit extension. He was about to ruin the life of a brother officer, as well as the life of his wife and three kids. It didn't seem right, considering that he'd been given a second chance for committing the same crime. But then again, no one ever said life was fair.

He punched in Hector's extension while his other hand removed the pair of handcuffs attached to his belt, and placed them on his desk.

49

Gerry Valentine had once read in *Newsweek* magazine that the biggest challenge for terrorists who made bombs was not to get blown up in the process. According to the article, over half the terrorists who made bombs either blew themselves up, or created a bomb that blew up prematurely and killed the wrong people.

The same thing appeared to be true of operating a flamethrower. Turning one on was relatively simple, provided you didn't set yourself—or someone standing nearby—on fire. Once you got past that part, handling a flamethrower was easy.

Luckily, the four men who'd been beating them up in the warehouse had not read the article, and were taking turns setting one another's clothing on fire while starting up the flamethrower Jinky had sent over. It was designed like a lawn blower, and spit out a terrifying, long, bright orange flame. Each time one of them caught on fire, Gerry prayed that the man handling the flamethrower would drop it on the ground and break the damn thing.

But it wasn't meant to be. The guy who'd brought the flamethrower to the warehouse stepped out of the shadows, crushed his cigarette into the ground, and cursed the men in Italian. The man went by a single name. Mario. His English was broken, and he frequently reverted to speaking Italian. He was skinny, and had hair and eyebrows so black they looked painted on.

Mario took the flamethrower, and showed the men how to operate it. As flames shot across the warehouse, they illuminated his face, and even though he was on the other side of the warehouse, Gerry instantly recognized him. It was the man he'd seen in the stairwell of the Atlantic City Medical Center ten days ago.

"That's Jack Donovan's killer," he said under his breath.

"You're sure?" Vinny asked.

"Yeah, that's definitely him."

"This is just getting better and better," Vinny moaned.

They watched Mario continue his tutorial. Gerry knew that the Mafia liked to use guys right off the boat to do dirty jobs because they were hard for the police to trace. Guys who came into the country illegally were called wops. It meant "without papers." Mario had an air of ruthlessness about him that was almost palpable, and Gerry imagined him ripping the oxygen tubes out of Jack Donovan's nose, and then pounding on Jack's chest with his fists, robbing Jack of his last breaths.

"That guy is a psycho," Vinny said.

"You think so?" Gerry asked.

"He's got Anthony Perkins written all over him. Just look at his eyes. There's no life in them."

Gerry stared at Mario's eyes. They looked like the eyes you'd find on a stuffed animal. His father had once told him that professional killers nearly all shared one thing in common. They'd been abused as children, and no one had done anything to stop it. This made them angry at the world, and allowed them to enjoy the work that they did.

Jinky's men still couldn't get the hang of operating the flamethrower. Mario got angry with them, and started to direct the action. He had one man get behind Frank's chair and wrap a steel chain around Frank's neck. Then Mario turned the flamethrower on, and brought the flame within a few feet of Frank's face.

"Tell us which one of you shot Russ Watson, or we'll burn your head off," the man strangling Frank said.

Frank stared wide-eyed at the flame hovering near his face. He seemed to be debating what to do, as if there was a choice at this point. He stubbornly shook his head. He wasn't giving in to these guys; not now, not ever.

"Tell me," the man said.

"Screw you," Frank said.

Mario brought the flame closer to Frank's face. Frank pulled his head back, and the guy strangling him jerked his head forward. Frank's head was turning colors, first purple from the lack of oxygen, then bloodred from the heat of the flame. Smoke poured off his face as his eyebrows began to catch on fire. The man doing the strangling turned his attention toward Gerry and Vinny, who sat bound in their chairs on the other side of the warehouse.

"You boys liking this?" he yelled to them.

"Turn the flamethrower off, and I'll tell you who did it," Gerry yelled back.

"Tell me now," the man replied.

"Turn off the flamethrower," Gerry yelled.

"Go fuck yourself," the man yelled.

"I hear you're the expert," Gerry yelled back at him.

"You're next, asshole."

Gerry had been silently praying for a miracle, and he got one. Frank's right hand—his hitting hand—had popped free of the ropes. Frank made a fist and brought his hand up in an arch, catching the guy strangling him flush on the side of the face. The chain came loose from around Frank's neck, and fell jangling to the concrete floor.

Getting hit by a boxer was different from getting hit by an ordinary Joe, and the guy who'd been doing the strangling came staggering around Frank's chair, his eyes rolling in his head. Frank grabbed him with his free hand, and threw him directly into the path of the flamethrower. The man's clothing and hair instantly caught fire, and he threw his arms into the air, screamed, and took off at a dead run.

Mario looked surprised at the turn of events, but not terribly upset. He extinguished the flamethrower by flipping off a switch, and stood with the three men and watched their partner do flaming pirouettes in the center of the warehouse. Within a few moments the flaming man fell face-first to the floor, his arms and legs twitching. Mario and the others stood silently and watched him die.

"We need to call Jinky, tell him what happened," one of the men said.

"I have better idea," Mario said.

"What's that?"

"We kill them, then call Jinky."

They all seemed to think this was a good idea. Mario drew an automatic handgun from behind his belt.

"I do them," Mario said.

"You want to kill all four of them?" one of the men said.

Mario nodded his head forcefully. "All four," he replied.

Frank had continued to pull at the ropes holding him to the chair. He was nearly free, his fingers nimbly pulling the knots apart. Nunzie was cheering him on while trying not to look at the men who were about to kill them.

"Come on, Frankie Boy," Nunzie said.

"Almost there," Frank said, breathing hard.

Gerry looked sideways at Vinny, and saw his friend's lips moving.

"You praying?"

"What else is there to do?" Vinny asked.

Gerry looked at the door. Shadows were dancing in the puddle of light streaming through the bottom of the door, indicating there were people standing outside.

"Start yelling," Gerry said.

"What?"

"You heard me. There're people outside. Start yelling."

Vinny started yelling like it was nobody's business. His voice was drowned out by a battering ram being applied to the door, the sound echoing across the warehouse's ceiling. The door buckled on its hinges, but did not give way.

"It's a raid," one of Jinky's men shouted.

The man drew a gun holstered beneath his sports jacket, aimed, and pulled the trigger. The bullet hit the door and ricocheted dangerously around the warehouse. His partners also drew their weapons and fired at the door, determined to shoot it out with whoever was on the other side. Within seconds bullets were flying, and Gerry was reflexively jerking his head while begging God to spare him from being shot.

"Look at Frank," Vinny said.

"Why?"

"He's almost free."

Gerry stopped jerking his head and stared across the warehouse. Frank had almost wriggled free of his ropes. He was taking his time, just like he had in the casino parking lot. Standing, he walked over to where the flamethrower lay on the floor, picked it up, and clutched it against his chest the way Mario had instructed. Then he got up behind the four killers. The flamethrower's flame was on low, and he jacked the flame up, then squeezed the trigger, causing a huge flame to leap through the air. It engulfed the men, catching their clothes and hair on fire. Within seconds they were screaming and running wildly in circles around the warehouse.

One by one, the men dropped to the floor, and stopped moving. The battering ram was still hitting the door, the sound like a clock ringing its final toll. Frank solemnly lowered the flamethrower while shaking his head.

"Enough of that shit," he declared.

50

One winter when Valentine was a detective on the Atlantic City police force, his wife had talked him into taking a few night courses at a local community college. She had thought the classes would help round him out and broaden his horizons.

The two courses that had made an impact were an English course, which had turned him on to reading Raymond Chandler and other crime writers, and a philosophy course, which had gotten him thinking about things he'd never thought about before.

In the philosophy course he'd read a problem by the French philosopher Descartes that he'd never forgotten. The problem was this: You take your son and his friend to the beach. The two boys go swimming, while you stay on shore. Suddenly, you realize the boys have been pulled out by an undertow and are drowning. The boys are far apart, and as you swim out to rescue them, it becomes apparent only one can be saved. You are responsible for your son's friend, since you're the adult in charge, but you're also responsible for your son, since you're his father. Who do you save?

According to Descartes, you saved your son.

Descartes' reasoning was perfectly logical. You might someday forgive yourself for letting the other boy drown, but you would never forgive yourself if your son drowned. It was a lesson that Valentine had never forgotten.

As the Metro Las Vegas Police Department SWAT team entered the warehouse where Gerry and his friends were being held, Valentine ignored the orders of the SWAT team's commander, and came in behind them. The warehouse smelled of smoke, and he stared at the four burning bodies lying on the floor, the three men tied to chairs, and a man with a horribly damaged face holding a flamethrower. Then his eyes found his son.

Of all the men in the room, Gerry looked to be in the best shape. Gerry hadn't been badly beaten up, and the look on his son's face said that his spirits were still intact. The others needed help in one form or another, but Valentine ignored them and ran to his son. He untied the ropes holding Gerry prisoner. His son rose and they hugged each other.

"Go outside and stay with the cops," Valentine said.

"I need to help my friends," his son said.

"Just do as I say. I'll take care of your friends."

Gerry tried to say something. It was unusual for him to be at a loss for words, and he started to walk to the open door with light streaming through, then turned and walked across the warehouse to one of the burning bodies lying on the floor. Gerry stared down at the corpse and balled his hands into fists.

Valentine came up next to him. "What's wrong?"

"This is the guy who killed Jack Donovan."

Valentine looked down at the blackened body and then up into his son's face. Many times he had heard wronged people say that there was nothing sweeter than revenge, but had never believed it himself. He placed his hand on his son's shoulder.

"Feel any better?"

"You mean because this bastard's dead?"

"Yeah."

"No," Gerry said. "I don't feel any better at all."

Gerry walked out of the warehouse, and Valentine untied Vinny and Nunzie from their chairs, and told them to go outside as well. As both men got to their feet, they shook Valentine's hand and thanked him.

When they were gone, Valentine went over to check on the man with the damaged face. The man had put the flamethrower on the ground, and was standing with his hands against the wall, and his feet spread apart. While one SWAT team member frisked him, a second SWAT team member pointed a rifle at him. The man's face looked like something out of a horror movie, and he grinned at Valentine.

"Hey, Mr. Valentine, how you doing?"

"Frank? What happened to you?"

"They tried to get me to talk," Frank said, still grinning.

"You tell them anything?"

"Naw. They would have killed us."

Valentine immediately understood. Frank had been willing to take the punishment on the slim hope that they'd be rescued. He was as dumb as an ox, but sometimes that was what you needed to survive in this world.

"Let him go," Valentine said to the SWAT team members.

The man holding the rifle shifted his attention to him.

"Excuse me?"

"You heard me. He's one of us."

The man looked at his partner, who'd finished frisking Frank. Then he lowered his rifle and they both walked away. Valentine went up to Frank and saw him smile.

He whacked Frank on the shoulder and the big man winced.

"Not so hard," Frank said. "That's my bad arm."

Valentine led Frank outside and turned him over to a pair of medics who'd come in an ambulance, and were attending to Gerry, Frank, and Nunzie. The medics had already inspected the corpses inside the warehouse, and were happy to have live people to be treating. Valentine walked over to the police van they'd arrived in. Bill Higgins stood beside the van, making a call on his cell phone. Bill had stayed outside with Jinky Harris, who sat in the back of a van in his electric wheelchair. Jinky had started singing like the fat lady in the opera once he'd heard that Detective Hector Frangos had been arrested, and was cooperating with the Metro Las Vegas Police Department.

"Mind if I talk to your prisoner?" Valentine asked.

"Be my guest," Bill said.

Valentine popped open the van's back door and climbed in. Jinky's chair was strapped to the floor of the van with pieces of rope, making him a prisoner. Jinky had the look of a caged rat, and started protesting before Valentine had shut the door.

"Get the hell away from me."

"Hear me out."

"No! Get away from me! Hey Higgins, get him away from me!"

Valentine slammed the door, then got down on his haunches and looked at Jinky. "If you had half an ounce of common sense, you'd play ball with me."

Jinky stared through the van's tinted window at Bill standing outside, talking on his cell phone. When he realized Bill wasn't going to save him, he calmed down.

"What do you want?" he asked.

"Some straight answers would be nice."

"I brought you here, didn't I?"

"That's a good start."

"What do I get in return?" Jinky asked.

Valentine glanced at his son and three friends standing outside the van. It was a miracle they hadn't died, and he wanted Jinky to pay for what he'd done to them. Only Jinky was the key to finding out what was going on at the World Poker Showdown, and he was determined to solve this case. Then he had an idea.

"Come clean with us, and I'll get Bill Higgins to persuade the prosecutor to cut you a deal."

The air-conditioning in the van had been shut off and the interior air was warm and sticky. Jinky removed a wadded-up Kleenex from the pocket of his tracksuit and dabbed at his reddening face. "Is that a promise?"

"Yes, it's a promise."

"Okay. What do you want to know?"

"How is Skip DeMarco cheating the World Poker Showdown?"

"You think the Tuna told me? Get real."

"You must have some idea what's going on."

"I'll tell you what I know," Jinky said. "The Tuna stole a poker scam from some sick guy in Atlantic City. Nobody knows what the scam is, but it's supposed to be perfect. No traces, no clues, nothing. There's only one drawback."

"What's that?"

"It can make a person really sick if they don't handle it right," Jinky said. "That's what everyone says, so it must be true."

Valentine thought back to his meeting with Ray Callahan at the hospital, and how Callahan had stared at the playing card Valentine was carrying in his wallet.

"Is that why two dealers in the tournament collapsed?"

Jinky shrugged. "Could be. Like I said, I don't know what the scam is."

"Next question. Why did you try to have my son and his friends killed?"

Jinky dabbed at his face some more. "There's a lot of mob money being bet on DeMarco to win the tournament. I have nothing against your son and his friends, but when they started screwing with DeMarco, I got told to whack them."

"By the Tuna."

"No, not the Tuna."

"Then who?"

"If I told you that, I'd be dead tomorrow."

"Even if the police put you in protective custody?"

"I'd still be dead tomorrow," Jinky said.

Valentine looked in the big man's face and knew he wasn't going to get the name. He didn't know anything more about how DeMarco was cheating the tournament than he had when he'd stepped off the plane at McCarran yesterday. Worse, he'd nearly lost his son in the process of trying to find out. He opened the rear door and started to climb out.

"What about my deal?" Jinky asked indignantly.

He turned. "What about it?"

"Are you going to talk to Bill Higgins, like you said?"

Valentine paused. As a cop, he'd prided himself on never going back on his word. The oath that went with being a police officer was something he'd always upheld. But being retired was different. He was his own man now.

"No," he said.

"But you promised me!"

"I lied," Valentine said.

51

One of the most depressing movies Valentine had ever seen was called *Leaving Las Vegas*. In the film, an alcoholic comes to Las Vegas, shacks up with a hooker, and proceeds to methodically drink himself to death. The title had summed up the plot perfectly. For some people, the only way to leave Sin City was in a pine box.

Valentine was not going to let that happen to his son, or his son's friends. He retrieved his rental car from police headquarters, then drove Gerry, Frank, and the Fountain brothers to their motel to get their things and check out, then straight to the airport. It was a tight fit in the car, but he wasn't going to let them out of his sight until they were safely on an airplane, and headed home.

"The four of you may have to come back out here and testify in a trial," Valentine said as he parked the rental in short-term parking. "If that happens, I'll come out as well."

"I don't want to ever come to Las Vegas again," Vinny said as they walked across the lot toward the terminal. "I used to think I understood how this town worked, but I was wrong. This place is like another planet."

Once inside, Frank and the Fountain brothers went to

the American Airlines counter and booked three seats in economy on a flight to Philadelphia that left in ninety minutes. The reservationist kept looking at Frank's battered face, as if she might consider him a security risk. Valentine leaned on the counter and spoke to her.

"He's a professional boxer."

"You his manager?"

"Sort of."

"He ought to consider another line of work," the reservationist said, printing out three boarding passes and sliding them across the counter.

"You should see the other guy," Valentine said.

They walked to the security screening area, stopping on the way to buy Frank a baseball cap and sunglasses so his face wouldn't cause any small children to burst into tears. As the three men got in line, they shook Valentine's hand and thanked him for all he'd done. Valentine turned to his son as they passed through the metal detector.

"Think they'll ever straighten up?"

Gerry waved to his friends. "And do what? Become monks?"

They returned to the ticketing area and went to the Delta counter, the main carrier into Tampa, and Valentine purchased a seat on the ten o'clock red eye for his son.

"Don't you think I should stay and help you?" Gerry asked.

"No. Remember what I told you before we came out here?"

"Sure. No job is worth getting killed over."

"Well, I have a new saying."

"What's that?"

"No job is worth losing your son over."

Gerry wanted to say something, only didn't know

how to say it. Instead, he gave his father a bear hug in the middle of the terminal with dozens of people swarming around them. They hadn't done enough of that kind of thing when Gerry was growing up, and when they were finished hugging, Valentine offered to buy his son a cheeseburger.

"You're on," Gerry said.

They walked around the terminal and found a food court where the prices were so high Valentine thought he was in Paris. But there were times when he was willing to pay just about anything for a decent cheeseburger with a slice of onion, and he tossed the menu aside and ordered for both of them. When the waitress had departed, Gerry said, "Hey, look. The tournament is on TV."

The restaurant had a horseshoe-shaped bar with a TV perched above the bottles of liquor. Valentine spun around in his chair, and saw Skip DeMarco being interviewed. DeMarco was wearing his familiar smirk, and the caption beneath him read *World Poker Showdown Tournament leader—$5.8 million in chips*. Valentine shook his head in disbelief. Only a few hours ago, Bill had told him that he was heading to Celebrity to shut down the tournament.

The story ended, and Valentine crossed the restaurant, and stood in a quiet corner before flipping open his cell phone and calling Bill.

"What the hell is going on?" he asked his friend.

"As of this afternoon, the World Poker Showdown is being classified as a private event," Bill replied. "Unless I can prove that cheating is taking place, I've been told to lay off."

"Told by who?"

"The governor of the state of Nevada."

The burden of proof that was required of the police

and other law enforcement agencies in the U.S. was not required of the Nevada Gaming Control Board. The GCB could shut down any gambling operation based on *suspicion* of cheating. And since the WPS was already on thin ice—from DeMarco rigging the first day's seating, to dealers with criminal records and a president who hung with mobsters—Bill didn't need an excuse to pull the curtains. If anything, it was long overdue.

"Can he do that?" Valentine asked.

"Yes," Bill said. "It's in his job description."

"But *why* would he do that?"

"Because the tournament is a huge success. You don't screw with success in this town, Tony."

Valentine put his hand on his forehead and left it there. No matter what it was about in Las Vegas, it was always about the money.

"I got some other bad news this afternoon," Bill said. "Ray Callahan, our crooked poker dealer, died."

"Somebody whack him?"

"No. Callahan died from cancer complications. Now we'll never know how he was involved with DeMarco's scam."

Valentine removed his hand from his forehead and pulled out his wallet. The playing card that Jack Donovan had given Gerry was stuck in his billfold, and he peeled back the bills with his fingers and stared at it. Ray Callahan had wanted to know what Jack had died from, and had not seemed surprised when Valentine had told him cancer. It was the clue he'd been looking for and it had been staring him right in the face.

"Let me ask you a question," he said. "If I can prove DeMarco's cheating, will the governor let you do your job, and shut down the World Poker Showdown?"

"He won't have a choice," Bill asked.

"Even if the WPS is the biggest show in the history of television, and drawing more tourists than Las Vegas has beds?"

Bill laughed into the phone.

"Even then," his friend said.

Valentine stared at the playing card in his wallet. He'd been baffled by scams before but always managed to solve them. If he couldn't solve one, then he needed to get out of the gambling business and into gardening or shuffleboard or whatever the hell it was retired people in Florida did.

"I'll call you later," Valentine said.

He heard Bill start to speak, then hesitate. "Are you still on the case?" his friend asked.

"You bet," Valentine replied.

Valentine said good-bye and folded his cell phone. His son was standing beside him. Valentine removed the playing card from his wallet, and handed it to him. "The secret of how DeMarco is cheating is in the hospital where Jack Donovan died. Jack found something there that can be used to mark cards. It doesn't leave a trace, and is dangerous if not handled properly. I know it's been a rough couple of days, but I want you to go to Atlantic City, look through the hospital records, and find out what it is. I'll ask one of my police buddies to accompany you, so no one tries to whack you."

Gerry blinked, and then he blinked again.

"I thought you wanted me to go home."

"I changed my mind."

"So I'm still working with you on the case?"

"You were never off the case."

"I wasn't?"

"Of course not. You're my partner, aren't you?"

The happy look in Gerry's eyes was one Valentine hadn't seen in a long time. There was a time in every man's life when he had to emerge from his father's shadow, and this was Gerry's time. His son slipped Jack's playing card into his shirt pocket, and hugged his father again. Valentine was surprised at how good it made him feel.

52

"My producer thinks this story would make a terrific made-for-TV movie," Gloria Curtis said, microphone in hand.

Valentine nodded, staring at the magnificently conditioned racehorse standing a dozen yards away. The horse's front legs were going up and down like pistons while a trainer held it in check with a lead rope. Valentine had put Gerry on a plane for Atlantic City, then driven to the University of Nevada football field where Gloria and several hundred gamblers were preparing to watch Rufus Steele challenge the horse in the hundred-yard dash.

"It isn't over yet," he reminded her.

"You sound awfully pessimistic," Gloria said, shivering from a breeze.

He continued to watch the horse, which had deposited a steaming pile of manure on the field. His late father had liked to bet on the ponies, and had always run to the betting windows after seeing a horse take a crap.

"Just being realistic," he said.

"Meaning this may not having a happy ending."

Valentine didn't say anything, not wanting to jinx Rufus, who stood on the fifty-yard line, doing jumping jacks in his Skivvies T-shirt and black boxing shorts while exhorting his fellow gamblers with nonstop banter.

"Come on, boys, what do you say? I'll give you even money I can beat that nag in the hundred-yard dash. That's even money!"

A group of gamblers stood around the horse, and appeared to be making sure the animal hadn't been doped. The group included the Greek, who asked the trainer to lift the horse's saddle, then peered beneath it to make sure there were no hidden electronic devices that might slow the animal down. Satisfied, he turned to his fellow gamblers.

"Looks good to me."

"Check its hooves," one of the gamblers said. "Maybe Rufus took off its shoes."

The Greek decided this was a good idea, and went to the noneating end of the horse and attempted to lift one of its hind legs. Before he could say Jack Robinson, the Greek was sitting on his rump in the grass, having been kicked solidly in the thigh. The other gamblers rushed to his aid.

"I'm okay, I'm okay," the Greek said, rising and dusting himself off. "That's one hell of an animal. I think we just might have a bet here."

The horse was led to the center of the field where it began to prance around on its hind legs. Valentine wondered if Rufus had bitten off more than he could chew, and glanced at Gloria. She looked equally worried.

"Maybe I'd better go talk to him," he said.

Rufus was still doing his exercises. He was all skin and bones, with some sinew thrown in for good measure. He winked as Valentine approached.

"Hey, Tony, you ready to help me fleece these suckers?"

"Are you sure you want to go through with this?"

"Of course I'm sure," Rufus said, stopping to suck down the cool night air. "Come on, don't tell me you're losing faith in me?"

Valentine looked across the field at the competition. The Greek had hired a professional jockey to ride the horse, unwilling to let Rufus provide the rider. The Greek's jockey was a diminutive man with a pinched face and expressionless eyes, his uniform the color of money. With the trainer holding the horse, the jockey climbed into the saddle, then took the horse down the field at a canter.

"A little," Valentine admitted.

"You don't think I can beat Greased Lightning?"

"Is that the horse's name?"

"Yeah. Raced in the Kentucky Derby a few years back, came in fourth," Rufus said. "The owners use it for stud now. A real nag, if you ask me."

Valentine knew enough about horses to know that nags weren't used for stud. The jockey had stopped in the end zone and turned Greased Lightning around. With a tip of the hat to the Greek and his friends, he took off at a dead gallop. A football field is exactly one hundred yards long, and Valentine clocked the horse with his watch. Greased Lightning went from end zone to end zone in seven seconds flat.

He turned to see Rufus removing a cigarette from a pack of Marlboros. The Greek and his cronies were standing nearby, and watched Rufus light up and take a deep drag.

"Rufus," Valentine said, "you can't beat what I just saw. Give up."

Rufus exhaled a thick plume of smoke into the still night air.

"Say that a little louder," he said under his breath.

"Why?"

"Because I want those boys standing nearby to hear you."

Valentine raised his voice. "Rufus, you can't beat what I just saw."

Rufus looked pleased and offered the pack. Valentine reached for it, then hesitated. He was going to quit smoking, even if it killed him, and withdrew his hand.

The Greek and his cronies stepped forward.

"We want to make a wager," the Greek announced.

Rufus ground his cigarette into the grass. "How much?"

"First we want to settle the odds," the Greek said. "We want three-to-one on Greased Lightning. Take it, or leave it."

Rufus held his chin and gave it some thought. Of all the gamblers assembled on the field, the Greek had the biggest bankroll, and his action would dominate the wagering. He said, "I'll do it, with one stipulation. You get in front of the TV camera, and say what you just said into a mike. That you want three-to-one odds on a champion racehorse beating a seventy-two-year-old broken-down cowboy in the hundred-yard dash. Say that, and it's a deal."

The Greek looked crushed. He had won a TV poker tournament recently, and was a celebrity in the poker world. He liked being famous, and was what gamblers called a trophy hunter. Using the palms of his hands, he smoothed out the creases in his bowling shirt, and let the appropriate amount of time pass before speaking again.

"Even money it is," the Greek said.

"How much?"

"I'll bet you a half-million that you can't beat Greased Lightning in the hundred-yard dash."

"Five hundred thousand dollars?" Rufus asked.

"That's right," the Greek said.

"Tony, you hear that?" Rufus asked.

It was more money than most people made in an entire lifetime, and Valentine slowly nodded.

"I heard," he said.

The Greek and Rufus shook hands, and the deal was struck.

"Good evening and welcome to the playing field of the University of Nevada," Gloria Curtis said, staring into the camera. "This is Gloria Curtis, reporting to you from Las Vegas, the city that never sleeps. Standing beside me is a man who never sleeps, Rufus Steele, legendary poker player and gambler. Tonight, Rufus is betting a sizable sum—"

"One half million dollars," Rufus said proudly.

"—that he can outrun a former Kentucky Derby hopeful named Greased Lightning in the hundred-yard dash. Rufus, how are you feeling?"

"Like a spring chicken," the old cowboy said.

"I must tell you that in all my years reporting sports, I've never seen a matchup as intriguing as this one."

Rufus was about to reply when Greased Lightning bounded up behind them, the jockey pulling back on the horse with his reins.

"What do you say we get this started?" the jockey asked them. "This isn't a pleasure horse I'm riding, folks."

"Right," Rufus said. "Just give me a second to set up our course."

Rufus walked over to a large beach towel lying on the ground. On the towel sat a jug of drinking water and a brown paper bag. Rufus picked up the bag and removed a plastic traffic cone painted in orange Day-Glo paint. He tossed it to Valentine.

"Tony, do me a favor, and go put that cone on the center of the fifty-yard line."

Valentine marched out to the middle of the football field, and placed the cone in the center of the fifty-yard line. When he returned to the sidelines, the Greek was shouting and wagging an angry finger in Rufus's face.

"That's cheating!" the Greek shouted.

Rufus flashed his best aw-shucks grin. "No, it's not. I said we'd be running the hundred-yard dash. I never said those hundred yards would be in a straight line." He turned to Valentine. "Did I, Tony?"

Before Valentine could answer, Rufus turned to Gloria. "Did I, Miss Curtis?"

"No, you didn't," they both answered.

Rufus pointed at the end zone. "We start the race from there, and when we reach the cone, we turn around, and run back to the end zone. Plain and simple."

A hush fell over the crowd of gamblers. The Greek had balled his hands into fists and his face resembled a pressure cooker ready to explode. He stormed across the field to where Greased Lightning and the jockey were standing. The horse was kicking at the ground and seemed to know that it was about to be asked to perform. The Greek had a short conversation with the jockey, then returned to the sidelines.

"You're on," he told Rufus.

There was too much artificial light in Las Vegas for any stars to be visible. Only the moon could be seen in the pitch dark sky, and it appeared to be slyly winking at them. Valentine followed Rufus to the end zone from where the race would start.

"The Greek sounds pretty confidant," he said.

"That's because the jockey thinks he can make the turn, and still beat me," Rufus replied, doing windmills with his arms to loosen up. "If the horse was a rodeo pony, I'd be in trouble. But not a racehorse."

"You sure?"

"Positive, pardner."

Greased Lightning came into the end zone kicking up a storm. The jockey had his riding crop out and was sitting high in the saddle. Valentine guessed the jockey was planning to take the horse down the field at half-speed, make the turn at the fifty-yard line, and come back at a full gallop.

"I don't know, Rufus," Valentine said.

From the paper bag Rufus removed a starting gun, which he handed to Valentine.

"Make sure you pull the trigger when the race starts," Rufus said.

The crowd of gamblers followed them into the end zone and stood behind the two participants. Rufus and Greased Lightning toed the starting line, the jockey practically standing up in his stirrups, the old cowboy in classic sprinter's pose.

"Tony, be our starter," Rufus called out.

Valentine walked over to where they stood. He paused to make sure Zack was filming them, then pointed the starting pistol into the air.

"Gentlemen, take your marks."

The wind blowing off the desert had died and the air was remarkably still. A jet passed overhead, the whir of its landing gear coming down shattering the stillness. Greased Lightning emitted a loud whinny.

"Get ready—go!"

Valentine fired the starter into the air. The cap in the gun made a loud *bang!* and the horse screamed like it had been shot. It fled ahead and went down the field at supersonic speed. Rufus appeared to be frozen, his legs stuck to the ground, as the animal passed him.

The gamblers let out a collective roar, with the Greek shouting the loudest. Rufus was huffing and puffing, running about as well as someone his age could run, which was to say not particularly fast. Before he'd reached the fifteen-yard line, Greased Lightning had reached the fifty and was still running.

"Come on, Rufus," Valentine yelled. "Come on!"

The jockey was pulling back on his reins with all his might. The horse started to break, its back legs tearing up the ground like hoes. When it finally came to a stop, it was near the opposing side's twenty-yard line. The jockey jerked the horse's head, trying to turn the animal around. The horse obeyed, and when it was turned around, came to a dead stop, as if the race was over. The jockey slapped its side with his crop while digging his heels into its side.

By now, Rufus had reached the cone in the center of the field, done a nifty spin, and taken off back for the finish line. The old cowboy still had some run in him, his long legs covering the ground with amazing agility. Sensing disaster, the Greek and his cronies stood at the finish line, jumping wildly up and down.

"Run!" Valentine yelled through cupped hands.

Rufus hit the ten-yard line as Greased Lightning crossed the thirty. It was a contest now, and Rufus took a half dozen giant steps, and then fell face-forward with his arms outstretched as the horse raced past him.

"I win! I win!" the Greek shouted while doing a juvenile victory dance.

Valentine hurried over to where Rufus lay and helped him to his feet. The old cowboy was covered in grass and dirt and took a moment to get his bearings.

"Did I lose?" he asked under his breath.

"It was mighty close," Valentine said. "Let's look at the tape."

Zack stood on the sideline with his camera pointed at the finish line. He rewound the tape, and let Valentine and Rufus watch the race on the tiny screen on the back of the camera. The ending was close, but the outcome was perfectly clear. Before Greased Lightning reached the end zone, Rufus's hand had broken the plane of the finish line.

Rufus called the Greek over, and let him watch the tape. When it was over, the Greek was crying. Rufus raised his arms triumphantly into the air.

"I win," he declared.

Poker Protection Tips

Poker is an amazing game. It requires aggression, bluffing, money management, the ability to read tells, and knowing how to play hundreds of different hands. It also requires luck and lots of hard work. Anyone can play, and practically everyone does.

But poker also has a dirty little secret and it's called cheating. Of the more than fifty books on poker in my library, all contain chapters on the subject. Cheating happens in friendly games, casino card rooms, and tournaments. It continues to be one of the largest unchecked crimes in America.

If you play poker on a frequent basis, it's safe to assume that you've been swindled at least a couple of times. It's part of the game, and something every player needs to guard against. There are a number of universal poker scams that are used to separate honest players from their money (unless you play in high-stakes games, the chances of running up against a skilled mechanic are slim). The following pages deal with those scams, while also explaining ways to protect yourself against them.

PEEKING

Ever notice when watching the World Series of Poker how zealously the players guard their cards when they look to see what they've been dealt? Ever wonder why? The obvious answer is that the players don't want their opponents to see their cards. But the chances of that happening are slim. The other opponents are looking at their cards at the same time. So why do players do it? The answer is simple: They don't want to be "peeked" by someone standing behind them. This person is called a confederate or an agent. Their job is to peek the cards, then signal their value to another player at the table. Peeking is a favorite method of cheating among professional card hustlers. Many great players (including world champions) have been scammed by peeking. Here are the card hustler's favorite methods, and how to protect yourself against them.

The Friendly Host

There is a card hustler from New England who holds weekly games in the recreation room of his house. He's very accommodating to his guests. During the game, his wife will enter the room, and ask if anyone would like a drink. She takes everyone's order, then reappears five minutes later balancing a tray, and serves everyone at the table.

The wife is the confederate. She spots the cards while taking the orders, then signals them to her husband while serving the drinks. She does this twice a night. It usually generates enough money to pay their mortgage each month.

Protection Tip: You can't stop people from coming into the room when you play (especially if you're a guest in their home). But you can stop showing them your cards. Whenever someone enters the room, put your cards facedown on the table and leave them there. If possible, look at your hand as infrequently as possible. Most pros look at their cards once or twice during a game.

The Friendly Player

Sometimes a player sitting beside you will drop out of a hand. This player might ask you to show him what you're holding. Most players will reveal their cards (especially in a friendly game). This is a huge mistake for two reasons. First, if the player is working with someone at the table, he can signal what you have. But even if the player isn't a cheater, he can still inadvertently signal to the other players if your hand is weak, or strong.

Protection Tip: The smart thing to do is shake your head no. If the player puts up a beef, tell him to sit next to someone else.

The Man with the Newspaper

People play poker everywhere—airplanes, hotel lobbies, trains, and anywhere else where people gather. One of the more subtle forms of peeking used in such settings involves a man sitting reading a newspaper.

Let's say the game is being played in the lobby of a swank hotel. There are four players. Three are cheaters, the fourth a well-oiled sucker. The cheaters position the sucker so he is sitting in a certain chair. Behind the chair sits a person reading a newspaper. This person is the cheaters' confederate. The newspaper the confederate is reading has a razor slit in its center. By peeking through the slit, the confederate is able to peek the sucker's cards. If the sucker were to turn around, he wouldn't see anything wrong.

Now comes the clever part. The confederate signals the sucker's cards to the cheaters by breathing through his nostrils. Short breaths indicate low cards, long breaths high cards. Hustlers call this The Sniff. It's one of the most deceiving ways to signal I know of. For all the sucker knows, the guy behind him has a cold.

Protection Tip: Avoid situations where people are sitting behind you, even if you think these people can't see your cards.

Binoculars

One of the most famous peeking scams was exposed in the James Bond movie *Goldfinger* (1964). Goldfinger is playing cards poolside at the Fontainbleau Hilton in Miami Beach while his girlfriend is looking at his opponent's hand through binoculars, then signaling those cards through a transmitting device. I saw this movie as a kid, and thought it was far-fetched. Little did I know that it is a favorite method of peeking among cheaters in high-stakes games. (The Fontainbleau scam is documented in the book *The Last Good Time*. According to the book's author, Jonathan van Meter, the scam inspired the scene in the film.)

A True Story

Stuey Unger was one of the greatest poker players who's ever lived. During his relatively short life (he died in his early forties) he entered thirty poker tournaments and won twelve of them, including the World Series of

Poker three times (a record). Even Tiger Woods doesn't have a win ratio that high.

One of the most famous stories about Unger occurred at the now demolished Aladdin Hotel in Las Vegas. Unger was playing Texas Hold 'Em in the card room, and realized he was being cheated by a peek. Unger didn't see the peek: he just knew that one was in use, because his opponents were dropping out whenever he had strong cards. Rather than leave the game, Unger decided to play on, believing he was a strong enough player to still beat his opponents.

When the night was over, Unger had won all the money, and his belief in himself had paid off. While this is not a strategy I would recommend, it does show that even with an edge, the cheater can still get beaten by a superior player.

SHORTING THE POT

Shorting the pot is one of the most common forms of cheating in poker. Often, it is done innocently, when a player gets distracted and forgets to ante up, or places the wrong amount into the pot during a round of betting. But there are also players who do this regularly and on purpose. It is the lowest form of cheating I know of.

Protection Tips: There are several ways to prevent a player from shorting the pot. The first is for the person dealing the game to keep track of each player's bets during each round. This is the dealer's responsibility, and a job that should be taken seriously.

Another way is to "spoke" your bets. This was developed by a group that I play with, and is especially good in games where players ante up if no one wins the pot.

The idea of the spoke is to place each bet behind the other on the table, so that your opponents can see that you've bet the correct amount for each round.

A third deterrent, and perhaps the most effective, is to politely reprimand any player who gets caught shorting the pot. This puts the guilty player on notice, while informing everyone else at the table what's going on.

HOLDING OUT

Holding out is when a player secretly takes a card (or cards) out of the deck, and switches them in later during a hand. While this might sound bold (or difficult), it's relatively easy to accomplish. A cheater can simply drop his hands below the table, remove a high pair from his hand, and slip them under his leg. He then declares he's dropping out of the hand, and discards his remaining cards. The high pair is later used to create an unbeatable hand.

Protection Tips: First of all, begin each game by counting the cards in the decks you're using, even if the cards are brand-new. Cheaters who hold out often remove the cards before the game, and then patiently wait to bring them into play.

Second, make it a rule that players cannot take cards out of sight at any time. This includes during the shuffle (some players like to shuffle on their legs) and during play, when everyone is holding their hand. Cards stay on the tabletop. Period.

Third, when a player discards his hand, it is the dealer's responsibility to make sure the proper number of cards have been discarded into the muck.

Adherence to these rules will make it difficult for a player to hold out during a game.

SHINERS

A shiner is a common method of peeking cards, and something most card players should be aware of. A hustler who uses a shiner is said to be "playing the lights."

A shiner is particularly effective in Texas Hold 'Em, where each player receives two face-down cards. Let's say there are five players. By using a shiner, the cheater memorizes the first ten cards dealt. Let's say the cards are the ace of clubs, king of hearts, two of spades, five of hearts, nine of diamonds, ace of hearts, eight of hearts, two of hearts, six of hearts, three of clubs. The cheater now knows the following:

Player one has pocket aces (a great hand).
Player two has the king and eight of hearts (a possible flush).
Player three has pocket twos.
Player four has the five and six of hearts, connected (also a good hand).
Player five (the cheater) has the nine of diamonds and three of clubs (a bad hand).

Based on this information, the cheater would drop out of the hand.

Shiners come in many shapes and sizes. Pros use small, coin-shaped mirrors tucked in their hands to spot cards during the deal; amateurs tend to favor mirrors stuck in pipe bowls or shiny rings to do the dirty work. Another favorite shiner is a common Zippo lighter, which sits on the table next to the dealer. As the cards are dealt, the deck is brought directly over the lighter, allowing the cheater to spot their values in the Zippo's reflection.

Protection Tip: Keep the playing area for your games clear of any foreign objects, no matter how innocent they might appear. Even a cup of coffee can be used as a shiner, with the liquid's dark surface reflecting the face of a card. If you think someone might be using a shiner, glance up at the ceiling. Any light reflected off the shiner will also be reflected on the ceiling, and will look like a tiny butterfly.

For a peek at James Swain's
next exciting novel,

DEADMAN'S BLUFF,

read on . . .

Coming soon from Ballantine Books

Big Julie, a famous New York gambler, once said that the person who invented gambling was smart, but the person who invented chips was a genius.

Poker had a similar truism. The person who'd invented poker may have been smart, but the person who'd invented the hidden camera that allowed a television audience to see the players' hands was a genius.

George "The Tuna" Scalzo sat on his hotel suite's couch with his nephew beside him. It was ten o'clock in the evening, and the big-screen TV was on. They were watching the action from that day's World Poker Showdown, which was generating the highest ratings of any sporting event outside the Super Bowl. His nephew, Skip DeMarco, was winning the tournament and had become an overnight sensation.

"Tell me what you're seeing, Uncle George," DeMarco said.

His nephew faced the TV, his handsome face bathed in the screen's artificial light. Skip suffered from a degenerative eye disease that he'd had since birth. He could not see two inches past his nose, and so his uncle described the action.

"They're showing the different players you knocked out of the tournament today," Scalzo said. " 'Treetop' Strauss, 'Mad Dog' McCoy, 'The Wizard' Wang, and a bunch of other guys. It's beautiful, especially when you call their bluffs. They don't know what hit them."

Bluffing was what made poker exciting. A man could have worthless cards, yet if he bet aggressively, he'd win hand after hand. DeMarco had made a specialty of calling his opponents' bluffs, and had become the most feared player in the tournament.

"Is the camera showing me a lot?" DeMarco asked.

"All the time. You're the star."

"Do I look arrogant?"

Scalzo didn't know what "arrogant" meant. Proud? That word he understood. He glanced across the suite at Guido, who leaned against the wall. His bodyguard had a zipper scar down the side of his face and never smiled. Guido came from the streets of Newark, New Jersey, as did all the men who worked for Scalzo.

"Guido, how does Skipper look?"

"Calm, cool, and collected," Guido said, puffing on a cigarette.

"Is he a star?"

"Big star," Guido said.

"There you go." Scalzo elbowed his nephew in the ribs.

The show ended, and was followed by the local news. The broadcasters covered the headlines, then a story from the University of Nevada's football field came on.

"What's this?" his nephew asked.

Scalzo squinted at the screen. The story was about Rufus Steele challenging a racehorse to the hundred-yard dash. Rufus appeared on the screen dressed in track shorts. Beside him was Tony Valentine, the casino consultant who'd caused them so much trouble. Scalzo grabbed the remote and changed the channel.

"Put it back on, Uncle George," his nephew said.

"Why? He can't beat no fucking racehorse," Scalzo protested.

"I want to see it anyway. This is the old guy who wants to play me."

The suite fell silent. Ever since they'd arrived in Las Vegas, his nephew had been challenging him.

"You're not going to play that son-of-a-bitch," Scalzo declared.

"If he has the money, I don't have a choice, Uncle George. This is poker. If I don't accept his challenge, he wins."

Scalzo did not like the direction the conversation was taking. He clicked his fingers, and Guido rose from his chair.

"Yes, Mr. Scalzo."

"A glass of cognac for me. What would you like, Skipper?"

"For you not to drink while we have this conversation," his nephew said.

Scalzo balled his hands into fists and stared at his nephew's profile. If someone who worked for him had said that, he would have had him killed.

"You don't like when I drink?"

"You get mean. Doesn't he, Guido?"

Swallowing hard, the bodyguard said nothing. Scalzo made a twirling motion with his finger. Guido walked into the next room, and shut the door behind him.

"This cowboy is the real thing," his nephew said.

"What's that supposed to mean?" Scalzo snapped.

"He's an old-time hustler, Uncle George. I can't scam

him the way we're scamming the tournament. It won't work."

Skipper had won dozens of poker tournaments on the Internet, and was a feared player in cyberspace. Live games were a different matter, with other players ganging up on him because of his handicap. Scalzo had found a way to level the playing field, and Skipper had gone along, wanting the recognition that he believed he deserved.

"But no one has figured out the scam so far," Scalzo said.

"Steele will. He'll feel a breeze."

"So let him put a sweater on."

"It's a gambler's expression, Uncle George. Steele will know *something* is wrong. Even if he doesn't know what it is at first, he'll figure it out eventually. I have to play him on the square. If I'm as good as I keep telling myself I am, then I should beat him."

"You want to play the cowboy legitimately?"

"Yes."

Scalzo scowled. Skipper was letting his mouth overload his ass. He wasn't going to play Steele head-to-head. The old cowboy knew too many damn tricks. Scalzo dropped the remote in his nephew's lap.

"I'm going to bed," Scalzo said. "Let's talk again in the morning."

His nephew stared absently into space as if disappointed with his uncle.

"Good night, Uncle George," he said.

Going into the next room, Scalzo was greeted by an unexpected guest. Karl Jasper, founder and president of the World Poker Showdown, was at the bar, talking with Guido while drinking a beer. The face of the WPS, Jasper had dyed hair, whitened teeth, and shoulder pads in his jackets that made him look trimmer than he really was.

"Nice place," Jasper said.

Scalzo and his nephew were staying in a high-roller suite, compliments of the hotel. It had a fully stocked bar, pool table, Jacuzzi, and private theater with reclining leather chairs. It was the best digs in town, and it wasn't costing them a dime.

A snifter of cognac awaited Scalzo on the bar. They clinked glasses, and Scalzo raised the drink to his lips.

"Did you see Rufus Steele on TV?" Jasper asked. "The man is becoming a menace."

Scalzo let the cognac swirl around in his mouth. It felt good and strong and made him wake up. He liked how Jasper addressed things. He was a product of Madison Avenue, and had gone from account executive to founder of the WPS in the blink of an eye. He was a smart guy who suffered from the same problem a lot of smart guys suffered from: He didn't know how to run a business. Within six months of starting, he'd run out of cash. In desperation he'd gone to the mob, and Scalzo became his partner.

Scalzo could not have envisioned a more perfect setup. The biggest mistake the mob had ever made was letting themselves get pushed out of Las Vegas. No other town in the world had the same kind of action. By partnering with Jasper, Scalzo could run a card game inside a Las Vegas casino without law breathing down his neck. It didn't get any better than that.

"Rufus Steele is a clown," Scalzo said. "The real problem is Tony Valentine. He wants to expose Skipper. He has a grudge with me."

The beer in Jasper's glass had disappeared, and Guido poured him another.

"You've dealt with Valentine before?" Jasper asked.

Scalzo nodded almost imperceptibly.

"Can he be bought off?"

"He used to be a casino cop. They called him the squarest guy in Atlantic City."

"So, what should we do?"

Scalzo stared across the suite at the picture window on the other side of the room. The curtains were pulled back, allowing him to see the pulsing neon spectacle that was the strip at night. For years he'd run a successful scam in Atlantic City that had made him a small fortune, but this was different. This was Las Vegas, and for as long as he could remember, he'd wanted a piece of it for himself.

"We need to get rid of him," Scalzo said. "Once Valentine's gone, Steele will fade into the sunset, and we can go back to business."

"When you say get rid of him," Jasper said, "do you mean, run him out of town?"

Scalzo put his snifter down and coldly stared at his guest. Jasper's face and hands were evenly tanned from playing golf three times a week. They'd been partners for over a year, and so far, Jasper had shown no regrets for having jumped in bed with the devil.

"I mean kill the bastard," Scalzo said.

Jasper blinked, and then he blinked again. *Making a Madison Avenue decision,* Scalzo thought. He put his hand on Jasper's arm and squeezed the younger man's biceps.

"We need to do it right now," Scalzo added.